9/15/1[c]

D0187357   N

What people

THE REAL
ENEMY

"Mysterious disappearances, a dangerous legend, and the emotional meltdown of a marriage. Kathy Herman pulls it all together in a riveting story that rockets to a conclusion that will keep you on the edge of your seat."

Lorena McCourtney, author of *Your Chariot Awaits*, an ACFW Book of the Year

"A good solid read with enough questions and twists to provide hours of entertainment. I'll tell my friends to read this book!"

Lauraine Snelling, author of *One Perfect Day*

"Kathy Herman's *The Real Enemy* will not disappoint. Her characters are full and flawed. Her plot moves swift and sure. Her ending is unexpected and profound. Don't cheat yourself out of a great read. Grab this one!"

Lyn Cote, author of the Texas Star of Destiny series

"A marriage is unraveling as fast as a town. *The Real Enemy* is an emotion-packed page turner that kept me up late ... and I loved every minute!"

Roxanne Henke, author of *After Anne*

"I loved *The Real Enemy*! Kathy Herman has given us a clever mystery and fascinating characters facing real-life issues. A thoroughly satisfying read. Highly recommended."

Gayle Roper, author of *Hide and Seek*

"Kathy Herman gives the reader a stunning read in *The Real Enemy*. The story kept me riveted to the page, and when I reached the end, I realized evil could not be muted."

DiAnn Mills, author of *Breach of Trust*

"In *The Real Enemy*, Kathy Herman skillfully weaves together a tale of supernatural legends and mysterious disappearances with the age-old problems of infidelity and unforgiveness that only a return to faith can mend. Suspenseful and engaging!"

DeAnna Julie Dodson, author of *In Honor Bound*

"With believable characters and a plot that kept me turning the pages, *The Real Enemy* had me looking over my shoulder on more than one occasion. A must read—with the lights on!"

Diann Hunt, author of *For Better or For Worse*

"In *The Real Enemy*, Kathy Herman has made a fine art out of combining true-to-life human drama with edge-of-the-seat suspense. She gives meaning to the concept of forgiveness. This was a great read."

Hannah Alexander, author of *A Killing Frost*

"Ms. Herman not only delivers a riveting story where the pressures of the present and shadows of the past collide, but adds a thought-provoking look at the high cost of unforgiveness.

Carol Cox, author of the A Fair to Remember series

"In *The Real Enemy* Kathy Herman masterfully pairs crime with family estrangement to redeem a marriage nearly destroyed by sin, in a twist that will surprise the reader."

Eric Wiggin, author of *Blood Moon Rising*

9/15/09

SOPHIE TRACE TRILOGY

THE REAL ENEMY

A NOVEL

KATHY HERMAN

David C Cook®

transforming lives together

To Him who is both the Giver and the Gift

ACKNOWLEDGMENTS

THE Great Smoky Mountains and rolling hills of East Tennessee provide the stunning backdrop for this story, and I'd like to thank my friend Rachel McRae for giving my husband and me a list of "must see" places to visit as we traveled this beautiful area. Though I've made references to numerous Tennessee towns and landmarks, Sophie Trace and its legend of the red shadows exist only in my imagination.

I want to acknowledge the late LaVerne McCuistion, perhaps my most passionate supporter, who slipped into the Lord's arms during the writing of this book. I will miss her sorely and will have to save her a copy of this book and those yet to come for when we meet again on the streets of gold.

In the writing of this story, I drew from several resource people, each of whom shared generously from his or her storehouse of knowledge and experience. I did my best to integrate the facts, as I understood them. If accuracy was compromised in any way, it was unintentional and strictly of my own doing. All information regarding organized crime and gangs was obtained from a broad range of newspaper articles and related Internet sites. The prototype I chose for the Sophie Trace Police Department was identical to that used in Athens, Tennessee.

I owe a debt of gratitude to Commander Carl H. Deeley of the Los Angeles County Sheriff's Department and also Chief Wallace

Fullerton of the Marysville (California) Police Department. The combined input of these seasoned professionals enabled me to better understand the work environment, protocol, and everyday challenges of police chiefs.

I want to extend a heartfelt thank you to my friend Paul David Houston, former assistant district attorney, for helping me understand specific statutes and criminal charges as well as plea-bargaining options; and my professional investigator friend, Will Ray, for providing valuable input concerning evidence collected during crime scene investigations.

I'm immensely grateful to Mark and Donna Skorheim, who sent cards of encouragement and prayed faithfully and fervently that, in spite of my rigorous physical therapy schedule, I would stay on deadline. The two of you are a powerful voice of intercession!

A special word of thanks to my tenacious prayer warrior and sister, Pat Phillips, and my online prayer team: Chuck Allenbrand, Judith Depontes, Jackie Jeffries, Joanne Lambert, Adrienne McCabe, Nora Phillips, Will Ray, Carolyn Walker, and Sondra Watson for your continuous support. There's no way to measure your importance to this writing ministry.

To Susie Killough, Judi Wieghat, Pearl Anderson, LaVerne McCuistion, my friends at LifeWay Christian Store in Tyler, Texas, and Nashville, Tennessee; and my church family at Bethel Bible Church for your many prayers during the writing of this book. There were times when your prayers seemed almost tangible!

To the retailers who make my books available and to the many readers who have encouraged me with e-mails, cards, and personal testimonies about how God has used my words to challenge and inspire you. He uses you to bless me more often than you know.

To my novelist friends in ChiLibris, who allow me to tap into your collective storehouse of knowledge and experience: What a compassionate, charitable, prayerful group you are! It's an honor to be counted among you.

To my agent, Beth Jusino, and the diligent staff at Alive Communications. Your standard of excellence challenges me to keep growing as a writer. I only hope that I represent you as well as you represent me.

To Cris Doornbos, Dan Rich, and Don Pape at David C. Cook for believing in me and investing in the words I write; and to your hardworking staff for getting this book to the shelves. What could be more exciting than being colaborers "on the same page" for Him?

To my editor, Diane Noble, for insightful suggestions that intensified and tightened this story and genuine praises that enabled me to see how my writing has grown. I love working with you. You've made editing something I actually look forward to.

To my husband, Paul, who has, over the course of my fourteen novels, listened with inexhaustible interest as I've read aloud every word of each book (at least twice!). You're the only other person who has witnessed God's hand at work during the creative process. What a privilege we share!

And to my Lord and my God, who has walked with me through every valley in my spiritual journey that I might live to tell of His mercy and grace. I pray that the truth of Your Word woven into this story will come to life in the heart of every reader. How humbling it is to be the vessel!

PROLOGUE

"Do not be overcome by evil,
but overcome evil with good."
Romans 12:21

ROSA Mendez crouched behind the rubble of a razed brick building and held her breath. Had he seen her? She listened for his footsteps moving toward her, but the only distinguishable sound was the squawking of two grackles fighting over a potato chip wrapper stuck in the storm drain.

She gingerly peeked around the side of the brick pile and caught a glimpse of her cousin Eduardo bounding up the front steps of the abandoned Pentecostal church, wearing red high-tops and the Super Bowl cap she gave him for his birthday. What was drawing him to this empty old building?

She wanted to follow him inside and ask what he was doing here. If he had been the Eduardo she had idolized nearly all her life, she would have. But this new Eduardo? Her heart trembled when she thought of how he might react if he knew she was spying on him.

Deep voices resonated from inside the church. They sounded mean, but she couldn't make out what they were saying. She glanced at her watch. Surely her younger sister, Carmen, could babysit four little girls by herself for a few more minutes. She might not have another chance to find out what Eduardo was up to.

She crept around to the side window and peered in through the broken glass. About a dozen men stood in a straight line, their arms folded across their chests, Eduardo and two others facing them. She ducked just below the windowsill, still as stone, and listened to what they were saying.

"We're unstoppable. The question is: Are you? Few men are smart enough or tough enough to succeed at this. Ready to show us what you've got?"

"*I* am."

"So am I."

"Eduardo?"

"Absolutely."

"Excellent. Make sure they never get the chance to scream." The man laughed. "Oh … and if you get caught? We never heard of you. Rat us out to the cops, and you're dead men. There's no place you can hide that we can't get to you. Any questions?"

Silence filled the room.

Rosa leaned against the side of the church, her knees about to buckle, her heart pounding like a kettledrum. What was her cousin doing with these thugs?

A few seconds later, feet shuffled across the creaky floor and it sounded as if the front door opened. She ran to the rear of the building and hid behind the overgrown shrubs near the steps, studying the guys as they crossed the street and strutted toward the railroad tracks. Their backs were to her, but Eduardo was easy to spot in his red athletic shoes.

Whatever it was they were up to, they had picked the most secluded part of town to meet. After the woolen mill closed down, blocks of old buildings on this side of Sophie Trace had been demolished and replaced with rows of corrugated metal storage facilities. This dilapidated church was about the only remnant left standing.

Rosa waited until the men disappeared, then sat on the crumbling steps, hugging herself and rocking back and forth. How could Eduardo be stupid enough to get pulled into something that might put lives in danger and get him sent to prison? Was she brave enough to confront him? Would it even do any good?

Until the past few months she could talk to him about anything. But along with his increasing indifference came a mean temper that frightened her. He had shoved her a few times when she pressed him about why he was avoiding her, and he had even started yelling at the younger cousins anytime they got on his nerves.

Rosa blinked the stinging from her eyes. What happened to the Eduardo she had looked up to for as long as she could remember? The doting cousin who taught her to swim when no one else could even coax her into the water? Who taught her to ride a bike? Not to be afraid of dogs? The math whiz who helped her make an adventure out of everything from times tables to algebra? Eduardo had always been her hero—the big brother she never had.

If only she hadn't eavesdropped. What if he was in danger? Clearly *someone* was.

Rosa's mind screamed with possibilities, and the skin on her arms turned to gooseflesh. What if they were smuggling illegals into the country? Or what if it was even worse than that? Her mind flashed back to a recent TV documentary about slavery in the twenty-first century.

She shuddered. Was Eduardo involved in *that?* The guy who threatened him sounded capable of anything.

A train whistle startled her. She shivered. The air had turned chilly, and the sun had dropped behind the metal roofs of the storage facilities. She pulled the windbreaker out of her backpack, her hands shaking, and slipped it on, the stranger's threat replaying in her mind like a stuck CD.

Rat us out to the cops and you're dead men.

Rosa began to run and then run faster and faster, lamenting that she had shirked her babysitting responsibility and had stumbled into something she had no business knowing but couldn't ignore. She raced past the high school, vaguely aware that the clock at city hall had chimed five times, and came to a stop at the red light at Stanton and First.

She leaned over, her hands grasping her knees, and tried to catch her breath. What should she do? If she confided in her parents, they would feel obligated to tell the police. No, Eduardo was the one she needed to talk to. Maybe she could reason with him and get him to stay away from these dangerous men.

The light turned green and she darted across Stanton and raced toward Mockingbird Lane. But what if it was too late? What if Eduardo had become just like *them?* What if he was capable of hurting her—doing whatever it took to shut her up? What if he knew she had followed him and decided just to deal with her later?

Make sure they never get a chance to scream, one had said. She swallowed a sob and kept running, trying not to think about what that meant.

CHAPTER 1

"OUCH!"

Police Chief Brill Jessup yanked her hand away from the stuck desk drawer and shook it a few times, keenly aware of her broken thumbnail and the embarrassment scalding her face. She stole a glance through the blinds covering the glass wall, pretending not to notice Detective Captain Trent Norris's amusement. She wasn't about to ask him for help. How hard could it be to get the stupid thing open?

"Everything okay, Chief?" Trent's voice sounded patronizing.

"Yes, just fine."

Brill reached for the stack of Thursday's mail in her in-box and sat back in the well-worn brown leather chair, her thumb throbbing, and her feet barely touching the floor. The desk chair was still too high, but she wasn't going to call the maintenance engineer and have him adjust it *again*. Why draw attention to the fact that she was a foot shorter than her predecessor and utterly useless with a screwdriver? She could live with it until she was off duty and could get her husband, Kurt, to help her.

She wiggled out of the chair and ambled over to the window, her back to the glass wall and Trent's curious glances, and looked out through the magnificent trees of gold and orange and crimson that shaded the grounds around city hall. In the distance, beyond the ridge of rolling hills, the hazy outline of the Great Smoky Mountains looked almost surreal against the bluebird sky. She had always admired the grandeur of the Mississippi River when she lived in Memphis, but it couldn't compare with the heart-stopping view on the other side of the state. Outside, anyway.

She turned around and cringed at the monstrous bookcase that swallowed up the entire wall behind her desk. The other walls were dingy beige and bare, except for a few framed pencil sketches of Civil War heroes and an abundance of nail holes—glaring reminders of Chief Hennessey's passing.

Brill remembered seeing the framed portrait of the chief that hung in the main corridor of city hall at the end of a long row of portraits of the other police chiefs who had served the community of Sophie Trace. How honored she felt to be counted among them, even if she was the first "redheaded spitfire" to run the department. She smiled. Trent would probably be embarrassed if he knew she'd overheard him refer to her that way while talking with his wife on the phone. Not that he meant any disrespect. Perhaps it was even intended to be complimentary. But she wondered if he would describe her that way if she were male.

She went over to her desk, took a nail file out of her pencil cup, and began to smooth her jagged thumbnail. Hadn't she made up her mind when she accepted this position that she wasn't going to allow gender to be an issue nor was she going to overreact if someone tried to make it one? Her eighteen-year record on the Memphis police force spoke for itself. Had any detective cracked more cases than she? It was her captain who first nicknamed her Brill—short for brilliant—and it eventually stuck. When she moved here, she planned to use her given name, but Kurt talked her out of it. She'd been known as Brill for so long that the only person who still called her Colleen was her mother.

Police Chief Brill Jessup *did* have a nice ring to it. She chuckled aloud without meaning to, recalling that when she was in the second grade, she announced to her teacher and classmates that she wanted to be a lion tamer when she grew up.

A voice came over the intercom on her phone. "Chief, line one is for you. It's Kurt."

"Thanks, LaTeesha." Brill picked up the receiver and pushed the blinking button. "So how's your day going?"

"Great," Kurt Jessup said. "I'm in Pigeon Forge at the new store. The SpeedWay sign was put up this morning. I thought it might look lost with all the glitzy signs along the main drag, but actually it's not hard to spot."

"I think your little quick-copy business just turned into a chain."

"Yeah, I'm starting to think five stores is enough unless I want to hire someone to handle HR. I've got all I can say grace over."

"Good. The last thing you need is time on your hands." Brill felt her neck muscles tighten in the dead air that followed. Had she subconsciously intended to turn the knife? She wondered if Kurt was thinking the same thing.

"What time will you be home?" she said.

"I'm not sure yet. I want to stop by the church and finalize my class notes for Sunday."

Brill sighed under her breath. What made Kurt think he was

qualified to teach Sunday school? And didn't he care that it put pressure on her to attend? It's not as though she could opt out without raising a few eyebrows. "So you're really going through with it?"

"I told you I was. I wish you'd at least pretend to be supportive."

"Sorry. I think you're biting off too much too soon." Okay, so she *was* turning the knife. Was she supposed to pretend he was worthy?

"I guess we'll just have to agree to disagree," Kurt said. "I've put the past behind me. I want to get involved at church, and I really feel called to do this."

Called? Convenient choice of words. How was she supposed to argue with that? "Did you remember Emily has gymnastics at four?"

"It's right here on my phone. I'll get her there on time. So how're things at the station?"

Brill leaned on the side of her desk and looked down at the cars parked at the meters. "Let's see … we investigated multiple vehicle break-ins in the employee parking lot at the tire plant. Responded to a domestic disturbance on Fifth. Racked up a few speeding violations. Made a report on a fender bender in front of the high school. Checked out a 'popping noise' on Beech Street—a possible drive-by shooting we haven't been able to confirm. Feels strange not having a big case hanging over me. The real challenge of the day has been trying to get this stubborn file drawer open. I got it open once, but I'm not sure what I did."

"Why don't you just ask Trent to show you?"

"I can figure it out by myself, Kurt."

There was that uncomfortable dead air again.

"What I *would* like help with"—she stood and turned around—"is making this office look like it's mine."

"I'll help. Where do we start?"

"With a coat of fresh paint—something cheery. These walls are disgustingly drab, and I doubt they've been painted since Chief Hennessey was sworn in. I could use a few plants in here too—something *alive* to offset the abundance of dead oak. I'll bet if we cut this conference table and chairs into firewood, there'd be enough to burn 'til the next century. We could burn this old desk chair while we're at it."

Kurt laughed. "So how do you *really* feel about your new office?"

Brill smiled in spite of herself. "Oh, you know how I am. When the walls look grotty, I feel grotty. I'm sure once it's brightened up, I can make do with what's here. But I would appreciate your lowering the desk chair a notch. I'll tell you one thing, I doubt there's a prettier view of the Smokies anywhere in town."

"I think you're right. It shouldn't take more than the weekend to do the job—unless you actually want that big bookcase moved. In that case, you'll have to wait 'til I can round up some young bucks to help."

"Forget it, you'd need a forklift." Brill scanned the rows of books that rose almost to the ceiling. "Let's just paint around it. I'll weed out some of the books and put a few family photographs on the shelves. At least there's plenty of light in here."

"It'll look more professional after we hang your diplomas and award certificates," Kurt said. "So, are you starting to feel settled?"

"I'm comfortable with my position, though it still feels strange being called 'Chief.'"

"Especially with a Cherokee reservation just across the border."

"Very funny, Kurt."

"Sorry, bad joke."

"Not to mention politically incorrect. You read the literature the chamber of commerce gave us. You know how Sophie Trace got its name. There's a rich Cherokee history in this region."

"And some bad blood that wasn't mentioned in the brochures. Wait'll you hear what I found out at the barbershop this morning."

Brill smirked. "And they say *women* are gossips."

"This wasn't gossip. There's a legend. Some people actually believe that the spirits of the Cherokee who were driven off this land have come back to get even with the descendents of white people who settled here."

"That's about the craziest thing I've ever heard."

"They refer to the spirits as red shadows. I kept my mouth shut and just listened to the barber and a couple old duffers bat the legend back and forth. Apparently there have been a number of bizarre unsolved crimes over the years, including an ax murder in 2006—seven people were found dismembered."

"Up in the foothills, not in Sophie Trace," she said. "And the victims were shot first. I read the case file. The sheriff, along with the FBI, ATF, and DEA determined it was drug related. The victims were tied to a Venezuelan drug cartel. It was likely a territorial issue."

"Try telling that to my barber and his cronies. They're convinced it was the work of red shadows—also last week's seven-car pileup on I-40."

Brill rolled her eyes. "We arrested a drunk driver at the scene with a blood alcohol level three times the legal limit. Come on, Kurt.

Those guys were pulling your leg. You're new in town, and they were having some fun."

"I don't think so. You should've heard them."

Brill, a grin tugging at her cheeks, got up and closed the blinds on the glass wall. "Well, you can tell the keepers of the legend down at the barbershop that I'll gladly get an arrest warrant for whichever red shadow or shadows poured a fifth of Jack Daniels down our drunk driver's throat. But I'll need names and addresses." She chortled into the receiver.

"I knew you'd find it entertaining. At least a little folklore will keep the case interesting."

"At the barbershop, maybe. Not here. The guilty party is already behind bars. Case closed."

"And now you're sitting around twiddling your thumbs?"

"I've got a stack of paperwork to keep me busy." Brill put the nail file back in the pencil cup. "Actually it's nice not to be stressed out for a change."

"I know. I'm just concerned this job isn't going to be challenging enough."

"Well, we both know I didn't pursue this position for the *challenge*." The words cut, and she knew it. Let him bleed a little.

There was a long pause, and she could hear Kurt's shallow breaths in the silence. Finally he said, "Maybe after dinner, we can go over to that big home-improvement center. You can choose the paint for your office." His tone was even and nondefensive.

"I'm leaning toward deep yellow." She let her gaze glide around the room. "Maybe a shade of mustard that won't make it look like a nursery."

"You pick the color, and I'll do the painting. You'll have a fresh new look on Monday morning. How's that sound?"

It sounded great. But was she *using* Kurt by taking advantage of his willingness to please her, especially when she had no intention of letting him back into her heart or her bed? Probably. But wasn't it better than shutting him out altogether? For Emily's sake she could pretend to love him. But she could never forgive him—not ever.

"Brill, you still there?"

"Yeah, I'm here. Okay, sounds like a plan." *But if you think being nice to me is going to change anything, think again.*

CHAPTER 2

KURT parallel-parked his Dodge Caravan across the street from Sophie Trace Elementary School and glanced at his watch. Right on time.

He leaned back on the headrest and looked down the wide avenue, lined on both sides with towering shade trees that formed a canopy of gold, russet, red, and purple. He admired the old-fashioned gaslights, historic brick buildings, and striped awnings that characterized the town he still couldn't call home.

At the end of the block, he spotted the white gazebo in Shady Park and pigeons bobbing in a blanket of colored leaves that covered the ground. Three backpack-clad boys who appeared to be of middle-school age stood at the light at the crosswalk.

Kurt heard the bell ring and caught his reflection in the rearview mirror and cringed at the lines that fanned out from his eyes.

He took his cell phone off his belt clip, accessed the menu, and reviewed the remainder of the day's calendar:

3:00 p.m. Pick up Emily at school/ice-cream date

4:00 p.m. Emily to gymnastics

4:15 p.m. Class notes for Sunday school

5:30 p.m. Pick up Emily/flowers for Brill

Brill. Would there ever come a time when she crossed his mind without his heart feeling weighed down? It helped to picture her as Colleen O'Reilly, the shapely redhead who dared to challenge the views of the political science professor their senior year in college.

Kurt remembered finally getting up the nerve to ask her out, surprised when she accepted. The chemistry between them sparked a battle with passion, but he knew after the first kiss that he was going to marry her.

She got him involved in Campus Crusade for Christ and the Baptist Student Union. He made a deeper commitment to Christ and to her. A month after graduation they married, virgins on their wedding night. They did everything by the rules.

He sighed. And wasn't there a lot to be said for rules? Once broken, the damage couldn't be undone, but merely managed. If he'd learned nothing else in the past year and half, that lesson was forever carved into his heart.

He stared at his calendar, wondering why he felt compelled to keep giving Brill flowers every week. What was done was done. He could neither undo it nor live with it, and his folly produced the kind of guilt that taunted him on a regular basis. Had his compulsory flower giving offered even a moment's respite from her indifference?

He was sure the only reason she wanted to move away from Memphis was to brush off the dust that had been kicked up by his unconscionable behavior. Did anything about Sophie Trace appeal to her other than being close to the Smokies?

Brill was a master at controlling her feelings, and he guessed that when her anger finally got bigger than she was, he would have to be strong enough for both of them.

He was aware of children's voices and footsteps pounding the pavement and turned just as the side door of the van slid open. Emily climbed in, her bright blue eyes dancing with the details of a school day yet to be discussed.

"Hi, Dad." Emily popped up between the seats and planted a warm kiss on his cheek, her sandy blonde ponytail swiping his ear. "I've been thinking about Chocolate Mud Pie Crunch since lunchtime. I want two scoops with peanuts and butterscotch syrup." She slipped out of her backpack and buckled up in the backseat.

"Okay, then," he said, "Chocolate Mud Pie Crunch it is. That ought to give you a burst of energy to work off in gymnastics."

"Don't worry, I've got plenty of *disgust* to work off. Mrs. Bartlett told us we could pick something to read when we finished our math problems. So I was minding my own business, trying to read my Little House book, when Heath Briggs kept pulling my hair. Then Jeremy Downs passed me a note and Mrs. Bartlett saw it and made everybody do ten more math problems."

"She punished all of you?"

"Uh-huh. Because no one would tell who wrote the note."

"Were you afraid Jeremy would make things hard for you if you told?"

A grin tugged at the corners of Emily's mouth. "Not for long. Pouncer will help me take care of *him*."

"You're not thinking of putting a dead mouse in his lunch box like you did to that kid's last year?"

Emily giggled. "He stopped bugging me, didn't he?"

Kurt coughed to cover his smile. Maybe that old tomcat she adored was good for something after all. Let her work it out on her own. "Ready for our date?"

"It's cool having a date. How come you're taking me out and not Mom?"

"I take your mother out sometimes. But ice-cream dates are reserved for the princess of the family."

"Did you take Vanessa for ice cream when she was nine?"

"Not as often as I wanted to. We were on a tight budget back then. There *are* advantages to being the baby girl. So what else happened at school?"

"I got all my spelling words right."

"Good girl."

"And I made a friend, Jasmine Mendez. She's smart too. Mrs. Bartlett said we could do our science project together, and we decided to do it on wind as an energy source. We might have to go to the library and also look stuff up on the Internet."

Kurt listened intently to Emily's girlish chatter, glad for a reprieve from the aching emptiness that never let him forget that he had a long way to go before he and Brill were okay.

Brill filled a glass vase with the fresh flowers Kurt brought to her and felt no need to comment. Hadn't she told him at least a dozen times that his guilt offerings were a waste of time and money?

She carried the vase out to the living room and set it on the end table, then returned to the kitchen, glad to see that Emily had cleared the table and Kurt was almost finished loading the dishwasher.

"I'm glad you didn't mind takeout." Brill took off her tie and unbuttoned the top button on her uniform shirt. "I intended to be home sooner, but we had an emergency come up."

"What emergency?" Kurt said.

Brill pulled Emily close and kissed the top of her head. "Why don't you give me half an hour to wind down and I'll come help you with your math?"

"Okay." Emily grabbed her cell phone off the breakfast bar. "I'm going to send a text message to Jasmine."

Brill watched Emily race up the stairs, glad that she seemed genuinely excited about making a friend.

"What emergency?" Kurt repeated.

"A forty-five-year-old supervisor out at the tire plant left for lunch and didn't come back. No one's seen him since. Name's Michael Stanton. His wife says he's a devoted husband and father and that there's no way he could be involved with another woman."

"I assume you don't just take her word for it?"

Brill fought the urge to turn the knife. "Of course not, but no e-mails were found on his home or office computer that would lead us to think he's cheating on his wife. No porn either. Or gambling sites. He's a deacon at their church. Helps homeschool their seven kids. She said if there's any way he could call her, he would. She thinks there's foul play involved and has filed a missing persons report."

Kurt lifted his eyebrows. "I thought someone had to be missing twenty-four hours before a report could be filed."

"We don't get real serious about it for the first twenty-four because the missing person usually shows up somewhere. But a family member can file a report anytime they want."

"Maybe the guy just wanted out. Seven kids is a handful."

"That's a possibility, but it doesn't fit what his family and coworkers say about him." Brill's cell phone vibrated, and she glanced at her LED screen. "It's Trent Norris. I need to take this call." She put the phone to her ear. "Chief Jessup."

"Ma'am, I'm sorry to bother you after hours, but we just located Stanton's black Ford Taurus in the parking lot at Nick's Grill. Unlocked. His BlackBerry was on the front seat. No immediate sign of a struggle. We're dusting for prints and gathering trace evidence."

"Do you know if Stanton ate lunch there?"

"As far as we can tell, he didn't," Trent said. "The owner, Nick Phillips, says he's a regular, and he didn't remember seeing him today. There's no credit card receipt with his name on it. It appears that something or someone changed his mind about having lunch there."

"See if his wife knows the password to his BlackBerry. It might give us a clue what's going on."

Brill came down the stairs and went into the living room, where Kurt sat on the couch, thumbing through the new issue of *News-week* and eating something crunchy. How he could snack the way he did and avoid a paunchy waistline was beyond her.

"Did you get the math problems worked out?" he said.

"Emily didn't need my help. I think she pretended she does because she wants my attention." Brill smiled. "I played along, but I think she's on to me. She's growing up fast. I can't believe how independent she is."

Kurt turned a page. "Don't let that fool you. She's still a little girl."

"She nine, if that's what you mean. But I don't remember Ryan or Vanessa being so self-sufficient."

Kurt started to say something and then didn't.

"What?"

He shook his head. "Nothing."

"I hate it when you do that. Just say it."

Kurt set the magazine on the side table. "Okay. I think Emily's putting on an act. I think she feels the tension between us, and our efforts to spare her the pain are failing miserably."

Brill flopped into the overstuffed chair. "Well, aren't you the bearer of good news?"

"You asked."

Pouncer jumped up on the chair and curled up in Brill's lap. "Have you talked to Emily about this?"

"No. I'm not really sure how much to tell her. The last thing she needs right now is to lose respect for me. I'm with her more than you are."

Brill stroked the cat and let his purring comfort her. She hated that Kurt was right. "We already explained to her that we've agreed to disagree about some things. And we promised her we're not getting a divorce. That has to mean something."

"There's more to being good parents than not getting a divorce, Brill."

"Don't lecture me. I'm doing the best I can. You think it's been easy for me these past eighteen months?"

The silence that followed screamed louder than words.

"Do you still want to go to the home-improvement center and get the paint?" Kurt finally said.

She glanced at the clock on the mantel. "Why not? I can probably decide on a color in five minutes. I know what I want."

"Good." He rose to his feet, calm as ever. "I'll tell Emily to get her coat."

Kurt brushed past her and she stood, stopping to stare at the family portrait on the bookcase. It wasn't her fault things were tense. He's the one who brought this evil into their marriage. He should count it a blessing that she even agreed to stick it out.

CHAPTER 3

PROMPTLY at nine Brill tucked Emily into bed, then went downstairs and out to the garage where Kurt was surveying the paint, rollers, and brushes they had purchased.

"I like this deep golden yellow you chose," he said. "It's going to look great in your office. I can start tomorrow night, work all day Saturday, then finish up Sunday after church."

This doesn't mean I'm coming to your Sunday school class. "I need to go check on our missing plant supervisor."

She took her cell phone off her belt clip and went back in the house. She ambled out to the kitchen and pressed the speed dial for Trent Norris.

Trent picked up after the first ring. "Hello Chief."

"What's the latest on Michael Stanton?" she asked.

"Still hasn't contacted his wife. Or any family member or anyone he works directly with."

"Did his wife know the password to his BlackBerry?"

"Yes, ma'am. We checked his contacts and personal information. Nothing of interest. We went over their home and cell-phone records. No red flags there. The last call Stanton made was to his dad at eleven fifty-three this morning. We talked to the dad, and he said his son sounded fine and was on his way to Nick's Grill to grab some lunch. Didn't say whether he was meeting anyone, and—"

"Did he use his credit card?"

"No activity on the credit cards since this morning when Stanton used the Visa to fill his car. No unexplained purchases or cash advances eith—"

"What about their bank statement?"

"The wife handles most all their banking online. We went over it with her. Nothing awry with checks, deposits, or withdrawals."

Brill switched the phone to her other ear. "What about fingerprints?"

"Only his were on the BlackBerry. We found numerous prints on the inside and outside of his vehicle, many were partials. Some have been matched to his wife and kids. We're still working on the oth—"

"Did you check to see if he booked a flight? Rented a car? Bought a bus ticket?"

There was a moment of dead air. She could tell Trent was still on the line and assumed she had insulted him with her barrage of questions. "I'm sure you thought of all that."

"Yes, ma'am. I've called in O'Toole and Rousseaux, and everyone we can spare. We're checking as fast as we can. Nothing so far."

"Good work, Trent," she said with a calmer voice that she hoped didn't sound patronizing. "How's his family holding up?"

"The wife's plenty scared. Kids are staring out the window like puppies waiting for their master to return."

Brill sighed. "Can you tell what kind of relationship Mrs. Stanton has with her husband?"

"Says they're soul mates. Real involved with the kids, too. If he was fooling around, she was clueless."

"I'm sure you've asked his coworkers?"

"*And* his administrative assistant. No one we talked to thinks he's up to no good or that he has any enemies. I'm not holding my breath for a ransom call either. The Stantons don't have much socked away."

"All right, Trent, keep digging. If anything changes, call me immediately. I don't care what time it is."

Brill ended the call. She opened the freezer and took out a half gallon of strawberry ice cream. She retrieved her favorite mug from its place, packed it tightly with ice cream, then grabbed a spoon and sat at the table. She closed her eyes and let the first creamy bite melt in her mouth.

Michael Stanton seemed a little too perfect. He certainly wouldn't be the first forty-five-year-old male to leave his wife and kids, much to the dismay of everyone who knew him. But if he was having an affair, why wasn't there a paper trail? Or a suspicious name and phone number in his BlackBerry? Or any suggestive e-mails on his work or home computer?

She licked the spoon and took another bite of ice cream. Maybe Stanton didn't leave of his own volition. Who might want him to disappear: his lover's spouse? A disgruntled employee? A jealous colleague?

Kurt breezed into the kitchen. "What'd you find out?"

"Entirely too little, and my detectives are stretched thin. I may have to ask Sheriff Parker to help, though I'd rather not involve him, especially when we don't have any evidence to suggest foul play."

"What does your intuition suggest?"

She locked gazes with him. "That we're missing something. And if I ask Sheriff Parker for assistance, he'll see me as the damsel in distress rather than a police chief who needs to pick his brain and borrow some manpower."

"You only met the guy once. Is he really that backward in his thinking?"

"Let's hope not. But I'm sure not eager to invite his big boots into my jurisdiction 'til I've got a handle on what's going on. Michael Stanton left his car and his BlackBerry, and there was no sign of a struggle. It's not out of the question that he just got tired of his life and walked away. I can't afford to overreact."

"You came here with an impressive track record, Brill. You don't have to prove yourself to Sheriff Parker."

"But I *do* need to prove myself worthy to lead the department. I think it's time to roll up my sleeves."

At nine thirty Brill pulled up behind Detective Norris's squad car in front of the Stantons' two-story brick house on Crawford Street, the number five-fifteen visible under the porch light.

She got out, the October breeze brisk with the promise of frost, and walked to the top of the driveway where Trent was standing. The orange glow of his cigarette seemed almost suspended in the dark.

"Those things will turn your lungs black," she said.

"Then they'll match the rest of me." Trent blew out a stream of smoke, then dropped the cigarette on the pavement and snuffed it out with his shoe. "I'm surprised to see you, Chief. I gave you a full report less than thirty minutes ago."

"I'm just used to being in the thick of things and prefer it to pacing by myself. Is Mrs. Stanton still up?"

"Yes, ma'am. I doubt she'll close her eyes tonight. She's sitting by the phone, hoping it'll ring. Her sister and brother-in-law came and got the kids. I'm sure she'd be comforted to know the police chief's here."

"Good. I'll go talk to her."

Brill knocked gently, then slowly pushed open the bulky metal door and peeked inside. A woman, her face ashen, her eyes vacant, sat at one end of the couch with a pink and white afghan wrapped around her shoulders.

"Mrs. Stanton, it's Police Chief Brill Jessup. May I come in?"

The woman nodded.

Brill went over to the couch and took Mrs. Stanton's hand in hers. "I'm so sorry for the pain you must be feeling. We're doing everything we can to find your husband.'"

"Something terrible's happened to him. Michael would never do this to us." A tear trickled down the woman's cheek. "And would you please call me Shannon? Mrs. Stanton sounds so impersonal. If one more officer calls me 'ma'am,' I'm going to scream."

"All right, Shannon," Brill said. "I just want to reassure you that my detectives are working hard to find your husband."

"How can a man leave for lunch and disappear without a trace—and in broad daylight, no less?"

"That's what we're working to find out."

"He never went anywhere without his BlackBerry." Shannon

seemed to stare at nothing. "He missed the deacon's meeting at church tonight. They're all praying for him. Everyone loves Michael. The kids adore him. He baptized Peter, our eleven-year-old, just last month. And he helped Patterson, our six-year-old, to memorize the Twenty-third Psalm. And Payton, our two-year-old, won't go to sleep unless Michael sings to her. He does something special with each of them, and the older ones are asking where he is. What do I tell them? I can't bring myself to lie. But I don't want them to be scared. Do you have children, Chief Jessup?"

"Yes, three. Our son and oldest daughter are in college. Our youngest, Emily, is a fourth grader at Sophie Trace Elementary."

"Ours are homeschooled. Michael teaches them math and science. I do the rest."

"That's quite a commitment," Brill said.

"Michael and I are totally into our children. He wouldn't just leave us. That's why I know something's happened to him."

"Can you think of anyone who would want to hurt your husband?"

Shannon shook her head. "That's just it. Everybody loves him."

"Was he prone to get depressed or moody?"

"He's the most even-tempered person I know. I'm the one who gets overwhelmed sometimes. Michael's a rock."

"It's not always easy to maintain a cool façade. Is it possible that your husband might have sought an outlet for the pressures of a busy life?"

Shannon sighed. "I know what you're getting at, and I've already answered this line of questioning for the detectives. Let me save you the time: Michael doesn't gamble. Isn't into porn. He doesn't drink or drug or deal. He doesn't have a girlfriend—or a boyfriend. He's never paid for sex. He isn't bipolar. Has no addictions. No dark secrets. And he would never ever walk out on us!"

"Okay." Brill put her hands on Shannon's shoulders and looked her squarely in the eyes. "We'll do everything in our power to find him. I promise."

Shannon's eyes welled and a single tear spilled down her cheek. "How could something like this happen *here*? I always thought Sophie Trace was a safe place to raise our kids."

"We don't know that your husband has met with foul play. We may find a good explanation for all this."

Or not. Brill's mind flashed back eighteen months to the precise moment when the shrill pitch of betrayal shattered her heart into a million sharp fragments. Nothing would surprise her anymore.

Kurt lay on the couch facing a crackling fire, the first of the season, and felt surprisingly cold. He smiled when Pouncer jumped up on the couch and curled up behind his knees, wondering if the cat had brought home a trophy mouse for Emily to shock Jeremy what's-his-name.

The clock on the mantel chimed twice. He wondered if Brill would wait out the entire night with Mrs. Stanton or if she would come home and lay wide-eyed in the dark. She wouldn't sleep. She never did when there were so many unknowns in a case, especially when children were affected.

"Daddy, why did you light a fire in the middle of the night?"

Emily, barefoot and dressed in her plaid flannel nightgown, came and stood between him and the fireplace.

"Your mom went out on a case and I'm waiting up for her. Why are you awake?"

She shrugged. "Can I stay here with you for a while?"

"Sure."

Emily flopped on the edge of the couch, then stretched out and nestled next to him, her back against his chest. "Is Mom working the case where the dad went missing?"

"How'd you know about that?"

"Well ... I kind of overheard you and Mom talking."

"If you overheard us, you were eavesdropping. You know better than that."

"I get curious when you talk softly."

"Sometimes Mom and I need to discuss things that little girls don't need to be bothered with."

"Did the man get murdered?"

"If you were eavesdropping, you already know as much as I do. Why don't we talk about something else?"

"I'm not a baby."

"I know you're not. But you're only a kid once. There's no need to clutter your childhood with scary stuff."

"I'm not scared. If the guy isn't dead, then why doesn't he come home to his family?"

"You know we're not supposed to discuss details of cases your mom is working on."

"Maybe he went away to think." Emily nestled a little closer to him. "I remember when you did that. Mom was really sad, and I stayed in my room with Pouncer. I never heard her cry before."

Kurt hadn't either. It was the worst weekend of his life. "You never told me you hid in your room with the cat. I'm sorry. You must've been really sad and confused."

"I was just glad you came home."

"The important thing now is that your mom and I are trying to work out our differences, right?"

Emily's silence crackled louder than the fire.

"Right …?" He gently stroked her hair, his heart racing. *Lord, if she's going to ask the question I've been dreading, please give me the right words—and the courage.* "It's okay, baby. Tell me what's on your heart. You can be honest with me."

Seconds passed, then Emily finally exhaled, and in a tiny voice said, "Is Mom really coming home, or are you just trying not to make me sad?"

"What?" Kurt, both surprised and relieved, turned her around and gazed into her wide eyes. "Your mother is definitely coming home. I would never lie to you about that or anything else. You hear me?" He ran his thumb down Emily's cheek. "She had to go out tonight and work this case, just like she did dozens of times in Memphis. What would make you think she's not coming back?"

"I don't know."

"I think you do."

Emily rubbed her eyes. "She just seems … kind of quiet and sad sometimes. I thought getting a new job would make her happy. But she doesn't seem happy to me."

"Well, we're not through working out our differences."

"I know … you and Mom have 'agreed to disagree,' but is that going to be forever?"

"I hope not. But you know what we totally agree on and always will? That we love you very much and are not getting a divorce."

She fiddled with the button on his shirt. "Promise?"

"Promise." *Again.* "So don't worry. Mom will seem happier after she's adjusted to the new job. She just needs time."

"I think you need time too."

Kurt smiled, though his heart felt like a lead weight. "What *I* need is laughter. Lots and lots and lots of laughter."

He tickled Emily until her giggling filled the room and caused Pouncer to jump down on the floor and meow as if to say he wanted in on the fun.

When his daughter quieted down, she resumed her nestling posture, her hand dangling off the couch and stroking Pouncer's back. Finally she said, "Daddy?"

"Hmm?"

"I hope the man comes home and the mom isn't sad and they don't have to agree to disagree."

"Me, too, Emily.

CHAPTER 4

BRILL sat at the desk in her office, poring over the notes in the Michael Stanton case file and trying to ignore the pain in her back caused by her inability to put her feet flat on the floor.

She captured a yawn with her hand and glanced at her watch: *3:10*. So much for a good night's sleep. Nothing her detectives had uncovered had led her to believe that Michael Stanton was anything but a model husband, father, employee, and friend.

Trent knocked on her open door. "You paged me?"

"I did. Come in. I wanted to commend you for doing a thorough job—and in a very tight time frame."

"Thank you, ma'am. Unfortunately we still don't know what happened to Stanton. His church wants WSTN-TV to run his picture on the morning news and has offered a three-thousand-dollar reward for anyone who helps us find him."

"Well, *somebody* knows where he is. Money talks." She grimaced and shifted her weight from one side to the other, trying to keep one foot flat on the floor.

"Why don't I lower that desk chair for you?" Trent said. "I think you'd be more comfortable."

Brill pretended not to notice the amusement dancing in his eyes. "Thanks. I'd appreciate that."

"Be right back." Trent left through the open door and went out to the detective bureau to his desk.

She got up and arched her lower back, then went over and looked out the window. A crescent moon hung in the darkness. She wondered if Michael Stanton could see it. Was he in trouble? Or was he just a middle-aged man who wanted a new life?

Trent came back, screwdriver in hand, and turned her bulky leather chair over as if it were no heavier than a toy.

"There's just nothing to suggest foul play," he said. "Stanton doesn't owe anybody and doesn't have any enemies. I might think he was having an affair. But with no money trail and nothing suspicious on his BlackBerry or his office and home PCs, there's only one logical conclusion: He was abducted by aliens." Seconds passed in silence, then Trent chuckled. "Don't look so stunned, Chief. I'm kidding."

Brill tucked a strand of hair behind her ear. "And just when I was beginning to wonder if you had a sense of humor."

Trent turned the chair upright and patted the seat. "There you go. Try it now."

Brill positioned herself in the chair, her back now supported and her feet flat on the floor. "Perfect. Thanks. Actually my back thanks you."

"You want me to show you how to get that file drawer open while I'm at it?"

"Sure, why not?"

Trent gave the top drawer of her desk a slight shove with his palm, and then pulled it out. "There you go."

Could she feel any dumber than she did at this moment? "Thanks, Trent. My husband reminds me a regular basis that I'm too independent and stubborn for my own good."

"Well, I'm pretty handy with stuff like this. Feel free to ask me for help if you need it."

"I'll remember that. Why don't you go home and get some sleep?"

"What about you, ma'am?"

"I'm thinking of doing the same. We've done all we can tonight. If Stanton doesn't surface by sunup, I think we need to go one-on-one with the people he supervised at the tire plant—and his superiors. I'll need to ask Sheriff Parker for help. What's been your experience working with him?"

"The sheriff carries a big stick in Stanton County. He and Chief Hennessey were tight, mostly because the former chief didn't care if the sheriff got the credit for everything."

"I see ..." *In other words the only thing bigger than Sam Parker's belly is his ego.*

"You going to call in the Feds, ma'am?"

She locked gazes with him, the corners of her mouth twitching. "If and when the evidence suggests Stanton might have been abducted by someone *other* than aliens."

Brill heard an obnoxious buzzing noise and realized it was her alarm clock. She groped the nightstand and hit the Off button.

She sat up on the side of the bed, all too aware that the other side hadn't been slept in. She ran her hands through her hair, then grabbed her cell phone and headed for the shower.

"Good morning," Kurt said from the doorway. "Rough night?"

"We didn't find Michael Stanton. So yes." She gave Kurt a quick overview of her experience with Shannon Stanton and explained where her detectives were with the investigation. "Their church is offering a three-thousand-dollar reward for anyone who helps us find him. One of the TV stations agreed to show his picture on the morning news."

"Yeah, I saw it just before I took Emily to school. WSTN did a good job."

"Not good enough if no one's seen him."

Kurt folded his arms across his chest. "You'd think someone would remember seeing him in the parking lot at Nick's Grill during a busy lunch hour. Especially when word gets around there's a reward."

"Rewards also draw out every nut in the county who's looking to make an easy buck. Determining which, if any, leads are legitimate just adds to our workload. I need to shower and get back to work. What do you have on tap today?"

"I'm going to drop in on the manager at my Knoxville store. I'll pick up Emily at school this afternoon and can start painting your office anytime after that."

"We may have to wait 'til things calm down. I need to get going, it's already after ten." Her cell phone vibrated in her hand and she looked at the display. "Here we go. It's Trent." She put the phone to her ear. "Did we find Stanton?"

"No, ma'am. But it's possible we have another missing person. A first-grade teacher at Sophie Trace Elementary School didn't show up for class this morning and no one's seen her. Name's Janice Evans. Sixty-one. Her husband saw her leave home at seven fifteen this morning, driving her red 2005 Ford Mustang. The school principal called home to check on her."

"Good grief. My daughter goes to that school. I assume you checked the accident reports?"

"No major accidents reported this morning and none on Grand Avenue, which is the route her husband says she would normally take. We've got a cruiser in that area trying to spot a red Mustang with her license plates."

"Did you check the ER at St. Luke's?"

"Yes, ma'am. No one by that name was admitted. I know she's only been missing three hours, and there could be a logical explanation. But under the circumstances, I thought you'd want a heads-up."

"You thought right. I'll see you in thirty minutes."

CHAPTER 5

NICK Phillips winced as a clap of thunder rattled the windows at Nick's Grill and reverberated for several seconds. The front door flew open, and Antonio and Tessa Masino scurried inside, wet leaves swirling at their heels.

"Hi, friends." Nick put his hand on Tessa's shoulder and shook Antonio's hand. "I was hoping the rain wouldn't keep you away. I added a new menu item just for you: a low-fat grilled chicken Caesar salad that'll knock your socks off."

"Sounds wonderful." Tessa set her umbrella in the corner next to the coat rack.

"It was nice of you to think of us," Antonio swatted the air, "but I already decided I'm having a Nick's Triple Bacon Cheeseburger Deluxe and plenty of fries." He patted Tessa's cheek. "Forget what the doctor says, love. If my ticker gives out, I'll go happy."

Nick followed the Masinos to the counter and winked at Maggie Cummings, green pad in hand, who scribbled the order nearly as fast as Antonio talked.

"Got it," she said. "I'll bring your coffee."

Nick stood next to Gus Williams, who sat on the first barstool, wearing the same plaid flannel shirt and overalls he had on the day

46

before, and waited for Gus and Antonio to go through their daily greeting ritual.

Antonio slapped Gus on the back and straddled the stool next to him. "How's it going, friend?

"Really can't complain. But I always do." A grin appeared beneath Gus's white mustache but faded as he spoke again. "So did y'all hear Michael Stanton went missin'—the guy who always smiles and says, 'God bless you,' when he leaves?"

"Hard to believe," Nick said. "He's been a customer here a long time."

Tessa nodded. "We recognized his picture on the news. The man has seven children, for heaven's sake. I hope nothing horrible's happened to him."

"Might've just up and left." Gus stroked his mustache. "Can't imagine tryin' to support a family that size in today's world. Then again, a nice-lookin' fella like that might've found him a lady friend, if you get my drift."

Nick felt a draft and turned toward the front door in time to see Clint Ames hurry inside.

Clint shook the rain off his London Fog and hung it on the coat rack, then sat at the counter next to Tessa. "Hi, everybody. Man, it's nasty out there."

The friends greeted Clint while Maggie set a Coke in front of Gus and began filling mugs with coffee.

"I've got some news I'll bet you haven't heard," Clint said. "A first-grade teacher at Sophie Trace Elementary is missing."

"How do you know that?" Nick said.

"Her husband's replacing the plumbing in my cabins at Hazy

View. The principal of the school called his cell while I was standing right there and asked why his wife didn't show up for class. He tried to reach her cell and she didn't pick up. Long story short: No one's seen her. Seems she disappeared between home and the school—just like that." He snapped his fingers. "Two people in two days. Anyone else find that disturbing?"

"I'll say." Nick slung a bar towel over his shoulder.

"Isn't it a little early to assume she's vanished?" Tessa said.

"Her husband's really scared." Clint pointed to his watch. "As of twenty minutes ago he still hadn't heard from her and the cops put out an APB but haven't spotted her car."

"There're still questions about those ax murders back in 2006," Gus said. "Let's hope this isn't round two."

"What questions?" Antonio waved his hand. "That mess was drug related. The victims were shot execution-style before they were dismembered."

"So we were told." Gus lifted his bushy white eyebrows up and down. "I asked Chief Hennessey once if he believed the red shadows did it. I could tell by his face he knew somethin', but he just walked off and never did answer."

Tessa laughed. "I'm sure he was speechless."

"I'd be careful about pooh-poohin' the legend," Gus said. "Y'all who weren't raised in this town don't understand how real the threat is. My great-great-granddaddy staked his claim on Cherokee land. The red shadows could come after me next."

"Maybe you should tell that to the new police chief who moved in next door to me and Tessa," Antonio said. "I'm sure she's not out chasing red shadows."

"Wouldn't do any good." Gus took a sip of Coke. "Nobody's seen one in years. But I used to hear my Grandpa Williams talk about red shadows all the time. Believe me, y'all, the legend's real."

Nick saw the disbelief on Tessa's face and waited for the rebuttal: three ... two ... one ...

"Yes," Tessa said, "but just because the Cherokee legend is real doesn't prove there's any substance to it. The principal chief himself has denied the notion that the spirits are responsible for any crimes, solved or unsolved. It's nonsense. I can't believe any rational person would live in fear of the spirits of the dead."

Gus took off his glasses and held them up to the light. "Well, with all due respect, Antonio's great-great *Italian* granddaddy Masino wasn't livin' here when the Cherokee were driven out, so y'all have nothin' to fear." He wiped his lenses with the bottom of his flannel shirt. "On the other hand those of us with British roots have good reason to fear the red shadows—and especially a guy with the last name *Stanton*."

Nick hid his amusement and waited for Tessa's comeback.

"Hogwash," she said. "There are more Stantons listed in the phone book than any other name. It's purely coincidence."

"By the way, the missing school teacher's last name is Evans," Clint said.

"There you go—another British surname." Gus put his glasses back on. "Wouldn't surprise me if her or her husband's ancestors came over here from England with the Stantons."

Antonio nudged Gus's arm. "The seven ax murder victims were *Latino*."

"That's what the authorities told the media. But what if they weren't? And what if the axes were actually tomahawks? If you investigated a gruesome crime like that and believed the red shadows were responsible, would you want to start a panic?"

"Oh, brother, you think it was a cover-up?" Tessa said.

"Yeah, I do. And I don't think it's the first time. Don't forget the Jones family that was found dead in their home last year."

"From carbon monoxide poisoning, Gus."

"So they say. What about the remains of that couple that was found near the old mill?"

"Authorities think they died of exposure—probably fifty years ago."

"Ah, probably," Gus said. "But no one really knows, do they?"

Tessa exhaled and shook her head slowly. "I can't believe we're even having this conversation. It's an insult to the Cherokee people for you to throw around this baseless drivel."

"It may not be politically correct to say it," Gus said, "but I'm tellin' y'all, the red shadows do exist. And I doubt they're real happy about bein' blown off in recent years. I know some folks who think that big pileup on I-40 last week was caused by red shadows."

Tessa rolled her eyes. "Not unless one of them was intoxicated and driving a Corvette."

Nick glanced over at the booths and noticed other customers were listening to the banter. He put his hand on Gus's shoulder and said loudly enough that the eavesdroppers could hear, "I don't think we're going to resolve this issue today. There are interesting arguments on both sides. One thing we agree on: It's pretty serious that two people are missing in two days. Any way you slice it, our new police chief has her hands full."

CHAPTER 6

LATE Friday afternoon Brill sat at the conference table in her office, finishing up a meeting with Detective Captain Trent Norris, Detectives Sean O'Toole and Beau Jack Rousseaux, and Sheriff Sam Parker.

"We've shared a great deal of information around this table," she said. "Before we leave, I'd like Trent to summarize what we know so far, just to be sure we're all on the same page."

"Yes, ma'am." Trent folded his hands on the table and seemed relaxed. "We've got two missing individuals: Michael Stanton, a forty-five-year-old Caucasian male. And Janice Evans, a sixty-one-year-old Caucasian female. It seems unlikely the two know each other. They don't work together. Don't go to the same church. Don't live in the same neighborhood. Haven't communicated by phone or e-mail.

"There's been no ransom demand in either case, and nothing to connect the two cases. Nothing that points to a motive. The spouses have independently expressed serious concern that foul play is involved.

"Stanton's car was found by Detective Rousseaux and myself in the parking lot at Nick's Grill at Third and Main. There was no sign of a struggle, and trace hasn't produced any evidence to suggest otherwise. His BlackBerry was in the car and contained nothing of interest.

"Evans's car has not been found even though an APB has been issued. I believe that covers the major points, ma'am."

"Thank you, Trent. Sheriff Parker and I will hold a press conference shortly to satisfy the persistent media that've taken up residence on our front steps." Brill made a tent with her fingers and gathered her thoughts, aware that what she was about to say would probably not set well with Sheriff Parker.

"Just before this meeting," she said, "I talked with a friend, Special Agent David Riley, who works out of the FBI field office in Knoxville. I apprised him of our situation, and he's of the opinion that we could benefit from the FBI's expertise and some additional manpower."

"I'll just *bet* he does." Sam leaned forward, his elbows planted on the table. "With all due respect, it would be ludicrous to involve the FBI when you're not even sure these people have been kidnapped. The Feds do it their way or no way."

"That hasn't been my experience with Special Agent Riley," she said. "I worked with him on missing persons cases during my time on the Memphis police force and always respected what he brought to the table. I also learned that every minute counts when someone's missing—and it's not the time to get territorial."

Sam's glasses rested on his nose, and his steely gaze went from one detective to another and then rested on her. "Well, of course it's time to get territorial. What happens in Stanton County is *my* business."

"And what happens in Sophie Trace is mine. I'm the one who has to answer to the city council. Two people have vanished, and we're no closer to figuring out *why* than when they were first reported missing. I owe it to the victims and their families to use every available resource to find them. I'd like to think we're both professional enough to handle concurrent jurisdiction."

Did she really just say that to Sam Parker, the man whose reputation for being a control freak was right up there with Attila the Hun's?

"All right, Chief Jessup, let me get this straight." Sam, an annoying grin plastered on his face, sat back in his chair, his arms folded across his chest. "You're actually prepared to invite the Federal Bureau of Investigation into your jurisdiction with zero—I repeat, zero—proof there's even been a crime committed?"

"I'd rather be wrong than sorry. I don't have time to wait for proof."

"What's your hurry, madam? Are you afraid we can't get the job done?"

"Actually I'm trying to ensure that we *can* get the job done. The FBI has more experience than either of us when it comes to missing persons. And I assure you Special Agent Riley is very agreeable to work with."

Sam exhaled loudly enough to show his disapproval. "You're jumpin' the gun on this, Chief Jessup. I can tell you that right now."

Kurt turned off the five o'clock news and set the remote on the end table. So much for worrying that this job wasn't going to be challenging enough for Brill.

"What did you think of your mother being on TV?" he said to Emily.

"Very cool." Emily leaned her head on the back of the couch. "But I'm really freaked out about Mrs. Evans. Everybody at my school will be too."

"I know, sweetie. I'm praying she's all right."

"What if she isn't? That dad who disappeared hasn't been found yet."

"How about we go scrounge up something for dinner?"

Emily jumped to her feet. "Can I make meat loaf? I love getting the hamburger all squishy in my hands."

Kurt walked into the kitchen just as the phone rang.

"Hello."

"So how'd I do?" Brill said.

"The press conference was very professional, Chief. I thought you handled yourself well. Your daughter was proud of you too." He winked at Emily.

"Good. I felt relaxed, even though I could feel Sam Parker scowling into the cameras. He's probably out marking his territory now that I've asked the FBI to help."

"The sheriff looked solemn, but I thought it was because of the situation. Everyone else probably did too. So when's David Riley coming?"

"Any minute. I considered postponing the press conference until he arrived and could be briefed. But we would've missed the five o'clock news, and it seemed too important to push it 'til ten. There's a lot of gossip, and people deserved to hear the facts directly from me. I certainly don't want anyone to accuse this department of holding back information."

"Are you?"

"No. We absolutely can't make a connection between the two cases and can't find a motive in either. Frankly I'm a little overwhelmed, which is ironic when, just yesterday, my biggest challenge was getting a file drawer open. It's as though these two people have disappeared into thin air, yet I have to believe someone out there saw something."

Kurt took the cordless phone over to the table and sat. "I think it was a good move to show their pictures and encourage people to call if they know anything. The missing woman's red Ford Mustang is the kind of car that shouldn't be hard to spot."

"If only someone would come forward and give us a clue we can actually work with. Maybe David will find an angle we haven't thought of."

Kurt picked up a pen and began to doodle. "So I guess you want me to scrap the idea of painting your office for a while?"

"Not necessarily. If you start tonight, how sure are you that you could be finished by Monday?"

"Positive. It's only going to take one coat. I can do a total makeover if I can work in there without anyone underfoot. I'll even hang your diplomas and certificates on the wall behind the conference table. Just tell me where you want me to put the plants. It'll be fun."

"All right, go for it." Was that a smile in her voice? "I'd be embarrassed for David to see my office the way it looks now. I can move what I need into the small briefing room until Monday."

Kurt smiled at Emily. "Why don't Baby Girl and I stop and get something to eat and then head your way and get things ready to paint? You want us to bring you dinner?"

"No, I had a sub sandwich a couple hours ago. Thanks anyway."

"All right. See you when I see you. I love you." He let the words hang there and knew she wouldn't respond in kind.

"I don't know when I'll be home, but I'm sure it'll be late."

Brill asked Trent to help her set up a makeshift office in the smaller of two briefing rooms, after which she sat at a table and became engrossed in the details of the missing persons case files. A knock on the door startled her.

"Hey, Red," said a familiar deep voice.

Brill smiled and looked up.

Special Agent David Riley filled the doorway, outfitted in cowboy boots, jeans, a tan corduroy sport coat, and a grin that turned his eyes to slits. His balding head was now shaved and had the same five o'clock shadow as his face. She decided the new look was rugged and quite becoming.

She stood and offered him her hand. "It's great to see you, David."

"Likewise." He shook her hand and held it several seconds before finally letting go. "I was surprised when I heard you took this job. Seemed a little too tame for you. But now here you are—two people missing and the Feds in your backyard again. You really know how to pick them. So how's Kurt?"

"Good. His SpeedWay business has turned into a chain of five stores. He's enjoying being his own boss. Did Patricia open her dance studio?"

"I expect she did." David rocked from heel to toe, his thumbs hooked on his jeans pockets. "We're divorced. She moved back to Dallas."

"Oh." Brill felt her cheeks flush.

"She complained I stopped talking to her." David's eyes were no longer slits but dark pools. "I guess after all the sick stuff I saw every day, the last thing I wanted to do was relive it with her over dinner." He blinked several times. "So fill me in on what's going on here. I'm intrigued that two people suddenly disappeared in a town this size and there's no evidence that the cases are related. I'm thinking they have to be. My first thought is serial killings."

"It crossed my mind," Brill said. "I personally checked to see if any animals were reported missing or abused over the past few months. Nothing. I would've expected to find a pattern of tortured animals if we were looking at a serial killer about to make his debut."

"Good thinking. Though it's way too early to rule it out."

She nodded. "I know. But we didn't find any sign of a struggle in Stanton's car—no blood either."

"All right, start at the beginning. I want every detail."

Brill pushed open the glass door at Nick's Grill, surprised when David Riley held it for her. She stepped inside, not expecting the cozy ambiance or the delicious aroma. The dining area was abuzz, booths and tables packed with customers.

She smiled at a waitress coming in her direction.

"Two for dinner?" the waitress asked.

Brill glanced at her nametag, "Actually, Maggie, I'm Police Chief

Jessup and this is Special Agent Riley. We'd like to speak with Nick Phillips, please."

"Wait right here and I'll get him for you."

Brill took a menu from the stack next to the cash register and perused it. "Oh, good. They've got veggie burgers. I got hooked on those in Memphis and wasn't sure if I could find them here."

"You always were one to eat healthy," David said. "I'll probably die with a cheeseburger in my mouth."

Brill smiled. "Veggie burgers are an acquired taste."

A fifty-something man with a full head of sandy brown hair and twenty extra pounds hanging over his belt moved briskly toward them.

"Chief Jessup," he offered her his hand, "I recognize you from TV. I'm Nick Phillips, the owner."

David held up his badge. "I'm Special Agent David Riley of the FBI. We'd like to ask you some questions about Michael Stanton."

"Sure. May I offer you dinner? Or would you prefer to talk in my office?"

"We just need a private place to talk," Brill said.

"Follow me."

Nick strode down the hallway off the kitchen and flipped on the light in the first room. He motioned for David and Brill to go in first and then followed them.

"Pull up a chair," Nick said. "What would you like to know?"

David sat in a folding chair, his hands resting on his knees. "How well do you know Michael Stanton?"

"He's a regular." Nick leaned against his desk, his arms folded across his chest. "Comes in once or twice a week for lunch. Alone.

Very pleasant. Always says 'God bless you' when he leaves."

"Do you remember what kind of food he orders?"

"Yeah, the healthy stuff. Grilled veggie sandwiches. Veggie burgers. Spinach salads. Not an ounce of fat on him. I've always wondered if he works out. Never asked."

"Do you remember anything else about him that stands out? Nothing is too insignificant. A name you heard him mention? Someone he might've talked to on his cell phone. Something about his clothing. His mannerisms. Anything?"

"Just that he has seven kids." Nick smiled. "Seems real proud of them and is quick to pull out his wallet and show their pictures. Says he helps homeschool them."

"Does he ever use his cell phone?"

"Sure. He calls his wife sometimes when he's here. Talks real nice to her."

"Did he call her by name?"

"I didn't pay that much attention."

"How'd you know it was his wife?"

Nick shrugged. "He called her honey and asked about the kids."

"Anything else?"

"Nothing comes to mind. I'm just sick that he disappeared."

David showed him a photograph of the second missing person. "Ever see this woman in here?"

Nick spent half a minute studying the photo. "Not that I remember. Attractive lady. Who is she?"

"Name's Janice Evans. She's a first-grade teacher at Sophie Trace Elementary. She's missing too."

"Yeah, I heard about that. Hope she shows up unharmed. It's

really weird that two people in two days are missing." Nick looked at his hands, seemingly conflicted about something. "Listen, this probably has nothing to do with anything, but are either of you familiar with the legend of the red shadows?"

"I am," Brill said. "Why do you ask?"

"Because I know people who think the red shadows might be behind these disappearances. Believe me, I'm not one of them. But you probably realize the legend holds a lot of weight with some folks in this town."

"I'm starting to." She turned to David, her eyebrows arched. "I'll tell you about it later. It's just folklore."

"If you don't mind, I'd like to hear what Mr. Phillips has to say about it."

"Sure, but I'd be more comfortable if you'd call me Nick." He cracked his knuckles. "You're going to need some background first or the legend won't make sense."

"Go on."

"Well, sir, it all goes back to Sophie Stanton, the little girl the town's named after. Shortly after her parents and a few other settlers arrived here from England, little Sophie wandered away from camp and later was found unharmed and living with the Cherokee."

"I read about that in the brochure the chamber of commerce gave me," Brill said. "The town was later named Sophie Trace because it was built on the backwoods trail the settlers followed to find the little girl."

"That's right," Nick said. "But let me rewind the tape and fill in some of the details. It's a fact that the Cherokee were fascinated by Sophie's fair skin, blue eyes, and blonde curls. And given the fact that she was seven years old, arrived on the seventh day of the seventh month, had seven buttons on each of her dress sleeves and seven days later, white men came looking for her; they took that as a sign from the Great Spirit that the white man and red man would live in peace."

"We all know that didn't happen," David said.

"It did for a while." Nick rubbed the stubble on his chin. "The Stantons and the others got along fine with the small tribes in this area. It wasn't until the government finally began to enforce the Indian Removal Act in the late 1830s that things started to change. Word reached the tribes here that the U.S. Army was driving thousands and thousands of their people out of Georgia. Many were dying."

David locked gazes with him. "The Trail of Tears?"

"You got it," Nick said. "No one knows for sure what happened to the Cherokee who lived here at the time, but many believe they fled to the Great Smoky Mountains and joined up with other Cherokee who escaped the forced removal. They became known as the Eastern Band of the Cherokee and still live there today."

David's eyebrows came together. "So what's the legend?"

"It's believed that the spirits of the Cherokee who once inhabited this region the red shadows—roam the countryside, seeking to avenge the descendants of the Stantons and the other white settlers who laid claim to their land."

The corners of David's mouth twitched. "You're saying that these red shadows had something to do with the disappearance of Michael Stanton and Janice Evans?"

"I'm not, but there're people who do. One of my lunch regulars was rehashing some old crimes that are still unsolved and a couple more recent ones he believes the authorities are holding out on. I have to tell you, the ax murders of 2006 left question marks in some people's minds. Gus is convinced the red shadows were responsible, and the victims were killed with tomahawks, not axes. He thinks the Feds covered the whole thing up. He believes the big accident on I-40 was caused by red shadows and the authorities won't admit it for fear of starting a panic."

"People here actually *buy* this stuff?" David said.

Nick held out his palms. "No, no, not everyone. But there are folks, especially some who grew up here, that blame the red shadows for every unsolved crime since the Trail of Tears. They're also the first to challenge the facts authorities have released about crimes in recent years. It doesn't help that a remnant of the Cherokee live just across the state line."

"Interesting." David shot Brill a look that seemed to say *I can't believe you have to live with this malarkey.*

"I realize it's just folklore," Nick said, "but I promise you some very sane people believe it. I thought you should know that."

"We should, thanks. You've been very helpful." David rose to his feet in perfect sync with Brill.

Nick escorted them to the exit. "I hope you find Michael Stanton and the missing schoolteacher."

"I won't rest until we do," she said.

David looked over Nick's shoulder and seemed to be sizing up the weather. "If we have more questions, we'll be in touch."

"All right. You folks take care."

Nick waved to someone in one of the far booths and headed in that direction just as lightning flashed, followed by a loud boom that shook the windows.

Brill pulled her collar up around her ears. "It's really coming down. I guess we just need to make a run for it."

"No point in both of us getting soaked." David took off his coat and pushed open the door. "Come on. I'll use my coat for an umbrella."

"You don't have to do that."

"Of course I don't. Would you rather get drenched?"

She laughed. "Not really."

"Then let's go."

She stepped out into the driving rain, David's arm around her, his coat shielding her, and realized she had just used her gender to her advantage—something she had committed *not* to do. Then again it was just David. Surely they were past all that by now?

CHAPTER 7

BRILL turned the key, pushed her shoulder against the heavy arched door, and stepped into the house that still felt like someone else's. She hung her umbrella on the coatrack, grateful that Kurt had thought to leave a lamp on in the living room. She went over and collapsed on the couch.

One nagging question dominated her thoughts: What had happened to Michael Stanton and Janice Evans? Her detectives had worked tirelessly with sheriff's deputies and FBI agents and torn open these two people's lives. Why were they no closer to an answer? Nothing was found to connect the missing pair. And neither had an enemy—at least none that could be named.

Brill hugged the couch pillow. She and David had carried on an amusing conversation about the red shadows after they left Nick's. They agreed that folklore so intertwined with the people of this community would need to be addressed with great tact and a straight face. They hoped Sheriff Parker's experience would help in that regard.

How could the fact that someone was missing and just happened to have the last name Stanton be anything other than coincidence? Stanton was the most common surname in the county. And didn't Sophie Stanton, though she married Robert Wiley Jones, have eight brothers who also raised families here?

"Welcome home, stranger." Kurt came into the living room and sat across from her in the overstuffed chair. "How's the investigation coming?"

"We're stumped," she said. "Did I wake you? I tried not to make any noise when I came in."

"No, we haven't been home that long. Emily got engrossed in one of her American Girl books, so I stayed late and primed the walls in your office."

"Thanks." She glanced over at him. "I'm probably being entirely too self-centered, but I would've been embarrassed for David to see it the way it was."

"It's not your fault Chief Hennessey had no taste."

Brill shrugged. "I guess my ego's bigger than I thought. The office didn't look very *chiefly* to me, and I think it should."

"Well, give me 'til Sunday night," Kurt said. "I'll make you proud of it."

For a split second she was almost numb to the sting of betrayal. But nothing Kurt did for her—no act of kindness, no guilt offering—would ever be enough to make her forget.

If only she could get past the awkwardness of being alone with him. What did they used to talk about?

"I'm going to hit the sack," Kurt said. "I want to get an early start. Oh, I almost forgot ... Tessa Masino came over when I was loading the paint supplies into the van. She invited Emily to come over and spend some time with her and Antonio."

"How does Emily feel about it?"

"You kidding? She hit it off with the Masinos from day one. She jumped at the chance. I thought we could try it for a few hours tomorrow. See how it goes. You have any red flags?"

"Not really. They seem nice. I trust your judgment." *At least with Emily.*

"Okay. Good night." Kurt got up and moved to the doorway and stood there in silence.

Brill held her breath, waiting for him to recite the ten empty words he seemed compelled to deliver and she seemed powerless to quell.

"I love you. I always have and I always will."

"I'm setting my alarm for seven," she replied flatly. "I may not see you 'til tomorrow night."

"Stick your head in your office if you get time. I'll be there most of the day."

Kurt shuffled down the hallway and turned into the bedroom across from hers and closed the door.

She stared at the ashes in the fireplace and wondered what happened to love when it died. Did it cool like fading embers? Or did it simply disappear—like Michael Stanton and Janice Evans?

Tessa pulled back the curtain of the bedroom window and looked over at the cottage-style craftsman bungalow next door and the new squad car parked in the driveway. She was glad to see that beautiful old place occupied again.

But something was wrong in that family. She'd felt it from the first time she and Antonio met the Jessups. Whatever *it* was, it wouldn't leave her alone.

She decided that God must have brought them here for a reason. She was particularly drawn to Emily.

"It's three in the morning, love," Antonio said sleepily. "What are you looking at? Is Mr. Quinlan roaming again?"

"No, I'm just restless. I'll go make hot tea. Maybe that'll relax me. Go back to sleep."

"How am I supposed to sleep with you tiptoeing around here? I like you right here next to me." Antonio patted her pillow. "Come let me hold you."

Tessa climbed into bed and into her husband's warm embrace.

"Now isn't this better than standing at a drafty window, looking out into the dark?"

"Much." Tessa nestled contentedly in Antonio's arms, her mind skipping from one thought to another like a flat stone across a pond.

Had she hurt Gus's feelings by laughing at his belief that red shadows were responsible for violent crimes and that the authorities were holding back information? Crazy talk—all of it. But couldn't she have been kinder? Was it Gus's fault he'd been brainwashed with this rubbish from the time he was a child?

Equally disturbing was the fact that the authorities didn't know what happened to the two missing people. It gave her cold chills to think that someone out there might be ready to strike again and no one knew why or how to stop them.

Antonio began to snore and then snore more loudly.

Tessa pressed her lips to his hand, then slipped out of bed and went downstairs to the kitchen. She filled the teakettle with water, set it on the stove, then sat at the table, her mind still in busybody mode.

Brill Jessup seemed terribly tortured about something. Perhaps it came with all the years she worked on the Memphis Police Force. But there was something troubling the new police chief.

Kurt Jessup was handsome. Nice hair. Dark eyes. Emily had inherited his good looks and her mother's round blue eyes. But Tessa saw the same pain in Emily's eyes as in her mother's.

So what business was it of hers? Antonio had finally sold the shoe stores and retired. They had time to do whatever they wanted. Even travel. Why would she even consider getting to know neighbors who had problems she would just as soon not know about?

Tessa set her elbows on the table and rested her chin on her palms. How could she ignore the persistent nudging that she should befriend the Jessups? It had to be the Lord's doing.

She was aware of Abby rubbing against her leg.

"Well, there you are, sweet girl." Tessa pulled a chair over next to her, and the cat jumped into the chair and rubbed against the arms several times before curling up into a black and white ball of fur.

She rubbed the cat's chin and it began to purr. "You're never late for tea, are you? Be glad you're oblivious to this ridiculous legend. It only has as much power as humans give it anyway."

With her other hand Tessa grabbed her Bible off the desk. She pulled the gold ribbon to the side and opened to the Psalms and kept turning the pages 'til she found the verse highlighted in yellow at the beginning of Psalm 91: "He who dwells in the shelter of the Most High will rest in the shadow of the Almighty."

She read it again. And again. How could anyone who truly believed these words live in fear of red shadows? Either there weren't many Christians in Sophie Trace, or the Christians weren't familiar enough with the Word of God.

CHAPTER 8

BRILL entered the police station at 9:45 on Saturday morning, her temples throbbing, her hair still slightly wet, and her uniform unpressed. She hurried passed LaTeesha's vacant desk and down the hall to her makeshift office.

David was already there working. "Well, hello, sleepyhead," he said. "How about this for a picture-perfect day after all that rain? The only thing missing is your pretty smile." His voice was resonant and playful.

"Sounds like someone's got a caffeine buzz." Brill spotted the coffeepot and headed straight for it.

"Kurt stuck his head in the door and told me you overslept."

"Not exactly." Brill filled a paper cup with coffee and added two packets of sugar, then sat in the folding chair across the table from David.

"I inadvertently set my alarm for seven p.m. instead of a.m. Kurt and Emily left the house before that or they would have gotten me up."

"I met Emily. She's a doll."

"Thanks." She turned her attention to the two case files he had open in front of him. "Did you sleep?"

"I caught some Z's in the officers' lounge. I hate motels."

Brill laughed. "Then you're in the wrong business."

"Nah … just helps me solve the cases faster."

"So are we still stumped?"

David winced. "Never use the S-word. Let's just say we're continuing to pursue all leads, though we haven't yet found our two missing persons."

Brill blew on her coffee and took a sip. "Have you talked with Sheriff Parker this morning?"

"Right off the bat. We're meeting with him at eleven."

Brill lifted her eyebrows. "Was he more agreeable?"

"I wouldn't go that far. But he knows it's time to handle these like kidnappings and it makes sense for me to take the lead."

"Just don't forget who it was that gave you the heads-up."

David lifted his eyes and locked gazes with her. "I never forget *anything* you do, Red."

Why was his tone suddenly provocative? Was he flirting with her? She shifted her weight and took another sip of coffee. "You've known me as Brill since the first time we worked together. Why are you calling me 'Red'?"

"You don't like it?"

"Not really. I don't see the point of having a nickname for a nickname."

"Ah, maybe you'd prefer I call you *Chief.*" The corners of David's mouth twitched.

"Now you're patronizing me. What's wrong with 'Brill'?"

"Don't get your feathers ruffled. I'm just having some fun with you."

"You're the only one who's amused." She took another sip of coffee and avoided eye contact.

"Sorry. I was trying to be cute. Guess it fell flat."

"I guess it did. Why don't we let the people in my department address me as Chief? Just drop the Red and call me Brill, okay?"

"Okay."

There was a knock at the door and Trent stood in the doorway. "Sorry to interrupt. Things just got a whole lot worse."

Kurt finished painting the wall behind Brill's conference table, then he stood back and admired his work.

"I like it." Emily sat cross-legged in a straight-back oak chair, her eyes peering over the top of her book. "The rest of the office looks yucky now."

"Not for long. It'll look a hundred times better when all the walls match."

"I didn't think I'd like this goldy kind of yellow. But it really looks cool."

"Think your mom will like it, eh?"

Emily nodded and set her book in her lap. "You've been really nice to her lately."

"I wasn't nice to her before?"

"Well ... kind of. I mean you brought her flowers all the time. But it seems like you do everything for her since we moved here."

"Your mom works hard, sweetie. I like to help when I can."

"You work hard. How come she never helps you?"

Kurt looked into her inquisitive blue eyes. "What makes you think she never helps me?"

"You take me to school. You pick me up. You take me to gymnastics. You do the grocery shopping. You mow the—"

"And who cooks our meals?"

"Mom. But we get takeout a lot."

"Who does the laundry?"

Emily giggled. "Okay, but I help."

"We all help, sweetie. That was my point."

Kurt dipped the roller brush in the paint and started rolling it on the wall to the left of the door. He could almost feel the wheels turning in Emily's head.

"Who do you think loves you more," she said, "me or Mom?"

"What kind of question is that? Love isn't a contest. Why are you asking me all these questions?"

"You said you wanted to have a little father-daughter time before I go to the Masinos' house."

Kurt smiled and continued rolling the paint on the wall. "Can't I enjoy your company without undergoing all this scrutiny?"

"What does 'scrutiny' mean?"

"It means you're being entirely too nosy."

"You told me I could ask you anything. Vanessa and Ryan ask you nosy questions, because I've heard them."

"They're a lot older than you. In fact they're practically adults. Of course I talk differently to them than I do to you." Kurt dipped the roller brush in the paint and decided he might as well get this behind him. "What questions?"

The room was silent except for the squishy sound of the roller spreading paint on the wall.

Finally Emily said, "Vanessa asked you if you and Mom were staying together just because of me."

"And how did I answer?"

"You said you and Mom made a vow to stay together long before I came along. And that you were going to work things out because it was the right thing to do."

"We are." He stopped painting and looked over at Emily. "So what did your brother ask me?"

Emily shrugged. "Nothing. I just said that."

Tessa set a turkey sandwich in front of Antonio and then sat next to him at the kitchen table to watch *Noonday News with Gloria Graves*.

"Hey, look. There's some breaking news." Antonio turned up the sound.

"WSTN News has now confirmed that a third person has been reported missing in Sophie Trace, a town of just over thirteen thousand that sits in eastern Stanton County in the shadow of the Smokies. We go live now to Hunter Desmond, who is standing outside city hall with some very dazed residents. Hunter, what can you tell us?"

"Authorities are being tight-lipped about the situation, Gloria. But a reliable source inside the police department has told me that the third missing person is an African-American male, twenty-nine-year-old Dr. Benson Vaughn, an intern at St. Luke's Hospital here in Sophie Trace. Vaughn worked a double shift in the emergency room and reportedly left the hospital just after the shift change at seven a.m. today.

"When he didn't come home, his wife, Lenora, left both voice and text messages on his cell phone. She also called the hospital and was told he had left. It was then that she began calling friends and family. When no one had heard from him by ten a.m., she called police and reported him missing.

"Vaughn's white 2006 Ford Focus was discovered in the reserved parking area near the emergency room at St. Luke's. The car was locked and authorities have impounded the vehicle and sectioned off part of the reserved parking area with crime-scene tape. It's not known at this time whether or not they found evidence of a struggle.

"Mrs. Vaughn told police that her husband keeps his cell phone with him all the time and would never fail to return her call. She feels certain that he has met with foul play.

"If anyone has seen Dr. Vaughn, whose picture is now showing on the screen, or knows his whereabouts, they are asked to immediately call the FBI or the Sophie Trace Police Department."

"Hunter, when can we expect to get a statement from authorities about this troubling new development?"

"Soon, Gloria. I understand that the Sophie Trace Police Department, Stanton County Sheriff's Department, and FBI will be handling this as concurrent jurisdiction and are scheduled to hold a press conference at one p.m. That's just under an hour from now.

"Authorities aren't saying whether they have any leads in the disappearance of Michael Stanton or Janice Evans. But Dr. Vaughn's disappearance makes three in three days. Folks here are shocked, as you might expect, and they're starting to wonder who might be next. This is Hunter Desmond reporting live from Sophie Trace. Gloria, back to you."

"We will follow this story and bring you breaking news as it happens. Stay tuned to WSTN News for live coverage of that press conference in Sophie Trace at one p.m.

"In other news today, Knoxville police cornered a gunman after an early morning car chase through an—"

Tessa looked over at Antonio, who held the muted remote in his hand.

"How can this be happening?" he said. "Maybe there's something to what Gus was saying."

"No, there isn't." Tessa cupped his cheek in her hand. "The authorities will get to the bottom of this. I think for now we should all lock our doors. Something very evil is at work here. But I think it's of the human variety."

"I wonder if Kurt will change his mind about letting Emily come over. He's probably afraid to take his eyes off her."

"Fear is a horrible thing to live with," Tessa said. "It's more crippling than this arthritis that's curled my fingers. I'll call Kurt's cell number. He said he'd be at the police station painting his wife's office."

Kurt stood with Brill in a corner of the busy detective bureau, trying to absorb the implications of a third missing person.

"Good grief," he lowered his voice. "How are we supposed to protect ourselves? All three of these people disappeared in broad daylight, going about their everyday business."

"Until we know what we're dealing with, I really think you and Emily should stick close together and don't go places where there isn't a crowd."

"Agreed."

Kurt's cell phone rang and he looked at the caller ID. "It's the Masinos. What should I tell them? You feel okay about Emily going over there?"

"As long as she stays indoors."

Kurt put the phone to his ear. "Hello."

"Kurt, it's Tessa. I suppose you've heard about the doctor that's missing?"

"Yes, I'm right in the thick of things down here."

"Do you feel comfortable leaving Emily with us, what with all that's going on?"

"We think she'll be fine at your house. Indoors is probably the safest place for all of us."

"We're not going out. Antonio and I are looking forward to Emily coming over. I've even got a scrumptious raspberry torte recipe I want us to make. And if she can stay for dinner, I'm making manicotti—my special three-cheese recipe. It's kid friendly."

"I'm sure Emily would love it. She's crazy about Italian food." Kurt looked at his watch. "Why don't I drop her off around two?"

"I can hardly wait. Tell that smart wife of yours that I'm praying she catches who's doing this."

"I will, Tessa. See you later."

Kurt disconnected the call and relayed the conversation to Brill.

"I'll order a pizza in, and then take Emily over to the Masinos and come back and finish painting."

"Kurt, you should be careful when you're out alone. Pay attention to your surroundings and avoid isolated parking areas. This is no joke."

"Copy that."

Brill glanced over at Trent, who was on the phone. "We can't rule out the possibility of a serial killer. But why would he target a middle-aged male tire plant supervisor, an older female schoolteacher, and a young intern? We know that the two men disappeared in parking lots and their cars were still there. Beyond that, all we know is the three are missing. The perp didn't even leave a signature—nothing to connect these crimes. No fingerprints. No DNA that we can trace to anyone. We're still going over the intern's Ford Focus. Maybe it will give us something."

"Let's pray you don't start finding bodies."

"Not finding them can be more difficult than closure." Brill put her hands in her pockets and looked down at the floor. "I hate it that the families will be exploited by the media, which I'm sure will, if it hasn't already, pick up on the red shadows nonsense and try to connect the disappearances to the ax murders of 2006. I'm going to be tied up here half the night. Don't plan on me going to church with you in the morning."

"I figured." *At least you have a legitimate excuse to skip my Sunday school class.* "What should we tell Emily? She's too smart not to know something's going on out here."

"Let's discuss the details with her on a need-to-know basis. And keep her away from the news as much as possible. Hearing it over and over again is enough to scare anybody."

"I'll reinforce that with Tessa and Antonio."

"Good. I'll go talk to Emily, and then I need to prepare for the press conference." Brill opened the door to her office. "Hi, baby. Wow, does this look great."

"Hi, Mom."

Kurt went in and closed the door behind him, just as Emily threw her arms around her mother.

"Doesn't your office look cool?" Emily said.

"It really does. Your dad's been working hard."

"Did he tell you I'm going over to the Masinos' this afternoon?"

"Yes. And I hear Tessa has something special planned."

"Mr. Masino said she's going to spoil me." Emily flashed an impish grin.

"Listen, sweetie. I need to talk about something serious, and you need to pay careful attention." Brill tilted Emily's chin and paused a few seconds. "Another person is missing: a doctor at St. Luke's."

Emily seemed distant for a moment, as if she were processing the information, and then said, "Three people in three days? You *have* to catch whoever's doing this."

"We will. In the meantime I don't want you going outside without a grown-up. Keep in mind that no one's hurt a child. And we don't know that the missing people have been hurt, either. So I don't want you to be afraid. I just want you to be smart, okay?"

"I'm not afraid." Emily took a step back, her feet planted on the floor, her arms folded across her chest. "I'm my mother's daughter, right?"

Brill smiled and tugged her ponytail. "Without a doubt."

"Okay, ladies." Kurt said, "The painter needs to get back to work. Emily, what kind of pizza do we want to have delivered?"

CHAPTER 9

BRILL waited until Special Agent Riley finished answering the last media question at the one o'clock press conference and then turned around and went inside city hall.

She hurried down the long corridor to her makeshift office, flipped the light switch, and went over to the closet where she had left her purse. She rummaged through the contents until she found the bottle of Excedrin and took out two.

"Was I *that* bad?" David said from the doorway. "Looked like you couldn't get out of there fast enough."

"You were fine. I just haven't mastered the art of seeming positive with the media when we don't know anything."

"That's what you've got me for."

"I have every confidence in you. But I only get one chance to make a good first impression in this town, and it's going to be associated with everyone's worst nightmare." She picked up the cup of coffee she had left on the table before the press conference and washed down the Excedrin.

"On the other hand," David said, "here's your chance to show them what you've got."

"I wonder if anyone will care what I've got if these three people show up dead."

"We've been over this. A serial killer would've left a signature."

"Maybe he did and we missed it."

"I don't miss anything."

Brill snickered. "Pride goeth before a fall."

"You got that right." Sheriff Sam Parker entered the room, half a foot taller than David. "As long as we have concurrent jurisdiction on this mess, I expect a heads-up on everything as it happens. And don't forget I had a relationship with folks in this town long before y'all showed up." Sam took out a handkerchief and blew his nose. "People trust me to talk straight with them, and I don't pussyfoot around their superstitions either."

"Meaning the legend?" Brill said.

"Precisely, madam. I might add that while I personally have not seen a red shadow, the legend *has* survived for generations in spite of naysayers. It's a mistake to ignore it. I promise you the media won't."

"And neither will the ACLU." Brill rubbed her temples. "To suggest that the spirits of the departed Cherokee might've had anything to do with the disappearances is not only ridiculous, it topples the scales of political correctness. For heaven's sake the principal chief himself said the legend's nonsense."

"Of course he did. You think the guy's gonna bad-mouth his ancestors?"

"Time out, you two!" David formed a T with his hands. "The media can jump on the legend like fleas on a hound dog, for all I care. We are about getting the *facts*. You got that? Now let's get busy finding something useful that will help us locate these missing people. This kind of bickering is a waste of taxpayers' money and it's giving *me* a headache."

Brill pored over her copies of the case files and couldn't see anything that would thread the three disappearances together. Finally she sat back in her chair and rubbed her eyes, aware that David was looking at her.

He took off his reading glasses, then reached over and gently squeezed her arm. "I assume you're ticked off at me for calling a time-out between you and the sheriff earlier. If I came off like a scolding father, I apologize."

"No apology needed," she said. "I'm not that thin-skinned. You were right. But so was the sheriff. The media's having a heyday with the legend."

"Power to them. We've got some serious stuff to work on, Brill. I don't have time or interest in the local folklore."

"Neither do I. But I have to live here after these cases are closed. I can't afford to be perceived as an outsider. Mayor Roswell and the city council are watching me like a hawk, and they expect results. If I'm going to be effective, I have to find a way to connect with the people."

"All right." David folded his hands on the table. "What would you do differently?"

"For starters, say something more encouraging than, 'I can't answer that while the investigation is ongoing.'"

"But that's the hard reality."

"Ours maybe, but not theirs. They're hurting. In a community this size, people know their neighbors and are bound to feel empathy for the family and friends of the three people who are missing. I don't buy for a minute that the majority of folks living here believe the red shadows had anything to do with it. But they're scared—and with good cause. For heaven's sake, I just told my daughter not to go outside without an adult."

"What could you possibly say to encourage them when we haven't made a dent?"

Brill steepled her fingers. "I'd just like to be a little more up front and personal."

"How? The media would back you into a corner and rip you apart."

"I don't want a Q and A with the media. I'm thinking more of giving a statement on WSTN News. I think the station would jump at the chance for an exclusive on anything that relates to the cases, and I could speak directly to people here. I'll be glad to write it out and let you look at it first. If you put the kibosh on it, I'll forget the whole thing."

David held her gaze and seemed to look into her heart the way Kurt used to. "You think it's that important?"

She nodded. "I really do. If I can come up with what I'd really like to say, maybe I can get it run on the ten o'clock news."

David slid a ruled pad across the table. "Have at it."

Kurt flopped on the couch, bone tired, and thoroughly happy with the way Brill's office turned out. In a strange way, painting her office made him feel connected to her—something that had been missing for a long time.

His cell phone vibrated, and he glanced at the LED screen before putting it to his ear. "Hello, Chief. I can't even imagine what kind of day you've had."

"It's been exhausting," Brill said. "I've studied the details of each case 'til I'm cross-eyed. How'd Emily do at the Masinos'?"

"She had a blast. She and Tessa made a raspberry torte that's 'to die for.' We saved you a piece in the fridge. Emily also got to stuff manicottis and have them for dinner. We saved a couple of those for you too. But the absolute highlight for Emily was getting into Tessa's trunk filled with old-fashioned dresses, hats, shoes, jewelry—you name it. Most of it belonged to her Aunt Nettie who came here from Italy, and Emily got to try on anything she wanted. I picked her up at eight thirty, but she would've been content to stay longer. She's asleep or she'd be talking your ear off about it."

"I'm sorry I missed her, but I'm delighted she had fun. Listen, I just poked my head in my office. I couldn't believe my eyes. It looks fabulous."

He smiled. "I'll get everything hung on the walls after church tomorrow. And I'll put those big plants in there like we talked about."

"Thank you. I really mean that."

"So how're the cases coming, or should I even ask?"

Brill sighed into the receiver. "We're still stumped. Obviously we didn't want to give that impression, but I thought the press conference was extremely impersonal. Most of the questions the media posed we couldn't answer. I feel really bad for the families. So much so that I talked David into letting me give a statement to WSTN News. I'm pleased with how it went. They're going to run it at ten, and I want you to watch it and tell me how I came across. It's the first time I really felt like I was talking to the people here."

He glanced at his watch. "It's almost ten now. How late are you going to work?"

"When I reach a stopping place, I'll head that way. Thanks again for painting my office."

Two thank-yous? "I'm glad you're pleased with it. Well, I guess I'll see you when I see you." He wanted to tell her he loved her but decided he'd rather bask in the warmth of her double thank-you than set himself up for more rejection. "Good night."

"Leave the porch light on."

"I will." Kurt disconnected the call and set up the DVR to record the news so Brill could watch it later.

He went out to the kitchen and grabbed a soft drink out of the fridge and popped the top, then sat on the couch just as the news was coming on.

He listened intently as the anchor reported the facts of Dr. Vaughn's disappearance and recapped the details of the previous two disappearances. Finally he made mention of Brill's statement to the people of Sophie Trace, which he was quick to point out was a WSTN exclusive. The picture went to a video clip of Brill, who appeared to be standing in the main corridor of city hall …

"My fellow citizens, I've been your police chief for such a short time that some of you are probably wondering if it's even possible for me to relate personally to what is happening here. I assure you it is. During my eighteen years in law enforcement, I've seen firsthand the daunting fear and helplessness that accompanies the unexplained disappearance of a loved one.

"My heart goes out to the families and friends of Michael Stanton, Janice Evans, and Benson Vaughn as they wait for the answers law enforcement is working around the clock to provide.

"I want you to know that I don't regard these three as merely missing persons but as spouses, parents, coworkers, and friends—valuable, productive members of this community. I, too, am your neighbor—a wife and mother who will not rest until we remove the veil surrounding these disappearances and bring to justice whoever is responsible.

"I ask for your support, your trust, and your patience as we examine every fact, every lead, and every hope. I've never been a quitter, and I'll be tireless in my quest to uncover the truth and restore peace and security to our community.

"I ask you to pray that I, and those who have teamed up with me, will succeed on every level, and that we can once again say with pride that Sophie Trace is 'the best-kept secret in the shadow of the Smokies.'"

"Way to go, honey," Kurt said out loud. He took his cell phone off his belt and pushed the speed dial. Brill picked up after the first ring.

"Well?" she said.

"I think you hit a home run. What you said was to the point. Touching. Serious. I liked that you included yourself as part of the community."

"How was my demeanor? Did I look nervous? Too stiff?"

"It's a hard for me to be objective, but I thought you seemed genuine. And tired."

"Or just genuinely tired."

He smiled. "You can see for yourself, I recorded it. So are you coming home?"

"David asked me to help him with something. I don't know when I'll be home. I did tell you I won't be going to church tomorrow, didn't I?"

"You did. I doubt if anyone will be surprised you're not there." *But I know one who'll be disappointed.*

Brill sat at the table in her makeshift office and realized someone had walked in the room. She looked up into Trent's bloodshot eyes.

"Do I look as awful as you do?" she said.

A slow grin exposed a row of pearly white teeth. "I can't answer that question without getting into trouble, ma'am."

"You're going home, I hope?"

"Yes, ma'am. Before I leave, I wanted to say how nice your office looks. Your husband was really sensitive to the craziness in the DB and stayed out of our way while he was working. I appreciated that."

"He'll be finished tomorrow."

"I also wanted to say that I thought what you said to the community was nice. I think folks will appreciate it right now."

Brill studied his face. "Trent, shoot straight with me … how seriously should I take the legend in dealing with people here?"

"Well, ma'am, the legend is what it is. The jury's still out on whether it's true or not. Personally I think it's laughable. But it's definitely a force to be reckoned with since about one in ten people in this community believe it."

"How'd you arrive at that figure?"

"Oh, just experience, I guess."

"What was Chief Hennessey's opinion on it?"

"His mother was a Stanton. I think he felt obligated to leave the legend alone."

"Did you ever ask him what he actually thought?"

"Sure. He just smiled."

"You're aware that some people are superstitious and believe the red shadows are responsible for the disappearances?"

Trent nodded. "Those same people blame red shadows when the weather's bad, ma'am. It's nothing new. But it did get touchy back in 2006 when seven drug traffickers were found executed and dismembered up in the hills. Some of the locals put their own spin on it, regardless of how the Feds reported it."

"I looked at that case file. The victims were listed as Latino."

"The Feds believed they were, ma'am, but it wasn't determined from the autopsies because the decomp was too advanced on all the body parts they recovered. The Feds tied the victims to a Venezuelan drug cartel that was smuggling cocaine through the port at Savannah. They think the victims were mules who were there to make a pickup and transport the blow to dealers in St. Louis and Chicago. Apparently someone didn't like the competition and decided to send a message."

"I'd say they made their point.… So there really *is* a legitimate question mark as to the identity of each of the victims?"

"There is, ma'am. Personally I think the Feds got it right. But some of the locals still won't leave it alone. They'd rather believe the victims were Anglo, that they were dismembered with tomahawks, and the Feds covered it up. Like I said, it's laughable."

"I agree with you, but I need to understand where people are coming from."

Trent smiled. "Oh, you'll get your chance, ma'am. Count on it."

CHAPTER 10

KURT Jessup ambled to the end of the driveway and picked up Sunday's issue of *The Gateway Gazette*. He filled his lungs with the crisp morning air and exhaled a cloud of white. Through a break in the crimson trees across the street, he could see the sunlight on the hazy foothills and the patchwork of autumn colors that had transformed the landscape.

He waved to Antonio and Tessa as they left for early church, and then went up on the stoop, surprised to see Pouncer waiting there.

"And where have *you* been?" Kurt pushed open the arched door and followed the cat inside.

He glanced down the hallway and saw that the door to Brill's room was still closed. He'd heard her come in after three and wondered what was so important that David needed her to stay that late.

He sat in the overstuffed chair, took the rubber band off the newspaper, and opened it on his lap. The headline jumped off the page:

THIRD PERSON VANISHES IN SOPHIE TRACE

Kurt read the article, which didn't give any details that hadn't already been reported on TV. He was disappointed that Brill's statement wasn't even mentioned, and then he remembered she had given it exclusively to WSTN. At least *The Gazette* had not capitalized on the legend or the local banter about it. That would probably change now that the cable networks had picked up on it.

He folded the newspaper and tossed it on the coffee table. Through the window he saw a couple strolling arm in arm on the sidewalk, the woman smiling, her face almost radiant. He enjoyed the sight until the two passed and wondered how long it had been since Brill smiled from the inside out. Would she ever? Or had he killed that part of her?

His mind flashed back to a hotel room … the scent of perfume … the pretty brunette with hair down to her waist that he'd had a crush on in high school. If only they hadn't bumped into each other. If only they'd parted ways at Starbucks. If only he'd said no.

Kurt groaned. He promised himself he wasn't going to wallow in the guilt. It was never ever going to happen again—not with anyone. His defenses were firmly in place now. But how could he have been so prideful as to ignore the biblical admonitions regarding sexual temptation as if they were meant for everyone else?

A shroud of doubt seemed to wrap itself around him. Should he be teaching a Sunday school class? Maybe Brill was right. Maybe he was biting off too much too soon. Maybe his weakness disqualified him from ever teaching at all.

"Daddy …?"

Kurt realized Emily was standing there.

"Well, *are* we?" she said.

"I'm sorry, sweetie. Are we what?"

"Are we going to come home after church and change clothes before we go back to Mom's office?"

"Uh, no. I'm done painting. All I have to do is hang her certificates and awards, put plants in there, and polish the furniture."

"So I don't have to worry about getting paint on me?"

"Not a drop."

"Then I'm going to wear my new dress and you can take me on another date." She folded her arms across her chest, a Cheshire-cat grin on her face.

"To the ice-cream parlor again?"

Emily gave a firm nod. "It was so good, I want the same thing: two scoops of Chocolate Mud Pie Crunch with peanuts and butterscotch syrup."

"Is that a fact?"

"Pleeeeease? If I eat a good lunch?"

"I think you're becoming an eating machine. I can't believe what you put away at Tessa's."

"Manicotti is good for me. It had three kinds of cheese, and I had seconds. And I ate a big salad and garlic bread."

Kurt smiled. "I'm full just thinking about it. You forgot to mention the raspberry torte. You had seconds on that, too. I'm not sure you need anything else sweet."

"Then could we try Nick's Grill? Mom said they have veggie burgers and yummy salads."

"Now that's an idea."

"And if I'm still hungry, then we might go get ice cream?"

Kurt pulled her onto his lap and squeezed her tightly. "You must be going through a growing spurt. Your ol' dad's not ready for you to grow any more. Can't you stay nine?"

Emily giggled. "I'll be ten before you know it."

Kurt considered the implications of Emily's getting older and how empty he would feel when no one needed him anymore. He wondered if once Emily went off to college, Brill would cite biblical grounds and finally divorce him. He certainly couldn't blame her. But neither could he imagine living his life without her.

Kurt stood with Emily in a long line of people he didn't know, waiting to greet the pastor following the morning service at Cross Way Bible Fellowship. He wondered if he would ever feel as comfortable with this body of believers as he had with his church family in Memphis.

He felt a tap on his shoulder and turned and recognized one of the couples that had attended his Sunday school class.

"Just wanted to tell you Jane and I enjoyed your teaching," the man said. "You have an interesting perspective about what it means to be a *living* sacrifice. Neither of us had made the connection between the flesh of animals sacrificed in the old covenant and our fleshly desires sacrificed in the new covenant. We're looking forward to hearing more."

Kurt stole a glance at the guy's name tag. "Thanks, Phil." *I needed that.* He shook the man's hand and then his wife's. "This is my daughter, Emily."

Emily flashed her prettiest smile. "Nice to meet you."

The couple made a fuss over Emily for a few moments and then moved on without asking about Brill and without Kurt mentioning her. He wondered if this is how it felt to be a single parent.

"Do we have to talk to Pastor Gavin?" Emily said. "I'm starving."

"Yes, we do. And I think you'll survive a few more minutes without food." He craned and peered over the heads in front of him. "We're almost there."

The line moved quickly and soon Kurt and Emily were shaking the hands of Pastor Gavin Bonner and his wife, Sally.

"I really enjoyed your sermon," Kurt said. "You gave us a lot to think about. And your style is so relaxed."

"Both come with prayer and practice." Pastor Gavin held his gaze. "I've heard some positive comments about *your* class."

"Really?" The voice of doubt that had played over and over throughout the morning was suddenly on mute. "That's encouraging."

"And not surprising, Kurt. It was no coincidence that you came to this church when you did and felt God nudging you to teach. He brought us the right person to teach Romans 12."

"It's a big stretch for me."

"Good." Pastor Gavin smiled. "That's when the Master does His best work."

"Tell your wife we're praying for her," Sally said.

"I will."

Kurt held tightly to Emily's hand and made his way through the congested hallway to the exit. He pushed open the door, and a blast of cold air flooded their faces.

"I'll bet you're a good teacher," Emily said. "What's Romans 12 about?"

"Oh … lots of things. It's about being transformed. About using our gifts. And about how we should treat people. It's hard to sum it up just like that."

"Is there a verse you like best?"

Kurt stepped off the sidewalk and walked toward the van. "Probably the last verse: 'Do not be overcome by evil, but overcome evil with good.'"

"Is that kind of like the war on terror?"

"Actually it's more like choosing not to do mean things to someone who does mean things to you. Like Jeremy, for example."

Emily grinned sheepishly. "Pouncer already brought me a dead mouse to put in Jeremy's lunch pack. I wrapped it in a paper towel and hid it in the freezer."

"What would happen if, instead of getting even, you were super nice to Jeremy every time he did something that bugged you?"

"He'd keep on bugging me, probably worse."

"And what if you just got nicer and nicer every single time—what do you think would happen?"

Emily shrugged. "Why would I do that?"

"Because the smartest way to deal with an enemy is to make him a friend. How long do you think Jeremy would enjoy bugging you if you never reacted and did something incredibly nice instead of getting back at him?"

"That would be really hard, though. And it might take a while." Emily was quiet for a few moments and then added, "I guess it's like what you're doing with Mom."

Kurt held out his key ring and unlocked the van. What would his precocious yet innocent young daughter think of him if she knew the ugly truth about why her mother rebuffed his repeated efforts at being kind?

He slid open the van door and helped Emily climb in the

backseat. "Did I tell you how pretty you look today? I love it when you wear your hair down."

"But it always gets tangled and it hurts to comb it out. I do it because I know you like it." She cocked her head and smiled with her eyes.

"Hmm … and not because you want me to take you out for ice cream?"

Emily pressed her lips tightly together and shook her head, then a grin slowly spread across her face. "Okay, but I'm just practicing my feminine wiles."

Kurt chuckled. "I don't think you need much practice." His cell phone vibrated; it was Brill. He put the phone to his ear. "Well, hello. Are you finally up?"

"Or stuck in my worst nightmare," she said. "A fourth person is missing."

Brill walked into the police station, angry enough not to care whether Sheriff Parker liked her statement to the community. Or whether ignorant people really believed red shadows were making people vanish. Or even how the media decided to spin the story.

She brushed past LaTeesha's empty desk and her newly painted office and went down the hall to her temporary office, where David and Trent sat in folding chairs at the table.

"I got here as quickly as I could," she said.

"You're fine." David pulled out a chair for her. "Sam isn't here yet."

She acknowledged Trent with her eyes and then sat next to

David. "I want whoever's doing this. And I want him *now*."

"Easy, girl," David said.

"Don't patronize me," Brill said. "Four people are missing from my town. I'm tired of telling everyone that we can't answer questions because the investigation is ongoing. Let's get it done. Let's find the good-for-nothing who's doing this and get him off the streets."

Sam Parker filled the doorway for a moment, then shuffled toward the table, looking unusually somber. "When you agreed to concurrent jurisdiction, I didn't know y'all were plannin' to make a way of life out of it."

"Glad you could make it, Sheriff." David glanced at his notes for a few moments, and then made eye contact with each person around the table, "Our fourth missing person is a forty-eight-year-old Caucasian female, Candi Eagan. Real estate agent. Last seen this morning at 7:00 a.m. when she told her husband she was going to her office to clear out her in-box before hosting an open house at noon.

"The husband called her cell phone and her office phone repeatedly throughout the morning and got her voice mail only. When she failed to return his calls, he was concerned and drove to her office around 11:30. Her car was parked out front, and the building was locked. He had a key, so he let himself in.

"He found the lights out, Mrs. Eagan's office empty, and no sign that she had been there. Her in-box was overflowing. And the coffeepot had not been turned on. He called family and friends, and none had heard from her. That's when he called the police.

"Responding officers questioned Mr. Eagan at length and have no reason to think he's hiding anything. He confirmed that a button we found on the pavement next to Mrs. Eagan's vehicle matches the buttons on the dress she was wearing, so there may have been a struggle.

"The vehicle has been impounded. We're dusting for prints and trace is going over it with a fine-tooth comb. That's it."

No one spoke for half a minute, and then the sheriff said, "So how're we gonna catch this slimeball?"

David took his pencil and bounced the eraser on the table. "We don't know that we're after just one person. And I can't build a profile yet. The victims are not gender- or race-specific. They range in age from twenty-nine to sixty-one. They have very different professional backgrounds. And in one case, the vehicle is also missing. About the only thing they have in common is they've vanished."

CHAPTER 11

LATE Sunday night Kurt lay on the couch, his mind replaying moments from weekends gone by when the kids had sleepovers or were staying with their grandparents. He enjoyed just being with Brill and didn't even mind her rambling on about everything from the kids to work to politics to spiritual things. Sometimes they went to a movie or browsed the shelves of a bookstore or tried a new restaurant. And when they were alone together in the house, they made love like newlyweds.

Kurt sighed. Why did all that change when she was promoted to detective? Whenever they could grab a weekend alone it became a time for her to catch up on sleep and get errands done. Sex seemed more like a chore, something to cross off the list. Why didn't she understand how isolated he felt—and how vulnerable?

Images he'd vowed never to revisit popped into his mind, and it was as though the serpent had slithered up on his shoulder, temptation dripping off its lips.

It's her fault you went to Victoria's hotel room. Men need sex. God gave you the appetite, and it must be satisfied. Your wife cut you off, and she's doing it again. Are you going to let her sentence you to a lifetime without sex? You're only human.

Only human? That's what got him into this mess. What he

needed was to be godly. He got up and stood by the fireplace, his hands gripping the mantel, his head bowed.

Lord, help me break this cycle of thought. I don't want another woman. What I really want is my marriage back on track and my wife in my arms.

Getting Brill to love him again would take a miracle. Not that he deserved it, but he believed in miracles. He was committed to doing nice things for her no matter how she treated him.

Kurt heard the key in the front door and turned just as Brill seemed to blow through the doorway with a gust of chilly air. She laid her purse on the entry table and took off her coat.

"I didn't think you'd still be up," she said.

"I was waiting for the fire to go out. You look beat."

"Beat is putting it mildly." She hung her coat in the closet. "We have absolutely no leads on any of the four missing people. Mayor Roswell and the city council are all over my case."

"Sorry. If you want something to eat, the manicotti Emily set aside for you is still in the fridge."

"I had Chinese takeout. The MSG gave me heartburn. I need to take something."

"I'll get it for you. Sit down and relax a minute."

Kurt went down the hall to his bathroom, took the bottle of Rolaids out of the medicine cabinet, and went back to the living room and handed it to her.

She had kicked her shoes off and pulled her legs up on the couch. "Do you realize I haven't even gotten to sit in front of a fire in this house yet?"

"Yes. I'm well aware of it. We've missed you." Kurt sat in the overstuffed chair. "Did you have a chance to see your office?"

"It looks wonderful. I should've called you. It's been crazy."

"Emily and I rubbed lemon oil on your furniture. Drank it right up. You should see a *big* difference."

"I was so busy admiring the paint, I didn't notice the furniture."

"I think your awards and certificates look great on that wall by the conference table."

"They do." Brill popped two Rolaids. "David and Trent were impressed."

"Really?"

"I think Sam Parker was too, but that stubborn redneck isn't about to give me credit for anything at this point. He and Chief Hennessey were really tight. I think he's got me under glass, trying to decide if I'm up to his standard."

"He's the least of your worries."

Brill arched her eyebrows. "And you were concerned I might not find this job challenging enough."

"Be careful what you pray for, eh? By the way, my Sunday school class went really well. Pastor Gavin already heard some positive feedback." Kurt sat perfectly still, the way he did when lightning flashed and he was waiting for a clap of thunder.

"I'm not getting involved in this discussion," she said flatly. "I told you how I feel about you teaching a class."

"I know. Just keep in mind I'm doing it because I feel called to."

"You're delusional, Kurt. You're not equipped to teach."

"God doesn't always call the equipped. He equips the called. I wish you'd support me. If nothing else, around Emily."

"I can't. Just don't bring it up, all right?"

Kurt studied her—the limp hair, the heavy eyelids and smeared mascara, the tough-yet-needy expression. Did he really want to get into a door-slamming discussion? He decided he didn't.

"Before I finished up at your office," he said, "Emily and I had lunch at Nick's Grill. The owner, Nick Phillips, introduced himself. I don't think I've ever talked to anyone you've questioned before. He seems really nice."

"Did he pass on any scuttlebutt about this red shadows baloney?"

"No, but I overheard some customers sitting at the counter talking about it, particularly a big fellow with a white mustache. Gus something. I'm surprised that any rational person could believe that people are vanishing by some supernatural means."

Brill captured a yawn with her hand. "Welcome to *my* world."

"You really should get some rest."

"I'd like to sit here for a while and just veg."

"I'll get out of your hair." Kurt stood, grabbed the fire poker, and spread out the embers on the grate. "After I take Emily to school in the morning, I'm planning to drive over to the Maryville store. I'll be back in time to pick her up, then we'll go get groceries. If you think of anything in particular you want, add it to the list on the fridge…. Okay?"

He turned around and saw that Brill's eyes were closed. Was she asleep already?

He went over to her and straightened her legs so she was lying on her side and put the couch pillow under her head. He took the afghan and tucked it up around her neck, resisting the urge to kiss her cheek, then went down the hall to his bedroom to spend another night alone.

Brill heard five chimes and realized it was the anniversary clock on the mantel. At least she didn't have to go to work for a few hours—not that being home was a refuge from stress.

The dreaded heaviness that made it difficult to face another day still bore down on her, taunted her, an ever-present reminder that Kurt had rejected her. Could she help it that she wasn't aging as gracefully as he? Whatever happened to "for better or worse"?

Her mind flashed back to the senior-class picture of Victoria Anne Shapiro she looked up in Kurt's high school yearbook—drop-dead gorgeous with sleek dark hair draping her shoulders. How much had *she* changed in twenty-eight years? Did she color her hair? Was she heavier? Did she have stretch marks? A roll of fat where there used to be a waistline? Was she still a natural beauty, or was she mostly pumped full of Botox and silicone?

What was it about this twice-divorced middle-aged woman that had caused Kurt to throw away his moral compass and choose an afternoon of carnal pleasure over a lifetime commitment? Was it merely a high school fantasy turned physical, as Kurt had confessed? Or something much more complicated?

Brill dispelled the yearbook image and the nagging question that seemed to have no answer and turned her thoughts to Emily and how she was being affected by the tension in the house. Wasn't the whole point of staying with Kurt to keep from shaking up Emily's life?

She sat up on the side of the couch and let her eyes adjust to the dark. She would just have to do a better job of pretending to care about Kurt. Emily deserved to have a daddy and certainly didn't need to know about Victoria Anne Whatever-her-name-was-now.

CHAPTER 12

BRILL approached her office door just before nine on Monday morning and noticed the lights were on. She stepped inside and saw David Riley working at the conference table, file folders open in front of him.

"Don't you ever sleep?" she said.

David looked over the top of his reading glasses and smiled. "I crashed for a few hours. Hope you don't mind me taking you up on your offer to use your office."

"Not if you don't mind the smell of paint."

"After a while you don't notice it." He took a sip of coffee. "Can't beat the view."

Brill let her eyes take in her fresh surroundings in the light of day. The heavy oak furniture she had despised was now rich with lemon oil and a surprising complement to the golden yellow walls.

Outside her window, beyond the painted trees and foothills, the outline of the Great Smoky Mountains looked as if it had been sketched ever so lightly on a hazy blue canvas.

"You have the look of a kid on Christmas morning," David said.

"It's just nice to have *something* back to normal. So are you studying the case files?"

"Yeah, I've been over the facts a hundred times. I'm not getting anywhere on establishing a motive. And the only common thread I can find is that each of the four victims went missing before noon."

Brill started to yawn and covered her mouth with her hand. "I need coffee."

"LaTeesha made a fresh pot just a few minutes ago."

"So you two've met."

"She has a pretty smile like yours."

Brill let his comment go by and glanced through her open door at the empty desk in the bustling detective bureau. "Have you seen Trent this morning?"

"He was in the DB before the last briefing. We're still waiting to see what trace found on Mrs. Eagan's Impala and the button from her dress. Her husband's hanging out in one of the interview rooms. I think LaTeesha got him coffee and a granola bar."

"I should go talk to him," Brill said.

"There's nothing new to tell him."

"He could probably use a little compassion, David."

"Never been my strong suit."

"I'll be back."

Brill breezed out the door and across the DB to another hallway. She spotted Mr. Eagan sitting in an interview room, his hands folded on a table, seemingly staring at nothing. She knocked gently on the open door and went inside.

"Any news?" His expression screamed with despair.

"Not yet, but we're working twenty-four/seven to fit all the pieces together."

"Why would anyone snatch four people?" Mr. Eagan's eyes were puffy and his face blotchy red. "And why Candi? She never hurt anyone in her life." A tear trailed down his cheek. "She's all I've got. We don't have kids."

Brill sat in the chair across from him. "I know this is hard, Mr. Eagan. But we *will* get whoever's doing this."

"What if you're too late? What if she's dead?"

"What if she isn't?" Brill folded her arms on the table and leaned forward. "Let's hold on to that thought for now, okay?"

He sat in silence for a few moments, cracking his knuckles. "What if the legend is true? What if this is happening because our ancestors stole this land from the Indians? What if the red shadows are for real?"

"I assure you whoever is doing this is flesh and blood. And we *are* going to stop him."

Mr. Eagan lifted his eyes. "What if the Cherokee have some hocus-pocus thing going? What if they won't give up until they've driven us all off the land?"

Brill reached across the table and put her hand on his and met his gaze. "I can only imagine the fear and pain you're experiencing. But you need to put aside the folklore and trust us to uncover the facts."

Brill heard a knock at the door and saw Trent standing there. "Could I speak with you, Chief?"

"Excuse me just a moment, Mr. Eagan."

Brill got up and stepped into the hallway. "What is it?"

"We just found Janice Evans's red Mustang.

Kurt turned off the radio and kept driving toward Maryville, glancing frequently in his rearview mirror at the silver Nissan Frontier that had been following him since he left Sophie Trace.

His cell phone rang. Brill's number flashed on the display. "Hi. I just heard breaking news that the red Mustang was found in the woods outside Sophie Trace. Can't be much doubt now that these people were abducted."

Brill sighed into the receiver. "It's even worse. A fifth person's now been reported missing—a female bank teller who didn't show up for work. No one's seen her since she left home this morning, and she's not answering her cell phone."

"Good grief. That's five in five days."

"Mayor Roswell's foaming at the mouth, and the media's gathered out front like a pack of wolves. When word gets out, panic will sweep through town at lightning speed."

"Count on it."

"My heart breaks for the families. When I got here this morning I talked with the husband of the real estate agent who went missing yesterday. It's all I could do not to cry with him."

Kurt took a sip of bottled water. When was the last time she showed that kind of empathy at home? "It must be hard to be positive when you don't have answers."

"That might change now that we've found the Mustang. The other victims' vehicles didn't yield any useful evidence. But we think the abductor was in the Mustang with Janice Evans and forced her to drive to the woods. I can't get into the details right now. But hopefully we'll get his fingerprints and DNA."

"Anything I can do?"

"Pay attention to your surroundings. And keep Emily close to you, preferably indoors or in high-traffic areas."

"You okay?"

"I can't afford not to be. This is horrifying for the community."

"I admit it's hard not to wonder who's next."

"Just stay alert. Where are you?"

"A couple miles this side of Maryville. I'll be fine." He slowed his speed 'til the truck behind him got close enough for him to see that the driver was a young man wearing a ball cap and talking on his cell phone.

"Listen to the news," Brill said. "I'm not sure I'll be able to call you again for a while. Don't plan on me for dinner."

"All right. I'll talk to you when I talk to you." He started to press the End button—

"Kurt, wait … pray that we catch this guy, okay?"

"Absolutely." *When's the last time you asked me to pray for anything?* "I'll pray you have wisdom. I think you've got every other resource at your disposal."

"Thanks. I've got to run."

He clipped the cell phone to his visor, relieved when the Frontier turned on the road to Stanton's Ferry. Was he any less vulnerable than anyone else in town? A chill crawled up his spine. What did this serial kidnapper want with all these people? He erased the graphic possibilities that popped into his mind, glad when he saw the Welcome to Maryville sign just up ahead.

Brill entered the large briefing room ahead of Trent, Sam, and David, not surprised to see it packed out with her officers and detectives, as well as sheriff's deputies and FBI agents.

David stood next to a big whiteboard in the front of the room and waited until the conversation silenced.

"We've got work to do, so I'll get right to the point." He turned around and created a fifth column on the board that already listed everything they knew about the first four victims. He wrote as he talked. "Victim number five is Sonya Nichols, a thirty-four-year-old Caucasian female. A teller at Smoky Mountains National Bank. Married with nine-year-old twin boys, who told investigating officers that she dropped them off at Sophie Trace Elementary School just before the bell rang this morning at eight.

"Her gray 2001 Ford Windstar was found parked in the employee parking lot at the bank, but she never clocked in for work. Her vehicle has been impounded, and we're going over every inch of it. That's it for the bad news.

"The good news," David stepped to his left and wrote under column two as he spoke, "is that we recovered victim number two's Mustang in a wooded area just east of town. An elderly man walking his dogs spotted the car with both doors open and realized it matched the description he'd heard about on the news.

"The crime scene was not compromised, and agents arriving at the scene found both the driver and passenger doors of the Mustang wide open. Keys were still in the ignition, and we've confirmed now that only the victim's prints were on them. No blood was detected inside the car or trunk. Hopefully we'll get DNA.

"Gas tank was empty, so it's possible the engine was left running. We found marks on the ground that suggests the victim was dragged to a second vehicle. And judging from the tire marks, it was probably an extended-cab truck or a van.

"In addition, a pair of high-heel shoes was found on the ground where the victim appears to have been dragged, and we were able to cast two other foot impressions: size eight and size nine men's athletic shoes. Tread patterns not distinct enough for brand identification. Janice Evans's husband confirmed the high heels are hers, and we can assume the shoe prints belong to her abductors.

"We don't see any immediate connection between victim number two, Janice Evans, being a first-grade teacher at the grade school, and victim number five, Sonya Nichols, having fourth-grade twins attending there. But we need to pursue it. Questions?"

The room was still. No lighthearted joking. No wisecracks.

Brill studied the whiteboard and tried to take it all in.

"Okay, people," David said, "let's get to work on victim number five. Chief Jessup, I want your detectives working with my agents to interview everyone who dropped kids off at the elementary school this morning. Let's see if anyone remembers seeing Sonya Nichols after she left the premises.

"Sheriff Parker, I want your deputies to get with my people and go talk to employees at the bank and see if anyone saw or heard anything suspicious in the parking lot."

Brill sat in her office, thinking back on the heart-wrenching encounter she'd had with Mr. Eagan earlier in the day. How odd it seemed that she could feel genuine compassion for a perfect stranger and none for the man she'd been married to for almost a quarter of a century. The aroma of something delicious wafted under her nose and brought her back to the present.

Trent stood in the doorway holding a sack. "Ma'am, I've got your order from Nick's: a grilled veggie burger with Swiss cheese on whole wheat and a bottled water. Hope you don't mind that I added an order of sweet potato fries—my treat." Trent flashed a big smile. "You're in East Tennessee now, and you haven't lived 'til you've tasted Nick's sweet potato fries."

"Thanks," she said. *I'd like to live—or at least feel alive.*

Trent glanced at his watch. "I'd better get back so Rousseaux can go to lunch."

"How's it going, working with the FBI teams?"

Trent paused, as if he wasn't sure how to answer, and then said, "We'll make it work, ma'am."

"Is there a problem?"

"Not really. The Feds tend to treat us like we don't have brains. I blow it off easier than Rousseaux and O'Toole."

"Have you confronted Special Agent Riley about it?"

"No, ma'am. In my experience the Feds either respect us or they don't. Griping about it just intensifies the problem."

"You want me to talk to him?"

"I really think we should leave it alone. In light of the fact that our friends and neighbors are missing loved ones and a serial kidnapper's on the loose, I'm sure my detectives can avoid the urge to mark their territory."

Brill studied Trent's expression for a moment and decided she liked him more all the time.

"Call me with updates," she said. "I'll be here working, trying to find some connection between the victims."

"I sure hope you do, ma'am. Enjoy those sweet potato fries."

Trent flashed a half-moon smile and then left.

Brill picked up a fry and took a bite, then stuffed it into her mouth. She ate another and another. Trent was right. These were delicious.

She unwrapped the top of her veggie burger and took a bite. There had to be a common thread in these crimes. She began reading the names out loud:

"Victim number one: Michael Stanton, age forty-five, disappeared around noon Thursday in the parking lot at Nick's Grill.

"Victim number two: Janice Evans, age sixty-one, disappeared on Friday between seven fifteen and eight a.m. on her way to teach first graders at Sophie Trace Elementary School.

"Victim number three: Dr. Benson Vaughn, age twenty-nine, disappeared Saturday shortly after seven a.m. when his shift ended at St. Luke's Hospital.

"Victim number four: Candi Eagan, forty-eight, disappeared Sunday between seven and eleven thirty a.m. in the parking lot of her real estate office.

"Victim number five: Sonya Nichols, age thirty-four, disappeared Monday between eight when she dropped off her kids at Sophie Trace Elementary and eight thirty when she was scheduled to work at—"

Brill heard footsteps and realized someone had come into her office.

"Who are you talking to?" David said.

"Myself." She took a big gulp of water. "The victims seem more real to me when I say their names out loud."

"Well, they're plenty real." David went over and stood at the big window, looking out, hands clasped behind his back. "We've got every cruiser, yours and Sam Parker's, out on the city streets. We need the strongest possible law-enforcement presence out there."

"We can't patrol every parking lot." Brill took another bite of veggie burger. "I think during the press conference we should suggest that people not go out alone for the time being. There really is safety in numbers."

"Can't hurt."

"You seem angry," she said. "Did something happen when you went to lunch?"

David turned around, his arms folded across his chest. "No. I'm just frustrated that the media is playing up this ridiculous legend. Do people think red shadows wear athletic shoes? Give me a break …"

"Forget the media." Brill folded her hands on her desk. "Let's spend our energy on the facts."

"I just can't get my arms around this one. Nothing about it makes sense, and I go nuts when I can't profile the perp. It reeks of a serial killer and his toady, but why is he choosing victims from both genders and such a broad age range? And why hasn't he led us to a body? Or left his signature?"

"Let's just pray he's done."

David shook his head, his hands pushed deep in his pockets. "He's not done. That's about the only thing I feel sure of. He's taken one victim every day for the past five. I'm sure with the media splash he's getting, he won't want to give up the limelight."

The front door of Nick's Grill opened, and a brisk breeze sent the napkins in booth one sailing across the floor.

Nick looked up in time to see Tessa and Antonio come inside.

"Hey, you two." He went over and shook Antonio's hand and put his hand on Tessa's shoulder. "Good to see you. Today's special is a heart-healthy grilled-salmon pasta that'll totally knock your socks off."

"Sounds delicious." Tessa elbowed Antonio in the ribs. "Doesn't it?"

Antonio flashed a sheepish grin. "A big juicy bacon cheeseburger sounds even better. But I'll treat my ticker nice today and have the salmon pasta. With hard rolls and lots of butter."

Tessa rolled her eyes. "See what I'm up against?"

Nick seated them at the counter.

Antonio slid onto the stool next to Gus, patted him on the back. "How's it going, friend?"

"Really can't complain. But I always do."

The two men chuckled, and Nick wondered how many years they had greeted each other that way.

Gus's face took on a somber expression. "Guess y'all heard a fifth victim went missin' this morning?"

"Yes, it's awful. Just awful." Tessa sighed. "They haven't released the name yet. I hope it's not someone I know."

"That police-chief neighbor of yours sure isn't solvin' anything," Gus said.

Maggie set a mug of coffee in front of Tessa and then Antonio. "You having the special?"

"We are, thanks." Tessa looked down the counter at Gus. "Chief Jessup is working impossible hours, trying to figure out what's happening. Antonio and I even kept her little girl on Saturday."

"Hey, we're *payin'* the chief to work hard, but she isn't comin' up with squat. And that big-shot FBI guy who's runnin' things refuses to give any details while the investigation's ongoing. But Feds are never gonna admit what's really goin' on here."

"Gus, you're a gentleman and a friend," Tessa said, "but you're totally duped by this legend. There's a logical explanation. People don't just disappear."

"Five of 'em just did."

"These are wicked, evil *people* doing this," Tessa said, "not spirits."

Gus stroked his mustache. "Guess we'll just have to wait and see."

"For heaven's sake," Tessa said. "Your own church teaches otherwise. Nothing in the Bible alludes to the spirits of the dead roaming the countryside and seeking to avenge anyone's descendents. When you're dead, you're either with the Lord—or separated from Him."

"So you don't believe in ghosts, either?"

"No, I don't."

"What about all those fortune-tellers who talk to the dead?"

Tessa rolled her eyes. "They can talk all they want, but the dead can't hear them. It's a racket, and—"

"Hi, all." Clint Ames came over to the counter and straddled the stool next to Gus. "I'll have the special," he hollered to Maggie, then turned to the others. "So'd you hear they found Janice Evans's Mustang?"

Everyone nodded in assent.

"Police told her husband they think she was forced to drive to the woods," Clint said, "and then was *dragged* to another vehicle."

Gus's face went pale. "I never heard that."

"Ed Evans told me himself less than an hour ago," Clint said. "I've been keeping in touch with him since his wife disappeared."

"Well …" Antonio turned to Gus, "that pretty much bucks the legend off the bronco."

"Does not. Red shadows can do anything humans can do. Don't forget the ax murders and the pileup on I-40."

CHAPTER 13

KURT hung up the phone and went into the kitchen where Emily was working on her math assignment, wondering if he'd ever get used to feeling as if he were a single parent.

Emily looked up expectantly. "Can I talk to Ryan now?"

"Sorry, sweetie. He hung up. We got interrupted by another caller. How's the math coming?"

"I'm almost done." Emily smiled and shook her head. "This stuff is so easy."

"Did you finish your science assignment?"

"Of course." Emily nodded toward her workbook. "Check it if you want."

"I trust you. Mmm ... the meat loaf smells good. I'm starved."

"Should be yummy since we made it the way Mom does."

Kurt pierced two baking potatoes with a fork and wrapped each in paper towel. He put them in the microwave and set the cook time for ten minutes, all too aware that the emptiness he was feeling was more than hunger.

"So did you tell Ryan everything?" Emily asked.

"Yeah, I did. He's been hanging out at the library, working on a research paper, and didn't know what was going on here until he saw it on CNN a while ago."

"Wow, my big brother might be the most famous student at Vanderbilt now that Mom's on TV. I wonder if Vanessa knows."

"Probably not or we'd have heard from her."

"Everybody at my school is talking about it. But we're all kind of freaked out, especially since Mrs. Evans disappeared."

Was this the right time to tell her the latest? Would there ever be a right time? He sat at the table and lifted Emily's chin. "Look at me for a minute. I need to talk to you about something really important, and I need you to be really brave. Your mom called when I was on the phone with your brother. They released the name of the woman that went missing today: It's Sonya Nichols ... Kevin and Devin's mother."

Emily face went expressionless the way it did when she learned her grandparents had died in a car wreck.

He held her chin and looked into eyes. "I wanted you to hear it from me first because it'll be on the news. And your classmates will be talking about it."

Emily nodded robotically and seemed to be lost in thought.

"Sweetie, I know this is scary and a lot to take in. I want you to talk to me about anything you're feeling."

Emily was silent for half a minute and then her eyes glistened. "Mostly I feel sad. I just went to their birthday party, and Mrs. Nichols was really nice. What if she's dead? What if Mrs. Evans is dead? What if *all five* people are dead?"

"I think we need to have hope. Your mom is working very hard to find them."

Emily was quiet for a few moments more, and then let out a mournful sigh. "I think I'll go to my room for a while, okay?"

"Sure. I was planning to have dinner in about thirty minutes, but if you need more time, it can wait."

Brill tried to read through the case file on Sonya Nichols but found it difficult to concentrate. She couldn't stop wondering how Emily had handled the news and was about to call home and check with Kurt when she heard footsteps coming toward her office. She turned and met David's drooping eyes.

"I hope I don't look as bad as you do," she said.

"You never look bad to *me*." His eyebrows went up and down. "Listen, I think we're about to get another break. The night janitor at Smoky Mountains National Bank thinks he might have seen Sonya Nichols's abductor."

"And he's just now coming forward?"

"He hardly speaks a word of English and didn't even know a teller at the bank had been abducted until his daughter came home from work and told him. Apparently he left the bank around eight fifteen this morning and saw Sonya Nichols with a man in the parking lot. That's all I know right now. The janitor's name is Carlos Ramos, and his daughter Maria just brought him in. They're waiting in the first interview room."

"Let's go."

Brill crossed the detective bureau and headed down the hallway, David right behind her. She went inside the first interview room, where a Hispanic man who looked to be in his fifties and a Hispanic woman in her early twenties sat at one side of the oblong table.

Brill and David introduced themselves, Maria Ramos interpreting for her father, and then they sat across the table.

"Ms. Ramos," David said, "we'd like to tape this conversation, if that's okay with you and your father. It helps us keep our facts straight."

Maria spoke to her father in Spanish and then turned to David. "No problem. My father wants to help."

David folded his hands on the table. "Mr. Ramos, I understand you saw Sonya Nichols this morning in the parking lot at the bank where you work. Are you sure it was her?"

Carlos Ramos began to speak in Spanish, and his daughter interpreted. "Yes, I know the woman whose picture was on TV—not her name but her face. I often see her coming to work as I'm leaving. She's very nice. She even greets me in Spanish."

"Tell us what you saw this morning."

"I saw her in the parking lot, getting out of her gray van. I also saw a man get out of a dark blue van and come over to her like he knew her. I thought it might be her husband. I walked to the end of the row and got in my truck, and when I looked up, the blue van drove past me toward the exit, and I didn't see the lady anywhere."

"And you weren't suspicious?" David said. "What did you think happened to her?"

"I didn't know." Ramos's dark eyes grew wide and fearful. "I never saw her get into the van. It all happened very fast."

"How fast? How much time would you say passed between the time you saw the man walk over to the woman and the time you saw the blue van driving away?"

"I don't know … maybe thirty seconds."

"You said you thought the man might be her husband. Can you describe him?"

"I only got a glimpse. I'm sure he was shorter than the woman, but she usually wears high heels. He had dark hair. I think he was Latino like me. I noticed his shoes were red."

"Could you tell what style they were?"

"Not for sure. Maybe high-tops. Nikes or something like that."

"Okay, good. What about his blue van? Can you describe it?"

"I'm sorry. I don't know the makes of vehicles very well. It looked old. The paint was faded. And it didn't have windows except in the front."

"Like a delivery van?"

Ramos nodded emphatically. "Yes. Yes. Like that."

"Was the man driving?"

"Yes. No one was in the passenger seat. I didn't see the lady in the parking lot and wondered where she went so fast."

"You never heard a scream?"

"No."

"Is it possible she called for help and you couldn't understand what she was saying?"

Ramos shook his head. "I didn't hear her call out. If I had thought she was in trouble, I would have called 9-1-1 because there's always someone there who speaks Spanish. I didn't realize what was happening. I'm so sorry." His eyes brimmed with tears.

Brill tented her fingers. "Mr. Ramos, no one blames you for what happened."

"*I* blame me. A woman was being kidnapped. And I just sat there, then came home and went to bed like I always do."

David sat back in his chair. "Is that why you didn't answer the door when my agents came to your house—you were asleep?"

"I heard the doorbell. But I never answer the door when I'm trying to sleep. I have to work nights."

Maria Ramos reached over and took her father's hand. "I called the minute I came home and found the FBI business card in the door. I heard on the news you were questioning employees at the bank. I knew you would want to speak with my father."

"Well, we appreciate your being so quick to respond. I think we got what we need. Your father is free to go." David stood. "If we have more questions, we'll be in touch."

Maria spoke to her father in Spanish. Mr. Ramos nodded politely, and they left the interview room.

Brill opened the blinds on the glass wall. "David, Sonya Nichols is five feet six. If the man in the blue van was shorter than she, Mr. Ramos is probably right about him being Latino. Seems consistent with the small shoe sizes we found next to Janice Evans's Mustang, too."

"You're reading my mind. My guess is the man Mr. Ramos saw talking to Nichols forced her into the van, and a second man was in back, waiting to subdue her. Probably the same pair that dragged Evans from her Mustang to the van.

"Two Latino men with size eight and size nine feet and who own an old blue van isn't much to go on, but it's a lot more than we had at this time yesterday."

CHAPTER 14

KURT was putting the last of the dinner dishes into the dishwasher as he heard the front door open and close. Several seconds later he heard footsteps moving toward the kitchen.

"Looks like I timed that poorly." Brill set her keys on the countertop, her hair uncombed, her mascara smeared, the skin under her eyes dark and puffy.

It was all Kurt could do not to put his arms around her.

"The meat loaf is probably still warm," he said. "Why don't I put a potato in the microwave for you?"

"No, I had a big lunch." She went over to the table and sat. "I came home earlier than I probably should've so I could talk to Emily. I'm concerned about her. Having her classmates' mother missing is a lot for a nine-year-old to deal with."

Emily appeared in the doorway. "I'm glad you're home." She ran over threw her arms around Brill and didn't let go.

"I'm sorry Kevin and Devin's mother is missing," Brill said.

Emily nodded, her head cradled in her mother's hands. "It's not fair."

"It really isn't." Brill stroked Emily's long sandy blonde hair. "How're you doing?"

"Fine," Emily said. "I'm my mother's daughter, right?"

"But it's okay to feel sad or even scared. Sometimes I feel that way."

"I'm not scared. Well, I do feel kind of sad. Scared, too ... a little." Emily's voice suddenly sounded babyish.

"That's okay, sweetie. Everyone is."

Kurt captured the moment so he could revisit it later in the privacy of his own heart, where he wouldn't feel like an intruder.

"I'm working as hard as I can with the sheriff and the FBI," Brill said. "We finally have some clues. I can't really talk about them now, but we're working as hard to find Mrs. Nichols and the others as we would if someone *you* loved was missing."

"Good." Emily pushed back and looked into her mother's eyes. "I like Mrs. Nichols. She was really nice to me at Kevin and Devin's birthday party when I was feeling lonesome because I just moved here and no one was hardly talking to me."

"I remember. How's your friend Jasmine? Have the two of you started on the science project?"

Emily shook her head. "It's not due 'til Thanksgiving, so we've got lots of time. I'm glad you're home. Can we pop popcorn and watch a DVD?"

Brill looked up at Kurt and then at Emily, fatigue seeming to scream from every fiber of her being. "Sure. Pick something and I'll be right there. I want you in bed by nine, though."

"Okay." Emily kissed her mother's cheek and dashed out of the kitchen, still talking. "I'm in the mood for *Beauty and the Beast*."

"You look like you could fall asleep on your way to the couch," Kurt said. "Had to be a rough day."

"It was. But we did get a couple of breaks in the case."

"Anything you can talk about?"

He listened while Brill told him everything that had happened from the time the authorities recovered the Mustang in the morning until she and David questioned Carlos Ramos just before she came home.

"I don't know if the shoe impressions will lead anywhere," she said. "They weren't distinct enough to identify the brand. But as of now, we're looking for two men, at least one of them Hispanic—perhaps a serial killer and a spineless accomplice. Obviously we're not making that public. If it's the work of a serial killer, he should be leading us to the bodies, or taunting us, or leaving a signature of some kind, and he isn't. David's about to go nuts."

"I can see why."

"Not only that, the mayor and city council are making sure I take the heat for this happening on my watch." Brill closed her eyes and rubbed her temples. "I need something for this headache."

"I'll get the Excedrin." Kurt said.

"I can get it."

"Then let me pop the popcorn. Okay if I watch the DVD with you and Emily?"

"I suppose our daughter would enjoy the three of us spending some time together."

And you'll be asleep in the first five minutes anyway, he thought.

Kurt tucked Emily into bed and listened while she said her prayers, which were more passionate than usual and included Kevin and Devin and Mr. and Mrs. Nichols.

"Good night, baby." Kurt kissed her forehead. "Sweet dreams."

"Dad …" Emily had that faraway look she got when she was about to ask a question he didn't know how to answer. "Do you think Mom will ever be happy again?"

"I'd like to think so. She's working awfully hard right now. You didn't say so, but I know you're disappointed she fell asleep before *Beauty and the Beast* was over."

"She didn't see hardly any of it. And you and I ate all the popcorn."

Kurt sat again on the side of the bed. "You miss her. I understand. I do too." *More than you know.*

"Being the police chief is a *very* important job."

"It is, and lots of people are counting on her. You should be very proud of her."

"I am." Emily sighed. "I just miss things the way things used to be when Ryan and Vanessa weren't at college."

"Look on the bright side: You're the only one left to spoil."

"I don't think hardly seeing my mother is being very spoiled."

"Hey, what about dear ol' Dad who took you on *two* ice-cream dates in the last week and routinely drives you to gymnastics, birthday parties, movies, and just about anywhere else you want to go? Don't I count?"

"You're always there, and I love you lots." Emily fiddled with his wedding band. "I just miss how we all used to laugh together … like when Ryan chased me and Vanessa around the backyard with that humongous water rifle. And when we were at the lake and those gross deer flies covered our camper and Mom totally freaked out." Emily giggled. "And remember that time it snowed, and we made the tallest Frosty the Snowman in our front yard and got on TV?"

"Sure I remember."

"Well, I liked it better in Memphis."

"We've only lived in Sophie Trace one month. Give it time."

"Time won't make any difference." Emily's eyes were suddenly brimming with tears.

He pulled her into his arms and she didn't resist. "What's wrong, baby?"

She shrugged.

He kissed her wet cheek and held her close. "It hasn't exactly been normal since we moved here, has it?"

"Like it was normal *before* we moved here?"

"Hey …" Kurt tilted her chin and looked into her eyes. "What's with the sarcasm?"

"I don't know."

"Well, we need to figure it out. Look at you. You're ready to start bawling."

"Maybe I'm just scared about Mrs. Nichols. What if she's dead?" Emily wiggled out of his embrace and lay back on the bed. "I have to go to sleep, Dad. It's past my bedtime."

He cupped his hand around her cheek, and she avoided looking into his eyes. "Okay. I get it. You don't want to talk about it right now. But we need to get to the bottom of what's bothering you." *Though I'm not sure I'm ready for it.*

"How could I possibly know anything? I'm only nine."

"You're wiser than you think, sweet girl."

"Good night." Emily turned on her side and hugged her pillow.

"Don't forget to cover Mom up before you go to bed. She can't get sick right now. She has to find Mrs. Nichols. She just has to."

Brill staggered down the hallway and into her bedroom. She shut the door, crawled into bed, and pulled the covers up to her neck. What time was it? How much of *Beauty and the Beast* did she watch with Emily? It was all a blur.

She heard a knock on her door and then Kurt's voice. "Do you need me to set your alarm?"

Alarm. Alarm. His words finally sank in. "I need to be up at six."

She heard the door open followed by footsteps and then saw him fiddling with the clock radio.

"You're good to go," he said. "Get some rest."

"Tell Emily I'm sorry."

"She knows."

"Did she get to bed by nine?"

"I just tucked her in. Go to sleep. You need to be alert tomorrow." He tiptoed to the door and then turned around. "I love you," he whispered. "I know you don't believe me, but I always have and I always will."

You're right. I don't believe you. She heard him pull the door shut and yielded every muscle in her body to the strong arms of the extra firm, king-size mattress. It was a big bed for just one person.

She'd asked herself a thousand times why she didn't just divorce Kurt since she had biblical grounds. But would divorcing him make her any less empty? Or their two decades of good years any less full?

Maybe his reckless fling would be easier to accept had they not "saved themselves" for marriage. But there was something special, almost sacred, about having given themselves only to each other. They could never get that back.

But neither could a legal document end the two becoming one. It seemed self-serving to just cut her losses and divide up the spoils. Emily deserved better—so did Ryan and Vanessa.

Brill pulled the covers up to her ears. Why was she doing this to herself? She had more than she could handle trying to find the five missing people and giving comfort and hope to the terrified loved ones who waited.

I've never been a quitter, and I'll be tireless in my quest to uncover the truth and restore peace and security to our community.

Right now the promise she made seemed impossible to live up to. Maybe after she got a good night's sleep, things would look better.

Tessa Masino pulled back the bedroom curtain and looked next door, glad to see the lights out and Brill Jessup's squad car parked in the driveway. She wondered if Emily had gotten to spend time with her mother. The pain she had seen in the child's eyes would not leave her alone.

Emily was bright, talkative, and articulate. Sensitive, yet outspoken. Sufficiently giggly and smiley for a nine-year-old. And certainly not afraid to try new things. But something was wrong. Was it discernment that told her so—or just her tendency to want to fix broken things? Tessa couldn't put her finger on it yet, but the girl needed her.

She wondered if Emily knew the twin boys whose mother disappeared today, or if they were in a different fourth-grade class. How scared the children of Sophie Trace must be, not knowing whose parent could be next.

Tessa's mind flashed back to that ever vivid, horrifying day when she was ten ... and three of her playmates lost their fathers in a tragic mining explosion. For years after that, she was afraid every time her dad went to the mine—and happy every time he came home with a black face and overalls that he peeled off in the mud room so he wouldn't track up Mama's kitchen floor.

Tessa squinted and watched a shadow moving on the sidewalk in front of that pretty Georgian colonial. She couldn't make out what it was until it entered the glow of the streetlight.

"Well, for heaven's sake, it's Mr. Quinlan."

Antonio sat up in bed. "Again?"

"I'll go call Junior."

Antonio reached for his sweatpants folded over the back of the chair. "I'll go after him before he gets away. Where is he?"

"On the sidewalk directly across from the Jessups' and headed this direction."

"Junior's going to have to consider putting him somewhere," Antonio said. "Poor guy doesn't know who he is anymore."

"Hurry, Antonio. He's standing in the middle of the street."

Tessa heard the neighborhood dogs barking as Antonio went downstairs and out the front door. She watched as her husband walked out in the street and gently took the confused old man by the arm.

She reached the bottom of the stairs just as the pair came in the front door.

"Hello, Mr. Quinlan." Tessa said. "How about a brownie and a nice cup of warm milk?"

The white-haired neighbor, clad in blue flannel pajamas and a pair of well-worn slippers, shuffled across the wood floor as Antonio led him by the hand into the kitchen.

Tessa put two cups of milk in the microwave and set the timer, then dialed Junior's phone number.

"Hello."

"Junior, it's Tessa. Guess where your father is?"

"Asleep in his room. I think."

"Actually he's at my kitchen table. Antonio found him in the middle of the street."

"Aw, you shoulda called, Tessa. I'd have gone after him."

"I know. But we thought it best to catch him while we could. Heaven knows where he was headed."

"I'll come over and get him."

"Bring his coat. You might as well stay a few minutes and have a brownie. I made a fresh batch earlier tonight."

"You're a doll. I'll be right there."

Tessa hung up the phone, then set a Tupperware container of brownies on the table. She took the warm milk out of the microwave and set one cup in front of Antonio and the other in front of Mr. Quinlan. Her mind flashed back to Saturday night when Emily Jessup knelt on the chair Mr. Quinlan now occupied and mixed the fruit compote for the raspberry tarts.

Tessa locked gazes with Antonio, fully aware that he was planning to take advantage of Mr. Quinlan's plight by snitching a brownie or two or three. She chuckled to herself and wondered if he would enjoy them as much if he realized that she had used a sugar substitute and margarine with zero trans fats in the mix.

She went over to the refrigerator and got out the carton of milk and poured a cup for Junior Quinlan and noticed the lights were on at the Jessups'.

Lord, I don't know what You've got planned for me and that sweet family, but I'm sure it's no accident they bought the house next door.

Kurt opened the front door and let Pouncer outside, then set the bolt lock and went into the kitchen.

As long as he couldn't sleep, why waste the opportunity to enjoy a turkey sandwich and get started on the procedure manual for his SpeedWay stores?

He piled turkey between two pieces of bread thick with mayonnaise and put it on a paper towel, then went over to the table he and Brill had bought with the money they got from their garage sale when Emily was a baby.

He pulled out a chair and sat, and for a moment he imagined the entire family gathered around the table. How long had it been since they'd all eaten a meal together? He couldn't remember. It seemed that Ryan and Vanessa had been absent for a long time.

Kurt turned on his laptop and took a bite of his sandwich. He was surprised and a little hurt that neither of them visited the weekend before the movers came. Was it too painful to say good-bye to the house they grew up in? Were they just preoccupied with getting settled at school? Or were they avoiding the rift between their parents that they were old enough to understand but young enough to wish away?

He took another bite of his sandwich and realized he wasn't even hungry. He looked around the empty table and felt an unexpected surge of emotion. What a mess he had made of his life. Brill would never forgive him for cheating on her—not that he deserved it. Two of his kids found any excuse they could not to come home. Emily was miserable that her family had been torn apart. And wasn't all of it his fault? And all because he let a woman draw him into her mind, into her problems … and into her hotel room? Why didn't he see it coming? Or maybe he did and just chose to play dumb?

If only Brill hadn't been so busy … if only she had been there for him, he wouldn't have felt a need to look elsewhere for the sex that was missing.

Kurt sighed. Who was he kidding? If he'd spent as much time and effort pursuing his wife as he did listening to Victoria's problems, he might have helped Brill not to be just another cop consumed by the job. She needed him as much as he needed her. How could he have turned to another woman merely to satisfy his curiosity and his lust? Did he not know it would cost him everything?

Kurt remembered the proverb that warned about the adulteress reducing a man to a loaf of bread. He pushed the sandwich aside and turned off his computer. Maybe he'd just take a sleeping pill and knock himself out. This kind of thinking never got him anywhere.

CHAPTER 15

THE next morning, Brill got out of her squad car and hurried past the frenzied media people, who were taping and snapping pictures and shouting questions from behind the barricade. She walked briskly through the crimson and gold leaves that covered the sidewalk and headed for the back steps of city hall, then stopped and turned around.

She moved her gaze across the throng of hungry reporters and held up her palms until the noise died down. "You're guests here. I expect you to conduct yourselves in a civil manner. As soon as I've had a morning briefing, Special Agent Riley and I will give you an update. You all understand the protocol."

"Chief Jessup," a woman in a brown coat shouted, "someone just snatched five people on your watch. What are you doing about it?"

"Are the Cherokee responsible for this?" a man yelled. "What are you hiding? What *can't* you say?"

A cacophony of voices chimed in, and she turned in disgust and walked up the back steps. She keyed in her code, then went inside and leaned against the door, the shouts of pushy reporters seeming to come at her like bugs on a lighted window. She brushed off her uniform shirt and straightened her tie, then hung her purse over her shoulder and went down the hall and into the police station.

She said her hellos and made a beeline for her office, not surprised that the detective bureau was crammed with people.

She went into her office and saw David working at the conference table.

"I'm convinced you're part bat." She put her purse in the bottom drawer of her desk. "Have you slept at all?"

"I took a few power naps."

"Any good news?" She poured herself a cup of coffee.

"Actually there is. Trace found a strand of coarse black hair in Janet Evans's Mustang—human. Male. And here's the best part, it was still attached to the root."

"Hello, DNA," Brill said. "Do we know whose?"

"Doesn't match anything in the system, but it's consistent with at least one of our unidentified subjects being Latino. We put out an APB with a description of the blue van Mr. Ramos saw. Maybe we'll get lucky."

"That's encouraging."

David smiled. "*And …* a clerk at Gas-and-Go watched the breaking news about the Mustang being found and recognized Janice Evans's picture. He remembers her stopping in there the morning she went missing. Said she filled her car with gas and bought three boxes of doughnuts and a large coffee. I'm thinking a woman with her hands full would be an easy target."

"Why didn't he speak up sooner? Her picture's been on the news."

"Said he didn't make the connection until he saw the car. We've also got the Visa card slip with her signature to confirm his story. At least now we have a consistent pattern. Our perpetrator is preying upon his victims in parking lots."

Trent stood in the doorway. "Sorry for interrupting. When you have a few minutes, Chief, I'd like to talk to you about something."

"We're done," David said. "Why don't I get out of here so the two of you can talk?"

"Stay put," Brill said. "Trent and I can use one of the interview rooms."

She led the way across the DB and down the hall to the first interview room. She flipped the light switch and pulled a chair up to the table.

Trent sat across from her. "You look rested, ma'am."

"Thanks, so do you. By the way, how's it going with David's people?"

"Truthfully we've been too busy to notice. I think we've interviewed more people in the past forty-eight hours than we have in my entire twelve years on the force."

"It's been crazy, I know. I feel like I'm back in Memphis. So what did you want to talk to me about?"

"This." Trent took a photograph out of his pocket and handed it to her. "One of the patrol officers spotted this gang graffiti on the north side of Woodall's Grocery. It wasn't there yesterday."

"That's all we need right now." Brill studied the graffiti, which had been spray painted in black on a tan brick wall:

SMARTz2RULE7X

"I'm not sure which gang," he said, "and was hoping you might know."

Brill shook her head. "Nothing about this is familiar."

"The Folk Nation tried to move in last year, and we really went after them. One of our informants said they moved on. We haven't seen any activity by them in nine months, and in recent weeks we've cleaned house of two homegrown gangs that were dealing drugs: Fat Cats and Ace High."

"Yes, I was impressed by the reports you submitted to the city council. Do you think your informant can help us identify *this* gang?" She handed the picture back to Trent.

"He's at school this morning, ma'am. We'll talk to him, but we don't want to be obvious. I'd like to find out if there's a connection to that possible drive-by shooting on Beech Street the other day. We need to nose around. But it'll mean pulling O'Toole and Rousseaux off the missing persons cases 'til we get some answers."

"Do it," she said. "When we say we have zero tolerance for gangs, let's mean it."

Trent locked gazes with her and seemed surprised and pleased. "Okay, we're on it."

"Was there anything else?"

"That was all I had."

"Keep me posted."

"Yes, ma'am." Trent stood and paused as if he were waiting for her to leave first.

Brill got up, walked down the hall, then crossed the DB into her office. She sat at her desk without saying anything to David, who seemed deep in thought.

She pulled a stack of papers out of her in-box and began to sort through it. All she needed right now was for street gangs to take advantage of the police department's preoccupation with five missing persons.

"I just finished reading the report from the lab." David took off his reading glasses. "The button from Candi Eagan's dress had her fingerprint on it, no DNA. Nothing useful was found on or in her car. Or Michael Stanton's. Or Dr. Vaughn's. Or Sonya Nichols's."

"That's disappointing," Brill said. "So the only real evidence we have is the strand of hair found inside Janet Evans's car, size eight and nine shoe impressions outside, and marks indicating she was dragged from her vehicle to an extended cab truck or a van."

"Yes, but it ties in with Carlos Ramos's statement that he saw a Latino man in a blue van talking to Sonya Nichols just before she disappeared. The DNA from that strand of hair might prove useful later."

Brill sighed. "*Later* could be the difference between finding our victims alive—or dead."

Kurt drove through Maryville toward his Athens store, lamenting that he still hadn't written a procedure manual for each of the Speed-Way managers to follow.

He opened his eyes wide and blinked a few times, but sleep was about to overtake him. He spotted an unmarked road and turned, then followed it up a steep grade until he came to a quaint cemetery.

He turned off the motor and rolled down the window and let the crisp autumn air flood his face. He gazed down at the sloping valley dotted with cattle and the painted foothills cloaked in haze and breathed in the vastness of the beauty. He rested there and let the Lord's creation revive him. Minutes passed with only the sound of the wind tingling his senses.

He moved his gaze across a sea of headstones that marked the hillside and homed in on a gray monument shaped like two adjoining hearts. The man and woman buried there had each lived almost ninety years. Why couldn't his parents have been as fortunate? His mind flashed back to the sound of the doorbell ringing … the police officer's whispered voice … news of a head-on collision … the trauma center … the doctor's pronouncement … placing a rose on two coffins … the heavy darkness that never seemed to let up.

Kurt's vision clouded over and he swallowed the knot in his throat. Why did his mom and dad have to die before he could prove to them and to Brill that he would do whatever it took to make things right? Why did they have to die thinking their only son was a total disappointment? And that everything they had modeled about marriage had been for nothing?

Lord, why couldn't You have waited to take them? Wasn't it enough punishment that I broke my wife's heart?

Kurt choked back the emotion and pulled himself together. This kind of thinking always landed him in a dark pit that was hard to climb out of.

He breathed in deeply and let it out. And then did it again. His phone rang and saw that it was his daughter Vanessa. He waited until the knot in his throat relaxed, then took it off the visor and hit the Talk button.

"Hi, honey."

"Dad, is everything okay there? I keep hearing all this awful stuff on the news."

"The only thing that's changed since we talked the other night is the number of people missing."

"It's getting ridiculous," Vanessa said. "Is Mom just freaking out?"

"No. You know your mom. She'll step up and do whatever she has to do."

There was a long pause, and he wondered if Vanessa was thinking that her mother's willingness to step up was the only reason her parents were still together.

"Your mom's an experienced cop," he said. "She's not going to crack under the pressure. If anything, she'll get more determined."

"What's all this about red spirits snatching these people?"

"It's baloney. Ignore it. It's just the cable networks exploiting an old legend that has absolutely no substance."

Vanessa sighed into the receiver. "Dad, Ryan and I are worried about you. This is creepy."

"We're fine, honey."

"You sound stuffy. Are you getting a cold?"

"No, I'm on my way to the Athens store to meet with the manager. Aren't you supposed to be in class this morning?"

"I'm on my way. I just wanted to touch base. Tell Mom I'm praying that she'll crack this case *soon*."

"I will. Try not to worry. She has the FBI and the sheriff working with her. They're going to get this guy."

"How's Emily holding up?"

"Okay, I think. We try to keep her away from the TV and all the hype. She's doing great in school."

Vanessa sighed into the receiver. "I'm never going to make straight As like Ryan and Emily."

"I don't expect you to be like them. Be yourself. I'll be proud if you get Cs."

"Really?"

"Really. But there better not be any Ds on your semester grades. We're paying for you to learn. Socializing comes second."

"I know."

"And if it makes any difference, Ryan and Emily got their smarts from your mother. I never made As and Bs either … are you *smiling*, Vanessa?"

She giggled. "You know I am. I love you, Dad."

"I love you too. Talk to you soon."

Kurt clipped the phone to his visor and sat staring at the stone hearts, missing his parents and wondering if they knew how hard he was working to fix the mess he'd made.

He put the van in gear and made a U-turn, then went back down the same road to the highway and headed for Athens.

Brill made a copy of the gang graffiti photo and gave it to David.

"This showed up this morning on the side of a corner grocery store," she said. "What do you make of it?"

David put on his reading glasses and studied the photo. "Looks like the gangbangers have been busy. I don't recognize this gang. Smart Z two rule seven X."

She went over and stood next to David and looked at the picture again.

SMARTZ2RULE7X.

"I'm only guessing," she said, "but I'm inclined to think the capital T and small Z are a syllable: *teeze*—Smarties. Which could be the gang name. And the seven and the X is the territory they're claiming to rule: Smarties to rule seven something."

David nudged her arm with his elbow. "You could be right. Probably some rinky-dink gang staking its claim."

"To what, though? There's absolutely nothing special about Seventh Street. Could be seven blocks of the downtown ... or seven square blocks. Hard to say."

"I'll e-mail this to our gang unit in the Knoxville field office. If Smarties are out there, they've heard of them. We've dealt with Folk Nation, Vice Lords, MS 13, Crips, Bloods, Latin Kings—dozens of others."

"We saw most of those in Memphis," Brill said. "The Folk Nation has been branching out all over the South, and Trent said we ran them out of here last year. And more recently we cleaned house of the Fat Cats and Ace High. But we've never heard of Smarties. My big concern is that the missing persons cases are so high profile in the media that the metro gangs will take notice and try to branch out here where they can feel like big fish in a little pond."

"Pretty bold move with all the law enforcement in this town. You said this graffiti showed up overnight?"

Brill nodded. "The patrol officer spotted it just after sunrise. Says it wasn't there yesterday. We've already removed it."

"Good. While we're passing this under the nose of the gang unit, let's see if another gang challenges this."

Brill sighed. "I sure hope not. I don't think I can handle anything else."

CHAPTER 16

NICK Phillips stood at the counter at the Grill and admired the dark green vinyl and faux wood tabletops on the new booths and wondered if his regulars had noticed. The place was filling up with the lunch crowd, and through the blinds, he saw Tessa and Antonio getting out of their car.

"Any idea how long I've been comin' here?" Gus asked.

"Going on twenty-four years." Nick patted him on the shoulder. "I was just a kid when I opened this place. And your hair wasn't white yet."

Gus smiled and stroked his mustache. "How old were you?"

"Twenty-six, and not half as smart as I thought I was." Nick chuckled. "I was so full of myself and my grandiose business plan, it's a wonder I didn't go bankrupt. Thank the Lord for a dad who was willing to float me a note—and a wife who didn't mind waiting tables."

"Does Robin ever miss workin' down here, now that your boys are grown?"

Nick shook his head. "Nah, the woman was born to be a domestic engineer; it's in her genes. She thrives at home and is never bored—and never boring. A real keeper, that one."

The door opened and the Masinos came in, hung up their coats, then took their places at the counter.

"How's it going, friend?" Antonio nudged Gus with his elbow.

"Really can't complain, but I always do."

The two men laughed on cue.

Nick pointed to the colorful writing on the chalkboard. "Today's heart-healthy special is grilled portobello mushrooms, sun-dried tomatoes, avocado, sweet onions, and low-fat provolone cheese—on homemade whole wheat."

Antonio shot him a wary look.

"I'll make you a deal. If you don't like it, you don't pay."

Antonio waved his hand. "Deal. I can't beat that with a stick."

"Sounds delicious," Tessa said.

Maggie scribbled something on her order pad, then turned and went through the swinging doors.

"Can you guys believe how much media is camped out at city hall?" Nick said. "I had to take the back streets to get here."

"So'd we." Antonio patted Tessa's hand. "Looked to me like there's more media folks here than residents. Hasn't been this much hype since the ax murders."

"Yep." The inflection in Gus's voice seemed to reiterate his opinion that the authorities were hiding something.

"I try not to imagine what might've happened to these five missing people." Tessa brushed the silvery curls away from her eyes. "But I can only imagine the repercussions for Michael Stanton's seven children. And Sonya Nichols's twins. And that young doctor's newborn."

"I hear you," Nick said. "This used to be such a safe place to raise a family. I'm glad my boys are grown."

Gus took a sip of water. "Tell me again where they're livin'."

"Nashville. They're sharing an apartment and doing some freelance work, managing Web sites. Robin and I sacrificed to send them to college. It's a shame neither can land the job he wants."

"Give them time," Tessa said. "Kids today are expected to choose a career path and pick the college they want to go to before they're old enough to really know themselves. Sometimes it takes a while to find their niche."

"I guess it's just a dad thing to want my sons to do well."

Antonio nudged Gus's arm again with his elbow. "You're awfully quiet."

"Yep."

"You still convinced the red shadows are responsible for this mess?"

"Yep."

"That's all you have to say? That's a first."

"Yep."

Nick patted Gus on the shoulder, glad he skipped the commentary for once and glad Tessa let it lie. But he couldn't help but wonder how much influence the media would have in hyping the legend in the midst of five unsolved disappearances.

Brill stood at the window in her office, her hands folded behind her, and craned to see how far the traffic was backed up on Main Street.

Someone coughed, and she turned around and saw Patrol Captain Pate Dickson standing in the doorway.

"Come in, Pate."

"Most of my officers have volunteered to pull a double shift," Pate said. "Sergeants, too. Sheriff's deputies are helping us manage the steady stream of media and curiosity seekers that are clogging the thoroughfares."

"I don't know what they think they're going to find," Brill said. "There's nothing here but a nervous community and a whole lot of tired cops."

"I imagine the red shadows legend has piqued their interest, ma'am."

"I expect you're right." Brill studied Pate's face. "How long have you lived in Sophie Trace?"

"Born and raised here, ma'am."

"What do you think of the legend?"

"It's good for tourism and that's about it. I believed it hook, line, and sinker when I was a kid. My sister and me used to sit on Grandma Dickson's front porch and listen to stories of how *her* grandma and Sophie Stanton use to play with the Cherokee kids on the reservation. Her stories were more entertaining than anything she ever read to us." Pate's face turned pink. "Sorry, ma'am. I'm sure you don't want to hear all this."

"I do. Please ... go on. It fascinates me."

"Grandma Dickson never ran out of stories. She had a doll her grandma had gotten as a gift from the chief's daughter, and she used to let my sister hold it while she told us stories about how the white kids and the Indian kids played hide-and-seek, had horse races, played in the waterfall at Foster's Bend—all kinds of things. Grandma Dickson's great uncle and the Stanton boys used to hunt with the Indians. The settlers and the Indians shared a meal together the first night of every full moon. One of the Stanton brothers married an Indian woman whose name meant 'sweet messenger.' You can't believe how many stories my grandma told us."

"How wonderful that she was able to pass on what her grandmother had told her."

"Yeah, it was. I tell my kids the same stories."

"Pate, did she say how the settlers reacted when they found out that government troops were driving the Cherokee out of Georgia?"

"They were sick about it, ma'am. Everyone was afraid the troops would come here next. Then one day, the Cherokee up and vanished. No one saw them leave, but everyone knew why. Grandma Dickson said the settlers, especially the kids, were sad to lose their friends. The Indians had become part of their culture here in America."

"Did your Grandma Dickson know where the idea of red shadows actually started?"

"Yes, ma'am. She said about twenty years after the Indians left, there was a series of barn burnings that involved the second generation of Stantons. No one saw or heard anything before the fires started, but there was always a feather left under a rock at their front door. Folks started to speculate about this and that, and before long folks came to believe that the fires were a supernatural phenomenon—that the ancestors of Cherokee who were forced off the land had come to take it back. Thus began the legend of the red shadows. To this day the red shadows get the blamed for every crime we can't solve. And even some we do."

Brill nodded. "Interesting."

"Like I said, ma'am, the legend's good for tourism, and that's about it."

She smiled. "I'm sure local retailers won't complain about the additional revenue. I do appreciate the extra effort on the part of your patrol sergeants and officers. I know it's a congested mess out there."

"We've got it covered, ma'am." Pate lingered a moment, then said, "I'm more concerned about the gang graffiti. We removed it as quickly as we could. Unfortunately a huge number of high schoolers pass by Woodall's Grocery every morning. If a rival gang saw it, I'd expect them to respond in short order."

Tessa breezed through the automatic door at Walmart and stepped outside. She surveyed her surroundings and waited on the curb until a family of six walked toward their car, then began walking with them. Even the air felt tense. Would Sophie Trace ever again be a peaceful town where a person could walk about freely without the ominous sense he or she could be the next victim?

She put her bags in the trunk and got in on the driver's side and locked her doors. Antonio would have a fit when he woke up from his nap and realized she had gone out alone. Maybe it was foolish. But she wasn't about to cower in fear and let whoever was snatching people run her life.

She started the car and drove to the exit, then pulled onto the highway and headed toward town. The traffic was much heavier than usual, and she was reminded why she and Antonio had moved away from the big city. She spotted media vans from TV stations she had never heard of. Some from out of state.

She came to Seventh Street and took a left. Why fight that mess when she could take the back way home and enjoy the fall foliage at the same time? As she approached the museum, she spotted a man in a hooded sweatshirt spray-painting something on the side of the building. She pulled into the almost-empty parking lot and slammed on her brakes about twenty feet away from him and honked the horn.

"Get away from there!" she shouted, incensed at his audacity and never letting up on the horn. "Stop that!"

The man turned and locked gazes with her, and then hurled something. In the next instant she heard a loud explosion, and the windshield cracked into a thousand pieces.

Tessa sucked in a breath, her hand on her heart, and out of the passenger side window, got a glimpse of the culprit running away.

She sat for a moment, her heart racing, and her car still running. She heard someone knock on the window and realized several people, all respectable looking, were standing next to the car. She rolled down her window.

"Are you okay, ma'am?" a tall man with kind eyes asked.

She glanced at his nametag and saw that he was Victor Nelson, a volunteer at the museum.

"I think so, Victor. Goodness gracious. I saw a man defacing the side of this gorgeous old building so I pulled in and honked my horn, hoping to scare him off. He threw something at me."

"Probably this." Victor bent down and held up a tall can without a lid. "Spray paint. It sure did a number on your windshield."

"I'll say."

"That was a gutsy thing to do, ma'am. You're lucky it was a can and not a bullet. The guy was probably a gangbanger."

"Oh my." She sat back in her seat and considered the implications. "What was he spray-painting on the wall?"

"Gang graffiti of some kind. It's not the first time they've chosen to use the side of the museum as a billboard."

"I called 9-1-1," she heard a woman say. "The police are on the way."

Late that afternoon Tessa sat with Antonio on the love seat in her living room, Police Chief Brill Jessup and Detective Captain Trent Norris sitting on the couch facing them.

"I appreciate your letting us come talk to you," Brill said. "I imagine you're tired of rehashing it."

"No, it's okay." Tessa held tightly to Antonio's hand. "I want to help any way I can, but I've already told the other officers everything I know."

"Would you mind going over it one more time?" Brill said. "Sometimes important details you might have forgotten immediately following a trauma will come out later."

Tessa told them everything she could remember from the time she spotted the man defacing the side of the museum until she saw him run away.

"Did you get to see his face before your windshield shattered?" Brill said.

"Yes, it was almost like slow motion. He was young. Hispanic, I think. Could've used a shave. He wore a navy blue hooded sweatshirt."

"Was there a symbol of any kind on the sweatshirt—perhaps a professional football or basketball team logo?"

Tessa shrugged. "I didn't notice. It all happened so fast. What I remember are his eyes. Dark. Desolate. And guilty—the way children look when they get caught doing something wrong."

"What happened after your windshield shattered?"

"I saw him through the passenger-side window. He darted across the parking lot and took off running down the alley. I could tell by the way he moved he was young."

"Was he tall, average, or short?"

"Short."

"What kind of pants was he wearing?"

"Oh, those awful baggy jeans. If he were my son, I'd burn them."

"Did you notice his footwear?"

Tessa's mind flashed back to the image of the young man running. "I didn't. Sorry."

"That's all right, you're doing great." Brill's voice was reassuring. "Was there anything that stood out about the way he ran, other than he was fast?

"Not really."

"Are you sure he went down the alley?"

"Positive." Tessa noticed Detective Norris was taking copious notes on his ruled pad.

"At any time did the man speak?" Brill asked.

"I was doing all the hollering until he threw the can and broke my windshield. But he did shout something at me when he ran off."

"Obscenities?"

"No, gibberish. 'Smarties roll seven dimes'—or some such. I'm not sure."

Brill glanced over at Detective Norris as if to make sure he was writing it down. "Okay, that's good, Tessa. Did you see anyone else near the museum at the time this man was spray-painting?"

"No, I zeroed in on that scoundrel half a block away. I didn't see anyone else until Victor Nelson from the museum heard me honking and came out to see if I was all right."

Brill took her phone off her belt clip and looked at the screen. "Excuse me a moment, I need to take this call." She put the phone to her ear and lowered her voice. "Yes, David ...? Trent and I are finishing up at the Masinos ... When ...? I assume you've already issued it ...? Give me ten minutes.... Thanks."

Brill fumbled to get her phone back on the clip. "Detective Norris and I need to get back to the station. Tessa, thanks for talking to us. You've been extremely helpful. For the time being, I'd appreciate it if you and Antonio would not discuss this with anyone, especially the media. If we have more questions, we'll be in touch."

Brill and Trent stood, shook hands with her and Antonio, then hurried out the front door and down the steps.

Tessa watched as they got in the squad car. "Something bad is happening."

"Something bad already did." Antonio stood behind her, his hands massaging her shoulders. "Thank the Lord you're all right."

"Amen to that. But something is dreadfully wrong. Didn't you notice Brill's hand shaking?"

CHAPTER 17

BRILL walked into the police station and crossed the detective bureau, aware of the somber faces there, and breezed into her office where David was waiting. She closed the door.

"Who's the child?" she said.

"A seven-year-old boy, Dade Tompkins. Sandy hair. Hazel eyes. Dressed in a Cub Scout uniform. Last seen leaving Pioneer Elementary School around 3:10 by a female crossing guard. Was on his way to a Cub Scout meeting at his den mother's house, three doors down from the school. Never made it. Den mother got worried and called the boy's mother. The AMBER Alert was issued at 3:44.

"We've already pulled officers, deputies, and agents from other cases to start questioning anyone who even breathed the same air as Dade Tompkins. You can imagine the fallout when this hit the news."

Brill fell into a chair and tried to process the implications of a sixth kidnapping in six days—and now a child. Her mind replayed everything they knew so far.

Finally she said, "This doesn't fit the MO. Are we even dealing with the same perp?"

"We have to respond as if we're dealing with a pedophile or possibly even a kidnapper that's going to make a ransom demand.

I've assigned agents to wait with the parents in case the kidnapper makes contact, but my gut tells me it isn't going to happen."

David got up and stood by the window, his hands pushed deep into his pockets. "The perp's messing with us, trying to throw us off. There was no way we could see this coming, and he knew it."

"I'm furious he got away with it on my watch." Brill brushed the hair out of her eyes. "When are we going to talk to the media?"

"We're not. I've assigned Special Agent Morrow to be the official spokesperson. We've got enough stress without taking a pounding from the media. By the way, how'd your interview go with Mrs. Masino?"

"Good. I found her to be extremely observant. And considering she tried to stop a gangbanger in the act of writing graffiti, she's lucky all he did was throw his spray can at her windshield." Brill took a picture out of her pocket and showed it to David. "It's exactly the same graffiti as what we removed this morning."

"Which reminds me, I heard back from the gang unit at the field office just before we got the word about the Tompkins boy. No one's heard of Smart-Ts or Smarties."

Brill put the picture back in her pocket. "Well, whoever they are, I don't want them putting their roots down in my town."

Kurt hung up the phone and sat at the kitchen table, where Emily was doing her math problems.

"That was your mother on the phone."

"She's famous," Emily said. "Now *everybody* at school knows my mom is the police chief and that she's going to find Mrs. Nichols and Mrs. Evans. Jasmine says the red shadows are just playing tricks again. That all the people who are missing will be found alive."

"Emily," he tilted her chin and looked into her eyes, "that legend isn't true. You know people don't come back from the dead."

"Well … maybe *these* do. Maybe they're just trying to trick everyone."

"Sweetie, listen to me … a little boy is missing now. Dade Tompkins, a second grader at Pioneer Elementary School."

Emily's eyes grew wide, and he saw his own fear staring back at him. "Sarah Tompkins is in my gymnastics class. I wonder if they're related."

"I don't know. But what I do know is that live humans are doing the kidnapping, not red shadows. And now that a child's been taken, I don't want you out of my sight, except when you're at school or gymnastics. I don't want you stepping outside either place until you see me there to pick you up. Understand?"

Emily nodded. "Where was Dade when he got taken?"

"A crossing guard saw him leave the schoolyard. He was supposed to walk to his den mother's house, just three doors down, for a Cub Scout meeting. No one knows what happened. I don't want to scare you, but this is so serious that I need you to understand we're dealing with real criminals and real crimes, not some kind of game with the departed Cherokee. Your mom and I need to protect you. In order to do that, you have to promise us you won't go anywhere alone."

"I promise."

Kurt pulled her into his arms and held her, wondering how scared and broken Dade's parents must feel tonight.

"Do you think Mom can find them?"

"It's not just your mother's responsibility, Emily. The FBI and sheriff's department are involved too. But I think we have to be prepared for the possibility that they might not find them alive."

"So you think someone killed them?" Emily pushed away from his embrace, her eyes searching his.

"I didn't say that, sweetie. Let's hope and pray that's not the case. But sometimes people make bad choices that hurt others."

"It's not fair." She folded her arms across her chest and pushed out her lower lip. "Why did God give us free will anyway? Everybody just gets in trouble."

"Not always. Think of all the good choices people make."

"But it's not fair that someone gets hurt because a person makes a bad choice."

"I know. But don't forget that sometimes we're the ones who make choices that hurt someone else." Kurt felt the sting of his own words and wondered if Emily noticed. "I'd still prefer having choices to being a puppet, wouldn't you?"

"I guess so." Emily's eyes brimmed with tears. "But I don't want Mrs. Nichols and Mrs. Evans and Dade Tompkins to be dead. Or any of those other people either."

"First of all we don't know that they're dead. But what *we* can do is take steps to make sure no one else is abducted."

Brill sat at her desk, looking through the case files, trying to find a connection—some sort of reason why the kidnappers had chosen these six people. Was it random? Or was it deliberate?

There was a knock and she turned and saw Trent standing in the doorway.

"Sorry to bother you in the midst of the other turmoil," he said, "but we just finished talking to our informant at the high school and wanted to give you a heads-up."

"Come in. What did you find out?"

"You were right. The gang name is Smarties. It's homegrown. Not much is known about it yet, other than the kingpin goes by Einstein. The word at the high school is that something huge is about to go down."

"As if we didn't already have something huge going on. Does the informant know the meaning of the seven and X in the graffiti?"

"No, but he thinks it's probably some kind of territorial challenge meant for Ace High, which I also learned is making a comeback at the high school."

Brill picked up a pencil and began to doodle. "Well, the Smarties put up the same graffiti twice in one day to make sure somebody saw it."

"We got rid of the second one almost immediately, but it's hard to say who read the first message before we erased it. If it was a challenge to Ace High, they'll have to respond. And if was intended to disrespect Ace High, they'll have to retaliate."

"Let's hope that our strong law-enforcement presence will deter them." She lifted her eyes. "Nice work, Trent. Sheriff Parker has actually offered to supply extra manpower to help on the kidnapping cases so you, O'Toole, and Rousseaux can clean house of the gangs. He doesn't want to see them gravitate here or anywhere in Stanton County. I promised the city council when they hired me that we would maintain zero tolerance for gang activity. I intend to keep my promise."

"Yes, ma'am. We'll stay on top of it."

Trent left her office and went out to the detective bureau and sat at his desk.

Brill sat for a moment, her mind racing, her energy drained. She started to get up and stretch when LaTeesha's voice came over the intercom.

"Chief, Mayor Roswell's here to see you. I explained you might be in a meeting, but he said to interrupt you."

"It's okay. Send him this way." Brill took a slow, deep breath, then rose to her feet and straightened her tie—a sick feeling in the pit of her stomach. What if he was coming to tell her she was fired?

She glanced out into the DB just in time to see Trent and Detective O'Toole rise.

"Mayor Roswell ...," Trent sounded surprised. "What can I do for you?"

"I'm here to see Chief Jessup. She's expecting me."

In the next instant Mayor Lewis Roswell knocked on the open door and came barreling into her office.

She started to extend her hand to the man whose salt-and-pepper hair was always perfectly in place and whose starched shirts and pleated pants were always without a wrinkle, but he brushed past her.

"Do you have any idea how upset the city council is that six of our citizens have vanished?" Mayor Roswell said.

Brill closed her door and pulled the blinds on the glass wall. "I think I do since I'm pretty upset myself."

"Well, what are you doing about it? That's what I want to know! Parents are panicking, now that a child's missing."

"We issued an AMBER Alert and released the boy's picture to the media within minutes of his mother informing us that he didn't make it to his Cub Scout meeting. We've got police officers, sheriff's deputies, and FBI agents interviewing parents, caregivers, students, classmates, teachers, crossing guards—anyone who might have seen this child. Every media outlet is asking anyone who has seen him to contact us."

"A kid can't just disappear off the face of the earth, Chief Jessup. Someone had to have seen him leave with the kidnapper."

"But the fact is, no one did—at least not so far."

"Well, the media is blaming it on the red shadows." The mayor threw his hands in the air. "This is not the kind of press this town needs. We've barely gotten over the stigma of the ax murders. How are we going to draw new industry into this community with another tragedy hanging over us? We want an arrest!"

"So do I, sir. But I can't pull suspects out of a hat. We've requested help from Knoxville, Maryville, and Athens. I assure you we will be working twenty-four/seven to—"

"I don't care how many hours you work if you don't get results." Mayor Roswell rubbed his five o'clock shadow. "We hired you to keep the peace in this town. You haven't been here a month, and six people are missing. That's worse than unacceptable."

"It would be worse than unacceptable no matter how long I'd been here." Brill paused and took the irritation out of her voice. "I assure you, I will find all six missing people and bring the kidnapper to justice. I have the best resources available to me, and I'm using them all. I'd like to think I have your support and confidence."

"Confidence? People are afraid to let their kids outside to play."

"With all due respect, sir, I didn't bring this monster with me from Memphis. I brought expertise, leadership, and experience. I need you to trust me to do my job."

"The city council's climbing all over me. They want to know why you haven't arrested someone."

"Because we don't have any suspects," she said. "I know that's not what they want to hear, Mr. Mayor, but that's the truth. We are making some headway, but we're nowhere near ready to make an arrest. The process takes time. Evidence has to be carefully reviewed. Waiting for results is difficult when everyone wants closure, but good police work requires that we do things right and don't miss a step."

Brill glanced at her framed degrees and awards, then turned around and leaned on the conference table, her arms folded confidently across her chest. "I'm willing to talk with the city council, but I need the freedom to work these cases thoroughly and methodically. Special Agent Riley and Sheriff Parker are both in agreement on how we're tackling this."

"The sheriff is not pleased with the way the investigation is being conducted."

"Really?" Brill felt her face get hot. "He's never mentioned that in any of our meetings."

Mayor Roswell shifted in his chair. "Sheriff Parker is of the opinion that the FBI presence was premature and invasive and that the Feds—and you—are running the investigation without his input."

"It's true the sheriff was not in favor of involving the FBI early on, but it was my call and it turned out to be the right one. But this has been concurrent jurisdiction almost from day one, and Sheriff Parker has been invited to every private briefing and has been as free to input as anyone else. If he has something to say, I suggest he speak up instead of complaining behind my back that he isn't being heard!"

In the awkward silence that followed, Brill was sure her face was as red as her hair.

She paused long enough to get her voice back and then softened her tone, "Sir, Special Agent Riley and I have bent over backwards to make sure Sheriff Parker is apprised of all aspects of the investigations. We have valued his insights and welcomed his willingness to supply manpower. Since our initial disagreement over the FBI's involvement, Sheriff Parker has never once voiced his disapproval."

Mayor Roswell looked away. "I-I may have misspoken. I suppose it was back when this thing started that Sam expressed his disapproval. Look … I'm in a pressure cooker and have to answer to the city council, same as you. They're not happy. We need results."

Brill nodded. "The best way to get results is to let me do my job. I can't afford to get sloppy just because the answers are not coming as quickly as we'd like. All I ask is that you and the city council put your mouth where your money is and trust that I can do what you hired me to do."

The mayor hooked his thumbs on his belt loops, and seemed to stare at his shoes. "Just don't forget we can unhire you."

"Are you saying my job's on the line?"

"You're being paid to protect this community, Chief Jessup. How safe do you think we are?"

Brill tugged at her shirt collar that was chafing her neck. "I would like the opportunity to address the concerns of the city council in person, Mr. Mayor. Just tell me when and where."

"I'll relay the message. But I assure you, they're not in the mood for excuses."

The mayor turned on his heel and left without shaking her hand. Brill closed the door, walked to her desk, and sat in the leather chair that now fit her perfectly, her hands resting on the arms. She looked all around her freshly painted office and saw nothing that reminded her of Chief Hennessey. The baton had been passed and the responsibility was hers now.

What if the city council booted her out before she'd had a chance to prove herself? What if the stellar record she had built crumbled under the weight of six corpses?

Could things get any more overwhelming? Why couldn't she drop to her knees and pray for guidance and wisdom and believe that God cared and would answer?

Her mind flashed back to the longest night she could ever remember … Kurt unloading the guilt of his affair … and then leaving like a coward to go hide with his shame.

Prayer doesn't change the pain. Or the brokenness. Or the betrayal. Prayer doesn't fill the deep, aching void that reminds me day and night that I wasn't woman enough for him. Prayer won't fix anything.

Brill sighed. Whoever said it was lonely at the top had probably never hit bottom.

CHAPTER 18

BRILL got out of her squad car and strode to the front door, the chimney smoke scenting the night air, transporting her thoughts back to their house in Memphis. For a split second she was sitting cross-legged in front of the fireplace, playing Monopoly with Vanessa, Ryan, and Kurt, while her baby girl did gymnastics inside her womb.

"You're home!" Emily sprang up from the couch and darted over to her and clutched tightly to her hand.

Brill stroked her daughter's ponytail. "I'm so sorry a little boy is missing."

"Why can't you catch who's doing this?"

"Because he or they aren't leaving much evidence, sweetie. Every law-enforcement person in the area has been working on it day and night since the abductions began."

"On the news they said no one even saw Dade Tompkins get in a car with anybody. He just disappeared."

Kurt walked up beside them. "Emily insisted on watching the news, so we watched it together. It was handled well—other than the hype around the red shadows legend. But Emily and I had a talk about that too."

"Yeah, there's no such thing as spirits coming back from the dead." Emily's wide eyes belied her confident tone. "The legend is just a made-up story. Somebody started it, and then somebody else added to it, and it got bigger and bigger and now everybody believes it."

"Everybody doesn't believe it," Brill said. "Just the misguided souls whose parents passed down what had been passed down to them. I had a conversation with Pate Dickson, my patrol captain. He grew up believing the legend. But he also got to hear true stories from his grandmother about how her grandmother used to play with Sophie Stanton and Cherokee kids on the reservation."

"How cool," Emily said.

"Let's go sit by the fire and I'll tell you some interesting things he told me, including how the legend got started."

Brill sat on the couch, Emily nestled next to her, and retold everything Pate had said about the different ways the settlers' kids and the Cherokee kids played together and how their families used to share a meal at each full moon. She explained how sad the settlers were when the Indians suddenly disappeared. And how the legend was unheard of until after the barn burnings two decades later.

Brill pulled Emily closer. "So even if it were possible for the Cherokee spirits to come back, which it isn't, the Indians weren't mad at the settlers. If anything, they would've been angry at the government troops. The legend is just a made-up story."

"So Captain Dickson believed in red shadows when he was a little boy but not anymore?" Emily said.

"That's right. When he grew up, he realized that just because someone put a feather under a rock on someone's porch and burned their barn didn't mean it was the spirits of the Cherokee. Pate's the first person I've talked to who actually seemed to know how the legend came to be."

"Wow. I can't wait to tell Jasmine."

"It'll be fun to hear what my barber has to say about it," Kurt said. "Would you like me to make you a sandwich or go get you some takeout? Emily and I ate at Nick's. If I'd known you were coming home early, we would've waited."

"That's okay. I'm not really hungry. It's been a grueling day."

"Then you should do something relaxing … like watching a DVD with me." Emily tilted her head and batted her eyes. "Pleeeease? Last time didn't count since you fell asleep."

"Actually it would be wonderful to forget about the real world and watch a story. What did you have in mind?"

"How about *The Lion, the Witch, and the Wardrobe?*"

"Nice try." Brill gave Emily's ponytail a tug. "But you have to be in bed by nine. Pick something that's less than two hours long. You choose."

Emily's smile stole across her face. "Okay. I'll go look."

Brill rested her head on the back of the couch. She waited until Emily was out of earshot, then said, "I can't believe a child disappeared on my watch. David is practically despondent. He's convinced it's the same perp that abducted the five adults, and that he changed his MO to catch us off guard. Heaven knows what he's planning next."

"Any leads on the boy?"

"No. I almost feel guilty that I get to watch a DVD with my child while Dade Tompkins's parents are agonizing. I was going to go over there, but David sent me home. His agents are waiting with them for a ransom call we know isn't going to come."

"It's frightening. I told Emily she's not allowed to step outside alone, not for any reason. I'm probably overreacting."

"Well, that's two of us." Brill took off her tie and unbuttoned the top button on her uniform shirt. "The mayor paid me a surprise visit in my office this afternoon. Basically threatened my job. I know the buck stops here, but like I told the mayor, it's not like I brought this monster with me from Memphis."

"What do you mean he threatened your job?"

Brill sighed. "He said the city council could unhire me."

"They're not going to do that," Kurt said. "Just show them how you get things done."

"What if I can't? What if this perp keeps eluding us—or moves on before we find the six victims? What if I can't even bring closure for the families?"

"Brill, stop it. You'll get it figured out. You always do. Don't let the mayor and the city council intimidate you because you didn't figure things out yesterday. Police work isn't like that, and they know it."

She lifted her gaze and studied his face. Considering she wanted nothing to do with this man, he was being entirely too understanding, and she was being entirely too transparent.

"I'm going to go change my clothes," she said. "You did a good job talking to Emily about Dade Tompkins."

The doorbell rang and Kurt put the DVD on pause, then got up and turned on the porch light and looked out through the peephole. A white-haired man wearing horn-rimmed glasses stood on the stoop, holding Pouncer in his arms.

Kurt opened the door and the cat leapt out of the old fellow's arms and into the house.

The man stared at Kurt blankly, his sweater sleeves snagged from Pouncer's claws. "Ginny's allergic to cats."

"I don't think we've met. I'm Kurt Jessup."

Brill came and stood next to Kurt.

"Uh, this nice gentleman just brought Pouncer home. I didn't get your name, sir."

"Well, for goodness sake." The man looked squarely at Brill. "Why didn't you tell us you were over here?"

"Have we met?"

"Don't change the subject," the old man said. "Ginny's been waiting dinner. Did you drive yourself?"

"Uh, I live here. I'm Brill Jessup, and you are …?"

"Mr. Quinlan!" Emily squeezed past her parents and took the old man by the hand. "You're not supposed to be out without Junior."

"Who's Junior?" Kurt said.

Brill threw her hands in the air. "Would somebody please tell me what's going on?"

"Mr. Quinlan lives in that three-story white house on the corner," Emily said, "with his son, Junior Quinlan, who's a fireman that has a real dalmatian named Darby and a parakeet named Winky. And his wife's name is Mary Ann. I met them when I was at Mr. and Mrs. Masino's house."

"Oh." Kurt's gaze collided with Brill's as he forced himself not to laugh.

"Mr. Quinlan can't remember things and gets a little mixed up,"

Emily said. "He's not supposed to be outside by himself. We need to call Junior so he can come pick him up."

Kurt saw two shadows emerge from the dark and move toward the stoop, and realized it was Tessa and Antonio Masino.

Tessa waved her hand in the air. "There you are, Mr. Quinlan. We spotted you out here. Have you all met?"

"Emily just gave us a heads-up," Kurt said. "Why don't you come in?"

"Good idea." Brill stepped out of the doorway. "It's chilly out there, and Mr. Quinlan doesn't have a coat on. Or socks either."

A few minutes later Junior had been notified that his father was at the Jessups', and Mr. Quinlan and the Masinos had made themselves comfortable in the living room.

Emily ran to the kitchen and got a plastic container of peanut butter cookies and offered them to the guests.

"So does Mr. Quinlan do this often?" Brill asked.

"Junior and Mary Ann do their best to keep track of him," Tessa said. "But he does wander sometimes. We just detain him 'til one of them can come get him. Just think of us as a 'neighborhood watch' of a different kind."

Emily held the plastic container in front of Mr. Quinlan.

He grabbed two cookies and bit into one. "Don't try to give me a flu shot," he said. "I've already been stuck."

"Don't worry," Emily said. "I don't like shots either."

Tessa's eyes glided around the room. "I've always loved this house. It's cozy. So are you completely moved in?"

"Pretty much." Brill's expression told Kurt she was relieved not to be asked about the kidnappings. "We've still got boxes in the attic we probably won't unpack. Most of it belongs to Vanessa and Ryan. One of these days when they're out of college and on their own, they'll have room for it. They're great kids. I miss them a lot. I'm still not quite used to them being gone, you know?"

Kurt listened to Brill's exchange with Tessa and wondered how long it had been since she let down her guard and allowed herself to be the lady of the house.

"I had so much fun at your house the other night." Emily sat cross-legged on the floor and looked over at the Masinos. "Can I come back again?"

"Emily," Brill said, almost under her breath, "it's not polite to invite yourself."

"Oh, we'd love to have her again." Tessa brought her hands together. "She can help me make my mother's special spaghetti sauce. When it's simmering, the entire house smells delicious."

Antonio winked. "Talk to her nice and she'll let you roll the meatballs too."

"I *love* spaghetti and meatballs," Emily said. "It's practically my favorite meal." The doorbell rang. "*That* would be Junior." Emily jumped up and ran to the door.

Kurt noticed that Brill took her phone off her belt clip and walked into the kitchen.

Brill put her cell phone to her ear. "Is anything wrong?"

"No, no," Ryan said. "I'm fine, Mom. I'm just thinking of you. Are you still at work?"

"Actually I'm at home, which at the moment is almost crazier than being at work. It's a long story, but we're having a close encounter with some of our neighbors."

"I hope they're nice."

"They are. So what's on your mind?"

"I heard that a Cub Scout is now missing. I'm really sorry. How are you holding up?"

"A lot better than the boy's parents."

Ryan exhaled into the receiver. "I've been camped out at the library, working on a paper, and every time I check the news, things have gotten worse there. I thought being police chief in a small town would be less demanding for you."

"So did I. Actually I don't mind the demands. I've never shied away from a challenge. I just wish it didn't involve missing people and a ridiculous legend that keeps people stirred up."

There was a long pause and she thought the phone had gone dead, and then Ryan began talking again.

"How's Dad?"

"Fine. Nothing's changed since you talked the other day."

"Are things any better—you know, at home?"

"It takes time to feel settled in a new place. But we're getting there."

"I meant with you and Dad?"

Brill was muted by her son's boldness and considered whether she really wanted to get into this. Finally she said, "We're about the same, Ryan. What can I say? I told you not to expect too much."

"Yeah, I know. You're not fooling Emily, though. She pretends to be oblivious, but it's tearing her up that you and Dad are phony with each other."

"Phony's an exaggeration. We're polite. And we made it clear to Emily that we're dealing with some things on which we've agreed to disagree. Frankly I see no reason to discuss the details of our personal struggles with any of our children, not even our eldest."

The line was silent again until Ryan spoke.

"Okay, I get that," he said. "And I've never once pressed you to talk about Dad's affair. But wouldn't it be easier on you if you forgave him and let it go? He's really trying, Mom. He loves you."

"Love? I don't see how a person can profess to love you and then deny it by his actions."

"Really? Peter did, and Jesus forgave him."

In the dead air that followed, Brill felt as if her words were stuck to the roof of her mouth. Even if she were able to form a sentence, how was she supposed to respond to that? Why was she having this conversation with her twenty-one-year-old son anyway? What did he know about heartbreak? Had he walked in her shoes? Fought her battles? Cried her tears? She hoped he never had to. But she wasn't going to allow him to boil down this huge betrayal into something she needed to forgive. It was all Kurt's fault.

"Look, Mom. I don't pretend to know the pain you're going through. I just know that you and Dad love each other and that things can get better if you'll let them." Ryan sighed. "I gather from your silence that you're mad at me for butting in."

"Not mad. But you're right, you don't know the pain, and I really don't think it's appropriate to discuss something this intensely private with my son."

"Sorry. I didn't bring it up to hurt you."

"I know. You just want your family together." She wished she were saying this in person so she could soften her words with her expression. "But it's important to be realistic. My relationship with your father will never be what it was. We're committed to raising Emily and to being there for each of our children. That might be as good as it gets."

"Or not. I'm praying that the Lord cracks the wall between you and Dad. If He can bring down the walls of Jericho, I think He can handle this. I've gotta run. My ride's leaving. I love you. Bye."

Brill listened to a few moments of dead air, then put her phone back on her belt clip. Ryan was so like Kurt. When he set his mind to something, it was almost impossible to dissuade him. But all his prayers and wishful thinking were not going to change the fact that she would never trust Kurt again.

"Who was on the phone?"

Brill looked up just as Kurt came through the doorway. "Ryan. Just checking in."

"I'm glad it wasn't a police emergency. You want to come meet Junior Quinlan before he takes his dad home?"

Brill smiled as she thought back on her introduction to Mr. Quinlan. "I noticed you about lost it when Emily gave us the rundown on the entire Quinlan household and their pets."

"That girl never forgets anything," Kurt said. "Did you notice how she played along with Mr. Quinlan about the flu shot? She never missed a beat."

"She really didn't ..." Ryan's words echoed in her head. *Emily pretends to be oblivious, but it's tearing her up that you and Dad are phony with each other.*

"Brill, you okay ...?"

"I'm fine. Let's go meet Junior."

CHAPTER 19

BRILL slid the rubber band off Wednesday's issue of *The Gateway Gazette*, not surprised to see the headlines in giant print:

Sixth Person Vanishes

Seven-year-old Dade Tompkins became the sixth person in six days to disappear in Sophie Trace, an industrial town of 13,000, located in eastern Stanton County.

Dade, dressed in his Cub Scout uniform, was last seen leaving Pioneer Elementary School at 3:10 yesterday afternoon by a crossing guard, who has asked to remain anonymous.

The boy's mother was notified when he failed to show up at his den's mother's house, which is just three doors down from the school. As of now, the police and FBI have not had any witnesses come forward with information on the missing boy.

Some residents in this East Tennessee community are calling the vanishings a "supernatural phenomenon," and an inevitable collision of past and present. They cite a legend that goes back to the days when the Cherokee inhabited this area …

Brill folded the paper and set it on the other side of the kitchen table. Would the media ever tire of entertaining the same ridiculous nonsense?

She took a sip of coffee and looked out the bay window. Branches of gold doubloons formed a canopy over Azalea Lane and, in between the houses across the street, she could see rich resplendent color where the sunlight had flooded the foothills.

How many times had she been here on vacation? How many times had she dreamed about living this close to the Smokies? So why did she feel displaced—like an alien on a strange planet?

Was she missing Memphis, or just a lifetime of memories, good and bad, that were locked up there? She closed her eyes and imagined herself sitting on the east bank of the Mississippi River, the breeze tussling with her hair, her gaze set on the barges and steamboats navigating the wide, snaking river. It seemed a lifetime ago that she had sought solace there when her home was no longer a refuge.

Home. She could clearly picture the brick fixer-upper that her in-laws had financed and Kurt had transformed over the years. The place had opened its arms to three newborns and witnessed three toddlers taking their first steps … hosted many rousing birthday parties … stood watch over sleeping children … and puffed out its chest as she hung her diploma from the police academy.

The house had made room for a crowd every Thanksgiving … and a bigger tree every Christmas … and a junk-food buffet on Super Bowl Sundays.

It had been captured in the background of countless photos taken on holidays, birthdays, graduations, and prom nights.

The house was her refuge when her heart lay crushed under the mud slide of Kurt's confession and she spent the weekend in her room, weeping, and wondering if she'd ever feel clean again.

She never did. And after that she lost herself in her detective work and found more and more excuses to come home late. The house became a place to crash—nothing more.

She wasn't surprised that Kurt didn't flinch when she applied for a job with a different set of challenges in a town that held no memories. Wasn't it wise to leave Memphis? To start fresh? To never look back?

So why, when the movers drove away and she locked the front door for the last time, did she feel as though she were leaving behind a part of herself?

"Mom, *do* you?"

Brill was aware of Emily's voice and realized her daughter was standing next to the kitchen table, a questioning look on her face.

"I'm sorry, sweetie. Do I what?"

"Do you want me to make you some oatmeal? I'm going to have some."

"Uh, sure. I'll have apples and cinnamon."

Emily smiled and grabbed the box of instant oatmeal packets out of the pantry. "I'm having maple and brown sugar."

Brill sat and just let her daughter serve her. She seemed so eager to do it. And so grown up.

Emily chattered nonstop about school, gymnastics, her friend Jasmine, and the mouse she decided *not* to put in Jeremy Downs's lunch pack. Several minutes later she carried a bowl of hot oatmeal topped with banana slices over to the table.

"There you go, Mom. That oughta stick to your ribs."

Brill chuckled. "Think so, eh?"

"I heard that someplace. It means you won't get hungry again for a while."

"Well, thanks for serving me breakfast, young lady. This is a real treat getting to share it with you."

"You're welcome. Breakfast is the most important meal of the day. You should never skip it."

Brill was amused at hearing her own words parroted by her nine-year-old.

Emily's ponytail never swayed as she carefully carried her own bowl of oatmeal to the table.

"I'll say the blessing." Emily folded her hands and bowed her head. "Dear Lord, bless this food and my mom, and please help her find the missing people. And please be with the ones who love them so they won't be so sad. In Jesus' name. Amen."

Brill was relieved that Emily hadn't asked her to pray. How could she delight in her daughter's communicating with God yet balk at the idea for herself?

Emily scooped a generous bite of oatmeal and banana onto her spoon and put it into her mouth. "Yum."

Brill thought about Dade Tompkins's parents and could only imagine how painful it must be for them to see the empty place at their breakfast table.

"I decided I don't want to be a police chief when I grow up," Emily said. "It's too stressful."

"Another way to look at it is that you'd be helping people by making cities safer."

"Only if you catch the bad guys."

"We catch an awful lot of them. Sometimes it takes a while."

Emily paused and met her mother's gaze. "There's a lot more criminals than police officers, right?"

"Always has been. Think back to the Wild West when the sheriff and his deputy were fighting all kinds of outlaws. And there have always been evil people: pirates, gangs, warlords, Mafia—and they don't differ much in their pursuit of power, regardless of what name they go by or what century they lived in."

"Yeah, and don't forget the bad angels." Emily took another bite of oatmeal. "They kind of started their own gang and they're still trying to trick people into joining."

Brill took a sip of coffee. "I never made that application before." *This child's mind never stops working.*

"I feel really sad about Mrs. Nichols. Kevin and Devin didn't come to school yesterday."

"I'm sorry, sweetie. Maybe the boys need a little time away so they don't have to answer questions. We're trying as hard as we can to find their mother and all the others."

Emily didn't say anything and kept eating.

"What's wrong?"

Emily shrugged.

"Since when can't you talk to me?"

Emily put down her spoon. She hesitated, then started to say something and stopped. Finally, she said, "When the kids at school first found out my mother was the police chief, they thought it was really cool. But now … well, they're gonna tease me, I just know it."

"Why?"

"Because people keep disappearing, and you can't find any of them."

Brill reached over and lifted Emily's chin so she could see her eyes. "Listen, sweetie ... *can't* isn't even in my professional vocabulary. Success in police work comes by hard work. By not giving up. By putting pieces of the puzzle together. Lots of people want to judge things too early and call it failure. I've got a pretty good record of cracking cases."

"Well, you have to admit it looks like the red shadows are playing tricks on the police."

"But now that you know the truth about the red shadows, why don't you tell the other kids at school that it's a made-up story?"

"Don't worry, I will."

"If it helps, I'm not angry that your classmates think I'm a fool. I've learned to turn anger into determination. That's the only way most cases get solved."

Emily sighed. "Do you think you can find these people? What if they're dead, Mom? What if you're too late?"

"I'm not God, sweetie. I can't do the impossible. But I promise you that I will work every conceivable angle to figure out what happened to them."

Later that morning Brill went in the back door of city hall, ignoring the taunts of reporters who swarmed behind the barricade.

She went down the hall and into the police station, amazed at the activity in the detective bureau. She went into her office and saw David working at the conference table.

"Well, Special Agent Riley," she said, "have you figured out who we're looking for?"

"I've worked up a profile." His voice was monotone and he didn't look up.

Brill pulled up a chair and sat across from him. "Am I going to have to give you a pep talk?"

"I'm not sure it would do any good. I just spent an hour with Dade Tompkins's parents. I'm trying to be positive, but the truth is, I'm just waiting for bodies to surface." David's hands turned to fists. "It's bad enough when a kid is abducted—but right under our noses? I've got a nephew who's a Cub Scout. It's just a little close for comfort."

"I'm interested in the hearing the profile."

"I'm not all that confident about it. How's that, coming from a Fed?"

"Honest."

David pulled his yellow ruled pad out of the stack of papers to his right. "You're the first to hear my thoughts. This is just a first draft. I'm brainstorming, but you'll get the idea."

"I'm listening," she said.

"Okay … the unidentified subject is likely a Hispanic male. Young. Angry. Craving respect and will go to great lengths to earn it. He's definitely capable of murder, but he's not a serial killer. Systematically snatching his victims and not getting caught has become his stage and is satisfying in and of itself. He's highly intelligent and insists on being recognized as such—so much so that the *predictability* of his actions spoiled it for him. That's why he switched his MO and kidnapped a child. He thrives on power—the ability to inflict fear on the entire community. He didn't kidnap these people to torture and kill them. He took them because he *can*. But at some point, he must dispose of them. I believe he's capable of killing them all—but quickly and impersonally. Perhaps injecting them with something deadly. Or forcing them to drink poison. Or throwing them in a mass grave and shooting them. But I think he'll wait until he's finished, until he's achieved his desired level of respect and fear—and then kill them all at once." David exhaled and was silent for a moment. "That's it."

"Pretty grim," Brill said. "No wonder you look despondent. So how do we begin to look for this guy? He has to be holding six people somewhere that wouldn't draw attention. Maybe a warehouse or an abandoned building?"

David's phone vibrated. He took it off his belt clip. "Yeah …? When …? You're absolutely sure …? Where's the wife now …? All right, I'll be right there."

He stared at his phone, a faraway look in his eyes. "Six just turned to seven."

Brill got up from her desk just as Kurt crossed the detective bureau and knocked on her open door.

"Come in." She pulled the blinds on the glass wall. "Close the door behind you."

She heard the door shut and turned around in time to see Kurt sit in the vinyl chair next to her desk.

"What's up?" he said.

"You know Billy Dan Harrison from the barbershop?

"Sure. He cut my hair. Why?"

"He's missing." Brill sat in the chair next to him. "Harrison's car was found in the barbershop parking lot by a colleague, who arrived at eight and found the place locked. Harrison was supposed to open at seven. He doesn't answer his cell phone. We pulled his phone records, and the last call he made was to a pizza place last night. He's been missing about four hours. His wife has left phone messages. Says he would return her calls if he could. Exact same response as the spouses of the other missing people." Brill let out a low moan. "I hate this. I wanted you to hear it from me. It'll be all over the news any minute."

Kurt laced his fingers and seemed to be processing.

She got up and paced in front of the windows. Had the whole world gone crazy? Seven people in seven days? Who was this wicked man that David felt inadequate to profile? How could they find the victims he was holding for some kind of mass murder?

"What now?" Kurt said.

"Trace is going over Harrison's car, looking for evidence. But the investigating officers found no sign of a struggle. So far the only vehicle that has given us anything useful is Janice Evans's Mustang."

"Has David created a profile?"

"He read me a rough profile of the man he thinks we're looking for. But until we get some substantial evidence or an ID on the DNA, it's still a wide-open field."

CHAPTER 20

NICK Phillips stood at the counter at the Grill and listened as his friends reacted to the news that a seventh person had been abducted.

Gus straddled the barstool, his elbows on the counter. "It's a serious situation we've got goin', y'all. I've half a notion to drive over to Maryville and hang out at my sister's place 'til the authorities restore some order around here."

"It's awful," Tessa said. "We hardly had time to realize the little Cub Scout was missing, and now this. It's just awful"

"It's worse than awful. It just turned personal." Gus took a sip of Coke. "Billy Dan's been cuttin' my hair nigh on twenty years. He's been warnin' folks about the red shadows all that time. Now they went after him. I wonder how long the cops think they can dance around the truth of what's really goin' on."

"Tessa and I were in the police chief's living room just last night." Antonio put his hand on Tessa's. "We didn't talk about the case. We were just there because Mr. Quinlan showed up at their door. But the chief seems like such a fine person."

"She can be fine all she wants," Gus said. "But if she's bein' schooled by Sheriff Parker and the Feds, she's gonna cook up some lie about what's happenin' to these folks—same as the ax murders. You

read the headlines this morning. I'm not the only one who thinks
there's a cover-up that's spanned more than a century."

Tessa shook her head. "Gus, I've known you for decades, and
we've had our differences. But this thinking is irrational."

Gus waved his hand. "The legend speaks for itself. Let the games
begin."

Maggie set a plate with a cheeseburger and sweet potato fries on
the counter in front of Gus. "There's no cover-up. No games. You're
out of your mind. But I love you anyway."

Gus blew her a kiss. "My offer still stands. Marry me, and we'll
go sailing around the world. Take one of those extended cruises."

"I get seasick on the ocean, Gus."

"I'll bring plenty of Dramamine. If you don't wanna elope, the
captain can marry us. How can you refuse this face?" He lifted his
white eyebrows up and down.

"Now *I'm* going to be sick," Antonio said. "Let's change the
subject. I think Nick here deserves a pat on the back for the new
booths and the new counter. This place looks pretty classy."

Gus held up his Coke glass. "I'll drink to that."

"Here, here." Antonio held up his water glass at the same time
Tessa did, and they toasted.

"I'm glad you like the changes," Nick said. "I don't know whether
this place is packed out because the food's good and the atmosphere's
crisp and new—or if folks are just looking for a place to commiserate
about our seven missing neighbors.

Brill sat at the conference table in her office, filling in a spreadsheet with the details they'd compiled on each of the seven missing persons. It seemed as if the perpetrator were picking these victims randomly. Six of the seven were abducted in a parking lot. Each in a different location. And if David was right about the perp going after a kid to break the predictability factor, then why did he go right back to the original MO?

David came into the office looking uncharacteristically exhausted. "Is this case making you crazy?"

"The jury's still out on that," she said. "How sure are you that our perp randomly chose his victims?"

"Everything's up for grabs, but it makes the most sense. I don't see a common denominator to link these cases together. Different genders. Ages. Backgrounds. My guess is he isn't picky. He just wants someone he can catch off guard. But I find it frustrating that, after seven of these, no one actually witnessed anything, other than Mr. Ramos, who saw a faded blue van driven by a man he *thinks* was Latino and *might've* abducted Sonya Nichols from the bank parking lot."

"Well, what evidence we do have speaks with clarity," she said. "We know that Janice Evans was dragged from her vehicle by at least two men, and the man who was in that Mustang with her had coarse dark hair, *and* we've got his DNA."

David flashed a phony smile. "Good. What I *want* is that kid."

"How long do you think the perp will keep his victims alive?"

"Until he's finished with his power spree or thinks we're getting too close to him. Special Agent Morrow is holding a press conference to warn people not to put themselves in harm's way. To avoid secluded parking lots and, better yet, avoid going out alone. Of course, the proponents of the red shadows theory can practically hear the war cry and the pounding of the tom-toms. The ACLU is all over it. The principal chief of the Cherokee emphatically denies there's any truth to the legend and wants no part of the media frenzy."

"Can you blame him?" Brill got up and walked over to the coffeepot. "You want coffee?"

"No, thanks."

"I have a feeling people are going to heed Morrow's warning. Anyone with a brain would think twice about being out alone."

"I don't know." David leaned against the window, his thumbs hooked on the belt loops of his Dockers. "Most people hear this stuff and don't think it could ever happen to them."

David's eyebrows formed a dark bushy line and suddenly he seemed miles away.

Brill carried her coffee over to the conference table and stole a few well-spaced glances at this special agent she admired and respected and had worked with numerous times before. His shaved head gave him a rugged, almost handsome look. She felt a twinge of chemistry and quickly dismissed it.

"A penny for your thoughts?" she finally said.

David blinked, then looked at her, the corners of his mouth twitching. "That's probably all they're worth."

"Actually I have the utmost confidence in you."

"Thanks. I want to hear *your* thoughts. You've been studying the cases. What's going on inside that brilliant head of yours?"

"I don't know how brilliant it is, but I'm not so sure the victims were taken at random." Brill glanced at her watch. "I have a meeting with the city council in fifteen minutes. But I'd like to use the afternoon to keep exploring the idea that there must be a common denominator in all this. It's just a gut feeling."

David nodded. "Go for it. I sure can't find one."

Kurt sat at his desk in the back bedroom he hadn't yet converted into his office and turned on his laptop to see what he had on Wednesday afternoon's calendar. How was he supposed to avoid going out alone or using out-of-the-way parking lots? He decided just to stay home and work on the procedure manual for his stores.

He smiled at Emily's picture on the screen and remembered how chatty she had been all the way to school. It was obvious that she loved spending time with her mom. So did he—even if all he got from Brill was her venting and sharing information.

He thought back on last night when the two of them looked at each other in silent amusement as Emily rattled off all the trivia she knew about Mr. Quinlan—*and* his pets. How long had it been since they had connected that way?

He decided he was going to give Brill flowers today instead of tomorrow. He'd been doing it every Thursday so he wouldn't forget, but he was actually enthused about it for once. She had told him repeatedly it was a waste of time and money. He wondered if it would make any difference to her that today's offering was motivated by affection instead of guilt.

Kurt took a few minutes and moved some of what he had on today's calendar to another day. But one thing he couldn't put off for long was preparing for his Sunday school class.

Why was he nervous about teaching again? He thought the jitters would disappear once he stepped out in obedience and got the first session behind him. The Lord got him over the first hurdle. Would He do it twice? Why was it so hard to trust Him?

Kurt sensed the all-too-familiar worthlessness bearing down on him, and the Enemy's taunts echoing in the chasm of his unfaithfulness.

Adulterer. Deceiver. Fool. You're nothing. They can see right through you. They pretend to listen, but they're laughing at you.

So what if they were? Hadn't the Lord called him to teach this class? And could anyone but God Himself know why He chose a sinner like Kurt Jessup to accomplish a task many other men could do better?

Kurt turned and looked outside. He could see the hazy foothills in the space between the houses across the street. In the distance, a gray-blue mist, like an Etch A Sketch screen, had magically erased the outline of the Great Smoky Mountains.

What, besides the natural beauty of East Tennessee, had he really expected to be better when he moved here? Hadn't Brill made it clear that she was allowing him to come along for Emily's sake? And didn't he willingly agree to switch roles with Brill and keep things together until their youngest child was grown?

Not that he minded living in a small town. The time he spent traveling between five stores provided him with a frequent change of scenery, plenty of people contact, and all the flexibility he needed to help with Emily.

The new house was a step up. And the church a good fit that forced him out of his comfort zone. He was confident that once the cops caught the kidnapper, Sophie Trace would be a decent place to live.

But could it ever be home? Could any place ever be home as long as he and Brill kept this arrangement? The choice to be celibate and stay married to her was even more oppressive than he had imagined—and perhaps a fitting punishment.

Brill studied the spreadsheet where she had listed every detail that was known about each of the missing people. There was just nothing here to connect the victims. The only thing remotely similar was that first victim, Michael Stanton, had seven children. And the third victim, Dr. Benson, was assigned reserved parking space seven.

She sighed. So if the perp chose his victims randomly, who would be next? How could this guy keep snatching people when every available patrol car was out cruising the streets and the law-enforcement presence was so strong?

She heard a knock on the door and looked up at Trent standing in the doorway. "Come in, Trent. What's up?"

He came in and handed her a photograph. "The Smarties's graffiti showed up again. Similar to what we found before."

Brill held out the photo and studied it.

SMARTZRULE7X

"I wonder why they left out the numeral two this time?" she said. "Trent, where was this spray-painted?"

"On the gazebo in Shady Park. We covered over it as soon as we found it. I'm encouraged that, so far, no gang has responded to what the Smarties put out there the other day. And our informant doesn't know anything about a possible drive-by on Beech Street. It's a constant battle keeping up with new gangs, like trying to wipe out termites before they have a chance to swarm."

"Well, stay with it. I don't want a gang infestation because we're focused on the missing persons cases."

"Yes, ma'am. By the way, how'd your meeting go with the city council?"

Brill arched her eyebrows. "I did my level best to sound positive, even though we don't have any suspects. I assured them we're utilizing all the manpower and resources available to us, and that we've now set up checkpoints on both sides of town. Every vehicle coming and going will be stopped."

"Good move."

"Thanks. Obviously we can't search a vehicle unless we see something suspicious in plain view. But anyone in a faded blue van will be detained until we find a reason to search it—whatever it takes."

"I sat in on the latest briefing, ma'am. Special Agent Riley's profile of the perpetrator was impressive."

"I hope he's wrong, but he rarely is. It's sobering that seven people might be alive and facing a mass killing."

"Maybe O'Toole, Rousseux, and I should get back on the case—just 'til something breaks?"

Brill shook her head. "No. When it's over, I don't want to have to deal with gang violence. We're getting help from departments throughout the region. I don't want you three to let up."

CHAPTER 21

BRILL sat at the conference table, her spreadsheet in front of her, and took a sip of cold coffee.

"Sometimes I wish I weren't so determined," she murmured to herself, "but there must be some connection other than one victim has seven kids and one uses reserved parking space seven. And one victim teaches at the same elementary school as another victim who has kids attending there.

"Wait a minute!" She opened the Tompkins boy's case file and looked at the missing persons report.

"That's right ... Dade Tompkins is seven years old. That's a third seven." She entered that fact under his name on her spreadsheet. "That's worth exploring."

She pulled out the other four case files and looked through them without finding any connection to the number seven. Should she give up on this line of thinking?

She decided she'd rather look foolish than be sorry. She opened Janice Evans's case file and looked for a home phone number. She almost hated to bother Mr. Evans with it. Then again, why would he mind if she bothered him? He just wanted his wife back. She punched in the phone number. At least he would know she was working hard to solve the case.

"Hello."

"Mr. Evans?"

"Yes."

"This is Police Chief Jessup. I'm following up on your wife's case and need to ask you a question. This is probably going to sound strange, but it might mean something. Is there anything in Janice's everyday life that involves the number seven?"

"I'm not sure I understand what you're asking."

"Is there a number seven that might be obvious to other people: seven grandkids, something special that happens on the seventh day of the month, anything that stands out?"

"Seven is the number of her classroom."

"You're sure?"

"Yes, it's on the door. Does that mean something?"

"I don't know yet. We're exploring some new angles. Thanks. That's what I needed. I'll get back to you as soon as we know anything new."

Brill disconnected the call, her pulse racing. She dug through Candi Eagan's file, found the home phone number, and entered the digits.

"Hello."

"Mr. Eagan, it's Chief Jessup. I need to ask you a question that might sound strange but could be important. Is the number seven significant in Candi's daily routine—something that would be obvious to other people?

"Like what?"

"Maybe Candi had seven house closings last month? Or seven new listings? Something like that?"

"No."

"Your anniversary date? Your birthday? Something special about the seventh day of the month?"

"I can't think of anything." His speech seemed thick and heavy, like he was either medicated or depressed—or both.

Brill picked up her pencil and bounced the eraser on the table. "Are you sure the number seven doesn't stand out somehow?"

"Not that I know of. Why are you asking?"

"We're digging deeper into each of the cases, looking for a possible connection."

"A little late for that."

Brill sighed. "I know it must seem that way to you, Mr. Eagan. But we're working twenty-four/seven. Exploring every conceivable angle."

"Candi's all I've got, Chief Jessup. How hard *you* have to work means nothing to me if I have to spend the rest of my life without her."

"I understand. And that's why I'm working so hard to find her. Thanks for your help. We'll let you know the minute we know anything new."

Brill disconnected the call and looked through Candi Eagan's case file again. She quickly read down one page, and then another, and another. She went back and reread the missing persons report. "She drives a 2007 Chevy Impala. That would certainly be obvious."

She wrote that information on her spreadsheet and wondered if she were grasping at straws. Then again, what did she have to lose? It was either this or a brick wall.

She rummaged through Sonya Nichols's case file, found her

home phone number, and keyed in the numbers. The phone rang once. Twice. Three times.

"Come on, pick up before I change my mind and—"

"Nichols residence," said a female voice.

"This is Police Chief Jessup. May I speak with Mr. Nichols, please?"

"He's not here. Can I help you? I'm Sonya's sister, Marcy Spellman."

"I would really prefer to talk to him, if—"

"Could you hold, please? I think he just drove up."

"Yes, I'll hold. Tell him it's not bad news."

Brill heard footsteps and voices on the other end and waited for what seemed an eternity, and then someone picked up the phone.

"Chief Jessup, it's Joe Nichols. What's going on? Did you find Sonya?"

"No, not yet. I need to ask you a question, though. I wouldn't bother you with it if it wasn't important. Does the number seven stand out in your wife's life somehow—in a way that would be obvious to other people?"

"Yeah, that's the number of her teller station at the bank. Why?"

Brill's heart felt as if it were pounding out of her chest, and she managed to say with a calm voice, "We're digging deeper into the cases. I don't have anything new to tell you right now, but we'll let you know the minute something changes. Thanks for your time."

Brill disconnected the call. Six out of seven was more than a coincidence. Now what about Billy Dan Harrison?

She sat back in her chair and considered how far-fetched this was. She could probably dig up the number seven in almost anyone's life. What about her own personal life? Was there any aspect of her life where the number seven stood out? She decided there wasn't. What about Kurt's life? Or Emily's? She couldn't think of anything significant about the number seven with them either.

She got up and walked out into the DB to Trent's desk. "Do you know if Mrs. Harrison is still here?"

Trent nodded and finished writing something, then looked up. "Yes, ma'am. She's in the second interview room. She insisted on waiting."

"Thanks."

Brill crossed the DB and turned down the hallway and stood outside the second interview room. She knocked softly on the open door and stepped inside.

"Mrs. Harrison, it's Chief Jessup. We met this morning."

Brill sat across the table from the bottle brunette with red, swollen eyes and took her hand. "We're doing everything we can to find your husband. We've even set up checkpoints at both ends of town."

"I know. I'm just so scared I'll never see him again."

"Let's not even go there," Brill said. "It's very possible that he's alive and needs our help. I have a question you can help me with. Is there anything in your husband's everyday life that revolves around the number seven—something that other people would notice?"

Mrs. Harrison's eyebrows came together, and she stared at Brill as if it were a trick question. Finally she said, "Everyone knows Billy Dan kept that 7UP can that Randy Travis drank from when he came through here years ago. It's in a shadow box, hanging on the wall in the barbershop like some kind of trophy. Is that important?"

"Every detail is important." Brill gave Mrs. Harrison's hand a squeeze, almost certain the woman must feel her pulse pounding. "The more we know about your husband, the better chance we have of finding him. Can I get you coffee or something cold to drink before I get back to work?"

"No. Just please bring Billy Dan home alive."

"I'm working on it with all my heart and soul."

Brill got up and left the room and walked as fast as she could back to her office and closed the door. *That* was definitely no coincidence.

Kurt opened the front door and let Emily squeeze past him, then followed her out to the kitchen.

"How come you're so quiet?" he said.

Emily shrugged.

Kurt got the Tupperware container of peanut butter cookies and set it on the table, then poured two glasses of milk and sat across from Emily.

"Rough day at school?"

Emily folded her arms across her chest, her lower lip pushed out. "I knew they would laugh at me."

"Because your mother hasn't solved the case yet?"

"They think the cops aren't telling people the truth about the red shadows. I told them the *real* story about how the legend got started. But Heath and Jeremy got the other kids not to believe me." A tear spilled down Emily's cheek. "Now everyone's calling me 'Jessup the *Mess*up.' I hate them. And I hate school. I want to go back to Memphis."

Kurt stuck a cookie in his mouth and bit down hard, hoping Emily couldn't tell how mad he was. Why did kids have to be so mean? "Was Jasmine in on the teasing?"

Emily shook her head. "She told them to stop."

"Well, see. You have a real friend."

"Could I ask her to come for a sleepover?

"That's a possibility. I'd like to meet her parents first. Or at least talk to them."

"They don't pick her up from school. They work at the tire factory."

"Does she stay with someone after school?"

"Her big sister, Rosa. She's sixteen. That's old enough to be the boss, if the parents say so. I remember when Vanessa was sixteen and I was little and she used to boss me around."

Kurt smiled to himself. Just four years ago and it seemed a lifetime. "I'm sorry the kids at school were immature and mean to you. Did Kevin and Devin Nichols come back to school?"

"No. Mrs. Bartlett said they're doing their work at home because they're really sad about their mom. I would be too."

"Well, don't you imagine Mrs. Bartlett is sad that Mrs. Evans is missing, since they're both teachers at the same school?"

Emily nodded. "There's a substitute teacher in the first-grade class. I think everyone's freaked out that Mrs. Evans and Mrs. Nichols might be dead."

Brill left a message on David's cell phone, asking him to call her, then sat at the conference table, a ruled pad in front of her. What was the significance of the number seven?

She got out her copy of the final profile David provided for each member of law enforcement and reread it.

> The unidentified subject is likely a Hispanic male. Young. Angry. A sociopath who has contempt for the law, and who considers himself to be the ultimate authority. Though capable of murder, he is not a serial killer.
>
> His thrill comes through the securing of a wide audience that reveres what he believes to be his superior intelligence. To that end he engages in the systematic abduction of his victims, not to torture and kill them, but to flaunt his intellectual prowess.
>
> He thrives on controlling every move and considers predictability to be the ultimate weakness. He must stay one step ahead of the authorities and will change his MO at any point to maintain a comfortable lead. He is most dangerous when he doesn't feel respected or gets bored with the game.
>
> His victims are the means to an end. And when the game is over, he will dispose of them, probably en masse, without a twinge of conscience.

Brill sighed. So what was his next move? Why and how did he choose his victims by the number seven? She made a column on the paper and wrote the victims' names and what she knew about the number seven in each case:

- Victim #1, Stanton, Michael. Seven children
- Victim #2, Evans, Janice. Classroom number seven
- Victim #3, Vaughn, Dr. Benson. Reserved parking space seven
- Victim #4, Eagan, Candi. '07 Chevrolet Impala
- Victim #5, Nichols, Sonya. Teller station seven
- Victim #6, Tompkins, Dade. Seven years old
- Victim #7, Harrison, Billy Dan. 7UP can/R. Travis

What prompted the perp to single out *these* victims? They had nothing in common. Was the seven really a factor, or was it just coincidence? All of a sudden she began to feel foolish. Maybe she was making too much of this.

Brill's phone vibrated; it was David. She put the phone to her ear. "Thanks for calling back so quickly."

"What's up?" he said.

"Would you come to my office? I've found something I can't ignore—a rather unexpected common denominator."

"I'll be right there."

Brill disconnected the call and studied the column she'd made on the ruled pad. The disappearances happened between October first and October seventh. If she was right, and the number seven was the common denominator, wasn't it logical to assume that the perp would stop his kidnapping spree now that he had captured seven victims? Or was that too logical for someone as delusional as he?

All of a sudden it was as though the first letter of each victim's last name jumped off the page. It was so obvious she could hardly believe she hadn't seen it before. S-E-V-E-N-T-H.

CHAPTER 22

BRILL leaned against the front of her desk, her arms folded, and faced David Riley and Sam Parker, who were sitting at the conference table. The smell of fresh paint wafted under her nose and reminded her that she needed to call Kurt and let him know she wouldn't be home for dinner.

"We're caught between a rock and a hard place," David said. "If we sit on this information about the sevens, we stand the chance that our unidentified subject will get bored because he's not getting the press he wants, decide to the end the game, and dispose of the victims. And if we release it to the media, they'll connect the sevens to the Sophie Stanton story and say it's a sign that the red shadows are taking their revenge. That'll start a worse panic."

"Well, it sure isn't gonna go away if we shut up." Sam's glasses rested on his nose, his steely gaze on David. "And there's a good chance someone will leak it anyway, which will just feed the conspiracy theory that law enforcement is coverin' up the truth about red shadows."

Brill took a sip of bottled water. "I agree. Why not go public with the fact that we think the number seven has been a factor in each of the kidnappings? Who cares how the media spins it? If our unidentified subject planned to snatch seven people, he's done with it—and we all know what that means. It's worth giving him the attention he wants in order to buy us some time."

David lifted his eyebrows. "I'm not sure that'll satisfy him for long."

"It might if we withhold the fact that we know first letters of the victims' last names spell the word *seventh*. He wants us to discover how clever that was. Let's make him wait."

"I hate being pulled into his game," David said, "almost as much as I hate feeding the media."

"With all due respect, this isn't about you." Sam's lips seemed to curl. "I promise y'all, those who believe the legend will make the facts fit no matter what we do. It's always been that way. For cryin' out loud let's do whatever it takes to buy some time. There are seven lives at stake here."

"Take it easy, Sheriff," David said. "I agree with both of you. I just don't like it. The perp will only give us a small window to figure out where he's holding these people before they run out of the time we're trying to buy."

Brill brushed the hair out of her eyes. "What if the word *seventh* is the clue to where they are?" She reached behind her and grabbed the ruled pad and read down the list of victims' names. "They all have Anglo surnames, even if Dr. Vaughn is African American. It's obvious the perp planned the kidnappings to look as though the Cherokee were making good on this legendary vendetta. He took great care to abduct each victim in the proper sequence so that the first letter of their last names spell the word *seventh*. There has to be a reason."

David sat back in his chair and rubbed his eyes. "It could be a clue. Or it could be his way of saying, 'Checkmate.'"

Tessa looked out the kitchen window, not surprised that Chief Jessup's squad car wasn't parked in the driveway. She carried two plates of baked chicken, new potatoes, and asparagus over to the table.

Antonio said the blessing and then picked up his fork. "This looks great. I suppose you're going to say it's good for me?"

"Of course." The corners of Tessa's mouth twitched. "I plan to keep you around for a long time."

"I'm disturbed by what was on the news tonight," Antonio said. "What's with all the sevens? You know I'm not superstitious, but this gives me the creeps. I keep trying to think of anything involving the number seven that would make either of us a target."

"Fear is so crippling." Tessa cut her asparagus into bite-size pieces and blinked away the memory of the man smashing her windshield. "We just have to use good sense and trust the Lord for the rest."

"Kind of hard to do when seven people in seven days have vanished into thin air."

"It's sobering, that's for sure. I wonder how Kurt and Emily are doing. Can't be easy on them to have Brill tied up with this case."

Antonio swallowed and took a sip of ice water. "Maybe we should have Emily over again. It was fun having a kid round."

"It was, wasn't it? She's such a delight. But she has sad eyes."

"She seems happy to me. It can't be easy moving to a new town and starting a new school. But it's obvious she's loved and cared for."

"I don't doubt that. She just seems deeply troubled about something. We're all troubled about what's been happening. But this seems deeper than that. I noticed it when they first moved here, before the disappearances."

"Yeah, I remember you saying that. You're good at sensing things about people."

Tessa felt Abby rubbing against her leg and resisted the temptation to give her a bite of chicken.

The doorbell rang.

Antonio wiped his mouth with a napkin. "I'll get that. If I don't come back, call Brill and tell her the red shadows got me." He grinned sheepishly. "Just kidding."

He walked to the door and opened it. Tessa listened to see who it was.

"Well, hello, Mr. Quinlan. Would you like to come in?"

Tessa heard footsteps and smiled when the old fellow with white hair and horn-rimmed glasses shuffled into the kitchen.

"Well, you're just in time for dessert," Tessa said. "I just happen to have some oatmeal raisin cookies. Your favorite."

Antonio poured a glass of milk and handed it to her. "Junior's going to have to do something. He can't keep this up."

"Thank heavens your father finally let you invite me over," Mr. Quinlan said. "If you're free Friday night, I'd be honored to take you square dancing."

Tessa linked her arm in Mr. Quinlan's. "Why, I would be delighted." She led him to the table and seated him, knowing that he had already forgotten what he said.

"Hello, Junior. It's Antonio. In case you're wondering where your father is, he's sitting in our kitchen.... Yeah, Tessa just made a date with him for Friday night ..."

Kurt opened the door at Nick's Grill and followed Emily inside. She slid into one side of a booth, and he slid in the other.

Nick hurried over to them and handed each a menu. "Hey, it's good to see you, Kurt, Emily. Welcome back."

"I like coming here," Emily said. "Even your *healthy* food tastes yummy."

"Glad you approve. The special tonight is grilled Alaskan salmon with fresh green beans and your choice of baked potato, garlic mashed potatoes, or wild rice. I'll give you a few minutes to look at the menu."

Emily handed the menu back to Nick. "I know what I want—I mean, I'll have the oriental chicken salad, please. And water to drink."

Kurt winked at her and gave his menu back to Nick. "And I'll have the grilled portobello and veggies, with Swiss cheese, on rye. And iced tea."

"If you're interested," Nick said, "tonight's special dessert is a honey-vanilla ice cream topped with a special blackberry compote." He hesitated for several seconds, then said, "I can't even imagine how hard it must be for your wife right now. There's some serious stuff going on in this town. It's got to be overwhelming for a new police chief. We've never had anything like this happen before."

"Yeah, it's been wild," Kurt said.

"Plus we've got this legend thing going on too. It's hard to understand it unless you were raised here."

Emily's eyes grew wide. "I know the real story about how the legend got started. Do you want to hear it?"

Nick glanced around at the customers in other booths and then smiled at Emily. "Sure."

"Give Mr. Phillips the short version," Kurt said. "I'm sure he needs to get back to work."

Kurt, aware that others were eavesdropping, listened as Emily retold what Pate Dickson had told her mother: that twenty years after the Cherokee disappeared there had been a series of barn burnings involving the second generation of Stantons, and how after each fire a feather was found under a rock on the family's front porch.

"Since no one knew who did it," Emily said, "they started blaming it on the spirits of the Cherokee. And that's how the legend got started."

Kurt heard chuckling and whispering behind him, and Emily took on the same indignant look her mother often did.

"They're not laughing at you, darlin'," Nick said. "It's just that everyone's heard so many versions of how the legend got started, no one really knows which is the right one."

"We need to let Mr. Phillips get back to work," Kurt said.

Nick smiled warmly. "It was good talking with you. Maggie will bring your drinks and we'll have your dinner out to you soon."

Kurt waited until Nick was out of earshot, then said to Emily, "Sorry, sweetie. I guess we keep learning new things about this legend all the time."

"I don't like being laughed at." Emily sighed. "Why does everyone keep talking about a stupid legend no one can prove?"

"I don't know. I'd much rather we talk about something else." Kurt's phone vibrated. He looked at the screen and then put the phone to his ear. "Hello Tessa."

"I hope I'm not calling at a bad time."

"Not at all. Emily and I are at Nick's Grill, just waiting for our dinner. What's on your mind?"

"Antonio and I were just wondering if Emily would like to spend the day with us on Saturday. We had so much fun before."

"Why don't you ask her yourself? Just a second, I'm handing her the phone."

"Hi, Mrs. Masino." Emily's eyes lit up the way they used to with her grandparents.

"Hi. Antonio and I would love it if you could come over on Saturday. I've got everything we need to make my special spaghetti sauce. We could go through another old trunk and see what we find. And we have Monopoly, Uno, dominoes, checkers—lots of games we can play."

Kurt could hear Tessa's voice from across the booth and nodded his approval.

"I'd really like that," Emily said.

"There is one thing we need to change first. I'd really like it if you would call us something less formal than Mr. and Mrs. Masino."

"Like what?" Emily said.

"Well, how about Aunt Tessa and Uncle Tony? Or just Tessa and Tony?"

Emily looked at Kurt, her eyes wide. "I'm not sure my parents would let me do that. It's kind of hard. I mean, I'm supposed to say Mister and Missus."

"I understand," Tessa said. "I grew up in the South too. But I expect us to become very close friends. I just wish we could come up with a name that didn't make me sound like a teacher."

"My real teacher is Mrs. Bartlett."

"Yes, I remember you telling me that. Emily, what would *you* like to call us?"

Emily hesitated. She looked over at Kurt, her face suddenly pinker than her sweater.

"Are you still there, honey …? Emily …"

"Yes, ma'am. Um, I think maybe I could call you Tessa and Tony. I might have to practice, though."

"I like the sound of it.'"

"And I could just call Abby, Abby." Emily giggled.

"I guess my little fluff ball doesn't need a nickname. By the way, have you gotten to know Jasmine a little better since we talked last?"

Emily nodded. "Yes, she's really nice. Dad said maybe she could come for a sleepover. I haven't invited anyone yet to stay at my new house. I have a really cool room, and it's upstairs. It was already lavender when we moved in, and I have this really cool purple comforter and one of those ruffley things at the bottom. Maybe next time you come over, you can see it."

"I would love to. Goodness, I'd better let you go so you can spend time with your dad and enjoy your dinner. I'll call again and we can decide on a time. We're looking forward to it."

"Me, too, Mrs.— I mean, Tessa. Bye."

"Good-bye, honey."

Emily handed the phone back to Kurt. "She's so nice, Dad. I really like spending time with her."

"I'm glad."

Emily's eyes seemed to search his. "Really?"

"Of course. You act surprised."

She didn't say anything.

"Emily, I know you loved Grammy very much. But developing a relationship with Tessa is a good thing. It doesn't take away from what you had with your grandmother."

"Does it bother you if I call her Tessa?"

"Not at all." Kurt tilted her chin and looked into her eyes. "It was horrible when Grammy and Poppy died in that car wreck. We miss them terribly, and I don't know if we'll ever be completely over their being here one day and gone the next. But the Masinos are obviously taken with you and vice versa. Your mom and I want you to enjoy time with them."

"I like the way I feel when I'm with them. Like I know they're not my grandparents, but it's fun because they treat me like they are."

Kurt held his daughter's gaze and didn't miss the sadness in those bright blue eyes. In a matter of eighteen months, her beloved grandparents had died tragically. A second sibling had left the nest. She had moved away from the only home she'd ever known and said good-bye to all her friends. She'd seen her normal parents evolve into a pair of robots who spoke niceties. And most of the time she lived in a single-parent family. What a huge number of losses for a nine-year-old. Kurt swallowed the ball of emotion in his throat.

"Don't cry, Dad. I promise I won't love them as much as Grammy and Poppy."

Kurt blinked away the moisture and forced his mouth to smile. "It would be okay if you did. I just miss them." *And your mother. And Ryan and Vanessa. And a home that feels like a home.*

Emily eased back into talking about her time with the Masinos and was soon chattering about all the fun she would have with them. As he listened, the words of Romans 12:21 echoed in his mind: *Do not be overcome by evil. But overcome evil with good.*

No one could dispute that his family was being overcome by evil—evil he had brought upon them. Hadn't his affair turned Brill into an automaton? And his college kids into nomads? And his baby girl into an only child starved for a sense of belonging? They were all slipping away from him, and he felt powerless to do anything about it.

But overcome evil with good. The words reverberated in his head until they seemed audible. In context, weren't they intended for the offended party—more for Brill than for him? And yet, he was being overcome by the very evil he had set in motion. Wouldn't the same principle apply?

"Dad, are you listening?" Emily said.

"Yes, you said you could hardly wait to dig into another of Tessa's old trunks."

"She reminds me a lot of Grammy. Not the way she looks, but the way she follows me everywhere and likes to spend time with me and teaches me to cook yummy things."

Kurt listened as Emily rambled on about this and that. He wondered how much good it would take to overcome the evil he had brought on his family. Could he ever do enough? He knew one thing: Unless he became proactive in the fight to win his family back, it was never going to happen.

CHAPTER 23

BRILL swished through the fallen leaves on the sidewalk and stepped up on the stoop, grateful that Kurt had left the porch light on. She turned the key and pushed open the heavy arched door and went inside. The TV was on and, out of the corner of her eye, she saw Kurt get up off the couch. Why wasn't he asleep? She really didn't feel like talking.

Kurt walked out to the entry hall. "Hi. Quite a day you've had."

"Unreal. How's Emily?"

"Good, overall. She got her feelings hurt a couple times today. First at school when the kids didn't believe her story of how the legend got started. Then at dinner when some customers in another booth laughed when they overheard her telling the story to Nick. Apparently there are numerous versions."

"Pate never alluded to that." Brill sighed. "It's times like this when I really feel like an outsider. How upset was she?"

"She'll get over it. Nick explained they weren't laughing at her—just the notion that her version was somehow the right one. By the way, Tessa and Antonio want her to come over Saturday."

Brill listened while Kurt told her about Tessa's phone call and how loyal Emily was to the memory of Grammy and Poppy.

"Are you okay with her getting close to them?" Brill said.

"Absolutely. Emily needs to fill that void with something. If hanging out with the Masinos can do that for her, I'm grateful."

"I'm exhausted." Brill opened the closet door and hung up her coat. "I'm going to bed. Why are you up so late?"

"I want to talk to you about something."

Brill shook her head. "Not tonight. I'm on overload. Whatever it is, it can wait."

"No, it can't."

"I need to sleep."

"I need five minutes."

Brill heard the determination in his voice and went into the living room and flopped on the couch. "What?"

Kurt sat in the overstuffed chair, facing her, his hands folded between his knees. "This rift between the two of us is causing our children a great deal of pain and emptiness. Ryan and Vanessa are using any excuse they can find not to come visit—they don't even consider it home anymore. And I'm extremely concerned about Emily. She seems lost."

"Lost how?"

"Like everything she's ever held dear is gone: both siblings, the house she grew up in, her school, her church, her friends, her grandparents, her *family*."

"That's *your* fault."

"I'm well aware of that, Brill. I just don't think my transgression should sentence Emily to an unhappy childhood."

"You should've thought of that before you ended up in bed with some homecoming queen has-been from high school."

Kurt paused for several seconds and then said, "I understand things will never be the same between us, but they can be better than this."

"I've got my life," she said. "And you've got yours. That's what we agreed to."

"Our kids have a life too. What about them? Our decision to stay together to raise Emily was made to benefit each of our kids. It's not working."

"We've been here one month." She glanced over at the family portrait they'd had taken before Ryan left for college and felt a pang of longing. "That's not enough time to know anything."

"It didn't start here. It's been going on for eighteen months. Why do you think Ryan and Vanessa didn't come home the weekend before the movers came?"

Brill put her face in her hands, then combed her fingers through her hair. "Kurt, I'm too tired to think. Seven people are missing, and I'm responsible to find them. I can only deal with one crisis at a time. Right now the case has to come first because lives are at stake."

"I understand that."

"Then what do you want from me?"

"I want you to take some time to consider what each of the kids, particularly Emily, is going through and tell me what *you* think we should do."

"You're not going to turn this around and make it my fault. You destroyed this family. You're lucky I even let you stay."

Kurt locked gazes with her. "I know what I deserve. This isn't about me. It's about our son and two daughters who deserve a home—not just a house with no memories. This place is a morgue. They deserve better. We can do better."

"If you think I'm ever going to be your wife again—other than in name only—you'd better forget it. And I don't have time to think right now."

"*Make* time. You can find time for whatever you think is important, Brill. The city council's not paying you to work twenty-hour days. You're not indispensable."

"Well, I *am* spent. I'm going to bed. You do remember Emily has gymnastics tomorrow?"

"Have I ever forgotten anything on her schedule?"

"No." Brill got up and stretched her lower back. "I'm so tired, I can't think straight. Once I've rested, I'll think about what you said."

"It's important," he said softly. "Good night. I love you. I always have and I always will."

"Spare me the mantra, Kurt."

She went down the hallway and into her bedroom. She closed the door and leaned on it. What kind of mother puts her job before her kids? Puts her own needs before theirs? She had never verbalized to anyone how hurt she was that Ryan and Vanessa didn't come to visit the weekend before the movers came and had made no effort to come see the new house. Then again it was just a house. Kurt was right. It wasn't a home.

And poor little Emily … she really had lost more than all of them. Nothing in her world was the same. Almost nothing had been salvaged. And now even her mother seemed to have abandoned her.

Brill fell across the bed, her mind racing in all directions, her flood of emotion barely contained. The situation with the seven missing people was consuming every ounce of her mental energy. If she switched her focus to personal problems, would she be effective on either front?

Why did her children have to suffer because of the chasm in her marriage? Why couldn't the problem be worked out privately between Kurt and her? Surely a year and a half was long enough for the kids to accept that things were going to be different?

She turned over and hugged her pillow. Who was she kidding? Even she hadn't accepted it. Her family situation was even more complex than the case.

And what was with her sudden attraction to David? She'd worked with him numerous times before and the relationship had always been professional. What she had felt today, however briefly, was chemistry.

Kurt glanced over at the fresh flowers he arranged in the vase and wondered if Brill had even noticed. At least he had gotten everything off his chest. Whether or not she would do what he asked was anybody's guess.

"Dad, do you need a hug?"

Emily seemed to materialize out of nowhere and stood in front of him, her bare feet exposed below her pink and white flannel nightgown.

"Where were you?"

She crawled up in his lap and wrapped her arms around his neck. "Sitting on the steps. I know ... I'm not supposed to eavesdrop. But I heard Mom's voice and came down to say good night. Then I heard you talking and decided I shouldn't interrupt."

"How much of our conversation did you hear?"

"Some. Well, a lot."

Kurt's mind raced in reverse. Had he said anything he needed to explain. "Do you have questions about what we talked about?"

The room was pin-drop still except for the sound of Emily's breathing.

"What's a *has-been*?" she finally said.

The answer formed a knot in Kurt's throat. She had overheard the one comment he didn't want to address, but there was no skirting the issue with Emily. "A has-been is someone that used to be popular but isn't anymore."

"So you were in bed with a lady who was homecoming queen that isn't popular anymore?"

Kurt felt a wave of nausea. He couldn't lie to her. But he didn't want to offer more information than she asked for. *Lord, help me say the right thing.*

"Yes," he said.

"Did you kiss her?"

"Yes, I did. It was totally inappropriate. And Mom has a right to be angry with me."

In the silence that followed, he wondered what was going through Emily's mind. How much did she truly comprehend about sex? How much detail had Brill revealed in their mother-daughter discussions?

"Oh, I get it now," Emily said.

Did she? Did he even want her to? He decided not to ask.

Emily pushed back and looked into his eyes. "Why did you even kiss her in the first place?"

Kurt held his breath and then let it out slowly. "It's complicated, sweetie. It's a grown-up issue."

"Well … if it's making me feel lost, and Ryan and Vanessa not wanting to come home, I don't think it should be just for grown-ups anymore."

"Good point." Kurt pulled Emily closer and laid her head on his shoulder. He had known there would come a time when he had to explain himself. That time seemed to be now.

"About a year and a half ago," he said, "I was in OfficeMax and ran into a lady I'd had a crush on in high school. She wanted to go somewhere and talk, so we went to Starbucks. At first we just talked about our families and about all the things we've been doing since we graduated. But she also shared some things about her husband that were making her very sad, and I felt sorry for her."

"And you just kissed her to make it better?"

"Something like that." He stroked Emily's hair. "But then I liked kissing her and didn't want to stop. I broke the marriage vows I made, and that's a very serious thing to do. But it's a private problem between your mother and me—an adult matter."

"Is that why they call it *adult*ery?"

"Not exactly." Kurt's vision blurred and a tear escaped down his cheek, and he quickly wiped it away. "Emily, this is something I'm not proud of and don't care to talk about. My behavior was wrong, and I'd give anything to go back and change it. I've asked the Lord's forgiveness, and your mother's, but her feelings are hurt worse than anyone can imagine. She's having a very difficult time."

"I remember the night you told her because after you left she cried and cried so hard, and I'd never even heard her cry before. I just hid in my room."

He pulled Emily closer. "I'm sorry you had to go through that. I was so ashamed I needed to go away and think. When I came back, your mother and I had more discussions."

"So what did you agree to disagree on?"

"I wanted us to start over the way we were. Your mom just couldn't do it. She agreed not to get a divorce and to live in the same house so we could raise you together. But she doesn't really want to be married to me. I don't exactly know how to explain that."

"I get it, Dad. That's why you have different bedrooms. I liked it better when you didn't. And when you and Mom hugged and kissed and she talked nice to you. She doesn't laugh anymore. I can tell she's sad, even when she's not frowning."

"Me, too, sweetie. She needs time. I'll keep working to win her back. I want us to be a family again."

Emily tilted her head back and looked into his eyes. "Do you love her?"

"Very much."

"Then why didn't you just tell that lady to talk to a counselor about her problems and save everybody all this trouble?"

Kurt arched his eyebrows. "That, sweet girl, is a question I've asked myself a hundred times. I can't undo the wrong. But I'm going to work as hard as I can to win back your mother's love."

"I think she still loves you but doesn't want to so she pretends not to. But she does."

"I actually understood that. And I hope you're right."

CHAPTER 24

BRILL sat at the breakfast table and savored the taste of a bagel and cream cheese with her coffee. Her eyes feasted on a blazing pink sky and the silhouette of a mockingbird that was chirping loudly enough to wake up the entire neighborhood.

"Hi, Mom." Emily pranced into the kitchen and sat across from her at the table, then took a bagel out of the wrapper. "Isn't the rose Dad put in the bud vase beautiful?"

"Yes, it's lovely."

"He put a bunch of fresh flowers in the living room. Did you see them when you came home last night?"

Brill glanced at the date dial on her watch. "*Today* is Thursday."

"He bought them yesterday, just because he was thinking of you."

"Hmm ..."

"Did you know he looks at lots of different ones before he chooses the one that's just right for you?" Emily's tone seemed a little too contrived.

"Is that so?"

"I think it's very special he does that, don't you?"

"Fresh flowers look nice in the house." Brill poured Emily a glass of orange juice and set it in front of her. "Be careful. You're about to get your sleeve in the jelly."

"Dad's thoughtful. He really likes doing nice things for you."

Sure he does—to salve his guilt. "So … I hear you're going to spend the day at the Masinos' on Saturday."

Emily bobbed her head, her mouth stuffed with bagel. She washed it down with a gulp of orange juice. "And Tessa's going to show me how to make her special spaghetti sauce that makes every room in the house smell soooo yummy."

"That should be fun."

"Then I'll be able to make it when Ryan and Vanessa come home and we all eat together like we used to—as a family."

Brill studied her daughter, who seemed to avoid eye contact. What was she *not* saying?

"Emily, is there something you want to tell me?"

"Like what?"

"Please don't answer my question with a question."

Emily sat silent, staring at her plate, the rubber heel of her tennis shoe bouncing off the leg of the chair.

"Sweetie, you know you can talk to me about anything. I can tell something's bothering you."

Emily glanced up at her and then seemed to focus on her juice glass. "I heard you come home last night, and I came downstairs to tell you good night. Then I heard you and dad talking so I waited on the step."

"You were eavesdropping?"

"Not on purpose. But I heard some things you probably didn't want me to. But it's okay," she quickly added, "Dad and I talked, and he told me about the lady you said was a has-been."

Brill coughed to cover her surprise. "When?"

"Right after you went to bed. I went over to him because he looked like he needed a hug. I told him I didn't mean to eavesdrop, and he wanted to know if I had any questions about what you two said." Emily traced the rim of her juice glass with her finger. "So I asked him what a has-been was."

"How did he answer?"

"He said it was someone who used to be popular but isn't anymore."

"What else did he say?"

Brill listened as Emily relayed the details of her conversation with her father, including his explanation of how he ran into the woman he had a crush on in high school and ended up listening to her problems, and eventually breaking his wedding vows. Did she really understand what that meant?

"He's so sorry, Mom. He really loves you. If you would just forgive him, maybe you wouldn't be sad all the time."

"It's not that simple, Emily. And I wish he hadn't talked to you about an intensely private matter that is much too complicated for a nine-year-old to understand."

"I looked up *adultery* in the dictionary." Emily kept her eyes on her plate and pushed the bagel crumbs with her finger. "What Dad and that lady did was wrong because only married people are allowed to love each other that way. Right?"

Brill felt the heat scald her face. She had never shied away from answering any of Emily's questions about reproduction. But the idea that her innocent daughter had formed a mental picture of her father's illicit behavior with Victoria disgusted and grieved her. Even if she'd been able to find her voice, she wouldn't have known what to say.

"I know you didn't want me to find out." Emily's chin quivered, her eyes brimming with tears. "But at least now you don't have to pretend around me anymore. I'm not a baby."

"Of course you're not." Brill felt as if someone else were speaking. "But you *are* a little girl. I didn't want to clutter your childhood with problems you shouldn't even have to know about."

"My childhood's already cluttered! You're not the only one who's sad, Mom. I hate it here. I hate every single day. I never see you. I never see Ryan and Vanessa. I don't even have a family anymore. And nobody wants to talk about it."

Brill felt as if her heart were breaking all over again. She went over and knelt next to Emily's chair and pulled her into her arms.

"It's going to be okay, sweetie. There're just so many changes all at once."

"I hate changes."

"Some changes are good."

"Which ones?" Emily started to sob, her tears wetting the front of Brill's uniform shirt. "I can't think of any."

Brill walked into the police station and across the detective bureau to her office. David sat at the conference table, files and stacks of papers spread out in front of him.

"Were you here all night?" she said.

A smile stole across his face. "I brought my toothbrush and jammies. You should've stayed. We could've had a sleepover. Or better yet, a lock in."

Was he coming on to her? She decided to ignore the remark.

"Did anything new surface in my absence?"

David shook his head. "Nope. But I'm sure you're right about the sevens being the link. I don't know that I would have ever picked up on the first letters of the victims' last names spelling the word seventh. Nice work. Once again the lady lives up to her nickname."

"At least I'm good for something."

David put down his pencil, his eyes probing. "What's wrong?"

"I just didn't sleep well." The lie pricked her conscience, but she wasn't going to discuss the fiasco of her personal life.

"Insomnia is one of the hazards of being a cop. You should learn to take power naps. That's how I deal with it. Ten minutes here and there, and I have all the energy I need."

What I need is a cure for reality.

"You're probably uptight because today is the day we find out whether or not our perpetrator stops with seven victims."

"Let's hope I'm right." Brill sat in the chair across from David. "It makes sense. Seven victims in seven days, between October first and the seventh, and something about each victim related to the number seven—all intended to stir up those who buy the whole red shadows legend. But I haven't quite figured out the guy's motive. The profile indicates that his thrill comes through the securing of a wide audience that reveres what he believes to be his superior intelligence. But the wide audience that he's duped consists of the very naive. Why would that make him feel superior?"

"Because he's delusional."

"But he didn't expect John Q. Public to figure out the word *seventh*. He wanted us to find it."

"So?"

Brill got up and went over to the window. "I don't know. We're missing something."

"Seems like you've hit the nail right on the head to me."

"It just doesn't make sense for a guy who thinks he has superior intelligence to revel in fooling people whose mental capacity he has little regard for."

David sat back in his chair, his arms folded, his weight balancing on the balls of his feet. "Go on."

"Don't you think he would need to outsmart someone sharp so he could feel even sharper?"

"I see your point. So what are you thinking?"

"I'm thinking that he planned this for some other reason and for some other audience." Brill looked out between the trees of crimson and gold and could just make out the shape of the Great Smoky Mountains in the distant haze. "I could be wrong. It's just a feeling."

"I never underestimate your feelings, Brill."

She glanced over at him. *Was* he coming on to her, or was she just mad enough at Kurt to wish he would?

He took his cell phone off his belt clip and glanced at the display. "I need to take this." He put the phone to his ear. "Special Agent Riley … No way. When …? Picked up by whom …? Who called it in …? Where are they now…?" He glanced over at her, his dark eyes wide and animated. "So what does Quantico say …? All right." He glanced at his watch. "I'll meet you there in one hour."

David sat staring at nothing, almost as if he were in a daze.

"What's going on?" she said.

"All seven victims were found alive and unharmed at a place

called Seventh Mound—on the Cherokee reservation just across the border in North Carolina. I need to get over there. The bureau chief wants this to stay under my umbrella."

Brill pulled the blinds on the glass wall and closed the door to her office, then went to her desk and dialed Kurt's cell phone.

"Hi, how's your day going?" he said.

"Surreal. You're going to hear breaking news shortly. I don't have time to get into it right now. Listen to the radio. I called to talk about Emily. How dare you discuss your sleazy affair with her and not even bother to alert me that you had."

"I waited to talk to you before you left this morning, but you were on the phone the whole time. I didn't want Emily to be late for school."

"You could've called my cell after you dropped her off."

"I didn't want to discuss it over the phone."

"Well, I do."

"All right," Kurt said. "She overheard most of what we said last night and was especially curious why I was 'in bed with a homecoming queen has-been.' I wasn't going to lie, but I answered her questions as delicately as I could. I didn't have much choice."

"Yes, I heard all about it at breakfast. Are you out of your mind talking to Emily about something so intimate?"

"Calm down. We had a very frank but appropriate conversation. I told her I broke my wedding vows, but that's as detailed as I got."

"Well, guess what, Kurt? She looked up the word *adultery* in the dictionary. Between your explanation and Webster's definition, our innocent nine-year-old knows *exactly* what you did."

"I explained how wrong it was," Kurt said, "and that I've asked the Lord's forgiveness, and yours, but that your feelings are hurt worse than anyone can imagine."

"Do you think?"

Kurt sighed. "I know this is shocking and embarrassing, but it was bound to come out. Emily is too precocious not to pick up on the tension and the cause. Don't you think she wonders why we sleep in different bedrooms?"

"I don't know. I keep thinking she's a child and we can protect her from all of it."

"Are you *sure* she understood the definition of adultery?" Kurt said.

"Look it up and you tell me. Think about *that* when you prepare your Sunday school lesson. I've got to get back to work."

Tessa sat with Antonio at the kitchen table working a puzzle when she noticed the words "Breaking News" on the TV screen.

"Antonio, look. Something's happening." She reached for the remote and turned on the sound.

"We interrupt this program to bring you breaking news. The FBI has reported that the seven people who disappeared from Sophie Trace over the past seven days have all been found alive on Cherokee land in North Carolina, less than seventy-five miles away.

"FBI spokesperson Special Agent Robert Morrow, would not disclose how the missing people were found, citing the ongoing investigation, but sources within the Cherokee Nation told WSTN News that a thirty-year-old Native American male was driving his pickup near Seventh Mound, an old Cherokee burial ground, when he saw six adults and a little boy walking on the side of the road.

"According to the source, the seven seemed disoriented and not sure how they got there. He drove them to the welcome center in the town of Cherokee and called the police, who then contacted the FBI.

"WSTN News was told by an anonymous source that the seven survivors have been detained for questioning and are currently undergoing medical treatment. But the FBI will neither confirm nor deny the report.

"This new development may cause the naysayers of the red shadows legend to take a second look at what many people here have said all along is a spiritual phenomenon. Is it possible that the spirits of the Cherokee who once inhabited this land seek to drive off the descendants of the white people who settled it?

"We posed that question to the principal chief of the Eastern Band of the Cherokee who would not comment other than to reiterate what he has stated emphatically numerous times before—that the legend is nonsense and that the ancestors of the Cherokee Nation rest in peace.

"Police Chief Brill Jessup was unavailable for comment, but our field reporter, Hunter Desmond, is standing outside the city hall in Sophie Trace with Mayor Lewis Roswell. Hunter, what's the tone there?"

"Shock and awe. That about describes the reaction of everyone I've talked to. Mr. Mayor, tell us how you feel at this moment."

"Stunned. Relieved, of course. Trying to make sense of it, as I'm sure everyone else must be. I don't have any more information than y'all do. I've not been able to reach Chief Jessup yet, and the FBI isn't saying anything. I understand the loved ones of the missing people have been taken to an undisclosed location. So I guess it's just a wait-and-see. My heart goes out to the families, who must be going through the gamut of feelings. I'm just so grateful. I think we're all eager to find out what happened to these folks."

"Mr. Mayor, what's your spin on the red shadows legend?"

"Well, you don't get to be mayor in a historic place like this without a strong connection to the people you serve. While I do not personally espouse the legend, it's been interwoven into our history since the Cherokee suddenly vanished in 1839. And since that time, there have certainly been unexplained crimes that could point to the possibility that red shadows exist."

"What's your explanation for seven people suddenly disappearing?"

"I have no explanation. I think we should wait and see what the FBI has to tell us before—"

"Well, for pity's sake." Tessa put the sound on mute. "Rather than give God the credit for bringing the seven back alive, they continue to let the Devil take credit by perpetuating this baseless legend."

"You can't just reason away this superstition. It's too ingrained." Antonio glanced at his watch. "It's almost time to go to lunch. Gus is bound to give us an earful."

CHAPTER 25

BRILL paced in front her office window. And judging by the wear pattern on the carpet, she wasn't the first. She heard a rap on her open door and turned just as Trent filled the doorway.

"You wanted to see me before lunch," Trent said. "Is this a good time?"

"Yes, come in and take a seat. Close the door behind you."

Trent came in and sat at the conference table.

Brill sat down across from him. "I wanted to fill you in on a couple things that weren't discussed in the briefing. I've been informed that the higher-ups at the FBI want the case to stay under David's umbrella. I'm not sure what my role will be. The questioning of the victims will be hush-hush. You know the drill. The Feds won't let them show their faces until they've been questioned and instructed on what they can and can't say. The last thing we need now is for one of the victims to misspeak and adversely affect the investigation—not that they're in any shape to come out in public."

"Were they harmed, ma'am?"

"The physical injuries are minor, but the jury's still out on the psychological damage. David said each of the victims woke up at Seventh Mound: Dirty. Dehydrated. Disoriented. Unable to remember anything—not even each other. The doctor who examined them found a considerable amount of Rohypnol in their blood."

Trent arched his eyebrows. "So our perp drugged them with roofies so they couldn't finger him or describe where they were being held. Pretty slick."

"It's possible they were drugged the entire time they were held. None of them remember anything, not even Michael Stanton who was held the longest." Brill sighed. "The poor guy has lost a lot of weight. David said he looks like a POW."

"It's a shame we're not going to hear how this went down," Trent said. "I'm just glad the perp's way of disposing of the victims didn't include murder. I never expected them to make it out alive."

Brill thought she should at least thank God for answering the prayers she had asked Kurt to pray. But she was just too depressed to get past her own pain.

"Let's switch gears for a moment," she said. "How are you and O'Toole and Rousseaux coming with the gang situation?"

"We're on top of it, ma'am. We just busted three drug dealers working the high school. Ace High members. Had enough prescription drugs on them to stock a pharmacy. We turned them over to juvy. Ace High is recruiting like nuts at the high school. Our patrol officers have been briefed and will be watching carefully for any sign of gang activity or drug dealing. Our informant says Fat Cats didn't like the law-enforcement presence here and moved over to Maryville. Still not much known about the Smarties."

"Last time we talked about this you mentioned that something big was about to go down. Any more on that?"

Trent shook his head. "No, ma'am. Guess it was just talk."

"Good. Maybe things will quiet down. We could use a break."

Nick held open the door at the grill and let Tessa and Antonio squeeze past him.

"Welcome, friends. I'm sure you've heard that all seven missing people were found alive?"

"We did," Tessa took Antonio's hand. "Praise God. I had my doubts it would end this well."

"Come sit at the counter," Nick said. "Today's special is grilled chicken spinach salad with my special low-fat dressing."

"That's what I'll have," Tessa said.

Antonio straddled the stool next to Gus and slapped him on the back. "How's it going, friend?"

Gus's grin appeared under his white mustache. "Really can't complain, but I always do."

"You want the special?" Maggie asked Antonio.

"I don't suppose my sweetheart's going to let me order a triple cheeseburger and sweet potato fries?"

"Order whatever you want, dear." Tessa patted his hand. "We'll just skip dinner tonight and breakfast in the morning."

"Guess I'll have the special." Antonio nudged Gus with his shoulder. "I'm sure you're dying to tell us how these seven people being found alive on Cherokee territory is tied to the legend. Get it off your chest."

"Before I do," Gus said, "can't we agree this is cause for celebration? This is huge, y'all."

Everyone nodded.

Before Gus could say anything else, Clint took his place at the counter. "What'd I miss?"

Maggie set a glass of Coke on the counter in front of Gus. "Our friend here was about to give us his spin on the big news of the day."

"Do you know something the FBI doesn't?" Clint said.

Gus took a sip of Coke and wiped his mustache. "They're sure not gonna come out with the real story. How do you think these people got to Cherokee land?"

"Uh … the bad guys drove them there?" Clint said.

"It's obvious: They were caught up by the red shadows and transported to the Indian burial ground—to send a message."

"What message?"

"That the Cherokee lived and died on this land and want us off it."

Antonio smiled. "You going to put your house up for sale?"

"I wouldn't rule it out. Seems to me they've been sendin' a lot more messages in recent years. We'd better start listenin'."

Antonio dropped his head, then shook it from side to side. "How can you honestly believe they were caught up? Michael Stanton was missing for a week. You think the red shadows were holding him in the great tepee in the sky?"

"Why don't we reserve judgment 'til we hear what Michael has to say about it?"

"Well, Janice Evans sure wasn't caught up," Clint said. "She was dragged from her car to someone else's? Doesn't sound very supernatural to me."

"Which raises another question." Nick stepped closer to the counter. "Let's suppose for a moment that the red shadows actually exist. If they dismembered seven people up in the hills and caused that seven-car pileup on I-40, why do you suppose they didn't harm these seven?"

"I can't read their minds," Gus said. "Their ways are not our ways."

Tessa exhaled loudly and rolled her eyes. "Did you even *ask* your pastor what he thought of this?"

"Doesn't matter. I know what I believe."

Clint turned and looked down the counter. "Gus, the Feds are going to find out someone's messing with the legend to stir up folks like you. It's a hoax."

"A very cruel hoax," Tessa added.

Kurt sat in his van across the street from Sophie Trace Elementary School, Brill's heartless words playing over and over in his mind. *Think about that when you prepare your Sunday school lesson.*

It seemed like the ultimate humiliation that his innocent young daughter should understand the raw mechanics of his adulterous act without having a mature concept of the issues that had lowered his defenses or the guilt that had tortured him since. Then again, sin was sin. Lust was lust. What difference did it make why he did it? Or how bad he felt afterward?

What *did* matter was preserving his relationship with Emily. What she thought of him was important, and he hoped her respect and trust in him had not been irreparably damaged.

Lord, I left my shame at the foot of the cross so why do I still feel overwhelmed by it? I'm doing my best to overcome evil with good. Don't let my past damage my present or future relationship with Emily—or change my resolve to win Brill back.

He heard children's voices and footsteps and turned to see Emily standing at the driver's-side window with a cute brown-eyed girl about the same height but stockier in build. He rolled down his window.

"Hi, Dad." Emily planted a kiss on his cheek. "This is Jasmine."

"Nice to finally meet you, Jasmine. Emily talks about you all the time."

"Nice to meet you, too." Jasmine's brown skin looked smooth as caramel in the afternoon sun.

"Do you need a ride home?" Kurt said.

"No, thank you. I'm supposed to walk home with some girls my big sisters watch after school."

"Jasmine's parents are coming to the open house on Tuesday," Emily said. "Maybe we'll run into them."

"We'll make it a point."

Jasmine reached over and hugged Emily. "Bye. I'll see you tomorrow. Nice to meet you, Mr. Jessup."

"Thank you. It was nice meeting you."

Emily came around to the other side, slid open the door, and let her backpack fall on the floor. She crawled up on the seat and buckled her seat belt.

"Are we going to have another ice-cream date?" she said. "I don't have to be at gymnastics 'til four."

Kurt caught her gaze in the rearview mirror. "Sure. Why not?"

"I really want you to meet Jasmine's parents so she can come over. Isn't she nice?"

"Seems very sweet. How'd it go today? You're awfully bubbly for a kid who's been having a hard time at school." *And just found out your dad cheated on your mom.*

"That's because Mrs. Bartlett told us that Mrs. Evans and Mrs. Nichols and all the other missing people were found alive on the Cherokee reservation. The other kids were too busy talking about it to bug me. But I decided I'm taking the high road if they start teasing me again."

"High road, eh?"

"That's what Jasmine does. She said people make rude comments because she's Hispanic, and her parents told her to take the high road and not be rude back because then she wouldn't be any better than them."

"Sounds like great advice."

Emily went on and on about her newfound friend and how they sat together at lunch, and then got permission to go to the school library and do some research for their science project. Everything felt normal. He knew it wasn't. But he wanted to hang on to this moment for a while.

Brill sat at the conference table, aware of David's empty chair and just how much she had gotten used to his being there. She wondered how the questioning was going and if the Feds had determined anything concrete about the person or persons responsible for the kidnappings.

She had gone back and reread the profile several times, trying to figure out what it was that didn't feel right. She was convinced the perpetrator had not staged the disappearances for those naive enough to believe in the legend. So whose attention did he want? Why would he go to all this trouble and then release the victims unharmed? What were they missing? The one consistent element was the number seven.

"Seven victims. Seven consecutive days. Victims had a personal connection to the number seven. First initials of last names spelled *seventh*. Woke up at Seventh Mound. For the plan to work, the perp had to succeed all seven times. Wait a minute ..." Brill's mind began to race in reverse. "Seven *times*. Seven X."

She sprang from her chair and rushed over to her desk. She rummaged through a stack of files and grabbed the one she was looking for, then opened it and pulled out the photographs of the Smarties's gang graffiti and held them out.

SMARTz2RULE7X

SMARTzRULE7X

"Smarties *to rule* seven times. Smarties *rule* seven times. The graffiti was meant for the cops, and we completely missed it."

There was a knock on the door and Trent stepped inside.

"Ma'am, we've got a problem."

"It can't be any bigger than mine. Come in."

Trent walked over to her and handed her a photograph. "We found this graffiti a few minutes ago sprayed-painted on the sidewalk in front of the police parking lot."

SMARTzDisCops7xLOL

CHAPTER 26

TWO hours later, Brill was back at the conference table in her office, sitting across from David Riley and Sam Parker and keeping her distance from an extra-large pepperoni pizza.

"I have to admit this is a first for me," David said. "I've been threatened, stalked, even shot at, but I've never had a perp use graffiti to dis me publicly. I guarantee he won't be laughing when I get him on *my* turf."

Sam picked up a slice of pizza. "With all due respect, Special Agent Riley, I believe it was intended to be an all-inclusive dis for law enforcement that worked this case—not just the Feds."

"I'm more than happy to share it with you." David popped a piece of pepperoni into his mouth. "We can't exclude the possibility that our perp may have an ax to grind with one of the three of us or our departments. We're checking the Internet to see if we can find anything online."

Brill moved her gaze from David to Sam and back to David. "I'm more inclined to think the perp designed the whole thing to be the mother of all gang initiations. According to information my detectives have compiled, this gang is secretive and exclusive. They don't go out recruiting like the others. They're selective about it. There's a reason they chose the name Smarties. They pulled off impressive serial kidnappings to prove their point. Seems like an oxymoron to say it, but this is a smart gang."

Sam rubbed his chin. "Geeks?"

"Not in the traditional sense." David took a sip of his soft drink. "Whoever's masterminding the whole thing is dangerous. He's cunning and clever, and his followers are probably thugs with high IQs. Trent said this is a homegrown gang, right? One that understands the legend and wanted to have some fun with it."

Brill nodded. "But the graffiti they posted was never intended to challenge or threaten a rival gang. That's what's so intriguing. The other gangs didn't know what it meant. None of us did until they accomplished what they set out to do and then threw it in our faces. That had to be the ultimate power trip."

"He's feeling juiced, all right," David said. "Unfortunately for us, there were too many media people in the area where today's graffiti was found to keep the dissing out of the news. But Special Agent Morrow merely told the media that we turned the graffiti over to our gang unit in Knoxville. We're not even going to acknowledge the gang name publicly. That would be the equivalent of showing them respect."

Brill brushed the hair out of her eyes. "Let's just hope the rival gangs don't try to outdo them."

"If the Smarties are really smart, they'll get outta Dodge," Sam said.

"They probably already did." David picked up a piece of pizza with one hand and with the other wrestled with the strands of mozzarella cheese until they broke. "In hindsight I probably should've set up the checkpoints sooner. But stopping traffic on a main thoroughfare not only creates congestion, it also increases public tension and sets the chamber of commerce's teeth on edge. It was really a last ditch effort. This perp is much too smart to have gotten caught that way."

"There was nothing we could've done to figure this out until it unfolded," Brill said.

David laughed. "What's with the 'we' stuff? Trent said you had already figured out the Smarties did the kidnappings by the time he came to you with the latest graffiti. You listened to your instincts and it paid off. Good work."

"Thanks." She smiled without meaning to, impressed that David didn't seem threatened by her.

Kurt sat at the kitchen table with Emily, pretending to enjoy the Tuna Helper he'd made, feeling even more dysfunctional than usual in his awareness that only two of five members of his family were seated around the dinner table.

"You're a good sport, sweetie. This isn't the greatest meal I've ever attempted. I'm not much of a cook compared to your mother."

Emily smiled and kept chewing, then finally swallowed. "I like it."

Kurt stabbed a piece of broccoli with his fork and put it into his mouth, at the same time studying Emily's demeanor. She had seemed overly cheerful since she got out of school this afternoon, almost as though she were hoping to avoid the subject that had caused such a rift in her parents' relationship.

Should he bring it up and put an end to the need to discuss it thereafter? Or should he let it die a natural death? He decided that if he were going to be proactive about getting his family back together, he needed to be up front about everything.

"Your mom told me about the discussion you two had at breakfast."

Emily's eyebrows came together. "Do we have to talk about it?"

"I just wondered if you had any questions."

"Not really. Mom was mad."

"At me?"

Emily seemed to stare at her plate. "No, at me. I started crying, and I told her she's not only one who's sad. I told her I hate it here because I never see her. And I never see Ryan and Vanessa. And I don't even have a family anymore. She hugged me, but I could tell she was mad."

"Emily, I know your mother pretty well. I don't see her getting mad at you for telling her how you felt."

"Well, maybe not exactly *mad*. But she wasn't happy."

"She was upset that you overheard us arguing last night—and that I talked to you about it after she went to bed."

Emily chewed her lip and pushed a piece of macaroni around her plate. "But now we don't have to have secrets, right?"

"Right. I just want you to know there's nothing in this world more important to me than being your dad. Your mother and I thought we could protect you from being hurt by *our* problems. But I see now that we couldn't. Even though it's painful for Mom and me, I'm glad we don't have to keep it a secret."

Emily glanced up at him and then at her plate.

"You might be disappointed in me," he said. "If you are, I hope you'll forgive me and try to think of the things I do right. I'm not a perfect man. But I have always loved your mother, and I always will."

"I've heard you say that to her before. She pretends she doesn't hear you."

"Maybe that'll change over time. I'm determined to win her back. It won't be easy."

"Dad …" Emily looked up at him. "I wish you wouldn't have broken your wedding vows and made Mom sad. But do I have to be mad at you?"

Brill sat in her office with David, reading through the preliminary statements given to FBI agents by the kidnapped victims.

"It's hard to believe not even one of the seven victims can remember anything." She covered a yawn with her hand. "It sounds as if they were in a stupor the whole time."

"Whoever masterminded the operation was clever," David said. "He knew how to mess with their memories. But after the Rohypnol is completely out of their system, they might remember what happened prior to the kidnapping. And we're processing the trace evidence we collected from their hair and clothing. Maybe we'll get DNA we can use. The waiting drives me crazy. Seems like everything's in slow motion."

Brill rubbed her eyes and leaned back in her chair. "Can you imagine waking up in the middle of nowhere with six strangers and not knowing how you got there or how to get out?"

"Pretty traumatic. The victims were dumped at the north end of the burial ground fifty yards from the road. The little boy woke up first and lay there crying. He thought the others were dead. Picturing that scene keeps me mad enough to keep pushing, even though I feel like someone threw me on the highway and rolled over me with an eighteen-wheeler."

Brill reached across the table and held his wrist. "Power naps can only hold you so long. You need to go to bed."

"Whose bed did you have in mind?"

She let go of his wrist, heat scalding her cheeks.

"I can't believe I said that." David's eyes were wide, his tone repentant. "Sorry, Brill. I didn't mean that the way it sounded."

"I certainly didn't mean to send the wrong signal." *Or did I?*

"No, no, it wasn't you. Patricia used to say those exact words, and I always used the same comeback. It was this thing with us. I popped off without even thinking. I'm sorry. Do I ever feel stupid."

"I've never seen you blush before."

David ran his hand over his shaved head. "I'm sure I look like a stoplight."

"Actually it's nice to see a more human side of you."

"Yeah, well, don't tell anybody." He sat for half a minute, just cracking his knuckles. Finally he said, "Truth is, whenever I held Patricia in my arms, I could close my eyes and forget the insanity of what I deal with every day. Be thankful you have Kurt. I didn't know what I had until it was gone."

"No chance for reconciliation?" Brill said.

"Not as long as I'm with the bureau. I'm torn between two loves and can't let go of this one. I guess it's like an addiction. I'd be more lost without my job than I am without my wife. I'm ashamed to even say it out loud, but I need the adrenaline rush."

"At least you're honest."

"I admire cops like you," David said. "You've been able to balance your career and personal life and raise a family. I don't know how you do it."

I don't. "It's not easy. I struggle with guilt because I'm not home more." She glanced at her watch. "Case in point: It's nearly ten p.m., and I'm still working on the case. I think I'll take my own advice and go get some sleep."

She stood and stretched her lower back, a part of her wanting to stay longer and see where the conversation might lead.

"Good night," she said.

"I'm really sorry about the remark, Brill."

"Forget it. See you tomorrow."

She left her office and crossed the DB, then left city hall by the back door. She was walking to her car when her cell phone vibrated. She figured it was Kurt, but the LED screen showed Detective Rousseaux.

This can't be good. She put the phone to her ear. "Chief Jessup."

"I hope I didn't wake you up, ma'am. But we've got a dead body I thought you should know about before news of it hits the airways."

Tessa held Antonio's hand and stroked Abby's back while she waited for a commercial to end and the meteorologist to come back on and do the weather segment.

She didn't feel like rehashing tonight's news, even with Antonio. All things considered, the news was good. The seven missing people were alive and would be back with their loved ones soon. The worst of the saga was over, though how could anyone rest easy until the guilty person or persons was found and brought to justice?

"I do hope we're going to have sunny weather," she finally said to Antonio. "The fall colors are stunning. Maybe we can take a ride. We haven't been to Cades Cove in a while."

"That'd be nice."

The meteorologist reappeared, but before he could say anything about the weather, the "Breaking News" header flashed across the screen.

"Folks, we have breaking news just in. Moments before this broadcast began, the Sophie Trace PD received a 9-1-1 call that a child's body was lying in the middle of Jackson Avenue. Minutes later, police and paramedics arrived at the scene and found a young Hispanic male dead from what appears to be a gunshot wound to the head.

"Police are not talking, but WSTN field reporter Wilson Farber is standing just outside the area that has been sectioned off with crime-scene tape. Wilson, what can you tell us?"

"The reports are sketchy, and none of these onlookers behind me will admit to seeing or hearing anything. But the man standing with me agreed to come on camera but won't give me his name. Sir, tell us what you saw."

"I was outside walking my dog. I saw car speeding around corner. Door comes open, boy falls out, but car does not stop."

"How far were you from where the boy was dropped?"

"Not far. I don't know English for this."

"Did you try to help the victim?

He shook his head. "Two peoples ran over to boy. He is dead. Who can help him now? This is work of street gang. Same problem in Mexico."

"Sir, do you know the name of the gang that did this? Do they live in the neighborhood?"

He put his hand over the camera lens. "I do not ask. Please, no more talking."

"Are you afraid?"

"Yes, and why not? These boys, they have no soul …"

A chill crawled up Tessa's spine as she remembered the desperation in the eyes of the young man who broke her windshield.

She got up and went in the kitchen and poured herself a glass of water. Half a minute later she felt Antonio's hands on her shoulders.

"You okay, love?"

She reached up and put her hand on his. "I'll be all right. I'm just appalled that things like this are happening here." She shook her head. "That boy is someone's child. Just tossed out on the street like that. It's so sad. Honestly I don't know how Brill does what she does."

Brill bent down and pulled back the sheet that covered the victim. For a split second she saw Ryan's face and wondered how any mother could deal with this.

"This boy can't be any older than twelve or thirteen. Too young to end up in a body bag."

She rose to her feet and turned to Detective Rousseaux. "Any witnesses?"

"Maybe we should ask the media," he said sarcastically. "They were questioning people before we got here."

"I'm asking *you*, Detective."

"We've got two witnesses, ma'am: a married couple that was getting into the red Pontiac parked there on the street when a late model silver Lexus came around the corner at a pretty good clip, dumped the body, and kept going."

"Did they see the driver? Or get the license plate number?"

"Negative, ma'am. This smells like someone trying to teach someone a lesson. Maybe the kid was dealing and infringed on another dealer's turf. Or he's the little brother of someone who dissed the leader of a rival gang. Or maybe he saw something he shouldn't have and someone wanted to shut him up."

"Do you know if there's been any more gang graffiti discovered since this morning?"

"Not that I know of, ma'am."

"Where's the couple that saw the Lexus?" she said.

"Over here. Miguel and Angel Garcia. They speak English."

Brill followed Rousseaux over to where a couple that appeared to be in their early twenties was standing with Captain Dickson.

"Mr. and Mrs. Garcia, I'm Police Chief Jessup," she said, extending her hand to the pair. "I know you're probably tired of answering questions, but would you mind coming down to the police station and going over it with us again? We'd like to get your statement while things are fresh in your mind. It could be very helpful to us."

"Sure," Miguel said. "But we already told the police everything we saw."

Brill studied Miguel's eyes and then Angel's. Not everything.

"Thanks. Detective Rousseaux will escort you. I'll see you there in a few minutes."

Brill walked back to where the body lay and watched investigators put the child in a body bag and zip it shut. She wanted to throw up.

CHAPTER 27

BRILL unlocked the front door and, with what little energy she had left, pushed it open. The fishy smell that lingered in the air suggested Kurt and Emily had made something with tuna for dinner.

She hung up her coat in the closet, cringing when she heard footsteps behind her. She had nothing left to give anybody, least of all Kurt.

"I figured you'd be late," he said. "I've been watching the news off and on all day. You must be exhausted."

Brill turned around. "Which is why I'm going straight to bed."

"Congratulations on getting all seven people back alive."

"Thanks, but I had nothing to do with that. And I suppose you heard that a young boy was murdered. Sort of trumps everything else at the moment."

"Yeah, that was a shocker. You think the cases are connected?"

"Kurt, I'm not *thinking* at all. I just saw somebody's son put in a body bag. I don't want to talk."

"Just listen for a minute," he said. "I talked with Emily at dinner. It wasn't the kind of discussion either of us had with her before, just a reinforcement that the truth's out and we don't have to pretend anymore."

"How did she act toward you?"

"Fine."

"Whatever." Brill started to walk down the hall to her bedroom and then turned around. "How could she be fine when she understands what you did? It's a disgusting thing for a nine-year-old to know about her father."

"Yes, but I think the truth is easier for her to cope with than the pretending. I don't think her innocent imagination feels the need to revisit whatever understanding she does have of my indiscretion."

"Thank God."

"Believe me, I have."

Brill shook her head with disdain. "You're getting off far too easy."

"Because Emily isn't 'making me pay' for my mistake? I would think you'd be relieved that she isn't bearing the burden of it."

"Of course I am. But it's a bitter pill to swallow that she's able to accept so easily something that's destroyed this family."

"Emily must've picked up on your anger because she asked if *she* had to be mad at me."

"What did you tell her?"

Kurt put his hands in his pockets. "I told her to be honest about how she really feels and not feel pressured into saying what she thinks either of us wants her to."

"I never told her she had to be angry with you."

Kurt hesitated, then said, "Well, that's the message she got. She loves us both, and I think she feels caught in the middle. I thought you should know. That's the very thing we were trying to avoid."

"This is giving me a headache. I need to take something."

"I'd be glad to massage your neck. That usually works faster than pills."

Brill tried to glare at him but was too tired to hold his gaze. "Why are you so nice to me when it's obvious it's not going to change the way I feel? And don't tell me you love me and always have. We both know where that got us. I just want to go to bed."

And whose bed did you have in mind?

David's words came out of nowhere and seemed almost audible. She felt the heat rush to her face with the realization that, for the first time in her life, she felt genuine desire for a man other than Kurt.

"I didn't mean to make you mad," he said.

"I'm not mad. It's hot in here. I'm going to check the thermostat."

Kurt went into his office in the back of the house, which still resembled a storage room with unpacked boxes stacked in the corners.

He sat at the desk where he'd been typing in his laptop. He'd almost finished the procedure manual for his stores and decided that tomorrow he'd drive over to the Pigeon Forge store and have the pages printed and bound for each of the managers.

Why did he feel empty, like his heart was a deep well that was dry to the very bottom? Was it because of his shame and embarrassment that Emily knew about his affair, or because he found it downright oppressive being a single parent and celibate spouse? Or was it just raw loneliness?

He drank the last of a Coke and crushed the can. He had no one to blame but himself. And Brill had never once led him to believe their life together under the same roof would ever be anything more than this. He just didn't know he would hate it so much.

He wondered how deeply Ryan and Vanessa had been affected by his affair and if they still needed to forgive him. He had offered them a nebulous explanation after he confessed it to Brill, but he'd never had the courage to discuss the issue openly with them the way he'd been forced to do with Emily.

Lord, how do I fix it? How do I put my marriage back together? How do I give my kids the family they deserve?

Kurt heard the shower go off in Brill's bathroom and glanced at the clock. He got up and turned out the light.

Do not be overcome by evil, but overcome evil with good.

He sighed and pulled the door shut. All he could do was give it his best shot.

Tessa looked over at the Jessups' house and saw that the lights were out and Brill's car was in the driveway. She couldn't imagine the burden on the chief of police, especially after the young boy was found murdered.

"Come get some rest." Antonio patted her side of the bed.

Tessa went over and crawled under the covers.

"I'm looking forward to Emily coming over on Saturday," she said. "I had no idea that her friend Jasmine was Julio and Juanita's daughter."

"Small world."

"They're such nice people. I wonder if Kurt would mind if I invite Jasmine to come over Saturday. It would be a perfect way for Emily and her to get to know each other better."

"Maybe Emily wants us all to herself."

Tessa smiled. "Oh, I doubt that. Little girls love having someone to giggle with, and Emily needs a friend. The two have already hit it off at school."

"You're meddling."

"Not really. It feels right. Maybe with two of them, the girls would be comfortable spending the night and going to church with us Sunday morning."

"The Jessups have their own church."

"There's no doctrinal difference between our church and Cross Way. I doubt if Kurt would object to Emily going to Sunday school with Jasmine."

Antonio turned on his side and stroked her cheek. "You're making an awful lot of assumptions, Mrs. Masino."

"I know. But it hurts me to see such pain in Emily's eyes. I can tell that moving here has been hard on her."

"Moving's hard on all kids."

"Well, I don't get the chance to help every child. I think God has brought Emily to us for a reason."

"And you think Jasmine's in on it, eh?"

"I don't know. Maybe." Tessa stifled a laugh and nestled next to him. "I think it would be fun to have the girls here at the same time. If it's okay with you, I thought I'd at least ask."

"Sure. I'm a pushover for little girls, and we—"

Tires screeched outside, the blaring of a car horn assaulting the quiet, and Tessa braced herself for a loud crash that never happened.

Antonio threw back the covers, jumped out of bed, and peered into the dark night.

"What happened?" she said, her hand over her heart, relieved when she remembered Abby was inside.

"I'm not sure." Antonio stood at the window a few moments and then shook his head. "Looks like some guy in a white Cadillac just about hit Mr. Quinlan."

"Is he all right?"

"Mr. Quinlan's fine. The driver looks pretty shaken. He's giving him what for."

Antonio put on his slippers and grabbed his robe off the chair. "I'll go get Mr. Quinlan. Call Junior."

CHAPTER 28

BRILL got out of her squad car, the October wind nipping at her cheeks, and stood admiring the thick streaks of hot pink and purple that blazed across Friday morning's sky. For a split second the shadows of light and dark on the hazy foothills appeared to be a caravan of Indians on horseback. She decided all this talk of red shadows must be playing with her imagination.

As she opened the door to Nick's Grill, the delicious aroma of fresh brewed coffee and bacon frying took her back to her grandmother's kitchen. She saw David and Sam sitting on either side of the corner booth by the window. She slipped in next to Sam and returned David's smile, wondering if he noticed her eyes were made up this morning.

"Thanks for coming," David said. "I thought we could all use a change of scenery to start the day. Things have been pretty intense."

Maggie came over with a stainless steel carafe of coffee and set it on the table with three cups and saucers.

"I'll be happy to take your order when you're ready. The special this morning is whole-wheat pancakes with blackberry compote. Comes with hash brown sweet potatoes or grits and turkey sausage or bacon. Or you can choose something from the menu. I'll give you a few minutes to decide."

As the waitress walked away, David filled a cup with coffee and handed it to Brill. "Update us on the murder case."

"I spoke with Detective Rousseaux on the way over here," Brill said. "He's got an ID on the boy. The parents called and reported him missing. Name's Hector Sanchez. He's twelve. Lived with his parents and four sisters on Beech Street, where a drive-by shooting was reported last week. His parents say he's a good kid. Never been in trouble. But they gave Rousseaux permission to search the boy's room, and he found several bags of cocaine hidden under his mattress—street value around five thousand dollars—and a pretty nice stash of prescription drugs."

Sam's eyebrows went up and down. "Whatever happened to doing odd jobs for spending money?"

"The temptation's enormous for these kids," Brill said. "Quick money—and lots of it. Not to mention status. The boy's tox report was positive for OxyContin and Valium. But not cocaine."

"A gangbanger just waiting to happen." David folded his hands on the table. "So, who wanted him dead?"

"We're still working on that one," Brill said. "At first we thought maybe someone was trying to get back at a rival gang leader by shooting his little brother, but Hector is the oldest child. We're looking into his parents' background. Dad works at the tire plant. Mom cleans houses. By all indications they're just hardworking folks. The parents are citizens. We can only dig so deep. My officers are already stretched thin."

"Why don't you pull your officers and get them busy on this?" David said. "Between Sam and me, we've got enough manpower to keep the kidnapping investigation going."

Brill took a sip of coffee. "The couple that witnessed the boy's body being dumped is suddenly not sure whether the vehicle was silver *or* a Lexus and won't admit to recognizing the driver. I think they know but are too scared to talk, which leads me to think it's either a drug dealer or gang member. The Smarties pulled off a serial kidnapping and dissed us in front of the entire world. Maybe Ace High or Fat Cats want to grab some of the limelight."

"I thought you cleaned house of those gangs," Sam said.

"We did, but it's an ongoing battle." Brill tucked her hair behind her ear. "Trent Norris spoke to this issue in the annual report to the city council. The Sophie Trace PD has zero tolerance for gang activity and has caused several gangs to move on just in the past few months. But homegrown gangs are springing up. And some of the Knoxville gangs are moving to smaller communities where they can get a foothold."

Sam traced his coffee cup with his finger. "Since we never had this problem in the past, it does cause me to wonder whether the gangs don't take a female police chief seriously."

"Well, they picked the wrong female to sell short." David tossed a sugar packet at Sam. "Do I need to remind you that *she* figured out the kidnappings were connected by the number seven, and *she* figured out the Smarties were behind them? I'd be hard pressed to think the late Chief Hennessey would've done any better."

Brill smiled at David with her eyes.

"My apologies, Chief Jessup," Sam said. "I certainly did not mean to detract from the good work you've done."

Sure you did, Brill thought.

"The important thing," David said, "is that we keep working in an attitude of mutual respect. We're still dealing with concurrent jurisdiction on the kidnapping cases, and we've barely scratched the surface."

The waitress came back and took their orders, then set a basket of warm bran muffins on the table. The trio each took a muffin and buttered it.

"This is delicious," Brill said. "I didn't realize how hungry I am." She glanced over at David. "Since you haven't brought it up, I'm assuming the kidnapping victims haven't told us anything useful."

David swallowed and took a sip of coffee. "Truthfully all seven were still somewhat disoriented last night when I left St. Luke's. The doctor wanted to observe them overnight and make sure they shook off the effects of the Rohypnol before we hit them with questions. I keep hoping that at least one of them will remember something that will help us get this gang leader off the street."

That afternoon, Brill decided to go with Trent to visit the parents of Hector Sanchez. They turned left on Beech Street and stopped in front of the clay-colored stucco bungalow on the corner. The drapes were drawn on the picture window, and she could almost feel the weight of the grief inside.

Brill breathed in and let it out slowly. "I never got used to this. No matter how many times I had to do it."

"Why did you insist on coming?" Trent said. "I saw your in-box. There are plenty of other things you could be doing."

"Yes, but confronting their pain keeps me mad enough to fight for them when I feel discouraged. I can't explain it."

"No need, ma'am. I understand exactly what you're talking about."

They got out of the car and went up to the front door.

Brill rang the bell and a short, stocky man came to the door. His red-rimmed eyes were a noticeable contrast to his smooth brown skin and dark hair.

"Mr. Sanchez?"

"Yes."

"I'm Chief Jessup, and this is Captain Norris. You said it would be all right if we stopped by and asked some questions."

"Yes, come in. My wife is in the living room."

Brill followed Mr. Sanchez into a small square room that had a white tile fireplace on one wall, where a woman sat, seemingly staring at nothing.

The four introduced themselves, and then Brill sat next to Trent on a couch with broken-down springs.

"First of all," she said, "we are very sorry for your loss. Captain Norris and I both have children and can only imagine what you're going through."

Mr. Sanchez straddled the arm of the big easy chair where his wife sat. He squeezed her hand and nodded.

"You both told Detective Rousseaux that you had no idea your son had drugs in his bedroom."

"We were shocked," Mr. Sanchez said. "We thought we knew Hector. This just doesn't make sense."

"Looking back, did you notice any change in Hector's behavior?"

"He seemed far away sometimes," Mrs. Sanchez said. "But he was twelve. His body was changing. I just thought he was moody."

Mr. Sanchez sighed. "He didn't want his friends to see him with his family. But isn't that normal for a twelve-year-old?"

"It can be, but if it was a change from his usual behavior, it's noteworthy." Brill glanced over to be sure Trent was adding that fact to his notes.

"Last Wednesday night your next-door neighbors called the police and reported hearing a loud popping noise around nine-thirty and thought it might be a drive-by shooting. Did you know about that?"

"We were folding laundry," Mrs. Sanchez said. "The washer and dryer were loud. We heard a noise, but couldn't tell what it was. I stuck my head in the hallway and listened. The house was quiet. The kids were in bed."

"Hector, too?"

"We thought so," Mr. Sanchez said. "But now we don't know anything for sure. There's a window in his room. Your investigators said his footprints were found outside and his fingerprints on the outside of the window. Maybe he was sneaking out at night."

"We also found a bullet lodged in the stucco near the picture window in the front of your house. We think the drive-by was intended to intimidate your son."

Mrs. Sanchez wiped the tears off her cheeks. "Does it matter now? A bullet finally found him. He was a *baby*. His voice hadn't even changed yet, and he was murdered and his body dumped like garbage."

"Maybe you see Hector as just another drug-dealing troublemaker," Mr. Sanchez said, "but he was our only son—our firstborn. We raised him to have values. We took him to church. We even monitored what TV programs he watched. And to have his life end like this …" He threw his hands in the air, his eyes brimming with tears, his chin quivering.

Brill paused until the tightness in her throat relaxed enough to talk without emotion. "I am so sorry for what you're going through. But we need to ask questions so that we can stop other parents from losing *their* sons."

Mr. Sanchez nodded. "We want to help."

"Did either of you ever hear Hector mention these names—Ace High? Fat Cats? Smarties?"

The Sanchezes looked at each other and shook their heads.

"But then we had no idea he had cocaine and prescription drugs in his room, either," Mr. Sanchez said.

"You told Detective Rousseaux that Hector didn't have any close friends. He never had sleepovers or campouts with friends?"

"Not since he was in grade school. Middle school has been difficult for him. He's not outgoing. Not an athlete. Or a high achiever. I think he got bullied and wouldn't talk about it."

"What did he do after school?" Brill said.

"He came home."

"With his sisters?"

"No, we pay the high school daughters of one of my coworkers to keep them at their house. Hector didn't want to be stuck with all those girls, so we let him come home. We trusted him."

"So he was by himself?"

"We both work, Chief Jessup."

"I understand. We're trying to get a feel for the world Hector lived in so we can figure out what would motivate someone to kill him."

"Your detectives said they found a list of names—clients he sold drugs to. Can't you question them?"

"Hector used first names and codes. We don't know who his clients were." Brill saw an eye looking through a crack in the door in the hallway. "How old are your daughters?"

"Eleven, eight, seven, and six."

"Was Hector close to them?"

"Why does that matter?" Mrs. Sanchez said.

"Sometimes siblings know a lot more than parents do."

"Our eleven-year-old, Anna, was closest to Hector. She won't even come out of her room."

"May I go talk to her?" Brill said. "I promise not to upset her."

Brill knocked gently on the door that had been cracked just moments before.

"Anna, it's Police Chief Jessup. I'd really like it if you let me come in and talk to you. Would that be okay?"

Brill waited for what seemed an eternity. Finally the door opened just enough for her to see a lovely girl with huge brown eyes and dark hair draping her shoulders.

"Okay," Anna said.

Brill stepped inside the girl's bedroom, which wasn't much larger than a walk-in closet. The room was cluttered with clothes, and there was a twin bed with a pink coverlet next to the wall.

"You can sit on my bed." Anna sat cross-legged on the floor and hugged a brown teddy bear that looked as if it had grown up with her.

"I have a daughter who's nine," Brill said. "Her favorite color is pink."

"Mine, too." Anna's eyes lit up. "Someday I'm going to have a swimming pool with a pink umbrella table and a pink cell phone and pink iPod."

"I'm very sorry about your brother. I can only imagine how sad you must feel."

"I want to see him, but my parents won't let me. It's not fair."

"You two were close?"

Anna nodded. "Are you a real policewoman?"

"I am. Actually I'm the chief of police."

"Does that mean you're the boss?"

Brill smiled. "Yes, that's one way to put it. Anna, did you know the kids Hector hung out with?"

"Hector didn't hang out with anybody. He was shy."

"So he didn't have *any* friends?"

"Not really."

Brill took her finger and traced the stitching on the pink coverlet. "Do you believe Hector came home after school every day?"

"He was supposed to come home, and my sisters and I always went to the Mendez's house. Rosa and Carmen babysat us."

"Did Hector do what he was supposed to do?"

Anna shrugged. "I don't know. I wasn't with him."

"Maybe you do know and you're not supposed to. I promise you won't be in trouble if you tell me. It's very important. And you might have to be very brave."

The room was pin-drop still. Brill wrapped herself in the quiet and waited for Anna to respond.

Finally the child said, "Hector knew someone named Doe who met him after school and gave him drugs to sell."

"How do you know that?"

"He had little packets of blow in his room. I saw them."

Brill was rendered mute for a moment by the irony of such an innocent-looking child referring to cocaine by its street name.

"How did you know what it was?"

"Hector told me and made me promise not to tell. He said he wanted to get enough money to buy Mom and Dad a big house so we all could have our own rooms and Mom wouldn't have to clean houses for other people anymore. I told him drugs were very bad for you and against the law. I learned that in health class."

"And what did he say?"

"He said he wasn't *doing* blow, only selling it—and that the people who bought it were going to buy it from someone anyway, so why not him? He said it was okay because it meant that someday Mom wouldn't have to work so hard."

"Did you believe him?"

Anna's huge brown eyes turned to pools. "No. But he said if I told anybody, he could get hurt or even killed. So I promised not to tell."

"Did you know someone shot at your house last Wednesday night?"

"No. Yes. Well, I heard it and I put my pillow over my head. The next day Hector told me he knew a secret and was in *really* big trouble. He wouldn't tell me what it was. He said if he told, they would kill our mom and dad." Anna started to bawl. "It's my fault Hector's dead. I should've told anyway."

Brill got down on the floor and held Anna in her arms the same way she would if she had been Emily. "Shhh. It's not your fault, sweetie. Hector got involved in something dangerous. None of this is your fault."

"I–I sh-should've t-told the police," Anna sobbed. "But I was afraid."

"Of course you were …"

"Hector didn't even tell, and they killed him anyway."

"Anna, did this Doe fellow know that Hector talked to you about the drugs?"

Anna shook her head. "Hector said Doe would be mad if he found out I knew, and that neither of us could ever tell anyone."

"Do you know where we can find Doe?"

"No. But maybe outside the middle school."

Brill kept her arms around Anna and let her cry, incensed that an innocent child got pulled into something this evil, and determined to rid the town of it before someone else got killed.

CHAPTER 29

BRILL'S stomach made gurgling noises. She glanced at her watch and could hardly believe it was after six. She put the Sanchez file on the top of the stack and looked up just as David came into her office.

"How's the kidnapping case coming?" she said.

David let out a low moan. "This perp is really good. The lab found traces of chloroform on their faces and in their hair, so we can assume he held something over their mouths to subdue them, which explains why we didn't find signs of a struggle. We think he kept them drugged with Rohypnol the rest of the time."

"So much for getting their testimonies," Brill said.

"Michael Stanton remembers talking to his dad on his cell phone and parking his car at Nick's Grill. He vaguely remembers male voices and a cold, musty room with a mattress on the floor, possibly a basement. Janice Evans remembers stopping to gas her car. She vividly remembers the smell of urine and a little boy on the mattress next to her. That's about it."

"Were any of the victims sexually assaulted?" Brill asked.

"There's no evidence of it. They were all malnourished and severely dehydrated and left to lie in their own filth."

"Did the other victims remember anything?"

David nodded. "Bits and pieces. We're putting it together.

Dr. Vaughn remembers entering the parking garage at St. Luke's and being grabbed from behind. Our real estate lady, Candi Eagan, thinks she may have been lying on the floor of a moving vehicle, someone's arm across her face. She heard two men speaking another language. Spanish, she *thinks*."

"Well," Brill said, "that adds credibility to Carlos Ramos's statement that he saw a Hispanic male approaching Sonya Nichols in the bank parking lot."

David nodded. "And Nichols remembers getting out of her car and seeing a young Hispanic man walking toward her. But she can't remember what he wanted or anything more specific about his looks. The next thing she remembers is desperately needing to use the bathroom and not being able to move or talk."

"What about the little boy?"

"Dade Tompkins remembers leaving the schoolyard and hearing someone calling him, then nothing until he woke up at Seventh Mound with six strangers he thought were dead. Poor little guy lay there and cried until the victims started waking up. And our barber, Billy Dan Harrison, remembers hearing a knock on his car window. Next thing he knows he was lying in a dark pit that 'stunk like death itself' and seeing red shadows moving in the dark and chanting. He was afraid they were going to scalp him so he kept his hands over his head." David lifted his eyebrows. "So you tell me what was real and what wasn't."

Brill folded her arms on her desk. "Does the doctor think their memories will come back?"

"If they were given Rohypnol the whole time, probably not. You've seen rape victims who can't remember a thing after being slipped a roofie. Not only can it wipe out huge chunks of memory, it can distort anything they do remember."

"At least they're alive."

"Yep. How's your murder investigation coming?"

Brill told him about going with Trent to visit with Hector Sanchez's parents, and also about the revealing conversation she'd had with Anna. "That's a heavy load of guilt for a child to carry," she said. "Of course, I'm determined to find out what Hector knew that got him killed. The medical examiner said he'd been dead an hour before his body was dumped."

David shook his head. "If I didn't know I was in Sophie Trace, I would think I was in an urban area of any major city in America. What in the world has slithered into this town?"

Brill locked her desk and went around to where David was standing.

"I'll let you know when I know. See you tomorrow."

David cocked his head and looked into her eyes. "I can tell by looking that you've got a doozy of a headache. You need someone to rub out those knots in your neck. May I? I'm pretty good at it."

Brill didn't resist his strong fingers kneading her knotted shoulders and neck, releasing the tension that had been building for days.

"Thanks," she said. "I had a great massage therapist in Memphis but I haven't even had time to look for one here."

"Well, I'm available. And you don't need an appointment."

Brill was too tired to consider whether this was inappropriate and how she felt surprisingly comfortable with David touching her.

Kurt had Emily set the table for two since Brill hadn't called to say whether or not she'd be home for dinner. The phone rang.

"Hello."

"Kurt, it's Tessa. Am I interrupting your dinner?"

"No, we're a few minutes away."

"I'm calling to see if it's all right with you if I invite Emily's friend Jasmine to come over tomorrow too. I wouldn't do that without asking you first. And Emily, of course."

"Do you know Jasmine's family?"

"Oh my, yes. They go to our church. Julio and Juanita Mendez are a precious Christian couple, and Jasmine and her two older sisters are dolls."

"Okay. I'll let you ask Emily. She's standing right here." Kurt handed the phone to Emily.

"Hi, Tessa … really? That'd be so cool … then you can spoil both of us.… Okay, I'll talk to you again soon. Bye."

Emily hung up the phone and threw her arms around Kurt. "I'm so excited, Dad. I finally have a real friend and make-believe grandparents. They'll never be like Grammy and Poppy, but it's okay to let Tessa and Tony spoil me, right?"

"Right." Kurt put a smile in his voice but wondered if he was emotionally prepared to spend most of the weekend alone.

"I'm gonna go send a text message to Jasmine."

"We're going to eat in fifteen minutes."

"Okay!"

The phone rang.

"Hello."

"It's me," Brill said. "I'll be home in about an hour."

"You want me to hold dinner?"

"No, I'm not hungry."

"Did you make any progress on the murder investigation?"

"I did, actually. I'll tell you about it later. How did Emily react to it?"

Kurt turned off the stove and took a pan of beef stew off the burner. "Actually it hasn't come up yet. She was bubbly after school, thrilled that Mrs. Evans and Mrs. Nichols are all right. I didn't want to spoil it. Plus Tessa invited Jasmine to come over tomorrow when Emily's there so the girls can get to know each other."

"I thought we agreed to meet Jasmine's parents first."

"We did. But Tessa's offer was too good to pass up. She says the family goes to her church and is wonderful. I trust her judgment. Plus we're going to meet Jasmine's parents Tuesday night at the open house."

"Okay. See you later."

Brill left city hall by the back door and slipped past the media unnoticed. She got in her car, the pleasant—or perhaps *too* pleasant—sensation of David's fingers kneading her shoulders still fresh in her mind.

Allowing him to touch her had awakened feelings she had thought were dead. They might as well be; she had no intention of acting on them. She wondered if David would be shocked to know that her marriage was a sham.

She couldn't even remember the last time she had made love to

Kurt. She wondered why she kept her wedding ring on. Was it just for show—something to give the mayor and the city council a sense that she had a stable home life? Was it for her children? Or just to avoid having to answer questions that were nobody's business?

She pulled out of the parking lot and decided to drive around and unwind before she went home and tried to step into the role of mother. She turned onto First Street, then drove several blocks and turned on Beech, noting that the drapes were still pulled at the Sanchezes' house. She drove up and down the narrow streets of this poorer side of town, where most of the homes were stucco, many with chain-link fences around property largely devoid of grass. Vehicles were parked along both sides of the streets, tricycles and Big Wheels abandoned in front yards.

She turned on Jackson and slowed when she drove over the place where Hector's body had been dumped. How wrong it seemed that life should go on as if someone's son had not lain dead on this street.

She crossed Main and drove into a neighborhood not unlike her own. The streets were wide and lined on both sides with grassy easements, sidewalks, towering shade trees, and well-maintained houses—craftsman bungalows, American foursquare, Georgian colonials, and others she couldn't name but loved to look at. Cars were parked in driveways or detached garages, and yards were manicured and free of children's toys. Privacy fences were common—and gunshots rare.

She drove several blocks west and turned on General Sherman Way. The town's upscale neighborhood consisted of stately antebellum homes set among live oaks, magnolias, evergreens, and hardwoods, the only fences around the properties neatly trimmed bushes that would burst into brilliant blooms in the spring.

She had read in the welcome packet given to new residents that a number of these pre–Civil War homes were open to the public for tours during the Christmas season. She wondered what Christmases had been like inside the walls of those homes.

Her mind flashed back to Memphis, where each year the scent of evergreen emanated from a fresh-cut scotch pine that filled the corner of their family room from floor to ceiling, every inch of it covered in twinkling lights and ornaments that each meant something.

Brill's eyes clouded unexpectedly and she blinked several times until the moisture cleared. Letting her thoughts drift to the past was *not* the way to unwind.

She turned onto Third Street and cruised slowly up and down the brick streets of the downtown. Gaslights added to the ambiance, and many of the buildings were made of the original brick and donned colorful awnings that hung over the sidewalks. She passed by Beanies Coffee Shop, The Cookie Crumb, Girls and Curls Beauty Salon, Mary's Alterations, Nick's Grill, The Toffee Emporium, and Klein's Deli.

She turned at the Civil War Museum onto Stanton Boulevard and stopped in front of the gazebo at Shady Park, pleased that no new graffiti had been spray-painted there.

She continued on past Sophie Trace Elementary School and wondered if she knew Emily as well as she thought she did. She couldn't imagine how shocked and devastated the Sanchezes must have been to find out that Hector was dealing drugs and had been killed because he knew too much. And he was only a few years older than Emily.

Brill tightened her fingers around the steering wheel. Knew too much about whom? Or what? Was Hector the only one who knew? Or were other kids at risk? She had Trent get his detectives together and form a task force to find this "Doe" character. If Anna Sanchez was telling the truth, Doe was a supplier and possibly a murderer.

Brill sighed. What was the point of driving around if she couldn't unwind? She left the downtown and headed for the cottage-style two-story at 416 Azalea Lane. Though it still didn't feel like home, she had a key to the front door and a substantial mortgage to prove it. What she wanted more than anything was to hug her daughter.

Brill pushed open the arched door and followed Pouncer into the house, no less uptight than when she left the police station.

"Hi, Mom!"

Emily jumped up off the couch and ran to Brill and threw her arms around her.

"Guess what? Jasmine's coming over to Tessa and Tony's tomorrow, and we're going to have a sleepover, and then I'm going to church with them and Sunday school with Jasmine." Emily leaned back and looked up at her mother, her bright blue eyes twinkling with sheer excitement.

"Really?" Brill said. "I thought you were just spending the day."

Kurt came out of the kitchen and went over to them. "Change of plans. I didn't think you'd mind."

"I probably don't. I just don't like being the last one to know."

Emily giggled, her mother's irritation apparently lost on her. "You're not the last one, Mom. I haven't told Ryan or Vanessa or Pouncer."

Brill reveled in seeing Emily so bubbly and decided not to make it an issue. "Sounds like fun."

"Jasmine has American Girl dolls too. She's bringing Samantha. Tessa has a *whole room* with a hundred dolls in it. She collects them just for fun."

"Sweetie, why don't you let me visit with your dad for a few minutes? Maybe we can play a board game later."

"Okay. I'm going to check my phone and see if Jasmine sent me a text message." Emily raced up the staircase, Pouncer on her heels.

"It's nice to see her excited about something, though I'm surprised she's not depressed after the frank conversations she's forced us to have about your affair."

Brill was sorry the second she brought it up and was glad Kurt didn't comment. She hung up her coat and went out to the kitchen.

"You want a soft drink?" Kurt said.

"Okay."

He took a can of Dr Pepper out of the fridge, popped the top, and handed it to her. "You look tired."

"Dealing with murdered children will do that to you."

She took a gulp of soda, then gave Kurt the short version of her experience at the Sanchezes'. "My life's mission at the moment," she said, "is to find this Doe guy and get him off the street. And then find out who killed Hector."

Kurt pulled out a chair and sat across from her. "It's hard for me to imagine anyone shooting a child in cold blood."

"He was shot in the head at close range. It was a deliberate, vicious act, possibly an execution." Brill wrapped her hands around the can. "I can't help but think it was intended to send a message. But to whom and for what reason is what I'm determined to find out."

"What about the kidnapping investigation?"

"Well, now that the victims are all safe, David and Sam can continue investigating without my officers so we can give the Sanchez case our full attention."

"Have the victims described the kidnapper?"

"Are you kidding? The Rohypnol wiped out their memories except for distorted sounds and images that David is trying to piece together. For example, your barber remembers being dumped into a smelly dark pit with chanting red shadows who wanted to scalp him." Brill lifted her eyebrows. "So you can see how unreliable their recollections are."

"Too bad. It would be great if they could help you get this guy."

"We know from the shoe prints we cast next to Janet Evans's Mustang that there were at least two men involved. I still think it was part of the Smarties' gang initiation. David thinks the perp is the leader and that he masterminded the whole thing."

Brill's phone vibrated. "I need to take this. It's David." She put the phone to her ear. "What's up?"

"I just talked to the lab. The DNA from the hair follicle we found in Evans's Mustang is a match with skin cell DNA we found on two of the victims."

"So it's the same guy, but he's not in the system."

"Yes, but we got a bonus."

She could hear the playful tone in his voice. "Don't make me beg. It's so unbecoming."

David chuckled. "We have DNA from sweat droplets found on five of the victims. Belongs to a twenty-year-old male, Raphael Guerrero. Last May he beat up a professor at Stanton Community College for giving him a B instead of an A in Logic because he didn't follow instructions on how the research paper was to be submitted. Guerrero served sixty days in the county jail and then dropped out of school and out of sight. His mother doesn't know where he is. Sounds like the perfect candidate for a smart gang."

"I'd say."

"We've issued a warrant for his arrest. Maybe we'll get lucky."

CHAPTER 30

AT noon on Saturday, Nick Phillips stood at the counter at the Grill, a bar towel draped over his shoulder, and looked out at the packed-out booths and tables.

"I can't remember when I've ever seen this many customers nonstop," he said to Gus. "There's always been a spike in business when the fall colors peak but never like this. It's got to be the media hype driving people to town."

Gus took a sip of Coke and wiped his white mustache. "Doesn't surprise me that folks are curious about what's been goin' on here. I'd love to be a fly on the wall when the Feds question the people who were kidnapped."

Maggie bent down and folded her arms on the counter. "Gus, why can't you just accept that someone set up the whole kidnapping spree to look like red shadows were behind it? It's bogus."

"Look, darlin', I talked to Billy Dan's wife, and he actually *saw* red shadows. That might be the first documented case in decades."

Maggie cupped his face in her hands, her expression softer. "But isn't it possible that Billy Dan saw what he expected to see? That date-rape drug, whatever you call it, messes with your mind. And why would red shadows need to keep them drugged? Wouldn't *supernatural* beings have powers beyond ours?"

"Can't answer that," Gus said. "But do you know anyone who can? Shoot, I don't know another person alive who's ever seen one. I can't wait to talk to him myself. I'll tell you one thing, he's goin' public with it. Has to."

Maggie straightened up and nodded toward the door. "Here come the Masinos. They've got two little girls with them. Let's change the subject."

Nick went over and put his hand on Tessa's shoulder and shook Antonio's hand. "Welcome, folks. Good to see you." He gently tugged on Emily's ponytail. "Hey there, sugar. Who's your friend?"

"This is Jasmine Mendez."

"Nice to meet you, young lady. I'm Nick. I've got reserved seats for you at the counter. And today's special desert that is *sooooo* chocolaty and so made for little girls, you'll have to take some home with you."

Emily lit up. "Yum. Come on, Jasmine. I never got to sit at the counter before."

Emily and Jasmine climbed up in the two empty places next to Tessa, then spun around on the stools, giggling all the while.

Antonio straddled the stool next to Gus. "How's it going, friend?"

"Really can't complain, but I always do."

Antonio chuckled. "We sound like a stuck record, you know."

"Let's hope we're a forty-five and not a seventy-eight." Gus poked his elbow into Antonio's ribs. "Can you even remember the last time you saw a record?"

"At a garage sale I think."

Tessa tapped Antonio on the shoulder, and he was sidetracked for a minute, seemingly amused by the girls studying the menu in great detail.

When Maggie finished writing on her green pad and left, Gus leaned over to Antonio.

"Listen, I need to talk serious about somethin', man to man." Gus stabbed the ice in his glass with his straw. "I know we've gone round and round about the red shadows legend … well, Billy Dan Harrison finally saw them."

Antonio's eyes grew wide. "Huh?"

"It's true. His wife told me. You know Beth Ann, don't you?"

"I've met her. Can't say I really know her."

"Well, I do," Gus said. "Have for years. She said Billy Dan isn't the same man that he was before he was taken."

"Taken?"

Gus lowered his voice. "You know, carried off by the red shadows."

"I never heard anything about them being carried off. I heard on the news they were all drugged, and I doubt any of them will ever be the same."

"Well, the Feds aren't tellin' the whole story. It's not the drugs that changed Billy Dan. He was only missin' for a day and a night. It's what he saw that's changed him." Gus looked down the counter at Tessa visiting with the girls and leaned over and put his lips closer to Antonio's ear. "He said red shadows smell foul as skunk—like death itself. And he saw them plain as anything."

"What'd they look like?"

"Shadows."

"Were they red?"

Gus took a sip of Coke. "Not in the dark. He was in a pitch-black pit of some kind. But he could tell by their shape they were Indians. He saw their tomahawks and heard them chanting. Had to hold his arms over his head for fear of bein' scalped. It was horrifying."

"I guess it would be. But from everything I heard and read, it was some drug messing with their minds."

"Antonio, Billy Dan is positive he saw red shadows. For cryin' out loud, all seven victims woke up in the Cherokee burial ground. Explain *that*. Beth Ann said he's afraid to go to sleep. Scared it'll happen again."

"Why do you suppose he saw red shadows and the others didn't?"

"How do we know they didn't?" Gus said. "Look, he's not makin' it up. He wouldn't do that."

Nick realized that Antonio didn't know what to say, so he stepped closer to the counter and slapped Gus on the back.

"You're absolutely right," Nick said. "Billy Dan wouldn't fabricate a story. But all the victims need some time to sort out what happened."

"Not much to sort out." Gus lowered his voice. "Billy Dan's sure what he saw and he's goin' public."

"How public?" Nick said.

Gus moved his eyes one way and then the other and spoke just above a whisper. "Don't be surprised if some night you see him on *Larry King Live.*"

"Aw, Gus. Don't let him do that," Antonio said. "People would just laugh at him."

"Billy Dan doesn't care."

"I know, but I do. Plus what he says will reflect on the majority of people here who don't believe the legend. They'll lump us all together."

Tessa laughed at something Emily said, then turned to Antonio and Gus. "So ... what are you boys whispering about?"

Brill sat at her desk, mentally reliving her conversation with Anna Sanchez. Something about it bothered her but she couldn't quite figure it out.

"Hello? Earth to Brill."

She looked up, surprised to see David standing at her desk.

"Sorry, I didn't see you come in."

"I thought maybe you were avoiding me," David said.

"Of course I'm not avoiding you. Though if I gave you the wrong impression last night, I certainly didn't mean to. Obviously I appreciated the shoulder massage, but—"

"Will you stop?" David's grin spanned his face. "I was just trying to help you get rid of your headache. Don't make a federal case of it—pun intended."

"I'm just not accustomed to being that familiar with colleagues. Kind of goes against everything we're taught."

"I suppose it does." David went over and sat at the conference table where his files were spread out. "You want me to take it back?"

She smiled without meaning to. "Actually it did the trick."

"Good. What are you working on?"

"I'm writing down everything I can remember of my conversation with Anna Sanchez. I wish I had it on tape. She knew a lot more than I thought she did. So where've *you* been?"

"Pulling out all the stops trying to find Raphael Guerrero. We've got his picture plastered everywhere we can possibly put it, and the media is only too glad to oblige. Meanwhile I'm trying to convince victim number seven to keep his mouth shut about his alleged encounter with *red shadows*." David rolled his eyes. "His story is right up there with UFO and alien abduction stories and does a disservice to the other six victims and the serious nature of this case."

"Isn't that the truth? So do you think this Guerrero is the brains behind the kidnappings?"

"He doesn't fit the profile, though I might have the mastermind pegged wrong. I knew the seven kidnapped victims were pawns, but I really thought he'd kill them before he discarded them. He didn't. So, in answer to your question, I don't know yet. I need more information. It could be that Guerrero is one of at least two kidnappers trying to get initiated into the Smarties."

Tessa savored the pervasive aroma of spaghetti sauce simmering on the stove and looked out the kitchen window at the swatches of foothills visible between the houses across the street. How she looked forward to the drive to Cades Cove with Antonio, and the chance to leisurely observe Mother Nature's finest jewels of red, orange, gold, and purple, which should be on display for at least another week or two.

The phone rang, and she went into the kitchen and picked it up. "Hello."

"Tessa, it's Juanita Mendez. I was just checking to see how Jasmine's doing. She forgot to pack her nightgown. I'll have Rosa run it over there."

"She's just fine. The girls are hitting it off great. We made my special spaghetti sauce this morning and then went to Nick's Grill for lunch and came back here. The girls are playing Monopoly with Antonio. Last time I checked, Jasmine had a hotel on Boardwalk."

"Does she seem subdued or distracted?"

"Not at all. Why?"

"I should've said something when I dropped her off, but I was afraid I'd start crying again and upset the girls. You heard about the twelve-year-old boy whose body was dumped on Jackson Street?"

"Yes, it was awful."

"Well, his father works with us at the tire plant, and Rosa and Carmen babysit his sisters at our house after school."

"Oh my goodness," Tessa said. "I didn't know. Jasmine hasn't mentioned it."

"In a way that's good. She's never met Hector, so we're trying to shelter her from the emotional drama. I'm glad she'll be with you and Emily tonight instead of at the funeral home. I just think it would be overwhelming for a nine-year-old."

"Oh, I agree. How are your older girls doing?"

"Carmen's holding up, but Rosa's devastated. Nothing I say seems to help. She didn't know Hector either, but she's very attached to his little sisters."

"Of course she is. Poor thing." Tessa shook her head. "Do they know who shot the boy—or why?"

"Not yet, but it's been all over the news that they found a

substantial amount of cocaine and prescription drugs in his room. He had to be dealing."

"At twelve?"

"Sad, isn't it? Since he's a minor, they won't release his name. The police don't have any answers yet, but he obviously knew some dangerous characters. His parents are just beside themselves. They had no idea. They're caring people. They didn't deserve this."

Tessa sighed. "It's such a difficult day and time to be raising kids, considering all they're exposed to."

"It's enough to scare you to death."

"Well, ease your mind. Antonio and I are taking good care of Jasmine. And if you need us to keep her longer, we'd be glad to."

"Thanks. Let's see how it goes. I'll have Rosa bring the nightgown."

Brill sat at her computer and scrolled down through the notes she entered after her conversation with Anna Sanchez. She couldn't remember everything Anna said, but she distinctly remembered two statements being contradictory.

Hector didn't even tell, and they killed him anyway.

He said if he told, they would kill our mom and dad.

So which was it—had someone threatened to kill Hector if he told what he knew? Or threatened to kill his parents? And Anna chose the word *they*. Did she know more than she was telling?

She sat back in her chair and rubbed her eyes, aware of footsteps moving rapidly toward her office. She looked up in time to see David stroll through the doorway, wearing a toothy grin the size of the Grand Canyon.

He rubbed his hands together. "Prepare to be wowed. We just picked up Raphael Guerrero. We heard his grandma makes tamales every Saturday night and the whole family gets together. My agents were waiting for him. I'm about to interrogate him. He hasn't lawyered up yet, and I thought you might like to play good cop/bad cop."

CHAPTER 31

BRILL did a quick read of Guerrero's rap sheet and two related newspaper articles, then followed David to the first interrogation room and went inside.

Raphael Guerrero sat alone at the oblong oak table, his hands folded, the shadow on his unshaven face accentuated by the thick dark hair that was drawn back in a ponytail. He was dressed in a navy blue hooded sweatshirt.

David introduced himself and Brill, and then they sat at the table opposite Raphael.

David sat in silence and appeared to be reading the notes in front of him, though she knew he was stalling to intimidate the suspect. Beads of sweat popped out on Raphael's upper lip, and he wiped it away with his sleeve.

"I know you speak English so let's cut to the chase," David finally said. "Do you know why you're here?"

"No. Is that English enough for you?" Raphael spoke with almost no accent, his dark eyes squinted in defiance. "I've done nothing wrong. This is harassment."

"Really? Well, let me tell you a story. Once upon a time there was this Latino gang called the Smarties that devised a very intricate initiation rite so clever and daring that it would earn them the respect of all other gangs and even law enforcement. At least two prospective recruits fulfilled the initiation requirements, then dissed the cops publicly and were received into the gang." David folded his arms on the table and leaned forward, a smug grin on his face, "Have you heard this story, Raphael?"

"I've never been into fiction, man."

"Then let me make it real: Michael Stanton. Janice Evans. Benson Vaughn. Candi Eagan. Sonya Nichols. Dade Tompkins. Billy Dan Harrison. Any idea what these people have in common?"

Raphael shook his head. "Never heard of them."

"Oh, come on," David coaxed. "You're not going to take credit for masterminding this remarkable serial kidnapping?"

"I had nothing to do with a kidnapping."

"That's right, there were seven kidnappings—each brilliantly executed."

Raphael shrugged. "Means nothing to me."

"Sure it does. You wanted the moronic public to believe the red shadows did it. And why wouldn't they? Each victim was somehow tied to the number seven. Oh, and it was absolutely ingenious that you chose your victims in perfect order so that the first letter of their last names spelled *seventh*. Great touch. And dumping them on Seventh Mound, the Cherokee burial ground—priceless."

Raphael pushed out his bottom lip and shook his head. "You're talking in riddles, man."

"Hmm …" David folded his arms across his chest and sat back in his chair, his weight balancing on the balls of his feet. "Then again, you're not all that smart. Your Logic professor robbed you of an A and messed up your grade point average because you weren't smart enough to follow his directions on how to submit the paper. At least he said you weren't."

"Who cares what he said?"

"You did. You beat him up because he dissed you. How dare he drop your grade to a B just because you didn't turn in the paper the way *he* wanted? Who is he to tell you anything? You were smarter than him—isn't that right, Raphael? And you're sure smarter than the deputies who bossed you around at the county jail?"

Raphael smirked. "I'm smarter than you, *Special Agent* Riley."

"Maybe you are. Maybe you aren't. Come on, *Smartie*, let's hear about the mother of all gang initiations. You're dying to tell me." David put his face within inches of Raphael's. "It was so profoundly genius, you can't keep it in."

"You hear me talking?"

"Oh, but you want to. You want us to know how clever you are. You wanted us to tell the media that the first letter of their last names spelled *seventh*, but you thought we didn't *get* it. You thought we were too dumb to figure it out."

"Don't know what you're talking about."

"You planned everything to the last detail, then sat back and laughed at us—at the whole world. You had people believing that red shadows really exist. People all over the globe are marveling at your brilliant scheme. They're talking about you on every continent, wherever the cable networks broadcast."

Raphael laughed with his eyes. "Make sure they spell my name right."

"So did you mastermind the whole thing or get initiated by it? Which of the victims was the most fun to capture—the Cub Scout?

Or maybe the old schoolteacher?" David got up in Raphael's face again. "Did it give you a rush to see them all drugged and helpless? To know you were in charge? To know they wouldn't remember a single detail because you kept them full of roofies?"

"Those are potato chips, right?"

"Oh, he's a funny man, too," David said. "Ever heard of Rohypnol?"

"Doesn't he play for the Titans?"

David jumped to his feet and grabbed Raphael's sweatshirt. "I'm done playing games. You're going to talk to me, one way or the other."

Brill took hold of David's arm and pulled him away from Raphael. "Down, boy. Why don't you go take a walk?"

"Oh, I'm just getting revved up."

"Well, go find a place and *unrev*. I think we should all take a break. There's no need to be this intense. Raphael, would you like something cold to drink?"

"Coke sounds great." He smiled flirtatiously at Brill and dismissed David with his eyes.

David opened the door to leave, then turned around and pointed his finger at Raphael. "I'll be back. I'm not done with you."

Brill stood. "Try to relax. I'll be right back."

She went out to the lounge and got two Cokes, then winked at David as she passed the two-way mirror and went back into the interrogation room.

"Here you go." She set a can of Coke on the table in front of Raphael and took a drink of the other. "Sorry about Special Agent Riley. You know how the Feds are."

"Can't say that I do. Never met one before."

"But you've had plenty of experience with law enforcement in the county jail."

"Definitely not the brightest people in the food chain, present company excluded."

"Then I'm sure someone as intelligent as you would just as soon spend as little time with them as possible."

"So how would I do that?"

Brill lifted her gaze. "If you tell us what you know and name names the judge might go easy on you. We could convince him the kidnappings were just a game you were playing with the cops. It'll work in your favor that you didn't do physical harm to any of the seven victims."

"Please. Victims sounds so harsh."

"They might beg to differ, Raphael. It was a traumatic experience."

"Traumatic how? They can't remember, what with being kept full of roofies and all. Isn't that what Special Agent Riley said?"

"It's not going to work in your favor that you spent sixty days in jail for beating your Logic professor with a lead paperweight.'

"The moron deserved it."

"The judge didn't think so." Brill glanced at the newspaper article. "It says here other students had to pull you off the professor and that he suffered bruises and contusions, a dislocated shoulder, and broken teeth. You've got quite a temper."

"What's your point?"

"My point is you're intelligent, prone to violence, and had every reason to want to get into the Smarties. And I, on the other hand, have zero tolerance for gangs. So … let's work together. Start naming names. Tell us how this went down. I want to help you, Raphael. But I can't do that unless you give me something."

"You really think I'm falling for this good cop/bad cop routine? I'm not telling you anything. You've got nothing on me." Raphael looked into the mirror. "You can come back now, Special Agent Riley."

"I wish you'd work with me," Brill said. "You're an extraordinarily bright twenty-year-old man with your whole life ahead of you. Are you really willing to take the fall for the others?"

Raphael snickered. "What others?"

"I'm serious."

"So am I. If I were a gang member and I ratted out the others, do you think I'd be safe *anywhere*?"

David burst through the door and started talking while he walked over to his chair. "You must've worn gloves, because we don't have your fingerprints."

"Because I wasn't involved."

"Oh, you were involved, all right. And make no mistake, we've got you."

"If you had anything on me, you wouldn't be conducting this lame interview trying to intimidate me, *Special Agent* Riley." Raphael faked a yawn.

"Is that so? What size shoe do you wear? Looks like a nine to me, wouldn't you say, Chief Jessup?"

"Sure looks like it," Brill said. "Or it could be an eight."

"Or it could be that I wear the same size shoes as several million other guys." Raphael's eyes moved up the front of Brill's uniform and then seemed to study her face. "You're much too pretty to waste on law enforcement. The red hair does something to me. I dig older women."

David folded his arms on the table and leaned forward, his nose about a foot in front of Raphael's. "Since you're having trouble focusing, how about we skip down to the bottom line? You *failed*, dummy. We've got your DNA. The Smarties are going to disown you."

"No way."

"We found a hair follicle in Janice Evans Mustang."

"It's not mine, man. I was never in that car."

"Correct. But you do sweat. We found sweat droplets containing skin cells on five of the seven victims." David pushed the DNA results across the table. "All we need is a sample of your DNA, and you're going away. The great thing about science is that it doesn't lie. But then, a genius like you knows that."

The cynicism seemed to melt off Raphael's face.

"But I'll tell you what. I'll give you a chance to start naming names. We know there's at least one other person involved in the kidnappings because of the shoeprints we cast where you dragged Janice Evans from her Mustang to your faded blue van. Yeah, we know about the van, too. Looks like this time cops dis Smarties—L-O-L."

Brill forced herself not to smile.

Raphael looked down at the DNA results, a drop of sweat trickling down from his temple.

"Oops, there's that pesky DNA again." David flashed a phony grin. "It would be a good move to tell me who the leader is. But whether you do or don't, I'm going to find him. And when I do, I'm going to give him the same opportunity to give you up. Only one of you is getting the deal. Want to know what they do to geeks in the pen?"

"You know what, man? I want a lawyer."

"Yeah, I thought you might."

Brill stood with David on the other side of the two-way mirror and watched as Raphael Guerrero met with his court-appointed attorney.

"Wasn't that fun?" David said.

Brill smiled. "It really was. It's been a long time since we teamed up like that."

"Guerrero's right on. If he gives us names, he's a dead man. It's a lose-lose. There's no good ending for him. Did you see his face when I told him we had his DNA, and the gang would disown him?"

Brill looked though the glass at the unkempt, bitter dropout with so much to prove and tried to picture him as a bright, eager student sitting in the front row of Professor Kilgore's Logic class.

"Had to be devastating," she said, "after the risks he took to get initiated into the Smarties. When you stop to think about it, it's pretty incredible what they pulled off. I'm sure whoever *they* is had a great laugh at everyone's expense, thanks to the cable networks."

"Yeah, and it was no small feat to dis the cops and get air time, either. Other gangs are bound to challenge them—and try to top them."

"Don't remind me," Brill glanced at her watch. "I need to get back to my murder case. I have a feeling Hector Sanchez's sister knows a lot more than she told me. I want to interview her again, but I'm torn. I should probably respect the family and hold off until after the funeral."

"Why? If you think Anna knows something, stay on her 'til she talks. That's what I've always admired about you—tenacity."

"You make me sound like a pit bull."

"More like an Irish setter with chutzpah. That might be an oxymoron. But you know what I mean."

"I have no idea what you mean."

"Well, it's a compliment. But then, you have a hard time accepting compliments. I don't think you realize that you're as much woman as you are cop."

"How do *you* know what I realize and what I don't?"

David shot a glance up and down the hallway and then looked at her as if she were the only other person in the world. "Because I pay attention to everything you do. Everything."

"Since when?"

"Since always. You've never noticed?"

The silence that followed was electric, and she sensed he wanted to kiss her. She knew she should get out of there, so why couldn't she move—wouldn't she move?

David stepped closer, held her face in his hands, and pressed his lips to hers with just enough tenderness to temper the passion.

The kiss thrilled her, and for a moment she forgot who she was and where she was. Finally, she pushed away from him, her heart pounding wildly, heat searing her cheeks.

"Are you crazy?" *Am I crazy?*

"Yeah, crazy about you."

"Tell me this did not just happen." She looked to see if anyone was watching and was relieved no one else was in the hallway.

"But it did. I've wanted to kiss you since I came here."

"It's unprofessional, David. Totally inappropriate."

"And wonderful. And exciting. Admit it." He traced her ear with his finger and she slapped his hand away.

"Listen to me. I'm serious."

"You think I'm not?"

"Look …" She brushed the hair out of her eyes. "I don't know what's gotten into you, but there is no chance this is going anywhere. For heaven's sake I'm married. I would've thought you'd respect that, if nothing else."

David's eyebrows came together. "But *you* don't. You've been giving me mixed signals all week."

Every fiber of her being burned with the scorching truth—and she felt suddenly inanimate, almost as if she were a wax figure that was melting. She forced her mouth to form the words: "This conversation is over."

"Brill, wait." He reached for her arm and held it. "Please don't leave mad. Let's talk about this."

"I just did."

"All right. I heard you. I'm sorry. I feel like an idiot." He let go of her arm. "I totally misread you. I promise this will never happen again."

"You had better mean it."

"I do."

Her eyes collided with his, and she softened her tone. "I'm sorry about you and Patricia. But you and I are never—I repeat, never—going to be romantically involved. And will you stop looking at me like you're afraid I'm going to charge you with sexual harassment? That's not what this is about."

David leaned against the two-way glass, his arms folded across his chest. "My attraction to you is genuine, albeit unprofessional. You have my word I'll never bring it up again or do anything inappropriate. Let's bury this right here."

"All right. I'm going back to my office."

Brill walked down the hall toward the detective bureau and stopped at the water cooler. She took a drink and let the cold water run over her lips as if that would somehow erase what had just happened.

CHAPTER 32

TESSA Masino stirred the spaghetti sauce and smiled at the sound of Emily and Jasmine's giggling as they played with Abby. The five o'clock news was on and Tessa saw "Breaking News" flash across the screen and turned up the sound.

"We interrupt this broadcast to bring you breaking news: The FBI has made an arrest in the serial kidnapping case in Sophie Trace.

"FBI spokesperson Special Agent Robert Morrow announced just moments ago that twenty-year-old Raphael Guerrero of Stanton's Ferry was arrested and charged with five counts of engaging in organized criminal activity.

"An unnamed source inside the federal prosecutors office told WSTN News that the charges are based on DNA evidence linking Guerrero to five of the kidnapping victims, but it is likely that the defendant will soon be charged in the other two kidnappings as well...."

Tessa heard a car and looked out the kitchen window as the Mendezes' white Ford Expedition pulled up out front and remembered Rosa was bringing a nightgown to Jasmine. She decided to invite Rosa to stay for dinner.

Just as the driver's side door opened, a late-model black pickup sporting a big dent in the front left fender stopped across the street, the motor still running. A man in a navy blue hooded sweatshirt, jeans, and red tennis shoes got out and strutted over to Rosa. He looked angry.

Rosa stood erect, her shoulders back, and faced this young male who wasn't much taller than she, their mouths moving at the same time.

Tessa wasn't sure whether she should intervene. Was this Rosa's boyfriend? Was it a private matter? Finally the young man put his hands on Rosa's shoulders and gave her a shove.

Tessa jumped up from her chair, rushed to the front door, and went outside.

"Rosa!" she hollered, wanting to go out to where the two were standing but deciding to stop at the edge of the stoop. "Come in where it's warm. I'll make us some hot tea."

The young man got up in Rosa's face, his hands turning to fists at his side, and said something, then jogged over to his pickup, climbed in, and sped away, his tires squealing as he turned the corner.

Tessa was sure Rosa wiped her eyes as she poked her head in the car and reached for something.

Half a minute later Rosa came up the walk, something pink draped over her arm, a smile pasted on. "Hi, Tessa."

"Are you okay, honey?"

"I'm fine." Rosa's eyes belied her pleasant tone. "That was just my cousin. He and I are having a disagreement. No big deal. Here's

Jasmine's nightgown. I'll see you at church tomorrow." She hugged Tessa and then turned to leave.

"Rosa, wait … why don't you stay for dinner? We're having spaghetti."

"Thanks, but I'm supposed to meet my parents. We're all going to the funeral home together."

"You have to eat. I doubt your mother is in the mood to cook."

"My aunt's cooking for us. That's what my cousin came to tell me."

Tessa gazed into Rosa's gorgeous brown eyes and saw an agonizing battle going on in her spirit. *Oh, Lord. Sometimes discernment is a difficult gift. What do I say?*

Tessa felt as if her feet were nailed to the stoop. "Honey, your mother told me how much you're hurting for the family of this young boy who was killed, that you and Carmen babysit his sisters after school."

Rosa nodded.

"I want you to know you can come talk to me *anytime* about *anything*. I've got broad shoulders and don't broadcast other people's business. Sometimes it's good to bounce your feelings off an old hen like me."

Rosa's eyes brimmed with tears. "Thanks. I'd better go."

Tessa stood shivering, her eyes on Rosa's back, her spirit screaming that something was terribly awry.

Brill drove down Main Street oblivious to the speed limit, her mind still reeling from her improper, and downright fatuous, behavior with

David. Why didn't she leave the moment she sensed he was about to make a move? She was still married, for heaven's sake. What was she thinking? Or did she even bother to think? And what if someone had seen them?

The silhouette of the Great Smoky Mountains looked surreal against the fiery sky and reminded her of the velvet paintings she had seen at roadside stands. Part of her wanted to walk into the scene and disappear. The other part just wanted to get this interview behind her.

She turned on Beech Street and parked in front of the Sanchezes' house. She picked up her recorder before she walked up to the front door and rang the doorbell.

A dog barked somewhere nearby, and then she heard footsteps inside the house and Mr. Sanchez opened the door.

"Come in, Chief Jessup."

Brill stepped inside the home and the delicious aroma of something spicy wafted over her.

"I'm sorry to intrude like this," she said, "but thank you for agreeing to let me talk with Anna again. I know you're greeting people at the funeral home tonight, and this isn't especially convenient. It won't take long."

"I don't understand why you need to record her statement," Mr. Sanchez said. "She already told you she knew Hector was dealing drugs—that some guy named Doe was his supplier."

"There are many officers working the case, Mr. Sanchez. This is valuable information, and I'd like to have her comments on tape where they can be accessed by other members of law enforcement." *And I think she knows more than she's saying.*

Anna walked up next to her father. "Hi, Chief Jessup."

"Hello, Anna."

"My parents told me why you were coming. Can we talk in my room again?"

"That's up to them," Brill said.

Mr. Sanchez tilted her chin and looked into her eyes. "Is that what you want, Anna?"

"Yes. It's okay, Daddy. I like Chief Jessup."

"You want me with you?"

Anna shook her head. "I'm fine."

"Okay, let me know when you're done." Mr. Sanchez stroked her hair. "I'll be out in the kitchen."

Brill followed Anna into her room, and Anna shut the door.

"You can sit on my bed like last time."

Brill sat on the side of the bed and noticed that Anna had picked up her clothes and straightened the tiny room.

Anna sat cross-legged on the floor, clutching the same brown teddy bear she held on to last time.

Brill explained she was going to record the conversation, then turned on the recorder and asked Anna all the same questions she remembered asking last time and got essentially the same answers.

"Thanks for letting me do this, Anna. This will be so valuable to the investigation. I have a few more questions. You said that Hector didn't tell the big secret he knew, but they killed him anyway. Can you tell me who 'they' are?"

Anna fidgeted and held more tightly to her teddy bear. "Not really. That's what Hector called them."

"How do you know Hector *didn't* tell someone?"

"Because he wouldn't do that."

"How can you be so sure?"

"I just am." Her eyebrows came together and she started rocking back and forth.

"Then why do you think they killed him?"

"Because they're just *mean*."

Brill paused and considered what she was about to say to an eleven-year-old. Was it necessary? She decided it was. "Hector also said they would kill your mom and dad if he told the secret. Should we be worried about them?"

"Hector didn't tell. I know he didn't."

"But someone killed him."

Anna hugged her teddy bear, a tear trickling down her cheek. "It's not fair. He didn't tell."

"You knew your brother better than anyone, didn't you? You were close."

"I know what you're thinking, but he didn't tell me the secret."

Brill turned off the recorder and sat in silence until Anna looked up. "Would your answer be different if it wasn't being recorded and no one could prove you said it?"

"Like what?"

"Like maybe your brother told you the most important secret he ever told anyone."

"But he didn't."

"He loved you. He trusted you. Why would he not?"

Anna exhaled as if she had nothing left. "I already told you: because they said they would kill him and our mom and dad. He *swore* he wouldn't tell and he didn't. But they lied. They killed him anyway."

"Criminals can't be trusted to keep their word, Anna." Brill got down on the floor and sat facing the girl. "But I can be trusted. If you know something, I promise you I'll use it to find whoever killed your brother. And I think Hector would want that, don't you?"

"He'd probably be really mad. If he knew they were going to kill him any way, he would've told the police."

"Maybe he wants *you* to."

"I don't know the big secret." Anna drew a line in the carpet with her finger. "But I heard him say a name once—not on purpose, but by mistake."

Brill drew a line in the carpet next to Anna's. "It might be important. Do you think you can trust me with it?"

Tessa sat in the upstairs bedroom with Jasmine while Emily was in the bathroom, taking her shower.

"I'm glad you girls are getting along famously. Tony and I are so enjoying having you here."

"I'm glad you invited me." Jasmine played with the bloomers on one of the dolls she had propped in a chair. "Emily's nice, and I don't have many friends."

"It was sweet of Rosa to run your nightgown over here. I'm afraid mine would be much too big. A young man driving a black pickup pulled up outside, just when Rosa did. She said it was her cousin."

Jasmine nodded knowingly. "That would be Eduardo. I wonder why he was with her? He hurts her feelings all the time, and they don't get along anymore."

"Why is that?"

"Eduardo's a pain. Rosa said he has a short fuse. That means he gets mad just like *that*." She snapped her finger. "I stay away from him."

"They both seemed angry," Tessa said. "I was a little concerned when Eduardo actually shoved Rosa. Is it usual for him to get pushy with you girls?"

"He never used to. He was really nice." Jasmine put the shoes on the doll. "I liked him when he brought Popsicles for all the cousins and gave us piggyback rides. But Eduardo's mean now, and I've seen him shove Rosa before. He's the oldest cousin and thinks he's the boss."

"How old is he?"

"Twenty-one."

"Does he have a job?"

"I'm not sure. But he got kicked out of junior college for fighting. My uncle says Eduardo is the dumbest smart person in the whole world. He's like this genius in math, but all he wants to do is fight with everybody."

"Do you have any idea why Rosa would be angry with him?"

Jasmine shrugged. "Not really. He hardly ever talks to her anymore."

Kurt closed his Bible. Tomorrow's Sunday school lesson was polished and ready to present. He hoped that by the time he got to the last lesson and Romans 12:21, he would have a handle on what it means to overcome evil with good. But right now all his good intentions seemed squelched by Brill's indignation and anger. He was no match for her.

He was disgusted with himself for missing Emily so much. It was healthy for her to grow more independent. But if this weekend was a test of his ability to live alone, he was failing.

He thought he heard the front door open, and then Pouncer jumped down off a cardboard box and shot out of the room.

He got up and went to the entry hall where Brill was hanging up her coat.

"I heard the Feds made an arrest," he said.

Brill nodded. "David interrogated the suspect and asked me to play the role of good cop. It was kind of fun, actually. It'd been a while."

"What DNA evidence do you have that got him five counts?"

"His sweat on five of the victims. We also have one other guy's DNA, but he's not in the system."

"This Guerrero character wouldn't give him up?"

"No. He knew he'd be a walking target if he told us anything."

"What about the murder investigation? Did you go back and talk to Anna Sanchez?"

"I did."

"Learn anything new?"

"Just a name she remembers Hector mentioning. It might mean something down the road. I'm exhausted and would really rather not talk about work." She went into the living room, kicked off her shoes, and flopped on the couch. "Have you checked on Emily?"

"She called after dinner. She and Jasmine are having a ball. I think she's made a genuine friend at last."

"You don't sound very happy about it."

"Of course I'm happy about it. Why would you say that?"

"You just sound blah."

Kurt sat in the overstuffed chair. "Right now I feel blah. But I'm happy for Emily."

"What are *you* blah about?" Brill said. "You've got everything you want."

Kurt was perplexed by Brill's sarcastic tone and studied her dark expression, aware that she didn't make eye contact. Should he even attempt to address her question or the answer she supplied? He wasn't going to let it go by.

"I don't understand why you would think I have everything I want," he said.

Brill rolled her eyes and put the couch pillow under her head. "Just a figure of speech. Forget I said it. I don't want to fight."

"Neither do I." Kurt kept his tone mellow. "But I'd like to understand your perspective. Because, except for my relationship with the Lord and with Emily, I don't have *anything* I want."

"Oh, give me a break. You've got this beautiful home. Great kids. A successful business that affords you total freedom to juggle your time. So now you can sleep around to your heart's content and your wife-in-name-only won't know or even care. Then again, maybe having a green light spoils it for you."

Kurt sat dumbfounded, not knowing what to say. What was eating her? Should he ask? Or just leave her alone and hope it would wear off? He decided he couldn't ignore it.

"Are you still mad at me because Emily overheard us arguing and we had to talk to her about my affair?"

"Do you honestly think I've ever *stopped* being mad at you for reducing our marriage to the level of a game show and trading our family's future for a few hours with the brunette behind curtain number one?"

Kurt could hardly stand to hear it phrased that way. But he opted not to water down his guilt by drawing attention to the fact that Brill lost interest in him and their marriage long before Victoria entered the scene.

"I really have no desire to rehash this," she said.

Kurt folded his hands between his knees. "Just for the record, I never strayed before that day and haven't since. Do I enjoy living like a monk? Absolutely not. But we *are* married, and for better or worse, I happen to believe it's for life. So don't tell me I have everything I want. It's simply not true."

"Whatever." Brill closed her eyes and folded her hands on her chest. "I don't have the emotional energy to care about how you feel."

Kurt sighed. She'd be asleep in a matter of minutes. The thought of his spending one more waking hour alone in this house was oppressive. He decided to go for a drive.

CHAPTER 33

KURT drove down Main Street, and traffic came to crawl when he reached the congested area in front of city hall. The media presence was impressive and so was the number of FBI jackets. Checking this out looked like a whole lot more fun than sitting home on a Saturday night.

He drove two blocks, looking for a place to park, and saw the taillights of a car parallel-parked along the street. He turned on his blinker, then as quickly as the car pulled out, he pulled his Dodge Caravan snugly into the space. He locked it up and walked back to city hall, a brisk north wind stinging his face.

The gaslights around the grounds at city hall revealed a group of marchers carrying placards and camera crews following them, holding even brighter lights. One of the placards read, *The Legend Lives*. Another read, *Red Shadows Have Spoken*. A third placard held high by an old man with a white beard read, *We Want the Truth*.

He spotted David Riley standing with a couple other guys in FBI jackets. He waited 'til David was alone and then went over to him.

"Fancy meeting you here," Kurt said. "Brill said you never sleep."

"Much too early for me to wind down." David looked out over the crowd, his hands in his pockets. "Since you're here, I assume Brill talked to you about what happened?"

"Actually I'd already heard everything on the news. She did say the two of you played good cop/bad cop with the guy you arrested. But she was beat and went to bed. Emily's at a sleepover. I just wanted to get out of the house for a while. So what's the demonstration about?"

David suddenly seemed friendlier. "Oh, just some nice folks who grew up with the legend and aren't sure who they can trust. They think we're lying to them about the kidnappings. Can't reason with them. The suspect we arrested, Raphael Guerrero, is no red shadow, and we found his sweat DNA on the clothes of five of the seven victims."

"I'm not sure even that will convince them." Kurt breathed out a stream of white vapor and looked over at David. "Hey, bud. You need to cover your head before you get frostbite. It's freezing out here."

"Yeah, my FBI hat's in my motel room."

"Here, take this." Kurt took off his stocking cap and handed it to David.

"I can't take your hat."

"Trust me, you're not going to get a better offer tonight, and I've got a hood on my jacket if I get cold."

David glanced at it before he put it on and pulled it down over his ears. "Thanks. I just happen to be a Titans fan."

"You want some hot coffee?" Kurt said. "I'm headed over to Beanies. Be glad to bring you a cup."

"Thanks. I'd appreciate that. I like anything. Decaf or not. Flavored or not. Just so it's black."

"Good man. I'll be back."

Kurt made his way slowly through the crowd of hometown folks who were now his neighbors and got the sense that most people who'd come out here tonight were just curious.

He crossed First Street and jogged a block to the next corner. He pushed open the hefty wood door at Beanies and was hit with the delicious aroma of hazelnut. The place was abuzz with customers sitting at tables, the best seats in the house those in front of two walls of windows that lined the sidewalk. He went up to the counter and smiled at a young man with a goatee and hair down to his collar.

"Two large cups of hazelnut—to go, please."

"Decaf or regular?"

Kurt glanced at the clock. "Decaf."

The young man filled two cups, put on the lids, and took Kurt's money. He was out of Beanies in less than two minutes.

He walked back to the square at city hall and spotted his stocking cap on a guy in an FBI jacket and walked over to him.

"Man, that was fast," David said. "How much do I owe you?"

"Nothing. Next time, you buy."

"Fair enough."

Kurt looked up at white clock tower of city hall that rose high above the red brick arches of the portico and listened to the clock chime nine times. "I think I'll go look around," he said. "By the way, that's decaf. I figured caffeine might work against you at this hour."

"You're probably right." David looked at him over the top of the cup and took a sip. "Thanks again. I owe you one. Well, actually two."

"Hey, you'd do the same for me. Stay warm."

"I'll do it."

Kurt wandered around the square, watching the locals and listening to what they were telling reporters, fascinated that their memories contained volumes of stories that had been passed down from generation to generation.

He thought back on the story Pate Dickson had told Brill of how the Indian kids and the settler kids played together, and how the families broke bread together at each full moon, and how sad the settlers were when the Cherokee disappeared. Those kinds of stories were worth preserving. He was glad that Emily had heard the Dickson family's story. But he also wondered if the Dicksons or anybody else really knew how the legend of the red shadows came into being. Maybe it just evolved over time.

"Kurt Jessup, is that you?"

Oh no. He cringed at the familiar voice, then turned around and found the face that went with it: a pair of indigo eyes framed in long dark hair and a white faux fur hat.

"Victoria," he said flatly. "What are you doing here?"

"Well, that's not a very friendly greeting."

"Sophie Trace is a long way from Memphis. Why are you here?"

"I'm a field reporter for KMPS-TV. They sent me out to report on the kidnappings and this interesting Indian legend. Could I get your comments? My camera crew will be here in a minute, and we can get it on film. It would be great to hear from a former Memphis resident who is now a Sophie Trace resident and—"

"I'm not interested in being on camera."

Lord, I can't exactly push my way out of this crowd without starting a ruckus, but I need You to get me out of here. Help me say and do the right thing.

"You don't have to be rude." She fluttered the eyelashes on her Elizabeth Taylor eyes. "I'm just here to do my job. Aren't you even going to tell me how you're doing?"

"Brill and I are working hard to put our marriage back together. I'm not letting anything get in the way of that."

"I heard she took you back. I'm happy for you. And how old is Emily now?"

"Nine, and totally adorable. So you'll understand if I leave now. And I'd appreciate it if you don't come looking for me. No matter what the question, the answer is no. I cannot see you, nor be seen with you."

"I've already driven by the adorable cottage house y'all bought over on Azalea Street. Such a pretty neighborhood. It's just a few blocks from that new Fairfield Inn, where I'm staying."

"Victoria, go home."

"I have to finish my assignment first. I'll be here several days."

She was forty-five and could easily pass for a woman ten years younger. At least she couldn't flaunt her figure while wearing a faux fur coat.

Kurt blinked away the memory and refused to open this door.

"Listen, my camera crew's coming and I need to get to work," she said. "Could we at least have coffee while I'm in town? I know of a place over on Second, Beanies. It's not Starbucks, but it's really quaint."

"You know I'm not going to have coffee with you. Or conversation. Or anything else."

"Well … if you change your mind, you know where to find me."

"Good-bye, Victoria. I'm going home to my wife."

Kurt turned, worked his way through the crowd and back to the sidewalk, and then exhaled. That wasn't so bad. *Thank You, Lord.*

A loud popping noise caused the drone of voices to fall silent. Everyone seemed to freeze. There it was again.

"It's gunfire!" someone shouted.

People started running and screaming, pushing and shoving. Parents grabbed their children and held them close as a tidal wave of frightened people began to stream away from the square.

Kurt stood where he was as dozens of people swept past him on both sides and a wave of others rushed toward him.

He scanned the grounds and spotted a young man in a blue hooded sweatshirt hunkered down behind the bushes in front of city hall. The guy got up and then eased into the crowd and was carried along in a river of bodies moving away from the square.

Kurt kept his eye on the guy and allowed himself to be swept along not far behind him. He turned and saw several FBI agents gathered around someone lying on the ground—someone wearing a Titans stocking cap.

Brill drifted between sleep and wakefulness, aware of loud ringing noise.

"All right. I'm coming. I'm coming." Brill groped in the dark and took her cell phone off her belt clip. "Chief Jessup," she said, or did she dream it?

"Ma'am, it's Trent Norris. I'm sorry to wake you. There's been a shooting in front of city hall."

"When?"

"Just minutes ago."

Brill sat up on the side of the couch. She opened her eyes wide and blinked several times. "What kind of shooting?"

"I don't know yet. The FBI's all over it. They have an agent down. Some of our officers were at the scene, helping with crowd control. Said they heard two shots."

"So the shooter didn't just open fire?"

"That's my understanding."

"Who's down?"

"I don't know, ma'am. But I thought you'd want to know."

"All right. I'm on my way."

Brill disconnected the call and her phone rang again.

"Chief Jessup."

"Brill, it's me. There's been a shooting at city hall. I'm stuck in the middle of a mob at the moment. I've got my eye on a guy I think is the shooter. A Hispanic kid in a navy blue hooded sweatshirt."

"Kurt, don't you dare approach him. Where are you?"

"Half a block west of city hall. The crowd's pouring down the sidewalk, but people are starting to break from the crowd and head their separate ways."

"Any idea who's been shot?"

"I'm pretty sure one of them is David Riley."

"David? How do you know?"

"I lent him my Titans stocking cap. The guy that got hit had on an FBI jacket and the Titans hat. It's got to be him."

"Listen to me, do not approach the kid in the blue hooded sweatshirt. I think he might be a gang member. The guy we arrested today was dressed that way and so was the young man who smashed Tessa Masino's windshield. The guy will kill you. He has nothing to lose. Do you hear me?"

"Listen, you're breaking up. I've got to go after him or he's going to get away."

CHAPTER 34

TESSA held on to the railing as she walked downstairs, Abby at her side, and went into the living room where Antonio sat watching TV.

"The girls are in bed," Tessa said. "But I'm under no illusion they'll be asleep any time soon. Oh my, it's wonderful to have the sound of giggling in the house. Anything interesting on the news?"

"I almost hate to tell you," Antonio shot her quick glance, "you're in such a good mood."

"What now?"

"There's been a shooting at city hall. Someone fired two shots into a crowd of demonstrators. An FBI agent was hit. That's about all I know."

Tessa peeked through the drapes and saw that Brill's car wasn't there.

"Looks like our police chief is gone again. I was hoping she and Kurt would have a night to themselves."

"You're meddling," Antonio said.

"Of course I am. That's what I do." She sat next to Antonio and linked her arm in his. "I can't believe we have more bad news. What is this town coming to—kidnappings, a dead child dumped in the street, and now a shooting? It used to be such wonderful place to live. Peaceful. Safe."

"Well, it isn't red shadows doing it," Antonio said.

"Do the authorities have a suspect in tonight's shooting?"

"Not yet. It just happened, and I got the impression it was chaos at city hall. Gus is down there. I saw him when they panned the crowd. Everybody looked dazed."

Tessa shook her head. "This is so disturbing."

"By the way, did you ask Jasmine about the guy in the black pickup?"

"Yes, she confirmed it was their cousin Eduardo. Apparently he's the oldest cousin and a bit of bully. Jasmine gave me the impression he used to be a sweetheart. But he and Rosa don't get along anymore, and he hardly ever talks to her. So I wonder why he followed her over here?"

"I thought he came to tell her his mother was going to cook dinner for the family."

Tessa nudged him. "Yes, but you didn't see them arguing. They were talking about something else. It looked heated, and it was obvious that Rosa was rattled by it. It didn't look as though she backed down, either."

"You're not going to be happy until you get every detail out of her." Antonio rolled his eyes. "Why don't you just leave well enough alone?"

"It seemed like a volatile situation to me. I don't want to see Rosa get hurt."

Kurt maintained a brisk pace about twenty yards behind the young guy in the blue hooded sweatshirt. There were only about a dozen adults and one little boy between them, all walking toward the light at First and Main. The frigid night air made his feet feel almost brittle and he wished he'd worn his wool socks. He heard sirens and thought of David Riley and wondered how badly injured he was.

The light at First Street was red. The young man stood at the curb with his back to everyone, jogging in place, his hands in the pouch of the sweatshirt, his head covered by the hood. He was five feet five or six. Medium frame. He wore Levis and blue and white Nikes.

The instant the light turned green the young man started across First Street, and when he got to the other side, he began to jog on the sidewalk. Kurt picked up his pace and had to make a decision. Was he going to risk being more obvious and run after the guy—or just let him go?

His mind flashed back to the moments after the shooting when he spotted the guy behind the bushes. If he was the shooter, he probably ditched the gun there and was likely unarmed. Kurt decided to keep following him.

The guy jogged across Second Street and then disappeared behind a doughnut shop. Kurt could barely see in the dark but followed the guy until he lost sight of him in the alley. Finally he slowed to a stop, his hands on his knees, and tried to catch his breath. He was too old for this. Whatever made him think he could catch this guy? What would he do if he *did* catch him?

He finally stood up straight and turned to go back to city hall. As he took a step, something grabbed the hood of his coat and yanked him backward. A second later he realized someone's arm was around his throat and something sharp was pushing into his neck.

"Why are you following me?" said a raspy male Latino voice that smelled of beer and cigarettes. "You'd better have the right answer or I'm gonna cut your throat from ear to ear."

"I'm not following anybody. I walked up to city hall to see what was going on, and there was a stampede. I don't even know what happened. I was running home and stopped to catch my breath, and the next thing I know, you've got me in a headlock and are threatening me. Come on, man. I've got kids. I just want to go home."

"Yeah? Where's home?"

Kurt opened his mouth and it was as if someone else were talking. "Three forty-eight Goldfinch Lane. Name's Roy Powell. We just bought that brick two-story. You know, with the rose bushes along the side?" *If he checks my wallet, I'm a dead man.*

Brill got out of her squad car and ran over to the yellow crime scene tape that sectioned off a swath of ground in front of city hall, where an ambulance was parked, its doors open, its lights flashing. Paramedics were working on someone and had an IV going.

She spotted Trent and ran over to him. "Who got hit?"

Trent dropped his cigarette on the ground and crushed it with his shoe. "David Riley.

"I'm fine," David hollered at her from the gurney. "Just grazed my left shoulder."

Brill went over and peered down at the man covered up to his neck with a blanket and wearing Kurt's Titans hat. She shook her head. "I leave you alone for an evening and you turn my town upside down."

"Two shots were fired. Semi-automatic."

"Kurt called and said he was going after a Hispanic kid in navy blue hooded sweatshirt he thinks is the shooter. I told him not to, that he might be a gang member, but my cell phone cut out. I've got to find him before he gets himself killed."

Brill heard a familiar whistle. And then heard it again. She turned toward the sound and saw Kurt strolling in her direction, carrying something on a stick.

"Thank God you're all right," she hollered. "What in the world were you thinking, going after a suspect?"

As Kurt got closer, she realized he was carrying a handgun on the stick.

"I believe this is your shooter's weapon," he said. "Looks like a Glock .45 to me, but I'm not the expert."

"Where did you get it?"

"Under the bushes in front of city hall. Here you go." Kurt handed her the stick. "I didn't touch it."

"How did you even know where to look?" she said.

"I heard shots and saw people panicking and running everywhere. I scanned the area for what didn't look right, and I saw a guy in a navy hooded sweatshirt hiding behind the bushes. He finally blended into the crowd and I kept my eye on him. I followed him all the way to Second Street until he cut behind the doughnut shop into the alley, and it was too dark to see. Next thing I knew he came up behind me, had me in a headlock, and threatened to slit my throat."

"So why are you alive to tell about it?"

"I convinced him I lived in the neighborhood—on Goldfinch Lane. I told him I had kids and wanted to go home—which *was* true.

He told me to run and not look back, so I hightailed it to Goldfinch and then circled back here. I had a hunch he'd stashed his gun in the bushes. I was right. Guess I learned a lot being married to a cop."

David laughed. "Good work, man."

Brill stared at Kurt, surprised at the gamut of emotions she felt. How could he do something so careless? What if Emily—and Ryan and Vanessa—had lost their dad? Brill wasn't prepared to take him back, but was she really ready to lose him, especially with David's inappropriate kiss still fresh on her lips? Had she even remotely come to grips with her bitterness? Or resolved the self-doubt Kurt's affair had generated and David's advances would seem to nullify?

"You okay?" Kurt said.

"Yes. I'm fine," Brill pulled her collar up around her ears, "considering you could be lying behind the doughnut shop with your throat cut."

"Had to think fast. Turned out good. I'd say the Lord isn't finished with me yet."

That's an understatement, she thought.

Brill pushed open her front door and picked up on the scent of flowers. Nice. She hung up her coat and went in the living room, where Kurt sat in the overstuffed chair reading *TIME* magazine.

"How's David?"

"Fine. The ER doctor released him."

Brill went in and sat on the couch. "I can't believe you actually followed a suspect and almost got yourself killed."

"It was hard to ignore someone who looked that suspicious. I guess I've been around law enforcement too long to just walk away." He turned the page. "Don't tell me I should've waited for the police. The guy would've been long gone."

"All I could think about is how devastated the kids, especially Emily, would be if something happened to you."

"Sorry. I just tried to do the right thing. I figured the guy ditched the gun and was unarmed."

"In all my years as a cop, I've never been that close to being a victim."

"Well, it helps that you have a badge and a gun."

"Good point. At least we've got trace evidence from your coat. If the guy's DNA is there, we'll find it." Brill leaned her head back on the couch and listened to the silence. "Seems weird with Emily gone."

Kurt nodded. "That's why I went out in the first place. I just don't enjoy being home alone on Saturday night."

"You weren't alone. I was here. Then again, the way things are with us, I guess it's the same as being alone."

"Actually it's much harder."

She wasn't going to ask him to elaborate.

"I need to tell you about something else that happened tonight." Kurt tented his fingers. "I was walking around the square, just kind of taking everything in, and I heard someone call my name. I turned around. It was Victoria. I couldn't believe it."

Brill tensed up just hearing the woman's name spoken out loud. "What is *she* doing here?"

"My sentiments exactly. She said the TV station sent her on assignment to cover the kidnapping case. It was awkward running

into her. I told her you and I are back together and made it clear I
didn't want to run into her again. I thought you should know."

"The woman's like a bad penny."

"Well, you have nothing to worry about."

"I'm not worried, because I don't care what you do."

Kurt set the magazine down. "There's no way you really mean
that."

"Yes, I do. I'm staying in this marriage to provide a safe haven for
Emily, but I refuse to worry about your fidelity ever again. It's pretty
hard to get hurt if I'm not emotionally involved."

"I understand your reluctance to trust me. All I can do is reiterate
my commitment. You are the only woman I've ever loved. I fell flat
on my face. I know that. But whether you care or not, I'm committed
to you and you alone."

Brill rolled her eyes. "Until the first time Victoria throws herself
at you."

"She did, actually. I walked away. I'm telling you because I *want*
to be accountable."

"Why? You have a green light to do whatever you want."

Kurt folded his hands between his knees and shook his head.
"Brill, think about what you just said. I'm a Christian, for crying out
loud. I don't have a green light to have sex with anyone but my wife."

"Well, your wife isn't interested."

"You weren't interested in sex back then either. That didn't
change the rules."

She looked over at him and studied his expression. "You've *never*
said that to me before."

"It would've sounded like I was making excuses. There aren't any."

"You felt like I wasn't interested?"

"What else was I supposed to think? You were so wrapped up in your job you stopped making time for *us*. I complained, but you stopped listening. That didn't give me the right to cheat. It just made it easier to deceive myself. Truth is, I find you more attractive than any woman on the planet."

"Why didn't I know that?"

Kurt shrugged. "Maybe I never said it exactly that way. Maybe I didn't even know it at the time like I do now. I've been on my knees a lot in the past eighteen months."

"Do you know I don't even pray anymore? I'm so far from God it's pathetic."

"He's only as far away as your own heart."

"My heart is a dark cave. It's empty." Her eyes filled with tears and Kurt was suddenly a blur. She hated it when she got emotional. It never made her feel better.

"The Bible says He'll never leave us or forsake us. Your heart may *feel* empty, but there's no way He left you."

"I don't know why I'm talking to you about this." She got up off the couch. "I'm going to bed."

"I wish you'd stay and talk. This is the closest we've gotten to real conversation in a very long time."

"Yes, and that's exactly why I'm leaving."

CHAPTER 35

THE next morning, frost covered the ground and the foothills looked as if they'd been dusted with snow. Brill sat at the table in front of the bay window, her hands wrapped round a mug of coffee, all too aware that Emily's place was empty.

Kurt came into the kitchen and gave her uniform the once-over, obviously disappointed that she wasn't dressed for church. Did he really think she had changed her mind about going to his Sunday school class?

"Tessa gave us some blueberry muffins, if you'd like to have one," he said.

"Thanks, but I'm content with just coffee."

She hoped he wouldn't bring up her teary moment last night. She should never have mentioned how empty she felt and wasn't eager to talk about it again.

"You ever going to take a day off?" he said.

"Not 'til we solve this case."

"You can't keep working seven days a week. You're going to burn out."

Brill took a sip of coffee. "I'm fine. Work's therapeutic. I guess you're teaching again this morning?"

"Uh-huh."

"I thought you hate getting up in front of people."

"I do. But I think it's what I'm supposed to do right now."

Oh, that's right. He was *called*. She wasn't taking the conversation that direction.

She studied Kurt as he opened a Tupperware container and put two muffins on a salad plate. He looked quite handsome in his starched and pressed light blue dress shirt and black trousers. She wondered what they used to talk about when they were alone together. Kids? Politics? Church? If she eliminated discussions about work and family, she'd had more meaningful conversations with strangers on a park bench.

Kurt was aging more gracefully than she. It didn't seem fair that three pregnancies had permanently padded her waist and behind while he stayed lean as ever. He had a slight thickening around the middle, but not much, though she hadn't seen him completely undressed in a long time. He had laugh lines and a few gray hairs mixed in with the brown but could still pass for Kevin Costner's brother, right down to the charming grin. No wonder Victoria couldn't wait to get her claws into him.

You weren't interested in sex back then either. That didn't change the rules.

Kurt's words had hit a nerve. Had she rebuffed his advances to the point where he was vulnerable to sexual temptation? Was she partly responsible for the emotional climate that precipitated his affair?

"Brill …?"

She was suddenly aware that Kurt was talking to her.

"I'm sorry, what?"

"Any idea when you'll be home?"

"No, I've got to deal with the shooting on top of everything else and clear out my in-box before it overtakes my office. Listen, about last night … don't make too much of what I said about my heart being an empty cave and all that. I get dramatic when I'm tired."

"I'm glad we talked."

"Why? It never changes anything."

"It might if we'd keep going. I'd much rather deal with your anger and frustration than live with indifference day after day. You have a right to be mad at me, Brill. But what's going on between us is hurting our kids more than my unfaithfulness. We need to resolve it. At least have some peace in our home."

Brill wiped her mouth with a napkin, her mind flashing back to the foolish kiss she wished had never happened. Her offense wasn't as serious as Kurt's, but she was more dishonest.

She downed the last of her coffee and then stood and carried her mug to the dishwasher.

"I don't have the emotional energy to resolve this right now," she said. "It's all I can do to deal with the fact that gangs have gotten a foothold in my town."

"I know. I just want you to think about last night's conversation with an open mind. I meant everything I said."

Tessa looked up as Emily and Jasmine came down the wooden staircase, each dressed from head to toe in her Sunday best, which included the feather hats they had found in Tessa's old trunk.

Antonio let out a wolf whistle. "Aren't you two something? Come down here and let me look at you."

The girls stepped into the entry hall, held out the bottom of their dresses as if they might curtsy, and then turned three hundred and sixty degrees.

"Now that's a sight," Antonio nudged Tessa with his elbow. "Aren't they beautiful?"

"Oh my, yes." Tessa put her hand to her mouth. "I wish my Aunt Nettie could see you. She just loved those hats."

"Can we keep them on at church?" Emily said.

"Yes, but we may have to sit over on the side so we don't distract people from the worship. You are just too cute."

Abby put her front paws on Emily's leg and looked up at her and meowed.

Tessa laughed. "I'll just bet you would love to play with those feathers." She cracked the front door. "Go find Pouncer."

"I'll back the car out," Antonio said.

The front door creaked and slowly opened until Mr. Quinlan, clad in blue and red flannel pajamas, was in full view on the front stoop.

He looked at the two girls, his faded blue eyes suddenly wide and animated. "Well, Wilma and Wanda Hollingsworth, you look positively stunning. I would be honored if the two of you would accompany me to the harvest dance."

Antonio rolled his eyes. "I'll call Junior."

Emily whispered something in Jasmine's ear, and then the girls took Mr. Quinlan's hands.

"Why, we'd be delighted to go to the dance with you," Emily said.

Tessa followed the girls as they led Mr. Quinlan out to the kitchen table.

He sat down and looked at up at the girls, his thin, white eyebrows forming a straight line. "Who are you?"

"I'm Emil—I mean, Wanda Hollingsworth. And this is Wilma."

"*Double trouble!*" He wagged his finger. "You have a lot of nerve showing your faces around here. Father made it clear that I'm not to cavort with the likes of you."

Emily pressed her lips together to keep from laughing, then looked over at Tessa and said, "What does 'cavort' mean?"

"It means our friend here is confused. Mr. Quinlan, why don't I get you a fresh-baked blueberry muffin while we wait for Junior?"

"I've had my fill of blueberries. Tommy Rickers and I ate so many we threw up. But we brought Mother a bucket load for cobbler."

Jasmine covered her smile with her hand. "Why is he saying that?"

"Mr. Quinlan has dementia," Emily whispered. "He gets a little mixed up."

Tessa cut a blueberry muffin in two and set it on a saucer in front of Mr. Quinlan. He devoured it without comment.

A few minutes later there was a knock on the door, and Junior Quinlan came inside, still in his bathrobe and slippers. Tessa saw the fear in his eyes.

"I am so sorry," he said. "I don't know what we're going to do with Dad. We keep thinking we can handle him by ourselves, but it seems like he's starting to wander almost every day. Thanks for calling. I hope he didn't make you late for church."

"No, we're fine."

Junior saw the girls and did a double take, a smile stretching his cheeks. "Is that you, Emily?"

"Yes, and this is my friend Jasmine. Tessa's letting us wear her Aunt Nettie's favorite hats to church."

"I see that." Junior looked at Tessa and winked. "Those are really fancy feathers. Mighty pretty. Come on, Dad." He took Mr. Quinlan by the arm. "Let's let these nice people get to church."

Tessa walked them to the door.

"Thanks again," Junior said. "Mary Ann and I are exploring options for Dad. I appreciate you being so caring while we're pulling our hair out. It's a hard decision."

Tessa patted Junior on the back. "I know it is. We're glad to help."

Brill stood at the window in her office and admired the hazy autumn landscape, lush in rich shades of crimson, burnt orange, and gold and the bluish outline of the Great Smoky Mountains in the distance. High above the foothills, a dozen vultures, wings fully spread, seemed to glide effortlessly in the thermals.

There was a knock on the door and David waltzed through the doorway, his arm in a sling.

"Good morning to you," he said.

"How are feeling?"

"I'm not." He laughed. "The Vicodin's working."

"Why are you here? I thought the doctor told you to take a day off."

"The doctor doesn't have to live with the nonstop action in my head. I've got a case to solve. I don't have time to be down."

Brill nodded. "I understand that emotion. Has any new evidence surfaced on the kidnappings?"

"No. Same old. Victim number seven won't keep his mouth shut about being snatched by red shadows. The media's eating it up. I wish we could match the hair DNA to someone, so we could announce another *human* suspect in the case. So far Guerrero's arrest hasn't stopped the red shadows hype. How's Kurt?"

"He's fine. I still can't believe he chased the shooter."

"Maybe the trace evidence from his coat will give you something."

"I hope."

"Brill, did you tell Kurt what happened between us?"

She felt her face get hot. "No. I'd just as soon forget it."

"Me, too. When he showed up last night, I almost blew it. I thought he'd come looking for me and asked if you'd talked to him. He thought I was referring to Guerrero's arrest."

"For heaven's sake, David. I feel bad enough about what happened. Don't you dare say anything to Kurt. If I decide to tell him, it'll be after the case is closed and you're back in Knoxville."

"Fair enough. I really am sorry. It's not going to happen again."

"No …" She looked out at the foothills. "It's not."

Her phone vibrated and she put it to her ear. "Yes, Trent."

"You're not going to believe this, ma'am. The Glock Kurt found last night is the gun that killed Hector Sanchez."

"Now, *that's* a twist I didn't expect."

"It's registered to a guy by the name of Allen Seconna. Lives in Knoxville. Works at night and bought it for protection but reported it missing about a month ago. There's more: Looks like the shooter tried to wipe it clean and missed. We found an index fingerprint that matches the driver's license fingerprint of Eduardo Mendez, who gave an address on Mockingbird Lane here in Sophie Trace. We've been to that address. His parents say he doesn't live at home anymore and doesn't come by the house very often. We've got the place staked out and are trying to locate our informant to see if he knows anything about this Eduardo Mendez."

"Good work, Trent."

"I saved the best for last, ma'am. You might want to sit down for this. Saliva DNA on the gun matches the hair follicle DNA found in Janice Evans's Mustang."

"Good grief. It's *all* connected." Brill caught David's gaze; his eyes were the size of quarters. "So Mendez was involved in the kidnappings, at least Janice Evans's. And he's looking good for Hector Sanchez's murder *and* last night's shooting."

"And the drive-by at the Sanchezes'. Same gun. This is huge. We'll have Mendez's picture out to the media shortly."

"Wonderful. Let's get this piece of trash off the street."

David's phone vibrated. "Special Agent Riley. Yeah, I just heard … amazing … after all that to get sloppy with a fingerprint. This Smartie's a real dummy. Get with Brill's detectives and keep me posted. I want this guy's head on a stick."

David put his phone in his pocket, looked at her, and laughed. "This is why I love this job. Come on. Let's go take a look at Eduardo Mendez's driver's license photo. We ought to have Kurt take a look."

"He never saw the guy's face up close. He can describe everything else about him to a T."

Kurt pushed open the side door at Cross Way Bible Fellowship, feeling very good about the lesson he presented to his Sunday school class. He almost felt as if he were someone else as the words flowed out of him. The only thing missing was someone to share his excitement with.

Thank You, Lord. We did it.

He got in the Caravan and put the key in the ignition when his cell phone rang. He saw on the LED screen that it was Brill.

"Hey there."

"Are you still at church?"

"Just leaving."

"I need you to come down to the station and take a look at some pictures. The gun you found last night was not only used to shoot David, it was used to kill that twelve-year-old boy, Hector Sanchez. We matched a print on it to a man named Eduardo Mendez. And the saliva DNA on the gun matches the hair follicle on Janice Evans's Mustang."

"So the same people were involved in the kidnappings and the shootings?"

"Sure looks that way. If we can get this Mendez character, maybe he'll lead us to the others."

"I never saw his face up close enough to identify him. I told you he sounded Latino."

"Come look anyway. Maybe something will stand out. Mendez's driver's license info says he's five feet six and weighs a hundred and seventy pounds."

"The kid I saw last night was about that height, but I doubt he weighed more than one forty. I put that in my statement."

"He could've lost weight. I just want you to take a look at the photo on Mendez's driver's license."

"All right. I'll grab a burger and be right there." *My class went great, thanks for asking.*

"Good grief," she said. "Eduar*do*. Doe. That's it. Doe. Why didn't I catch it sooner?"

"Brill, what are you talking about?"

"I'll tell you when I see you. I've got to go."

CHAPTER 36

BRILL sat with David across the table from Raphael Guerrero, who was outfitted in an orange jumpsuit and a very sour expression. His attorney, Robert Harris, sat next to him, his hands folded on the table.

"We're about to bust your pal Eduardo Mendez," David said. "I told you when we get the other guy I'd offer the same deal to both of you, and the first one to take it wins. Here's your chance to get a head start."

"I'm not dealing."

Harris leaned over and lowered his voice. "Raphael, you need to listen to—"

"Are you deaf, man? No deals. I never even heard of this Mendez person."

"As your attorney, I must advise you—"

Raphael shook his head. "No. No. And no."

"I thought you guys were supposed to be *Smarties*," David said. "This Mendez is a moron. He left his fingerprint on the gun used in last night's shooting, and ballistics said it's the same gun that killed Hector Sanchez. Does murdering a twelve-year-old and dumping his body on the street make you feel *smart*, Raphael?"

"I had nothing to do with that kid's death."

"You're in it up to your ears," David said. "We're not just talking five counts of engaging in organized criminal activity anymore. We're talking capital murder. Do you get that, smart boy?"

"Raphael, I think you should consider—"

"I said *no*."

"You'd rather rot in jail the rest of your life than finger a loser like Mendez?" David threw his hands in the air. "The jury won't feel sorry for you. As far as they're concerned, you're a kid killer. You know what they do to kid killers in prison?"

Brill leaned forward, her arms folded on the table. "Raphael, we know Eduardo goes by the name Doe and is dealing cocaine. Give us the name of his supplier. Tell us why Eduardo killed Hector Sanchez. We know Hector was dealing blow at the middle school. What did Hector do that got him killed? The DEA is on the way, and once they're involved, there's nothing we can do to help you."

Harris put his lips to his client's ear and whispered something.

Raphael shook his head. "I never heard of Eduardo Mendez. I don't want a deal."

"I strongly advise you to—"

"Shut up! No deal."

"Then you're going away, *stupid*," David said. "You want to rot in jail for the rest of your days, it's your choice."

Raphael snickered. "It's not all bad. And it's better than being cut into pieces like a side of beef."

"Look," Brill said, "I know you've been told you can never get out—that you either do things their way or pay. But if you help us, we can protect you."

Raphael slammed his hands on the table. "No, you *can't!* Forget it. I don't want a deal."

"Suit yourself," David said. "I'm done with this weakling."

Brill locked gazes with Raphael and couldn't seem to let go. "I believe you had nothing to do with killing Hector Mendez. Are the people you're protecting really worth it? They'll disown you without a second thought. Why sacrifice the rest of your life to protect them? They lied to you, Raphael. You *can* get out of the gang. You don't have to wear this ball and chain for the rest of your life. But you have to work with us."

"Listen to her," Harris said.

Raphael looked from Brill to David and back to Brill. "You have *no* idea who you're dealing with. I'd rather have three squares a day and keep all my body parts."

David smirked. "And you don't think the DEA will take you apart?"

"My client's done talking," Harris said. "Raphael, don't say anything else."

"Guard! Take me back to my cell." Raphael rose to his feet and looked down at Brill. "Look … if this Mendez guy, whom I've never met, ends up in the hands of the Drug Enforcement Administration, don't assume they're working with the right premise. I'm sure you'll figure it out, but I doubt this windbag next to you even knows what I'm talking about."

Tessa and Antonio sat at a booth at Nick's Grill with Emily and Jasmine, who were still wearing Aunt Nettie's feather hats and were quite the spectacle. Nearly every eye in the place was on them.

Nick came over to the booth, a smile tugging at his cheeks.

"I have to say those are about the coolest-looking hats I've ever seen. I wonder what other fun things a person could find in Tessa's old trunk? Maybe I'll come over and take a look."

"Oh, we found lots of fun things," Emily said. "We even found a Navy uniform that her big brother, Larry, wore when he was in World War II in the Philippians."

Tessa patted Emily's hand. "That's *Philippines*, honey."

Emily giggled. "Oh, yeah. Philippians is in the New Testament. Anyway, we each got to try on the Navy uniform and the tie and the white hat."

"We also got to wear these really soft silk robes," Jasmine said. "Larry bought them when he was in the Navy. They're really pretty colors, and my favorite one was black with a red dragon on it."

Nick smiled. "My parents had a cedar chest full of fun stuff my dad saved from the war. He even had some Japanese money. Bills. My brother and I were allowed to play with it once in a while."

"We found something I'll bet you never got to play with," Emily said. "Guess what it was."

"Hmm …" Nick looked up, his eyes moving one way, and then the other. Finally he shrugged. "I give up."

"Dolls!" Emily nudged Jasmine with her elbow.

"Okay …" Maggie set a large tray on a stand. "I've got three orders of chicken salad on whole wheat with sweet potato fries. And one triple bacon cheese burger deluxe with onion rings."

"That's mine," Antonio said sheepishly. "Tomorrow I'll eat celery and carrots."

"I should think so," Tessa mumbled.

Emily's phone rang, and she looked surprised. She reached in her small purse and put the phone to her ear.

"Hello. Oh, hi, Mom. We're at Nick's Grill with Tessa and Tony. We got to play in this big trunk and wear Aunt Nettie's feather hats to church and everybody said they loved them. And I got to go to Sunday school with Jasmine, and I won the prize because I already knew the Bible verse. I want you to meet Jasmine at the open house Tuesday night—and her parents. What are you doing …? Well, I hope you arrest all of the kidnappers so you won't have to work so hard …"

Emily looked over at Tessa. "Um, I think we're going to take Tony home so he can watch the football game, and then we're going to Walmart with Tessa and then back to their house and play dress-up some more.… I've already done my homework, and I'd really like to stay longer.… Okay, I love you, too. Bye."

Brill sat at the conference table in her office, going through the case file on Hector Sanchez. The photographs taken at the crime scene and in the medical examiner's lab were disturbing. Not only because he was so young, but because he was shot in the head at close range, consistent with an execution-style killing. What could a twelve-year-old have done that was serious enough to warrant this? Couldn't someone have roughed him up to teach him a lesson? It wouldn't be difficult to intimidate a child that age.

Brill sighed. When Ryan was twelve, he was in Little League and the worst drugs he encountered were refined sugar and caffeine in his soft drinks.

She pictured Anna and Hector, much like she remembered Ryan and Vanessa when they were growing up, lying on their backs in a grassy meadow, gazing up at a bright blue sky painted with white billowy clouds, and talking about imaginary things like faraway kingdoms, giant slayers, and superheroes. Telling secrets and dreaming about what they wanted to be when they grew up.

She thought about Anna and Hector's immigrant parents and the tiny, stucco home in which they had been living with five children. Did their kids even dare to dream? Or did they assume that one day they, too, would hold jobs that paid too little money and demanded too many hours? Always owing the landlord and credit card companies and always going to the emergency room when they needed medical care?

What a temptation it would be for a kid like Hector to buy into the mind-set that, if people were buying drugs anyway, he might as well get in on some of the profit. Doesn't every middle schooler want an iPod and an iPhone and clothes with designer labels? Wouldn't a Latino male from a low-income family want "juice" from his classmates instead of scorn? Wouldn't he jump at the chance to "be somebody"?

So who was this Eduardo "Doe" Mendez, and what was his relationship to Hector? How did they first meet? What promises did Doe use to lure a twelve-year-old into the underworld of drugs, deception, and danger?

She looked through the information her detectives had compiled so far. Eduardo Luis Mendez. Age twenty-one. Born in Houston. Parents U.S. citizens. No siblings. No arrests. Never been in trouble with the law. Parents said he was once a happy kid. Outgoing. Highly intelligent. In the past twelve months he'd had a personality change. Seemed belligerent and unable to get along with people. Got kicked out of junior college for fighting. Stopped bringing his friends home. Parents didn't see him much. Had no idea where or if he was working. An APB had been issued on his 2009 Black Ford F-150 pickup.

She heard a knock on the door and Trent walked in.

"Sorry to bother you, ma'am, but I know you're waiting for the lab results on the trace evidence found on Kurt's coat. We've got skin cell DNA, but it doesn't match Eduardo Mendez's."

"So there's a *third* party involved," she said.

"Yes, ma'am. But number three's in the system. DNA is a match to twenty-two-year-old man by the name of Jorge Alvarez. He was arrested last year for assaulting and spitting on the president of Langley College. He paid a fine and did community service. We've put out an APB out for his vehicle: a red 2005 Silverado.

"Interesting … each of these guys seems to have some kind of grievance with the education system. That certainly goes along with the idea that the Smarties had something to prove."

Tessa walked into Walmart, enjoying the sound of Emily and Jasmine's chattering.

"I shouldn't be long in here," Tessa said. "You girls see if you can remember fertilizer for my orchids and cat food for Abby. I forgot to write those on my list."

Tessa smiled at George Franklin, the delightful African-American man with white hair that always greeted customers on the weekends.

"Hello, Mr. Franklin. How are you doing?"

"I'm doin' splendidly. And you?"

"Oh, I'm having the best weekend. Well, as you can see, I have some special visitors."

Tessa introduced the girls to Mr. Franklin, who scratched his chin, his smile lighting up his eyes.

"My, my, my," he said, "What marvelous hats. My mama wore the finest hats in all of Mississippi, and when she passed, my sisters saved every one, thinking they'd have granddaughters someday." He chuckled. "Between us we had thirteen grandsons, but the first granddaughter is due in January. Think that child will be just a little spoiled?"

"Wow," Emily said, "she'll have *all* those hats to herself."

Jasmine nodded. "Cool."

Mr. Franklin pulled a cart loose from the stack and pushed it to Tessa. "You ladies have a nice time shopping. I enjoyed meeting you girls."

"Nice meeting you," Emily and Jasmine said at the same time.

Tessa pushed the cart to the pharmacy department and picked up a few items, and then moved over to garden center and got fertilizer, then to the grocery department and added what she had on the list.

"I think that's everything," Tessa said.

"You wanted to remember cat food," Emily said.

"You're absolutely right. It's in the next aisle."

Tessa turned the cart around and almost ran headlong into a young Hispanic man. She locked gazes with him, her heart doing flip-flops, and felt the heat color her cheeks. Did he recognize her, too?

"Excuse me," she said. "Come on, girls. We're in this young man's way.

Jasmine turned. "Eduardo! Why are you here?"

"You think I don't eat?"

"Everybody, this is my cousin Eduardo."

The young man nodded, his eyes seeming to survey whatever was in the aisle behind Tessa. "Have to run. I'm in a hurry."

Eduardo brushed past Jasmine and several other customers, then turned the corner and disappeared.

"He didn't used to be rude like that," Jasmine said.

"Tessa, why is your face so red?" Emily took her arm. "Are you okay?"

"It just feels a little warm to me. Let's go get these items checked out."

Tessa hardly remembered walking to the checkout. She paid for the purchase and left Walmart, barely aware of Emily and Jasmine thanking her for the Skittles.

She got in the car and looked in the rearview mirror as she backed out of the parking space, conscious that Eduardo stood leaning on his black pickup in the row behind them, talking on his cell phone. She'd seen those dark, empty eyes before—and she was certain he knew it.

CHAPTER 37

KURT, still dressed in his church clothes, sat in Brill's office and studied the mug shot of Jorge Alvarez.

"So this is the little punk who held a knife to my throat …?" Kurt said. "I really never saw his face, but I'd sure be able to identify him if I could see him on the move."

"We don't really need you to ID him," Brill said. "We got his DNA off your coat collar and have an APB out for his arrest." She laid another picture in front of him. "Humor me and take another look at this driver's license photo of Eduardo Mendez."

Kurt shook his head. "I don't recognize him."

"His fingerprint was on the gun you found, and we know the gun was used to shoot David and also to kill Hector Sanchez. DNA from your coat almost nails Jorge Alvarez as David's shooter. I think Eduardo Mendez looks good for Hector Sanchez's murder, but I'm a long way from proving it. I believe Eduar*do* is the *Doe* Anna told me was supplying Hector with cocaine. I just don't know what went wrong that would cause him to execute a child."

"Wait a minute," Kurt said. "I'm confused. I thought you said you found Mendez's DNA on the gun?"

"Just his fingerprint. We don't know whose DNA is on the gun. It doesn't match anyone in the system, but it does match the DNA from the hair follicle in Janice Evans's Mustang. So we know this perp is tied to the shooting and at least one of the kidnappings."

Kurt looked again at man in the photo. "So if you find this Eduardo Mendez and his DNA matches, it'll prove he shot the boy and kidnapped Janice Evans?"

"It'll prove he handled the gun and was in her car." Brill lifted her eyebrows. "We still have to work our magic to get Mendez to confess."

Kurt shook his head. "It's so weird coming down here to look at photos. In all the years you've been a cop, I've never been a witness before."

"Your deciding to follow a suspect was reckless," she said. "But as it turns out, finding the gun was a huge break."

Tessa pulled the car in the garage and let the door close behind it, her mind still reeling from her unexpected encounter with Eduardo Mendez. There was no doubt in her mind that he was the young hoodlum she caught spray-painting the side of the museum and who hurled his paint can and shattered her windshield.

The gang had used the same graffiti to taunt the police and claim responsibility for the kidnappings. Is that what Rosa was arguing with her cousin about? Did she know Eduardo was involved?

Tessa rubbed her temples. Should she call Rosa and try to get answers before she called the police? How she hated to ruin a delightful weekend for Jasmine and Emily by embarrassing poor Jasmine this way.

"Tessa, are you sure you're okay?" Emily said. "You want me to go get Tony?"

"No, honey. I'm fine. I was just distracted with something else. Okay ... let's get the groceries into the house. And then you girls can rummage through that second trunk and see what you can find."

Tessa carried as many sacks as she could from the garage to the kitchen, and the girls carried the rest.

"I'll put this away," Tessa said. "You girls go have fun."

Emily and Jasmine ran up the stairs, squealing, Abby on their heels.

Antonio came into the kitchen and kissed her on the cheek. "That didn't take long. What happened to your smile? When you left here an hour ago, you were glowing."

"I saw him," she whispered. "I saw the ruffian that broke my windshield."

"Where?"

Tessa stopped and listened until she was sure she heard two sets of footsteps overhead, and then told Antonio about her brief and uncomfortable encounter with Eduardo Mendez.

"I will never forget those dark, empty eyes," Tessa said. "I'm positive it was the same young man. And he recognized me, too. I'm sure of it. What should I do? He's dangerous. And I don't know if Rosa's safe. You didn't see how rough he was with her."

Antonio took her hands in his. "Let's think about this a minute. The girls will probably be here until after dinner. You can't wait that long to call Brill. If this Eduardo is dangerous, she needs to know. And if he knows you recognized him, he might try to leave town. He has to be nervous that they already got one of his gang members on five counts of kidnapping or whatever it was."

"Engaging in organized criminal activity." Tessa stopped and inclined her ear toward the kitchen door. "What was that noise?"

"It's just the girls, love. Don't lose your train of thought. We were talking about your not waiting to tell Brill."

"Well, you're right, of course. I *can't* wait."

"Oh, I think you can."

Tessa froze, her heart filled with dread. She didn't have to see the young man's face to recognize his voice.

Brill sat in her office going through every detail of Hector Sanchez's case file. What did this kid do that got him killed? Or what did he know? How was he connected to the kidnappings? Or were they two independent crimes?

David stuck his head in her office.

"They just sat Jorge Alvarez in the interrogation room."

Brill stood. "What a break getting his DNA off Kurt's coat."

"Be glad he didn't know Kurt was married to the police chief or he would have slit his throat." David said. "I'm going to pin this guy to the wall and get him to finger Mendez."

Brill hurried to the interrogation room, where a Hispanic man dressed in a navy blue hooded sweatshirt sat, his hands folded on the table. His hair was pulled back into a ponytail like Raphael Guerrero's.

Brill sat opposite him, David next to her.

"Let's cut to the chase," David said. "We got your DNA off the coat of the guy you put in a headlock last night and threatened to cut from ear to ear. He saw you shoot me, stash your gun under the bushes, and then try to blend into the crowd. You're nailed, *Smartie* pants. Unless you start naming names, you're going away for capital murder."

"Murder?" Jorge's dark eyes grew wide. "I didn't kill anybody. I admit I shot into the crowd, but I wasn't trying to kill anybody."

"Really?" David leaned forward. "What *were* you trying to do? You're too smart to think I'm that dumb."

Jorge sat silently staring at his hands.

"Maybe you were dissing the cops for arresting Raphael Guerrero?" David said. "You know the drill. If you get caught, the gang disowns you. So unless you start talking, your DNA will talk for you. We both know Eduardo Mendez killed Hector Sanchez. But your DNA's on the gun. Unless you help us, you're going to prison and he walks."

Jorge wrung his hands, beads of sweat popping out on his forehead.

"You can't prove I killed that kid because I didn't. I should be talking to an attorney."

"Go ahead," David said. "Get a legal mouthpiece. It just proves you've got something to hide. But it really doesn't matter. Your DNA was collected from the collar of the witness you threatened to cut and who saw you shoot into the crowd. Getting a jury to believe you killed that twelve-year-old will be a slam-dunk."

"It wasn't me."

"I know." David flashed a fake grin. "It was Eduardo Mendez. But I don't really care who goes down for it. You can take the rap or tell us the truth. Right now, *your* DNA is on the gun. And we've got an eyewitness to the shooting. Who do you think the jury's going to believe?"

Brill studied Jorge's face and wondered if he was buying what David was telling him.

"There's no way my DNA is on that gun."

"Oh, but there is. Maybe you had an itch on your face and scratched it with the side of barrel."

"I didn't."

"Look, Jorge. You're nailed for the shooting. The only question is whether you're going to get charged with capital murder in the death of Hector Sanchez."

"Come on, man. I didn't kill that kid. It was no secret he was dealing blow at the middle school. I don't do drugs, and I don't sell them. Maybe he stepped on someone's toes or infringed on someone's territory."

David's eyes turned to slits and he leaned forward. "Did Eduardo Mendez supply Hector Sanchez with cocaine?"

"How should I know?"

"Don't answer my question with a question, Jorge. It ticks me off. And you don't want to tick me off!" David pounded the table with his fist. "*Did* Eduardo Mendez supply Hector Sanchez with cocaine—yes or no?"

Jorge started to say something and then didn't.

David stood and pushed back his chair until it fell over backward and crashed to the floor.

"Yes or no, Jorge? You've got five seconds to answer, and then I'm done with you. One. Two. Three. Four—"

"Okay! Eduardo was supplying the kid!"

"Much better." David picked up his chair with his good hand and sat. "Now ... *did* Eduardo Mendez shoot Hector Sanchez?"

"I don't know, man."

"Yes, you do."

"How could I know something like that? I wasn't there."

"Mendez was one of your comrade gangbangers. Maybe it was part of the initiation."

Jorge shook his head. "It wasn't. The kidnappings and dissing the cops were the initiation. You saw the graffiti. There was no killing involved."

"So Mendez shot the kid on his own, independent of the gang?"

"I don't know. How many times do I have to say it?"

Brill put her hand on David's arm and squeezed to silence him. "Jorge, look at me." She saw raw fear in his eyes—fear of something worse than being charged with capital murder. "What are you really afraid of? What is it you aren't you telling us?"

"Nothing."

"I don't think you're protecting Eduardo Mendez. What you're protecting is the *reason* he killed Hector."

Jorge shook his head. "I've got nothing to say."

"But you *know*."

"Ask Eduardo. Let him speak for himself."

"I'm asking you. Why did Eduardo kill Hector? It's eating you alive. Just say it. Get it off your chest."

Jorge wiped the sweat off his lip with his sleeve. "I can't talk to you. Do I look like I want to die?"

Brill studied his face, her mind racing, and could almost hear the gunshot ring out as her intuition kicked in.

"No wonder you're afraid. Eduardo was *ordered* to kill Hector, wasn't he?"

Jorge flinched.

"That's it. Eduardo was Hector's cocaine supplier, and he couldn't keep his mouth shut. He bragged to the boy about the kidnappings *before* you even finished the job. And the boss found out, didn't he, Jorge? He had to punish Eduardo, so he made him kill Hector. Am I right? Is that how it went down? The boss ordered Eduardo to murder a little kid in cold blood? And you all had to watch? That must've made you all feel *very* smart."

"Shut up!" Jorge put his hands over his ears, his eyes brimming with tears. "I want a lawyer. Just get me a lawyer."

Brill stood outside the interrogation room and looked through the two-way mirror as Jorge Alvarez met with his court-appointed attorney.

"You did a good job in there," David said.

"I won't feel good 'til we have Mendez, his boss, and every one of the Smarties behind bars. I'm busting up this gang for good."

"A bunch of losers."

Brill sighed. "But each of them is somebody's son. What a waste of brainpower. If they'd spent half as much effort using their intelligence for something good, they could've made a real difference. They were just so busy being mad. Bitterness was the real enemy. It's probably killed more people than guns."

"You going to get philosophical on me?"

Brill turned around and leaned her back against the glass. "Haven't you ever been bitter?"

"Sure, I'm bitter about Patricia leaving me. But I'm not going to join a gang and plot out an elaborate kidnapping."

"That's a relief. You'd be a bear to interrogate. Besides, you don't have the hair for it."

David laughed and rubbed the stubble on his head. "What—you don't think I could grow my hair out long enough for a ponytail?"

"By the end of the century, maybe."

Trent came around the corner from the detective bureau and stood in the hallway.

"Ma'am, one of our patrol officers spotted a 2009 Black Ford F-150 like the one registered to Eduardo Mendez. He followed it to the four hundred block of Azalea Lane, where it's now parked. The suspect is not in the vehicle. Rousseaux and I are headed that way."

Before Brill could react, her phone beeped and she took it off her belt clip and looked at the text message:

MOM, COME TO TESSA'S ASAP.
JASMINE'S COUSIN IS GOING TO KILL US.

CHAPTER 38

Tessa sat at the kitchen table with Antonio, Emily, and Jasmine, acutely aware of two things: that the barrel of Eduardo's gun was shaking, and that she was liable to start retching at any moment.

The afternoon sky had turned dark gray and pellets of sleet were lightly falling.

Eduardo turned his head and looked out the kitchen window and swore under his breath.

Tears rolled down Jasmine's cheeks. "You're in big trouble, Eduardo."

"Save it, brat. You think I don't know that?" Eduardo glared at Tessa. "You're the only person who can tie me to the gang. I should've just shot you at Walmart while I had the chance."

Antonio took her hand and held it. He was shaking too.

"Where'd all these cops come from?" Eduardo said. "I ducked in here to hide from the one who started tailing me, and now they're swarming like termites out there."

"They probably had an APB out for your arrest," Emily said.

Eduardo snickered. "Big talk for a little girl. You've been watching too many cop shows."

"My mother is the chief of police. She's never going to let you go."

"Is she serious?"

Jasmine nodded. "You're holding a cop's kid hostage. I don't think that's a good idea."

"Are you kidding?" Eduardo went over to the table and stuck his gun flush against Emily's forehead. "Barbie here is my bargaining chip."

Emily sat up straight and showed no emotion, but Tessa figured the poor thing was terrified.

The phone rang and all four hostages jumped.

"Do you have an answering machine?" Eduardo said.

Antonio nodded. "It's set up to answer on the fourth ring."

"Let the machine get it." Eduardo waved the gun. "Everybody just stay put."

Tessa wondered if four rings had ever seemed so long. Finally the machine clicked on. *You've reached the Masinos. Sorry we missed you. Leave your number and we'll call you back.*

"This is Special Agent David Riley of the FBI," came the voice from the speaker. "Eduardo Mendez, I know you're in there. Pick up the phone ..."

"Why should I talk to him?" Eduardo said. "I'm not turning myself in. He's not going to do anything as long as I've got what's-her-name over there."

"My name's Emily. And you really should pick up the phone. It's sleeting outside, and if the weather gets worse, none of us are going anywhere. I doubt you want to be stuck with no options. Make some demands. They'll work with you."

"For a pipsqueak you make a lot of sense." Eduardo moved his gaze from Emily to Jasmine to Tessa and Antonio—and back to Emily. "You answer it. Put it on speakerphone."

Emily got up and pushed the button for speaker. "This is Emily Jessup."

"Emily, this is David Riley. Are you all right?"

"Yes, we're all fine. Eduardo told me to put you on speakerphone. Everyone in here can hear you."

"Eduardo, this is a dead end for you. We've arrested Raphael Guerrero and Jorge Alvarez. They told us everything. We know you shot Hector Sanchez because you were ordered to. It's over."

"There's no way they told you that. They don't want to die."

"Not only did they sell you out, your fingerprint and DNA are on the Glock .45 Alvarez used to shoot me and that was used to shoot Hector Sanchez. And your DNA matches the hair follicle found in Janice Evans's Mustang. You're nailed, buddy. It's over. Come out with your hands up."

"You think I'm nuts, man? I don't believe you."

"All right, let me remove any doubt. We know you were supplying Hector Sanchez with cocaine and bragged to him about the kidnappings and the gang initiation before you and your buddies had finished the job. And to punish you, the boss made you go get the kid and kill him in front of the others."

"There's no way Raphael and Jorge told you that!" Eduardo ran his hand through his hair and walked in circles, waving the gun. "This is a trick."

"What trick, Eduardo? Your gang betrayed you. It's over. Come out with your hands up. No one has to get hurt. We don't believe you ever intended to kill the Sanchez boy. You were caught between a rock and hard place. The gang boss said jump and you did. A jury will understand that."

"No, they won't! You're just trying to confuse me." He went over to Emily, grabbed her by the hand, and pulled her to her feet. "I've got my gun to Emily's head. If I even smell the SWAT team, I'll kill her."

"Emily, you okay?"

"I-I'm fine." Her voice shook. "I'm my mother's daughter, right?"

Brill put her hands to her mouth and choked back the emotion. She could picture how brave Emily was trying to be. She wanted to talk to her, to reassure her, but she promised David she would stay in the background and let him handle it. She knew the drill. Don't give the perp an emotional edge.

"You okay?" She felt Kurt's hands on her shoulders and was actually glad.

"No. Are you?"

"You kidding?" Kurt said. "My knees feel like Jell-O, but it's all I can do not to storm the house, grab the guy, and beat the tar out of him."

"And get them all killed."

"Yeah, I know. That's why I'm standing out here in the sleet."

Lord, I am so scared, she thought. *Please protect my baby. I haven't said a dozen words to You in eighteen months. But I'm pleading for Emily's life. Please don't let her die. If You're trying to get my attention, You have it.*

"Are you praying?" Kurt said.

"Like nuts."

"Me, too."

"Should we call Ryan and Vanessa?"

Kurt slid his arms around her and held her back to his chest. "Let's not rock their world unless the cable networks show up. Maybe David can talk Mendez into giving up before then."

Brill gave in to Kurt's embrace, feeling at the same time guilty for using him and guilty that she had allowed David to enter her private life. It was awkward resting in Kurt's arms with the man she had allowed to kiss her not five feet away.

"Eduardo, stay cool," David said. "I'm not sending in the SWAT team. We can work something out. Give us the boss's name. Tell us the names of the others. Cooperation is the name of the game. Work with us. We can cut you a deal."

Brill felt every muscle in her body tense. The FBI SWAT team gathered in her side yard.

Lord, intervene. Please don't make us use them.

Tessa stroked Emily's ponytail as she came back to her chair at the table and Eduardo closed the kitchen curtains before he moved to the other side of the room.

"Eduardo, talk to me," David said.

"Nothing to talk about, man. I'm not betraying the gang. I wouldn't last a day in jail. It's a death sentence."

"You overestimate their power. They're nothing but thugs with high IQs. The boss made you shoot a twelve-year-old, for crying out loud.

He didn't do it. The loser's big at barking out orders but he's a coward. He handed you the gun and let you hang yourself. It's eating you up."

"You don't know anything!"

"The only thing I don't know yet is the boss's name. But I will. If you save me the trouble, the bureau will work with you. Give us his name and make things easier on yourself."

"Why do you think Raphael and Jorge didn't rat him out?"

"Because I asked them to rat *you* out. You're the one with blood on your hands. The question is: Are you going to take the fall for the boss? He humiliated you in front of the others and then forced you to do the unthinkable to gain back respect. You didn't want to shoot that kid. Are you going to let him walk while you go to prison?"

Eduardo paced, waving his gun. "You don't know who you're dealing with, man."

"I don't know his name. But I know what he's made of. And he's a coward. Are you brave enough to hold your head up and make him pay? Look what he's done to you, Eduardo. Every day you hear that gun go off in your head. Every day you see yourself dumping a dead kid's body on the street. Look what he's reduced you to. Do something. Fight back. Give us his name."

"Shut up!" Eduardo pointed the gun at the table and moved it from person to person. "I need to think. I don't want to talk anymore."

"He hung up." David looked down at the ground and swore under his breath.

Brill's mind flashed back to the moment she lifted the sheet and viewed Hector Sanchez's face when he lay dead on Jackson Street, a bullet through his head. Could she trust David to get Emily out safely? She'd seen him do it before. But she'd also been there when the outcome was tragic.

"What now?" Brill said.

"Let's wait a couple minutes and I'll call him back." David's words turned to white vapor in the late afternoon air. "I still think I can talk him down. He's not as agitated as he was."

"The guy killed a twelve-year-old in cold blood." Kurt turned to David, his eyes fierce. "He really doesn't have anything to lose. Either get your people in there or I'm going in after him myself."

David put his hand on Kurt's shoulder. "The SWAT team doesn't have a clear shot. Trust me, the best approach for now is to keep Eduardo calm. I'm sure the wood floors creak in that old house. If he hears us come in, he's liable to start shooting."

Brill brushed the sleet out of her hair. "David's right, Kurt. We just have to wait it out." *Lord, please don't let Emily die. I'll forgive Kurt. I'll stop being hateful. Just don't let her die.*

"Could I make you something to eat?" Tessa said. "Or get you something to drink?"

"Trying to butter me up, old woman? It won't work!"

"She just wants you to calm down," Emily said. "You're scaring us and we didn't do anything to you."

"Well, I'm not letting her pick up a knife to make me a sandwich. You think I'm stupid?" Eduardo held up his fist.

"I've got pizza rolls in the freezer," Tessa said. "They just need microwaving. It's very simple. And they're quite tasty."

Eduardo paced and then stopped to look at Jasmine.

"All right. Let Jasmine do it. You try anything, little cousin, and I'll blow your pretty head off and not think twice. Go."

Jasmine pulled the pizza rolls out of the freezer as Tessa gave her directions on how to microwave them.

"May I ask you a question?" Tessa said.

"Whatever."

"How did you get those seven people to the Indian burial ground? I'm fascinated. It really was a brilliantly executed plan to make people think the red shadows did it."

"We spiked their orange juice with Rohypnol, better known as roofies, then put them in the back of the van, and drove them there. Seventh Mound isn't far from the town of Cherokee."

"That's it?" Emily said.

Eduardo curled his lip. "That part was easy. The kidnappings were perfectly timed, and the number seven thing was clever. It was a blast dissing the cops."

"I'm glad you had blast," Emily said flatly. "One of your victims' twin boys are in our class at school, and another teaches the first grade there. We were all sad and really scared."

"I guess I should feel real proud of myself, is that what you're saying?" Eduardo pointed the gun at Emily, the barrel shaking. "I killed a twelve-year-old, right? And kidnapped a seven-year-old. I must be capable of *anything*."

"The pizza rolls are done," Jasmine said louder than she needed to. "Bring them over here and get me something to drink."

Jasmine carried the container over to Eduardo and then went to the refrigerator.

"They have Diet Coke."

"Bring me one."

Jasmine did as she was told and then sat again at the table.

Eduardo let the pizza rolls cool a minute and then devoured them and drank the soda in several gulps.

Tessa wondered what would happen when he needed to use the bathroom—or when one of the others did.

CHAPTER 39

A barrage of sleet pummeled everything in sight at 418 Azalea Lane, and the eerie sound of it battering the cars just upped the tension.

Brill pulled her jacket up around her ears and went over to David. "It's going to be dark in an hour."

"Trust me," David said. "This thing will be over before that."

"Don't play with my daughter's life!"

He turned to her, his eyebrows forming a bushy line under the brim of his hat. "You know me better than that."

"Sorry." She pushed her hands deeper into her jacket pockets and looked down at the ground. "I feel like I'm going to break in two. I mean it."

"You're stronger than you think. Everything's going to be fine."

"That sounds like a cliché, now that I'm the worried parent and not the cop." She took her hands out of her pockets, pushed up the sleeve of her jacket, and looked at her watch for the umpteenth time. "Where are Eduardo's parents? What's taking so long?"

"They were with Jasmine's parents, visiting a nephew in Knoxville," David said. "His baby got baptized and there was a big family gathering. They should be here soon."

Sheriff Parker stood staring at the house, the brim of his hat white all the way around with sleet. "The way I see it, y'all, Eduardo

361

Mendez doesn't have any good options. He knows what they do to child killers in prison. And he knows if he fingers the gang boss, he's a dead man. I think he'll kill himself and save the SWAT team the trouble."

"Let's hope you're wrong." Brill didn't bother to hide her annoyance. "Those two little girls will have a hard enough time dealing with the trauma of being held hostage."

Kurt came over and put his arm around her. "How're you doing?"

"I'm fragile. How about you?"

"I'm praying. It helps. I called Ryan and Vanessa. They each wanted to jump in the car and come home."

What's home? "So what did you tell them?"

"I told them to hang tight and I'll call them the minute we know Emily's safe. They're going to call the prayer chain at their churches. And I called Pastor Gavin. There're lots of people praying."

Brill was glad. She wondered if God even listened to her prayers after the way she had ignored Him. She sensed someone approaching and looked up, shocked to see Nick Phillips.

Kurt went over to him and shook his hand. "Hey, Nick."

"I heard on the news a gunman was holding an old couple and two little girls hostage in the four hundred block of Azalea Lane," Nick said. "I put two and two together. I can't believe this. The Masinos were down at my place with Emily and Jasmine after church today."

"How'd you get past the barricade?" Brill said.

"The cops all know me." He held up a big white sack. "I brought you hot coffee. Thought maybe you could use some about now.

You've got to be half frozen, standing out here."

Kurt took the sack and patted Nick on the shoulder, too choked up to say anything.

"He needs to get behind the barricade," David said. "It's not safe here."

Tessa sat at the kitchen table with Antonio, Emily, and Jasmine, listening to the *tick tick tick* of the clock, and the *drip drip drip* of the sink and the rumbling of empty stomachs.

Finally Emily's voice broke the monotony. "Why don't you make a demand? See if they'll give you a plane and a pilot? Anything is better than this."

"They're not going to give me a plane," Eduardo said.

"How will you know if you don't ask?" Emily shifted her weight, her feet jiggling. "I can't stand to just sit here anymore."

"Well, you don't have much choice now, do you, Barbie?"

"If you fly to Mexico," Antonio said, "you wouldn't have to go to jail."

"Nice try, old man, but I'm wanted there, too."

Jasmine rocked back and forth in the chair, her arms folded across her chest. "Then go somewhere else where you might not get caught. If you stay here, you're in big trouble for sure."

"Shut up! All of you! I'm not asking for a plane. The SWAT team would take me out the first chance they got."

Tessa stroked Jasmine's hair and spoke as calmly as possible. "Eduardo, why not just cooperate with the authorities? I've watched enough TV to know the authorities will cut you a good deal if you give them names."

"Yeah, well, those *names* will make sure I die in prison."

The phone rang and they all jumped. Eduardo cursed and hit the speakerphone button.

"What?"

"It's going to be dark soon," David said. "And the weather bureau just changed the forecast. These sleet pellets are going to turn to freezing rain. Which will mean downed power lines. You want to be cooped up with four people and no electricity or heat?"

"You're making that up."

"Turn on the TV. See for yourself."

"Yeah, right. So the SWAT team can get a clear shot."

"There's a TV here in the kitchen," Antonio said. "I'll turn it on."

Eduardo gave a nod. "Go."

Antonio got up and turned on the TV to the Weather Channel, and then sat at the table.

Tessa stroked Emily's ponytail as the commentator talked about a front on the West Coast, heavy snowfall in the Rockies, and snow flurries throughout Kansas and Missouri.

"Most of the southern U.S. will experience heavy rainfall, but a winter weather advisory is now in effect for Tennessee, Kentucky, Ohio, and West Virginia. Expect freezing rain and hazardous driving conditions throughout the night and into tomorrow as this front makes its way—"

Eduardo turned off the TV. "So what? You going to stand out in the ice all night?"

"I think we need to do some serious negotiating," David said. "I want you to let the hostages go. They're not going to do you any good. And I don't believe you want to hurt them."

"How do you know what I *want*?" Eduardo walked back and forth along the far wall. "For all you know, I want to kill them all and then kill myself. Isn't that how it usually goes down?"

"With calculated shooters who plan it that way, yes. But hostage situations don't usually turn deadly. I don't think you want to die."

"Shut up! You don't know anything. You don't know the first thing about me."

Tessa heard people whispering on the other end of the line.

"*I* do," a woman finally said.

"Mom?" Emily started to stand until Eduardo pointed his gun at her.

"It's okay, sweetie. Eduardo, I know you've got a mother who loves you. I've talked to her. This is breaking her heart. She wants you to put down your weapon and come out."

"Right. So let *her* tell me."

"Your parents and Jasmine's parents went to visit your cousin Javier in Knoxville. His baby was baptized today. They're on their way back as we speak."

"There's no way my parents care what happens to me now. I've disgraced the family."

"You're wrong. Parents never stop loving their kids. Just like your aunt and uncle love Jasmine, and I love my little girl. I want you to let them go."

Eduardo looked over at Emily. "Why should I?"

"Because you're out of options. We can work with you. The Feds have ways of making sure you're protected. If you help us, this can have a good ending for you."

"You're telling me that if I give you the name of the Smarties' boss, they can guarantee protection?"

"Absolutely."

"How much jail time?"

"Minimal."

"What's minimal?"

There was a long pause and Tessa heard whispering. Finally Brill started talking again.

"Special Agent Riley says that, with a good deal, you could get off with as little as ten years. You'll serve half of that with good behavior. You've still got your whole life ahead of you. It doesn't have to end *here*. You don't have to kill anyone. You don't have to kill yourself."

"Maybe I want to."

"And maybe you don't. Surely you realize it takes more courage to face this head-on? You have it in you to do the right thing. All you wanted all along was respect. What could earn you more respect than choosing not to hurt those four people in there and accepting responsibility for your mistake?"

He banged his head against the wall, seemingly fighting an inward battle.

"It's cold out here, Eduardo. We're tired. You're tired. You were brutally coerced into taking one child's life. Now you have the chance to save two."

"How do I know you're telling me the truth about the Feds protecting me?"

"You don't. You have to trust me. This is about you doing the right thing. Each of us is given a moment in time when what *we* do makes all the difference. This is your moment. What you do here will affect dozens of lives, including mine, forever. You have all the power. No one's forcing you to do anything. What's it going to be?"

Eduardo's eyes welled and he tilted his head back, his face contorted with anguish. "I didn't want to kill the kid."

"I believe you."

"Einstein told me I had to. He said I dissed the others by telling Hector about the kidnappings before we were done. That I put the gang initiation plan in jeopardy."

"It was such a brilliant plan, you just wanted to tell someone."

"I didn't think Hector would say anything, but he bragged to the kids who were buying from him. I guess he thought he was hot stuff because he was in the know about what was going down. It got back to Einstein. I'd never seen him that mad."

"What's Einstein's real name?"

"Miguel. Miguel Lopez. He cut me out of the initiation." Eduardo's face was wet with sweat. "He said he was going to make an example of me. He held a gun to my head and pulled the trigger. And then he did it again. He was going to keep doing it 'til he killed me. I pleaded with him to give me another chance, that I wanted to be in the gang and would do whatever it took."

"And Miguel made sure it was something that fit the offense."

"He said if I wanted to prove my loyalty, I had to kill the kid I told. So I went and got Hector and brought him to the warehouse where we were holding the people we kidnapped. He was just a little kid. He was so scared." Eduardo let out a sob and then seemed to inhale it. "He begged me not to hurt him. I didn't want to hurt him. God knows, I didn't want to hurt him."

"But you did what you had to do."

"I shot him. I'm sorry, Hector. I'm so sorry." Eduardo slid down the wall into a sitting position, tears streaming from his dark eyes.

No one breathed.

Finally Emily rose to her feet, and Tessa grabbed for the bottom of her dress and missed. Why was she walking toward Eduardo? He was so emotional he was liable to do anything.

Tessa squeezed Antonio's hand and watched as Emily got down on her knees directly in front of Eduardo, her hands held out to him.

"If you give me the gun, Hector will forgive you. He'll know you saved our lives. You're not a bad person, Eduardo. My mom says nobody is *all* bad. You just made a bad mistake."

"Emily? Eduardo? What's happening?" Brill stood with Kurt, David's phone to her ear, her hands shaking, her heart pounding in her ears.

"They're not responding," she said. "I hear voices, but I can't tell what's happening.

"The front door is opening." David signaled the SWAT team. "Don't anybody move. Just stay cool."

Brill felt Kurt's fingers press into her shoulders as they waited for what seemed an eternity for the door to finally open wide.

She sucked in a breath.

There stood Emily, clad in her white dress with tiny pink roses embroidered across the yoke, one hand in the air, the other outstretched and holding gingerly to the handle of a large gun, the barrel pointed downward.

David spoke into his walkie-talkie. "Hold your fire. Repeat, hold your fire."

"Mom, don't shoot! This is Eduardo's gun. He's giving up."

Emily bent down and set the gun on the stoop as carefully as if it were a baby chick, and then made a beeline for her mother, her ponytail swaying as she ran.

Brill opened her arms and enveloped this little girl who had spent the afternoon staring death in the face—and wondered what had happened in that house and how close she had come to losing her.

Thank You, Lord. Thank You.

She was aware of the SWAT team converging, people applauding, and Emily's salty tears spilling onto her jacket.

"I'm so glad you're safe. I've never been that scared. Are you okay?"

Emily nodded, her small body trembling from fear or cold—or both.

I-I know how to be smart. I'm my mother's d-daughter, r-right?"

"Oh, sweetie, there's no doubt. I'm so proud of …"

Brill's words turned to whimpers and her vision clouded over, but she didn't need her eyes to tell her it was Kurt's arms, strong and resolute, comforting and calming, that had embraced her and Emily like a circle of light.

She allowed herself to rest there, not knowing exactly what it was that had changed between Kurt and her—or even if it would last. But at that moment she opened her heart and emptied it of the bitterness she had used to punish him and hoped it would make room for whatever good might come with a second chance.

CHAPTER 40

Six Weeks Later

BRILL stood at her office window and watched the work crew in cherry pickers wrapping every bare branch of the trees around city hall with Christmas lights in preparation for the annual Festival of Lights.

In the distance the foothills were lightly dusted with snow and the bluish silhouette of the Great Smoky Mountains looked almost like a chalk drawing on the late November sky. She heard a knock at the door and turned around.

Kurt stood in the doorway, looking handsome in his black trousers and tan suede jacket.

"Want to go to lunch, Chief?"

"Sure. It's dead around here." She smiled and quickly added. "Believe me, that's not a complaint. It feels great having Miguel Lopez and the Smarties off the street. I think the rest of the criminals went home for Thanksgiving. I just wish they'd stay there. Where's Emily?"

"At Tessa's."

"So is this a date?"

"It's a surprise."

"Well, that's intriguing."

"Come on. I warmed up the passenger seat for you."

Brill walked across the detective bureau and down the hall and exited by the side door. She spotted Kurt's Caravan and hurried over to it, her hair being whipped about like a flag in the icy wind. She got up in the passenger seat.

"Brrrrr." She put her hands in her jacket pocket. "I can sure tell the holidays are here. Emily wants it to snow so badly. But I'm ready for spring. I just want to get the holidays behind us."

"It's going to be strange having Thanksgiving in Sophie Trace."

"Especially with Ryan and Vanessa in Colorado skiing." Brill sighed. "I know the kids are getting older and have their own lives, but I miss them. It just won't be the same without them. I miss Memphis, too. We had so many wonderful holiday memories there."

Kurt reached over and took her hand. "We can make new memories, honey."

"You're right. We probably have to cycle through the first year."

"Okay, now for the trust part."

"What?"

"I need you to wear a blindfold."

"Why?"

"It's a surprise."

Brill chuckled. "Okay, I'm game. The chief of police, in uniform, wears a blindfold around town. Weirder things have happened."

Kurt opened the console and handed her a black blindfold with an elastic strap. "Don't peek. You'll be glad you waited."

Brill put the blindfold on. "I feel ridiculous. And conspicuous."

"No one will notice." He laughed. "If they do, they can always call the police."

"Funny."

Kurt started the car and she could tell they were moving.

"How long will it take us to get where we're going?"

"Less than five minutes."

"I feel silly."

"Call me Tonto, but you look cute."

"A cop in a blindfold is not my idea of cute."

"That's why I'm married to a cop and you're not."

Brill nestled in the warm seat and let her cold body relax. The lack of conversation that followed was comfortable. It sounded as if they were in the downtown, and then the traffic noise grew distant.

"Are we there yet?" She smiled without meaning to. "And this from the grown-up who's answered that question a thousand times."

"Almost."

Kurt made a turn and then stopped the van and turned off the motor.

"Now don't peek," he said. "I'm coming around to your side."

She heard the door slam shut, and seconds later he opened the passenger side door and helped her out of the van.

"Okay, hold on to my hand," he said.

"I hate being out of control. I never did well in those leadership seminars where we had to just let go and trust someone to catch us."

"Trust me, I'm not going to let you fall." Kurt pulled her along slowly. "You're doing great. Now step up. That's it."

"Where are we? I feel like a spectacle—a masked bandit with red hair and a badge."

"You're fine. Come on. One more step."

Brill stepped into a room and caught the faint, familiar fragrance of roses. "Are we home?"

"Surprise!"

Brill fumbled to take off the blindfold and stood dumbfounded. Her eyes brimmed with tears. "Vanessa! Ryan! I can't believe this. You said you weren't coming for Thanksgiving."

In the next instant the entire family was pulled into a group hug. Brill hugged everyone at least twice and then stood back to take a good look at them.

"I'm sorry we lied." Vanessa's blue eyes were even more striking, now that she'd let her dark hair grow long. "But we wanted to surprise you."

"Shock is more like it."

Ryan flashed the irresistible smile that would surely give him an edge with juries as a defense lawyer someday. "Are you going to make that cornbread dressing I love so much?"

"And the sweet potatoes with the yummy marshmallows?" Emily said.

Vanessa raised her eyebrows up and down. "And green bean casserole? It's not Thanksgiving without that."

"Well," Kurt slid his arm around her, "as long as everyone else is putting in an order, I have a hankering for your sweet potato pie. No one makes it like you do."

"Yes!" Brill said. "Yes, to all of it. I am so happy to have us all together. I'm still in the state of shock. Oh, my goodness, I need to get busy if we're going to have a feast. I can't make everything in one day."

"We'll help," Vanessa said.

Ryan shook his head, his palms out. "Wait a minute, I don't do food. But I'll shop. Do errands. Do chores. You've got me 'til Sunday. Use me up."

"Did you choose your rooms?" Brill said.

"Peanut here did it for us." Vanessa pinched Emily on the arm. "She put me in the other room upstairs, and Ryan down here across from you and Dad. This is a great house. I actually like it *better* than the house in Memphis."

Emily cupped her hand and whispered something in Vanessa's ear.

"Oh, I almost forgot," Vanessa said. "We made lunch. We need to go make sure the dining room table is ready."

Ryan's eyebrows came together. "We already did that."

Vanessa nodded toward the kitchen and pulled him by the arm. "You've got rolls in the oven, remember? I think I hear the timer."

Ryan smiled knowingly, and the trio left their parents alone in the entry hall.

Brill turned to Kurt and saw the man she fell in love with. "You engineered this, didn't you?"

"Let's just say that I knew our kids would enjoy Thanksgiving here more than anywhere else on the planet. They just needed something to come home to."

"We're *something*, all right." Brill put her arms around his neck. "There is one problem, though. Emily gave away your bed."

"That's what I heard."

"I guess you'll just have to move in with me. I've got room."

"Should I bring my sleeping bag?"

Brill blinked the stinging from her eyes and titled her head back, giggling like a coed. "Something tells me the kids have made sure we can't find it."

"Well, then, Mrs. Jessup," he said, linking his arm in hers, "I'm totally open to suggestions. Come on, let's go sit around the table as a family. We've both been waiting a long time for this."

Brill strolled with Kurt toward the dining room of this house that suddenly felt like home, the delicious aroma of fresh baked rolls wafting under her nose, and the indescribable fragrance of new beginnings permeating her heart.

Kurt and the kids had pulled off the surprise of all surprises. But she knew that this unexpected, unfeigned, totally unblemished reunion was just the outward sign of an inward miracle—and that it was going to be a marvelous Thanksgiving after all.

... a little more ...

When a delightful concert comes to an end,
the orchestra might offer an encore.
When a fine meal comes to an end,
it's always nice to savor a bit of dessert.
When a great story comes to an end,
we think you may want to linger.
And so, we offer ...
AfterWords—just a little something more after you
have finished a David C. Cook novel.
We invite you to stay awhile in the story.
Thanks for reading!

Turn the page for ...

- **A Note from the Author**
- **Discussion Questions**

A NOTE FROM THE AUTHOR

"SEE TO IT THAT NO ONE MISSES THE GRACE
OF GOD AND THAT NO BITTER ROOT GROWS
UP TO CAUSE TROUBLE AND DEFILE MANY."
HEBREWS 12:15

Dear Friends,

Is it ever right or fair that we should be saddled with pain and sorrow as a result of someone else's poor choices? Most of us have experienced betrayal on some level and have felt anger that was understandable and even justified. Certainly Brill Jessup did in this story.

Romans 12:21 admonishes us, "Do not be overcome by evil, but overcome evil with good." The implications of this Scripture seem obvious. But I chose to explore this idea from a different angle. I wanted to see what it would look like if the offender applied the same principle and used good to overcome the evil he himself had caused. I thought Kurt passed with flying colors.

Though his adultery cannot be minimized, neither can his sincere commitment to winning back his wife and family. Brill's pain and humiliation cannot be minimized, nor can the bitterness she allowed to steal her joy, her peace, and her relationship with the Lord.

Good trumps evil every time. As hurtful as Kurt's adultery was, the real enemy in the aftermath was the sting of Brill's bitterness. Until she emptied her heart of the bitterness she had used to punish Kurt, there was no room for anything else.

I absolutely loved writing this first book in the Sophie Trace Trilogy, and hope you'll join me in book two when we'll join up with the Jessups again and see how they're doing. Oh my, it promises to be another page-turner! Mystery and suspense abound.

I love hearing from my readers. You can write to me through my publisher at www.DavidCCook.com or directly through my Web site at www.KathyHerman.com. I read and respond to every e-mail and greatly value your input.

In Him,

Kathy Herman

Kathy

DISCUSSION QUESTIONS

1. What do you think is meant by Romans 12:21, "Do not be overcome by evil, but overcome evil with good"? Can you give an example of how that looks from your own life or someone else's?

2. What do you think would happen if someone decided to behave kindly toward a person, institution, or business that wronged him or her? What are the dangers of doing this? What might be the rewards? What did Jesus have to say about this?

3. Is anger sometimes just? Did Jesus get angry? Was Brill justified in her anger? What's the difference between anger and bitterness? Did Jesus ever seem bitter? Did Brill seem bitter? If so, describe what her bitterness looked like. Was her bitterness justified?

4. Do you believe the person who has wronged someone can overcome the evil he's done by doing good? In other words, do the words of Romans 12:21 apply to the offender as well as the offended? How successful was Kurt in this regard? Were his actions consistent with his repentance? Why, or why not?

5. Is adultery an unforgivable sin? Why do you think it's so destructive? Do you think women are affected by adultery differently than men? Explain your answers.

6. Why was Brill unwilling to accept Kurt's gifts and kindness? If you had not been privy to Kurt's thoughts, would you

have been skeptical of his motives? What actions of his, if
any, might have swayed you to believe his recommitment
was sincere? If you were Kurt and wanted to win Brill back,
what, if anything, would you have done differently?

7. According to Matthew 5:32, Brill had biblical grounds to
divorce Kurt. Do you think that having grounds always
means that divorce is the best choice? Why? In your
opinion, would Brill have been better off without Kurt?
Would Emily? Do you believe that the mystery of the
two becoming "one" is instantly dissolved when a spouse
commits adultery? Do you think God is pleased when a
couple survives the heartache and begins anew? Explain
your answers.

8. Was precocious nine-year-old Emily hurt more by finding
out that her repentant father had had sexual intercourse
with someone besides her mother, or by seeing her mother's
bitter claws take swipes at her father and never knowing
why? Which is worse? Explain your answer.

9. Is forgiveness always the correct response when we've been
wronged? Can you support your answer with a Scripture?
Does forgiving mean that whatever happened to hurt or
anger you didn't matter? Does forgiving someone negate
that person's responsibility in any way? Why?

10. Do you believe Matthew 6:14–15 should be taken literally?
"For if you forgive men when they sin against you, your
heavenly Father will also forgive you. But if you do not
forgive men their sins, your Father will not forgive your
sins." When do you find it most difficult to forgive? Do you

think forgiveness can be complete without God's help?

11. Does true forgiveness mean forgetting? Is it possible for a person to get to the place where he or she can remember an incident without the pain and anger associated with it? Who benefits most when you forgive someone?

12. What role do you think bitterness played in the actions of Raphael Guerrero, Jorge Alvarez, Miguel Lopez, and Eduardo Mendez in the story? How might their lives have turned out differently if had they had forgiven teachers and parents who had hurt or disappointed them?

13. Do you think there are many offenders in the criminal justice system who let their anger turn into bitterness, and their bitterness into violence?

14. Which character could you relate to the most and why? Which character could you relate to the least? Do you believe what Emily said her mother had told her—that no one is all bad?

15. Who or what was the real enemy in the story? Why?

Coming soon ...

The next book in the

SOPHIE TRACE TRILOGY

from best-selling author

KATHY HERMAN

Fall 2009

(ISBN: 978-1-4347-6785-1)

David C Cook

transforming lives together